WOMEN'S WORK

WOMEN'S WORK
Anne Tolstoi Wallach

NEW ENGLISH LIBRARY

For Dick

First published in the USA in 1981 by The New American Library Inc.

First published in Great Britain in 1982 by New English Library

First NEL Open Market Edition 1982
First NEL Paperback Edition February 1983

NEL Books are published by
New English Library,
Mill Road, Dunton Green,
Sevenoaks, Kent
Editorial Office, 47 Bedford Square,
London WC1B 3DP.

Typeset by Rowland Phototypesetting Ltd
Bury St Edmunds, Suffolk
Printed in Great Britain by
Hunt Barnard Printing Ltd,
Aylesbury, Bucks.

0 450 05460 8

Men work from sun to sun,
But women's work is never done.

Domina

Domina Drexler
The Potter Jackson Company
8 East 40th Street
New York, N.Y. 10016
555-8700, ext. 2198, 2865

Experience:

1971–present	Vice-president, creative director Potter Jackson, on fashion, food, and cosmetic accounts.
1969–1971	Vice-president, copy director Gibbons Advertising, Inc., on fashion, food, and fragrance accounts.
1968–1969	Vice-president, creative director Triano Loeffler Arbib, all agency accounts.
1966–1968	Copy supervisor Hudson Advertising Co., American Foods products, Boutique Bonnell.
1964–1966	Domina Drexler Associates, Chicago, Ill., Boutique Bonnell, Dial-A-Maid, Steero products.
1962–1964	Trimble's Fashion Shoppes, Elkhart, Ind., starting summer and part-time work, to ad department copy chief, 1963–1964.

Education:

Harvard Management Seminar 1972.

The New School, 1966–present: courses in art, sociology, history, psychology, textile chemistry, management planning, mathematics.

St. Joseph's School, Elkhart, Ind.

Additional Activities:

Member Yale Club of New York.

Young Management League.

Past member Advertising Women of New York, Fashion Fair, Ad Club, NOW Council.

Lecturer Dover School of Technology, 1970, 1971. Guest lectures, New School, NYU.

Author 1965: *How to Begin the Boutique*, how-to volume serialized in *Cosmopolitan*, published as course book.

Personal:

Single.

Two children, 18, 16.

The bed was enormous. Three big pillows lined the back, and little ones, square and round and sausage-shaped, were tucked in between them.

Domina Drexler ignored them all as she sat with her long legs crossed and her back straight. Her breakfast tray was in front of her, firmly settled on its stubby legs. Most mornings it looked to her like a picture from a glossy magazine. On its Chinese-red lacquer surface were a heavy silver thermos of coffee, a crystal goblet of orange juice, and a fat brown brioche, neatly split and mounded with butter. It was a fantasy breakfast, carefully planned and put together to extend the night hours that belonged to Domina, and ease the transition to the long working day, when time was never her own.

Today the tray was not doing its job. The coffee had poured out like gravy. The brioche felt damp. The juice had sloshed against the side of the glass, stranding bits of orange pulp along the side.

It's me, Domina thought. That damned meeting this morning. Everything depends on it. It'll either make everything right or destroy the best dream I ever had. No wonder my shoulders ache so much my neck won't turn. No wonder the tears are right behind my eyes, waiting to spring.

Domina lifted her chin and looked for some comfort from the room around her. Usually she felt a throb of triumph in surveying the things she alone had chosen, paid for, and placed. She had insisted on the wine silk of the wall covering, when everyone had told her that the fabric was too fragile to mount. She had haunted the painters to make sure that the line where the red met the cream of the ceiling was measurably straight. She had polished, and polished again, the pink marble of the elaborately carved fireplace.

9

What met her eye this morning were a square of dust underneath the armoire and an irritating tilt to one of the framed antique fans. There seemed to be a mountain of grubby cigarette ends in the big ashtray by her bed.

Nothing was going to help her ease into this day.

Domina willed her shoulders into relaxation again, and bent her neck the way the exercise teachers at Elizabeth Arden said would relieve tension.

One thing could, she thought. A simple promotion. Senior vice-president. One long word. All I need, all I want now.

Then get up, she told herself. Put on something terrific for extra courage. Your diamond stud earrings. They shine with success. Especially when you're going to face a man who knows you bought them for yourself. A man who once joked: if you give a woman a Christmas bonus, you can be sure she'll have new jewelry the first working day after the holidays. That bastard.

She pushed the covers back with determination. The top corner of the quilt promptly folded itself into the orange juice. Damn.

Domina folded the dripping corner into the bulk of the quilt and took it to the bathroom sink, where she began solving this newest problem with warm water.

It's your own fault, she thought as she carefully squeezed the soggy padding. He didn't ask to see you. You're pushing him. Complaining to him about a boss who never bothers you, who's only a name somewhere on an organization chart. And just when things are going so smoothly. Work fine. Clients happy. Enough money, enough even for the kids' school and college bills. So why take the chance of blowing it all just because *you* have to be the boss? Every other woman in advertising would be delighted to have made it *this* far.

But I *should* be the boss, thought Domina stubbornly. In the last two years I've brought in more new business, won more creative awards than anyone there. I look around at the other supervisors, the men, and I *know* I'm better. And Brady Godwin knows it, too. He doesn't like it, but he knows it.

Anyway, she thought, I've always lived on risks. If I hadn't, I'd still be in Elkhart writing tacky ads about house-dresses for half-size ladies, married to a man whose idea of a big night was watching one football game on television and listening to another on the radio simultaneously.

She hung the quilt over the shower rod and plunged into the business of getting ready for work.

Everything in Domina's morning make-ready was planned to move with the precision of a surgical procedure. Twelve minutes to warm her toes and get her face glowing in the world's hottest bath. Nine minutes to finger makeup gently on her face, then scrub it down briskly to look natural again. Thirteen minutes to stroke on pantyhose, snug into a satin camisole, wriggle into tight velvet jeans and tug on a heavy Irish sweater. Six minutes to undo and brush and twirl and pin up the mass of thick, dark hair. Another minute for shoes, and to check the briefcase full of yellow copy paper, readied the night before. Ten seconds for a chill blast of perfume spray.

She turned to leave the bedroom but not with her usual satisfied look back. Out in the hall music was throbbing from Michael's room. The closer she came the more the sound rose, sending drumbeats straight into her temples. Kids never learn, she thought, knocked furiously at his door, and marched in to do battle.

Michael, incredibly, was dead asleep.

The cast on his leg looked enormous, chalky and smooth against the crumpled coverlet. He lay awkwardly twisted, a book crunched beneath his arm, lamplight beaming into his face. A stale smell came from the backpack near the bed. Clothes which someone at school had hastily packed after the accident were still spilling out of the canvas bag.

Domina's anger died down. She thought of the telephone call from the baseball coach, his rasping voice strangely out of place in her office. Something about a terrific line drive, straight for Mike's kneecap – a common enough accident at a position like shortstop. With the phone slippery in her damp hand, Domina had instantly imagined Michael face-

11

down in the dirt, then on crutches, limping, his gypsy grace gone forever. And all for a stupid game, she'd thought grimly, a primitive male ritual like baseball.

She crossed the room to look closely at her son.

He breathed as deeply as if he were stretched on a sunny beach. When she touched the rough cast, her own knee ached.

Domina wanted to smash the cast, set Michael free again. Instead she reached over to turn off the noisy radio, then the hot lamp, slid the book out from under his arm. Michael asleep, lanky, angular, his dark hair falling over his eyes, seemed to her Michael in his crib again. He had never stayed neatly put, always lumped crosswise, a fat baby arm poked through the crib's slats. Oh Michael, she thought, heal, run again, grow strong. Walk up for your diploma on a sunny green lawn, kick the leaves in Harvard Yard, stride up and down the living room bursting with talk about your first job the way you do now about the team.

Then she realized it was late, and that Michael had better get well, go back to Choate, leave her in peace to work for all of them, for him, Maria, herself.

She moved out, went to the closet in the hall and tipped her jacket off its padded hanger.

'I'm going,' she called to the kitchen. 'Leota? Keep an eye on Mike, okay? Would you set the table for us tonight? And fix a casserole, salad? And ice in the bucket?'

'Do I ever forget ice?' demanded the alto voice from the kitchen.

The swinging door pushed out, followed by Leota's sleek head and plump chocolate arm.

'Leota. If only you could write ads,' said Domina.

Leota waved once at her boss while she took a good look at the crazy outfit Mrs Drexler had on today. Heels like on the chippies who used to walk the New Orleans waterfront. Now they went to big downtown offices. Imagine. Pants, too. Till Mrs Drexler taught her different, Leota thought that big career ladies wore tweedy suits, frilly blouses with bows in front, to look nice and feminine. Well, she was a pretty lady in whatever she wore, Leota thought. And she had a lot to handle for a white woman. Man walking out on her, leaving two kids. But Mrs Drexler made more money for herself now than any woman Leota had ever heard of in all her sixty years, made it all, enough for the big apartment and the schools and the trips to everywhere. And money for me. Leota smiled to herself. More money than anyone ever paid for me.

'You write the ads and I'll fix the dinner,' she said firmly.

Domina waved, and moved fast to get to the taxi that waited for her every weekday morning.

Beautiful, abundant Leota, Domina thought, who let herself in silently in time to fix that heavenly breakfast tray, who vacuumed and polished and laundered till afternoon. Leota, who got broken things fixed without talk, who filled the refrigerator and the liquor cabinet, who arranged dinner to wait for any number at any hour, without a word. Who but Leota would patiently dust in the kids' empty rooms, lifting the glass animals and the records and the trophies, putting them back precisely, even though the kids weren't living home now? Every working woman needs a wife, thought Domina, and for three hundred dollars a week, Leota's mine.

In the cab she reflected that both she and Leota had learned how to act toward each other by watching countless old movies. If nobody had ever read a book, nobody would ever fall in love. If nobody had ever seen a Warner Brothers movie, nobody would ever know how mistresses and maids should behave together.

She looked out through her cigarette smoke at Madison Avenue as they crossed it, its shop windows X'd out by iron gratings against New York's night bricks and burglars. Madison Avenue, home and namesake of the advertising business. She wondered why. The big agencies had been huddled on Third and Sixth for years. Her own agency, Potter Jackson, had been settled on Fortieth Street since the early twenties.

There had been years when Domina di Santis woke at the tinny trill of a dented alarm clock in a house that smelled of damp and bacon grease and cheap wine. In those days, Domina's first chore had been to cover her mother, snoring and rumpled, on the worn couch in the parlor. She would empty the chipped ashtray, put the inevitable wine bottle out the back, wrapped up in newspaper, and then find something to nibble while she waited at the corner for the school bus.

There had been years when Domina Drexler was shocked awake by her children noisily demanding a referee in one of their endless war games. In those days, Domina would squeeze oranges, toast muffins, pour milk. She would find lost mittens and homework, zip stubborn zippers, edge both of them toward the crosstown bus. She would skip them to school, wave them in the door, and quicken her pace to the subway entrance. With all of it, she could still make it to the office cubicle she occupied then, with a bag of doughnuts and black coffee, by nine sharp.

And there had been years when Domina had needed to open her eyes to decide who was with her in the softness of her bed. The men changed in shape and sleeping habits. But the scene she woke to always seemed the same. Usually, soft music left over on the radio from the night before, clothing tossed on her Shaker rocker or on the floor. Domina would sit up silently and explore the sheets for her nightgown. She would slide its coolness over her naked body and rise stealthily to take away the amber-stained drink glasses on her bed table, turning off the radio, so that whoever it was could wake up to a peaceful morning room.

Nowadays, though, she had moved to the middle of the bed, got used to sleeping stretched out like a star, and had no need of anybody. Well, maybe she had a need, but one she'd decided wouldn't be met. Everything she wanted in just one man? No. The best she could hope for was different pieces of what she wanted from several men. One for brains, the most important – bright, quick, easy to talk to. One for sympathy – friendly, patient, ready to listen if she called in the night. One for decency – helpful, dependable, kind. A fatherly man for the kids. A handsome man for parties and showing off. A man to travel with – resourceful, competent, cool. A man for silly fun and drinking and kidding around, so she could feel young and adorable once in a while. A man to sleep with all night long, to lie down with and make love to and get up in the morning

14

with. How many men was that, altogether? Too many. It was as if she needed a patchwork of men to make up her quilt, a warm wrapping against the cold.

Love was supposed to be for always. But for her, always had lasted only five years. When you depended on yourself, you at least knew what to expect. With anyone else, especially with men, you could never be sure.

Domina stopped herself from thinking about needs and beds and got her mind back to the meeting an hour away in Brady Godwin's office. She hated his office. It looked as if it had been dismantled in Edwardian London, and put back together in New York, piece by numbered piece.

Domina had worked in advertising agencies that looked like warehouses, like greenhouses, like whorehouses. She knew that agencies were decorated to look special and fascinating, so that visitors and clients would understand immediately that the ads would also be special and fascinating. The agencies, out of trying so hard to look different, she thought, ended up looking very much alike. So did most of the advertising.

Potter Jackson, one of the oldest and largest of all agencies, had been decorated in the hope that the place would not look like an agency at all. Born in the days when young men from Yale and Princeton and Harvard went into banking and teaching if they could, and when only black sheep from good families were tucked away into dubious commercial enterprises like advertising, Jackson had aimed to look like a place where nobody really had to work for a living at all.

Jackson behavior kept to that illusion, too. It was the only agency Domina had worked at where no paychecks were handed out. Instead, a discreet system deposited checks twice each month in everyone's bank account. Like members of the British royal family, Jackson employees never had to handle cash.

Domina went past the famous Art Deco clock in the lobby, and up in the elevator to white marble halls and floors, white desks and flowers, white doors. There were even receptionists with white hair on each of the nine floors the agency occupied in the huge building. The effect was somewhere between a hospital and a cathedral, with sound-proofing that produced a stillness appropriate to either.

There were no signs on doors, no ads in frames, no products on display to impress visitors at The Potter Jackson Company. The whole agency look, Domina thought, stated clearly that if you didn't know the work, the clients, or even where you were supposed to go from the reception room, you undoubtedly had no business being there at all. A favorite Jackson story concerned a stupid mail boy, who asked after a year at work just exactly what it was all these people *did* in these offices.

As Domina walked briskly down the long corridor to her own office in the corner, her high heels alternately clicked on the marble and were muffled on the pale blue-and-white Chinese rugs.

Each office she passed was furnished in a different way, like a series of model rooms in a department store. One of Jackson's proudest claims was that its executives could choose furniture and paintings from any period of decoration. Domina had seen priceless treasures in the agency's own warehouse, met Jackson's own curators, carpenters, and restoration experts. It was always a small surprise to her that you were not expected to dress in costume to match the period of your office. Her own choice, beautiful Italian provincial furniture, sturdy and mellowed and simple, would have been the appropriate background for a peasant girl, in the chorus of an Italian operetta. Domina had chosen it and seen it in place before she had realized that all of it might have belonged to one of her Neapolitan ancestors. Because it had all ended up looking so chic, so rich, she almost always came to work in blue jeans and disco shoes, to provide a little contrast.

She turned on her lights, put her jacket in one of the closets, pulled up the blinds on all four windows. The cleaning people always screened out the daylight in offices they knew belonged to women. It was assumed that ladies would want soft shading about them as they worked. Domina liked sunlight and brilliant electric light, lots of light, in spite of the laugh lines around her eyes and mouth.

After all, at thirty-seven, you had lines. Time enough to sit in the gloom when you were seventy.

She sat down at the trestle-table desk, flicked on the red electric typewriter that matched absolutely nothing in the office, and reached for a piece of yellow copy paper from the neat stack in the wicker basket.

Rolling the paper in, she started to sort out her feelings.

From childhood, almost as soon as she'd learned to put letters on paper, Domina had relied on the written word as an outlet for anger and fear and love and hate. She had developed the habit of writing letters to nowhere. She would think carefully and put down precisely what she felt, what she wanted to make happen, so that her thoughts became physical, things she could hold in her hand and pore over. Then she would tear the letter in tiny pieces, doubling and redoubling as much as the paper would permit. Often the problem would be destroyed along with the paper it was written on, and nobody in the world but her would know anything about it. Once you had declared your adoration for somebody, and outlined the details of your intense desire to spend afternoons in hotel bedrooms with him, you could manage to get through a session of office night work together without dropping your notes on the floor and blushing. The practice had not only spared Domina the cost of a psychiatrist but also helped her become one of advertising's top copywriters.

Now to write, as she wished she could speak aloud, to Brady Godwin.

She considered him as she typed his name.

A tall man, massive, marvelously tailored. Handsome for his age when you saw him on a platform or across a room, but strangely bland when you came closer to him across a desk. His eyes were empty, navy blue, without sparkle or depth. At her first meeting with him Domina had noticed, as he was hiring her, that even when his mouth curved into a smile, nothing changed on the rest of his face. His hand, as she shook it, felt dry and rasping. Godwin's voice had chilled her, too, even when the words spoken were pleasant. He talked softly and perfectly evenly, making people strain forward to catch the words, and giving no clue to his feelings beyond the words themselves. Domina, trained to assess body language and speaking tones in her clients, so that she could act on the smallest hints of their likes and dislikes, felt lost with this man. Conversation with him, even on happy subjects, was frightening. Everything in Godwin's manner reminded you strongly that he could make your whole working life easy and profitable or that he could have you standing in a long line at the unemployment office by tomorrow morning. A confrontation with him was something to steel yourself for.

Domina had faced him twice before with the same question she had ready for him this morning.

A year earlier, after she had worked nights and weekends in the unheated office, coaxed and bullied an art director into complying with her exact directions, she had captured the US Mills breakfast-food account from another agency. The advertising press then singled her out. She was photographed and interviewed. Headhunters began to call her for top jobs everywhere. Brady Godwin had invited her to his office, the first time she had been alone with him since the day he had hired her. He had seated her on a soft couch, offered her a cigarette from the silver box on his desk that marked his thirty years' service to the company, and folded himself into a wing chair that hid most of his body from her view. Then, leaning forward with his hands clasped between his knees, he had gazed earnestly at her and smiled in a fatherly sort of way. He had told Domina that now she would work without a creative supervisor, and be responsible directly to him as head of the creative department. Her present supervisor would remain, but only as a figurehead. The man would on no account interfere with her work. Godwin had said that his faith in Domina's ability was great and that he alone had taken a chance on giving her this unusual independence. Domina, bewitched by his voice, could hear in her own mind the echo of the voice of the US Mills president as he had said, 'I want you running this show, just you, Domina, and I don't want any of those Ivy League bastards in that agency getting their oars in.' She had felt the stirring in her insides that always signaled fury, the kind that grew hot and swollen because you couldn't let

18

it burst out in obvious anger. Trying to keep her voice just as even as Brady Godwin's, she had asked if the title of senior vice-president would go with the responsibility for handling the account. Godwin had assured her that, in time, it would. In time, she had thought. In how much time? She had yearned to pin him down, to make him mark a day on his leather calendar for the announcement, but she had said nothing. She had waited for her rage to subside, telling herself that it couldn't be long before they had to promote her.

Six months later, with the first market reports on the breakfast foods coming in at incredibly high levels, Domina had herself asked to see Godwin.

This time she had refused his offer of a cigarette, and had chosen to sit on a straight chair. She had launched immediately, without preamble, into her request for the title.

Brady Godwin had listened to her without moving. When she had finished, he looked closely at her and said that nothing would personally make him happier than to add her name to the company's management list. He had actually put her promotion into the works; it was, as a matter of fact, in the hands of the board of directors, who must approve such an addition. He most certainly understood her charming show of impatience – his own wife often seemed to expect things to happen overnight, too. However, he told her, he had something to offer her right now that might make the waiting somewhat more bearable. The corner office on her floor was to be hers, as of that very moment. Furthermore, she was to decorate it precisely as she wanted, without limits to her spending. Within reason, of course.

Domina had felt a rush of pleasure. It would make a lot of people realize how important she was to the company, to have a huge corner office with four windows. But somewhere back in her head she had known that she was being given a bone, a token to distract her from what she really wanted. And would they say next that since she had the office, the visible evidence of promotion, that she really wouldn't need the title? She had stated, a little flatly, that she thought the office would be a wonderful setting for the agency's first woman senior vice-president. And she had removed herself quickly from Godwin's peculiar eyes.

That evening she had asked her best friend to come over and see the office that was to be hers. Afterward the two of them had gone down for a drink in the pub in the lobby that the whole office used as a recovery room. While they had been talking cozily in one of the high wooden booths, Domina had heard a man's voice rising over a conversation at the bar. 'Give that bitch a big couch in her corner office, Billy. Maybe she'll figure out what couches are for one of these days.' Domina had turned to see who had spoken, but she couldn't match the voice to any face she knew. Some gnome on the office decorating staff, probably, she thought. But she had had no doubt that she was being discussed. Fireworks went off in her head, fireworks that returned each time she chose a chair or a fabric for the new office. There was some joyous revenge in choosing the costliest and finest objects in the company storerooms.

And then, just last month, there had been the business of the man from the Brussels office.

Domina had been asked to help orient him to American ways, show him around, explain the working patterns of the New York office. The man had been attractive, intelligent, and appreciative. He had noted down much of what Domina said, in a flattering way. She had enjoyed going over her accounts with him, presenting her special creative triumphs, introducing him to her clients and employees.

Last week the office mail had brought her one of the agency's general memos, the kind that always announced important changes. Domina had often typed the announcement of her own promotion on this form, read and reread it, and then torn it up. This memo, stiff and whole in her hand, had informed everyone that the man from Brussels was being transferred permanently to New York, and was being promoted to a senior vice-presidency.

Domina had dissolved into misery. She had locked her office door and allowed herself, for once, to weep with frustration and rage. She had even considered storming Godwin's office to announce that she was going to quit on the spot. Then she had calmed herself, dried her tears, and put on her darkest sunglasses to mask the damage done to her face. A while later her secretary had knocked on the door and brought in a long white box of flowers which had just arrived by messenger. The man from Brussels had sent Domina a fantastic bouquet, a poem of pink roses, baby's breath, and tulips. She had lifted the cover of the box, read the card of thanks, looked once at the flowers, put back the top, and jammed the whole mass into her wastebasket. Then she had cried again, cried so hard that she had had to wait until almost nine o'clock, when the office would be empty, to get out and home unobserved and cry some more.

Memo to Brady Godwin, thought Domina. You shit.

'Memo to Brady Godwin,' typed Domina. What a dumb name, she thought. You could use it forward or backward, like a – what was it – a palindrome. Like all the worst upper-class names that all the worst upper-class bastards in management always seemed to have. No wonder a tough guy like Lido Iacocca got to be president of Ford and Chrysler. Unreal palindrome people like Edsel Ford – or Ford Edsel, if you like – were simply no match for him.

Memo to Brady Godwin. It's time we talked about my promotion. For ten years I have handled every problem, built up every product, charmed every client for this agency. I have surpassed everyone's expectations of a mere woman. I am never sick. I get to meetings absolutely on time. I am always calm and even-tempered. The fact that I go home and cry is unknown to you, and cannot be used against me. I am talented, attractive, steady. People who work for me respect, admire, and even like me.

Every single other person in this office who does the kind of work I do is already a senior vice-president.

I know you're giving me a chance to shine. I know you pay me seventy-six thousand dollars a year. I know you think I'm impatient. Why do they always call men eager and aggressive, while women are called impatient?

Domina grabbed a pencil, impatiently, from her desk and wrote all across the page she had been typing, FUCK, in big black letters. That was progress, she thought. Five

21

years ago she couldn't whisper the word, let alone write it down. Maybe in five more years she'd be able to say it directly to someone. To someone like Brady Godwin.

Try the memo again, thought Domina, and get it into the language of persuasion, the advertising language you know so much about. That meant writing, not in the order *you* cared about, but in the order your audience would want to hear. Domina knew that you never write a toothpaste ad to tell how terrific your own manufacturing process is. You write about the reasons why people like toothpaste in general, and then explain how amazingly your product matches those reasons.

She reached for still another piece of paper and centered it carefully in her typewriter. The typewriter was getting warmer, losing its buzz as it heated to smooth working temperature. Maybe her writing would warm up, too.

Domina wrote, 'The advantage in the modern world of having a woman on your executive team.'

That was their language, all right; any expression borrowed from sports and soldiering was business-management talk. Targeting, strategy, gaming, pitching – all men's words and images. Even 'campaign' – advertising campaign – she suddenly realized.

'The news value to a traditional company like Potter Jackson of promoting a woman to senior vice-president.

'The importance to the agency of confirming her permanently as one of their very own people, the family.' Senior vice-presidents did not look for other jobs. The only way they ever left the company was to retire honorably, to die, or to become presidents and owners of their own advertising agencies.

'The promise Brady Godwin had made that the title would be hers before the end of the year. Last year.

'The fury she would unleash if she didn't have that title by the time she left his office that very morning.

'The unfair, lying, male shit they were trying to con her with.'

In one sweep Domina yanked the paper out of the typewriter and crunched it into a yellow ball, threw it across the office. Then she got up and retrieved it, so no prying eyes and hands could uncrumple it and read it.

It wasn't any good writing it all down. She would simply have to say what she wanted to say, in the order God put in her mouth. Logic always brought her back to the same place. They owed it to her. They weren't giving it to her. Impasse. Immovable object. But, thought Domina, nothing is really impossible. You have to find the right lever, that's all.

She got up and looked down on the street. Far below, traffic was in its usual morning snarl. The sound of a hundred horns blending rose up. Impatience, thought Domina, that's how it sounds. All those cars competing for the right-of-way. How do you beat the crowd and get yourself where you want to go?

The creative department of Potter Jackson was a traffic jam, everyone frantically trying to get ahead of everyone else.

There were sixteen separate creative groups, each divided into bunches of copywriters, art directors, and television producers, as well as business managers, assistants, and secretaries. At the head of each group was a supervisor who reported to the chief creative director, Brady Godwin. All these supervisors had the title of senior vice-president except Domina. She alone had an extra boss, an elderly gentleman who came in at eleven o'clock, lunched at the Princeton Club, went home on the 4:10 to Riverside, Connecticut, and who approved everything Domina did without question. He was rather a dear, and he didn't bother Domina. But *he* was the senior vice-president listed for her group, and that bothered her enormously.

It was ridiculous, it was unfair, it was demeaning and wrong, and today she was going to tell Godwin plainly. She would say that he was in danger of losing her, along with whatever she could take away with her in the way of business.

How she would adore to announce her immediate departure, the way people did in books and movies. How she would love to face down the whole board of directors as they met, explaining calmly and clearly why they had been idiots to relegate her to second place. But in the real world

23

Domina knew that the way to get a new job is to have a job while you look around. She had better be patient and keep still, even if it made her burst at the seams.

She turned from the window and looked around at her magnificent office. The pencils twinkled at her, the special black-and-gold ones Jackson had manufactured to order. The sun twinkled at her from the glass skyscraper going up across the avenue. Everything could be so sunny for me, she thought, so why can't I just leave this alone? I don't want to go out on that hard pavement and start all the tension of looking for a new job. I don't want to leave what I've got here.

But I can't let them do this to me, she thought. I will not be condescended to. I will not be treated like a simpering mistress who wants a new jewel. I will not be distracted by new offices and smiles. The general is not the general because he has a larger tent, Domina remembered, but because he had the command.

Ten o'clock was getting closer, and she wanted to leave time for a good look at herself in her closet mirror. If she knew she looked her best, she could at least concentrate on dealing with whatever Godwin would try to palm her off with this time.

'Domina? Excuse me, got a minute? I just want to show you the cereal layouts. I worked half the night getting them just right for you,' said the soft voice from the doorway.

M.J. Kent. And without a knock to announce her intrusion.

Domina would put a stop to that when she had time. But now she smiled a welcome to her newest and youngest employee.

M.J. was probably the most beautiful girl Domina had ever hired, far too beautiful for any but the most secure woman executive ever to hire. But Domina had seen instantly how talented the girl's drawings were, how filled with visual ideas. And Domina believed that brains and looks went together. She knew that today's broad standards of good looks allowed all but the dumbest girls to get themselves together and put on some kind of a show.

M.J.'s show was special by any standards.

The girl was tiny. Her wrists and ankles were like a child's. She had explained to Domina in her first interview that she had grown up dirt-poor in Eufaula, Alabama, where they never set eyes on a vitamin or a mineral. She was pale, too, without a touch of pink in her creamy skin. Her ivory pallor made Domina think of fried foods and hot biscuits and the things they were supposed to do to your complexion. Only, M.J.'s complexion made you want to eat nothing else but, for the rest of your life.

Domina thought that M.J. looked color-corrected, like the packages of products designed especially for television, when an artist makes the reds redder and the words larger, so that the design looks its best when it comes over the home set.

For one thing, M.J.'s hair was pure marmalade, orange-red, glistening, heaped generously in a toss of curl.

For another thing, her eyes were violet, fringed with the kind of lashes so long and thick and dark they looked glued on, expensively, one by one.

M.J.'s size and posture made Domina think of a ballet dancer. But her coloring belonged to a movie star. So did her breasts, full and independent beneath the snug knit tops she wore, which came just to the waistband of her denim jeans. Domina knew that M.J. was just twenty, older by a few years than her own daughter. That knowledge stirred her with a distant early-warning feeling that she always put away quickly, because what could you do about growing older? In the sunlight blazing now through the windows, M.J. looked like a small, round tabby cat, tiny, touchable, endearing.

M.J. looked sharply at her boss. She knew that Domina had been in early, typing furiously at something or other. What? Couldn't have been a new piece of copy – they were pretty much all set for the week, unless she'd missed something, and she sure tried not to miss things. A new idea for one of the other accounts? Not this morning, M.J. decided. Domina looked a little grim today, not quite as morning serene and plantation-lady cool as usual. That's what you get, thought M.J., from spending your nights all alone, lady. It wakes you up cross and unsatisfied, that's

25

what it does. And Domina Drexler, ma'am, when I have a job like you've got and money like you've got, and a colored maid popping in mornings behind a big breakfast tray, you can just bet there's going to be breakfast for two on that tray.

M.J. had not awakened on her own since she was going on sixteen, not if she could possibly help it. Of course, some nights were better than others, and some were just to get yourself a little ahead in this world of woe, but still and all, there was usually someone nice to share your coffee with.

Right now there was someone really cute to wake up to, and flirt with the rest of the day, too, right here in this very office.

M.J. kept her face still, the way she had always known just how to do, while she thought a little bit about last night.

They had gone to the movies, but this one was all war and noise and guns, the kind she hated paying mind to. So she had begun to fiddle around with her nice little account executive. And by the time she got her hand in his lap, he was more than ready to get up and hurry home. Home was his apartment – a walk-up, to be sure; but then, he was young yet, he hadn't properly got started making a lot of money. They'd gone to bed and really torn at it, falling asleep exhausted at dawn, waking with their legs still entwined together. Poor old Domina.

Domina watched M.J. put down the layout pad she was carrying. The girl held a bright orange felt-tipped pen in her small hand. Domina noticed the way the pen picked up the precise shade of M.J.'s hair. It looked almost as if she had art-directed her own appearance.

'Sorry,' said Domina, 'I haven't time. I've got to be up in Godwin's office in a few minutes, and there are some things I want to do before I go up. Leave them, and I'll check them out the minute I get back down.'

'Oh. Then maybe I'll just hang on to them. I could keep on working till you get back.'

'Suit yourself,' said Domina, standing up. It was a signal for M.J. to leave, but the girl seemed to be taking her time about picking up the layouts. The reason became clear when she spoke.

'Domina? Would you be mad if I just let the account men have a little peek? They're just dying for these, the ads are on extension already. I don't guess they want to wait much longer.'

Domina had been a supervisor far too long to fall for that. If the account men liked the ads as they were, she could neither add nor subtract, much less change anything drastically later on. And if they didn't like the layouts, the fault would still be Domina's, since she was supposed to make time to look things over. Defense, thought Domina – there's a military word, and that's what working in an office is all about. She swept the whole pile off the table and into her cupboard in one swift move, closing the door on them firmly.

'They'll be here all ready for me to see later on,' she said. 'I won't keep them long, M.J. You tell those guys to hold up till later. And don't let them bully you. There's a whole day left to make that closing date.'

M.J. smiled. 'I'm glad,' she said. 'I'll tell them, when they ask, that you have everything.'

Domina looked sharply at her. Did M.J. understand that she was now in a position to tell the account men that her supervisor was holding up the work? She could see no hint of this on M.J.'s face.

The hell with it. If her meeting with Godwin went wrong, she certainly wouldn't be worrying about food layouts. She'd be worrying about the maintenance for her apartment, the tuition for the children, the doctor's bills for Michael, the insurance bill coming up, and Leota's salary. She'd be worrying about which jobs might be open for her at other agencies, and which of these jobs might be good enough to show Brady Godwin and the whole rest of the world how stupid Jackson had been not to promote her and hang on to her.

A quick picture of her bankbook shot into Domina's mind, like a flash cut in a television commercial. The last figure in the little book, the one that counted, was $3,200.89. Domina's money always seemed to flow out and away just as fast as it came rolling in.

It wouldn't be easy to find a job better than this one. It

27

could be done, but it would take time. In a hurry, you grabbed at jobs that weren't good enough. And then you woke up and were sorry you had made such a fuss over a word, a name, a title. You can't pay bills with a title.

Well, then, she thought, I'll be just as icy as he is, no matter what he says. I'll keep my temper and I'll stare right back into his horrible eyes and I'll act like a lady. And when I leave, I'll plot and plan for new jobs just the way a man would do. I've done it before, haven't I?

But that was years ago, she thought suddenly, with dismay. And I didn't have a job nearly this good to lose. And I had a husband, who helped out with money some, and listened to my problems, sort of. But now I'm alone. Alone.

She looked up and realized that M.J. still waited, and was looking at her in concern.

'Domina? You all right?'

'Of course,' Domina said crisply. 'See you later.'

Now it really was time for her meeting. She would have to forget about a final check on her appearance, a final stop in the ladies' room. You had to leave time for Jackson's stately elevators, gliding up and down at their own calm prewar pace. There were eight of those elevators, but all of them always were going down when you were in a hurry to go up. And she was in a hurry to go up.

A little rushed, ruffled, unsettled, more than she had planned to be for this crucial meeting, Domina walked determinedly down the corridor.

Maran

Maran Milne Slade
27 East 45th St.
New York, N.Y. 10016
555-1897
Service will pick up by third ring

Owner and president of Maran Milne Slade Associates. Fashion finds for television, film, advertising, theater, and personal consultation by annual retainer only.

Credits:

Grey Advertising Inc.	Pan-American Phoenix
MGM	Shop
J. Walter Thompson, Inc.	ABC
Benton & Bowles, Inc.	Triano Loeffler, Inc.
William Hanson Bradley	Trager Rosen, Inc.
Associates	William Esty, Inc.

References:

Jacob Sternn	Domina Drexler
2 East 17th St	Potter Jackson
New York, N.Y.	8 East 40th St
	New York, N.Y.

Janie Hitch Enterprises	Peter Bosch
9887 Sunset Blvd	978 Pico Blvd
Hollywood, Cal. 90017	Los Angeles, Cal. 90090

Winner Lamée Award for Creative Fashion, 1979, 1978.

Sources worldwide: New York, London, Paris, Milan, Munich, San Francisco, Copenhagen, Stockholm, Helsinki, Tokyo, Hong Kong, Singapore, Sydney.

Maran Slade was waiting for her husband to finish making love to her.

She lay back with her slim legs apart to accommodate Bill's bulk, her head tipped a little sideways to avoid the rasp of his morning beard. While he pumped away at her, she rested her hands on his back so he would feel her encouragement. Heat seemed to steam from his body.

Thank God he likes the morning, she thought as she waited patiently for him to get it over with. At night, with the crazy hours my work get me home, I'd never get any sleep, much less get my face and hands fixed right for bed. This way it's fast, and I can get right into the tub, to feel clean again.

Bill always awoke with an erection, an achievement he believed was his alone, and one he honestly thought was the result of his love for her. Maran knew better, but wouldn't have disillusioned him for anything. She was thankful that he wanted her, glad that he reached for her before she was fully awake, so that he'd be inside her before she had to pay real attention. Maran loved Bill, but sex had always bothered her. She could never believe any woman who said she actually liked the whole process. But then, Maran had no patience with women who refused to do their job in bed, especially with husbands who were good to them. And Bill had been awfully good to her, rescuing her from the shameful state of having no man at all after her second husband had moved out. Maran felt she owed him a lot. Plus, she really did believe that sex was good for your looks. She smiled over Bill's head to think of him as a kind of giant one-a-day vitamin shot.

Come on, Bill, she thought. I've got the studio at eight.

31

I've got to get Jake Sternn alone. This new job he mentioned sounded so big, could be a terrific break for me. Domina had picked up a little news about it, something about Israel, how they could sell more clothes to the American market.

Just thinking about a job like that, she gave Bill a warm little hug. Then, to be safe about the time, she twisted her back so she could reach down and stroke his balls the way that always hurried him up.

It worked. He was pushing deep inside her, leaning heavily on her, breathing hard, and making embarrassing sounds in his throat. Bill at least measured up to her unusual height. In all the lovemaking she'd had to do in her lifetime, she disliked most the short men whose toenails scratched at her ankles as they moved on top of her. Maran tensed herself to receive his climax, and gave a couple of little screams to signal one of her own. Bill rolled off her, patted her once hard, and got heavily out of bed. When she heard the shower rush in the bathroom, Maran knew the day was begun.

She did her stretches and bends in bed, feeling the proper pull at her ribs and thighs. Then she moved to the other bathroom to dress, never looking in the mirror until she had finished. Her six-foot-one frame looked its usual elegance in the fitted black pants and matching turtleneck that were her uniform. Her hair was sleek in its small knot, ready to behave perfectly during her long working day. She felt trim and alert, happier up on her feet than she ever felt on her back. Almost everything bad that had ever happened to Maran had been when she was lying down: sex, the birth of her daughter, pneumonia, fainting in stuffy studios, sunburn, awful night arguments. She put on the stack of bangle bracelets she always wore, fitted her tinted prescription glasses to the top of her head without disturbing a hair, and went to the bedroom for her mink coat.

Bill was still in the bathroom. She could hear the radio blaring and see the steam that came through the door at the cracks. She banged on it for a good-bye.

Maran moved fast to the lobby of her building. The doorman, accustomed to her generous tips, jumped to help her get the tin trunk that had been taken down the night before, and find her a taxi.

At Sternn's today it was going to be an important shot for a new lipstick color, Revlon, she knew. Once there, everything was buzz and confusion in the front office. Maran pushed through the camera assistants, makeup and hair experts, writers, art directors, and Revlon people with their coffee and bagels, smiling at everyone, stopping for no one.

She didn't see Jake Sternn anywhere. He was probably hiding out in an equipment room until the actual shooting started. Photography always took forever to get going. All the helpers fussed to stretch out their special work – the makeup man, hairdresser, lighting guys, prop people, even the gofers. It wasn't surprising. They were all, except Maran, paid by the hour. She had years ago progressed to a daily rate, now seven hundred dollars. No need to prolong her actions. But Maran had always given full measure, whatever she was paid.

In the cluttered dressing room, the lanky model was being painted, brushed, nail-polished.

Maran quickly steamed out the designer dress dyed precisely to match the new lipstick color for the ad. Then she chose jewelry from her boxes, a first try that would be discussed and changed several times. A few jokes got the model hurrying a little, coaxed the makeup man into finishing, spurred the hairdresser into his final flourishes with the spray. Maran led the model through the crowd into the corner where the camera was, the two of them towering over everyone else in the studio.

Maran knew that most stylists, once their fashions are in front of the camera, sit comfortably drinking coffee in the dressing room, watching their racks of clothes and boxes of accessories. When the model comes back in, they come to life again, unpinning dresses, washing out sweat and stains, sewing up rips, packing what they have brought to the shoot.

Unlike the others, Maran never let her fashions out of her sight. She would jockey for a place slightly apart from the crowd which clustered around the model, and stay there, alert, watching for creases, pins that glinted, hems that sagged, anything that might mar the perfection of the photograph. It was one of the reasons her work was in demand.

Watching so carefully, Maran was the first to notice that the model was beginning to crack up.

For a few moments the girl's actions had lagged behind the directions the photographer was calling to her, to turn, to smile, to blow a kiss.

Abruptly she broke the pose, put her head back, and began to scream.

Everyone in the studio froze.

The girl shifted into loud sobs.

The assistants all watched in horror. Makeup that had taken two hours to accomplish began to mix with her tears, mascara sending hideous blue veins all down her lovely neck. Spots began to form on the front of the primrose gown. Sternn turned and walked off the set. The makeup man seemed about to burst into tears of his own. The art director stood transfixed. Even the secretaries were tip-toeing in from the outer office, so that the shrilling telephones added to the confusion.

Maran stepped forward. These fucking European girls, she thought. No control, no brains, no professionalism. Not like when I modeled. We held a pose for five whole minutes if the photographer told us to. Didn't even breathe, outdoors in the cold, so the pictures wouldn't show a cloud around our mouths. And we got forty an hour. These temperamental bitches get six hundred and they act retarded. There goes my lunch with Domina. Shit. And she's got a meeting with that old bastard Godwin this morning, so she'll be needing me, too.

She walked up to the model, by now working herself up to racking noises, drew her hand back as far as she could, and swung, spanking the girl so hard on her small, flat rear that one of the diamond earrings she wore flew out into the crowd.

While everyone scrambled to find it, Maran drew her arm back for another shot, but could see it wasn't going to be needed.

34

The model hugged herself, gasped, sniffled, and became human again. Her sobs subsided.

Somebody giggled, and everybody relaxed.

Maran took the girl by the hand and yanked her back to the dressing room. It would take them an extra hour to clean her up, mask the damage to her face, and start shooting again. And there were stains – *stains* – on the front of the layered organdy gown that cost four thousand dollars. Maran would have half an hour's work with alcohol and a hot iron to get it in condition again.

The beautiful black model who had been sitting in the dressing room waiting to repeat the picture for *Ebony* and *Essence* once the first girl had been photographed, smiled at Maran. 'Better not try that on me,' she drawled. 'I'm the only chocolate drop you've got today.'

'You've got too much sense, Sally,' said Maran.

'Maran? Jake wants you,' said one of the secretaries.

'Sure,' said Maran, her spirits leaping. 'Just let me get this going.'

She pushed the model into the chair and looked for the assistants. The makeup man was still shaking with fury, but his helper, a beautiful young man who had been soothing him in and out of bed for months, Maran knew, was comforting him. She felt the situation was under control.

Now Sternn, and this new job.

Jake Sternn was sitting on a tall stool in a storeroom, far away from the commotion. He looked hunched, worried, like a forest elf perched on a toadstool, knees up under his chin. But his small body straightened and he smiled as Maran came near.

'Never again,' he said as she shut the door. 'Never. She may be the most glorious thing since Suzy Parker and Helen of Troy, but I'm going out and find a new brunette.'

'She's a cunt,' said Maran agreeably. 'You wanted to talk to me? I desperately want to talk to you. Who first?'

Sternn looked up at her. Still the fabulous cheekbones, still the length of neck, still the stunning litheness she had shown years before, the first time he had ever seen her. He had warmed to Maran the moment he saw her upside down through a camera lens, and his admiration for her spirit had

35

grown year by year. Modigliani now, he thought, but she was all Renoir then. Today I'd shoot her in black and white to catch the lines in her face. Or in a ruff like Queen Elizabeth. Maybe with a pencil behind her ear.

How in hell am I going to tell her she maybe can't have this job? Why do I have to be the one to break it to her?

Look at that face. Would she work again in front of the camera? Could I do a thing on beauties grown old?

Maran waited patiently, as she had long since learned to do, letting her mind float. She was a little surprised by his silence, since Sternn was almost never silent. But she trusted this man as she did no other.

Maran had met Sternn in the glorious days when she was young. Her skin had been like cream silk, her waist twenty inches around, and her legs firm all the way up. The head salesclerk in the store where she worked had told her to try modeling. The first model agency she approached had taken one look at her and put her in a taxi to Sternn's studio.

Maran had adjusted only a year before to the idea that anyone would look at her twice. Through adolescence she had been far too tall and gawky. Her cheekbones were too pronounced, her feet too large, her eyes too slanted to interest the high-school boys around her. She had gratefully married the first man who took her up. And he had soon let her down, leaving her with a tiny daughter and with no real training for any kind of work. She had parked the baby with her mother and found a job behind a counter at Macy's.

Maran walked into Sternn's studio dressed in the best style of the day, in a wide cinched belt, a ruffled skirt and petticoats, spike heels, and a tiny hat pinned back on her high pompadour.

The man she met looked about twelve years old. He was small, with a mass of black hair and the most enormous eyes she had ever seen in any face. He wore blue jeans like a workingman, and tennis sneakers on his tiny feet. He had looked at her hard, and when told her name, had repeated it to himself several times. 'Marian. Marian? You shouldn't have such a nothing name. Why not skip the *i* and call yourself Maran? I mean, *nobody* is named Maran, you know?'

She'd been amused, but hadn't dared show it. However, when he had asked her to rinse out her hair and put on a wrapper, she had balked. Her hair would go all straight, she had told him. 'That's what I want,' he had said. Maran had thought: brother, wait till you see me uncurled.

When she had come out of the tiny dressing room, feeling chilled and ridiculous, there had been a tall stool waiting in a corner. And a camera, a kind she had never seen, small, with two lenses instead of one. Sternn had turned on some strange lights with umbrellas behind them, peered through his camera at her, and then exploded. 'Jesus,' he'd said, 'your neck is absolutely fantastic.' My neck, she had thought. Whoever looked at my neck before? But she had smiled in wonder, Sternn had caught that smile on his film, and everything had changed for her at that moment.

For nine marvelous years Maran Slade was fashion's top model. Her face and figure sold lipstick, dresses, refrigerators, cars, airplane tickets. She posed against the Golden Gate Bridge, the Eiffel Tower, the Pyramids, the Taj Mahal. She worked in the ateliers of Paris, where fashion was being revived after the war, in the studios of every postwar fashion photographer in New York. She married a handsome advertising account executive, divorced him a year later in Juarez. After the second divorce, she worked even harder to keep from thinking, from feeling like a failure at everything real. Through it all, Sternn was her mentor, her friend, her Pygmalion. She would drop any booking to smile, run, kiss, jump in front of his cameras.

Then she lost a job for a cosmetic ad to a seventeen-year-old German girl with a face as smooth as marble.

Maran went into a panic. Within six months her teeth had been capped, her hair tinted, and her face lifted, the surgeon cutting and stitching as skillfully as she herself could alter clothes. Feeling better about herself, Maran had accepted new bookings.

At her first photography session, after checking and re-checking her heavy makeup, especially around the faint

37

scar tissue, Maran felt positive that her face again looked smooth and perfect.

The pictures were meant for a cosmetic ad. On the set was a skinny dark girl from the agency named Domina Drexler. She had known precisely what she wanted. Tight close-ups.

Maran heard the photographer as he examined the test photo, telling the girl that Maran couldn't take tight close-ups. He wanted to put Vaseline on the lens, to soften and blur her image. The Drexler girl said she didn't want softness and blur. The photographer had shouted, then, that Maran would look like a hag and the pictures would flop. At that point Maran's heart had flopped. Feeling desperate, suicidal, furious about the time and money she'd wasted on the surgery, she'd burst into tears and fled for the ladies' room. In the mirror, her face looked as youthful as it had ever been. In the camera eye, she'd realized with horror, every line and wrinkle, every flaw, was magnified.

Domina had waited a decent five minutes. Then she had come in and asked Maran to come and have a cup of coffee. They had gone out together and sat over a small restaurant table until midnight. It had been the start of a friendship that shared every emotion, every problem, and every triumph in both of their lives.

It was Domina who put Maran on the road to success as a stylist, by introducing her to Janie Hitch.

When the black gospel singer from Alabama was persuaded by a smart agent to get out of her choir robe and switch from records to television, Janie starred in some commercials Domina had written. Domina insisted on Maran as the stylist for the job.

Since Maran had worn every important fashion for a decade, met every designer, furrier, costumer, hairdresser, and makeup person in the business, knew clothes from the drawing board to the thrift shops, she felt confident about setting styles and making them work. She got Janie to grow out her pomaded and straightened chignon and let her natural frizz round out into its own halo. Then she painted Janie's mouth a rich blue-black and her nails a frosty white. She chose clothes that emphasized the huge breasts and soft buttocks, in colors that almost glowed in the dark. The commercials were a tremendous success, and Janie was booked for a series of concert tours. Everywhere, she mentioned Maran Slade. After that, Maran Slade Associates was born.

At a press party for a designer opening a few years later, Maran accepted a drink from a tall newspaperman. In bed, Bill Hammond was just as long as she was. Then one day, after a terrific breakfast he cooked for them on her tiny stove, he asked to move in with her.

After the years of loneliness, Maran responded to Bill's warmth and admiration with joy. She liked his willingness to let her lead, decide, command. She liked being able to look up at him, which she could do by keeping her chin tucked down just a little. She liked his friendliness toward Dawn, her daughter, who was a sulky schoolgirl with none of her mother's looks.

When they married, Bill soon gave up his job and settled into being what he called a househusband. Maran paid the bills and thanked God she had found a steady escort and a sympathetic listener at home, all in one man. She was nearly happy. Only her appearance troubled her, the lines deepening again in her forehead, the brown spots showing up on her hands. She bought pink light bulbs for the apartment, altered her passport age by ten years by changing one digit, worked out a system of dressing that kept her from mirrors. Age was Maran's nightmare, a nightmare that grew worse, woke her shivering in the night, gave her headaches when she caught glimpses of herself.

Now she stood waiting for Sternn to speak. Just in back of his stool, lined up in rows on the floor, were slabs of mounted photographs. Maran thought of her own favorite of herself, the famous one in the satin Chanel gown with the circus tigers. It was undoubtedly there somewhere. She wondered suddenly if anyone, seeing her this minute, pins on a magnet at her wrist, alcohol spills down the front of her shirt, would ever identify her with the magic creature in that picture.

'Maran,' said Sternn finally, 'the agency has been after me about the Israel thing. I know I promised you. I know you'd do it the best. There's no question.'

Maran's stomach lurched. She wanted to put her hands in front of her face to warn him off speaking anymore, to stop him from saying one other word. He had promised, *promised*. She wanted this job. It would be worth a hundred small dumb jobs like the one today. A fashion promotion for a whole country? It could take her up, out of the world of stylists, away from standing on her feet pinning dresses and calming idiot girls. It could launch her into a new universe of consulting, advising planners who wanted to put hungry people to work in underdeveloped countries. Not that Maran gave a flying fuck for hungry people she had never met. But this work could be a stepping-stone to a special place, a world where it was good for you to be experienced, to be old. How long could she go on acting young and eager? She had felt so tired lately. Harder to get up every morning, wearier taking her clothes off at night. Screw it, she wanted this job so her years could be an asset instead of a hideous, disfiguring, shameful thing.

'What is it, Jake? What are you trying to tell me?' she said, struggling to keep her voice even.

'Maran, I can't promise. The agency made some kind of crazy commitment of their own, they're thinking about somebody else, someone who's worked with Tel Aviv before, who knows the fashion people there.'

Maran's voice was coming out shakily now. Was she quavering with age? Was even her voice going to betray her now? 'Well, who is it? Who is it that knows so fucking much?'

Sternn looked down at the floor again. 'They're talking about Belle Rosner,' he said softly.

Electric shock stabbed through Maran's forehead. Talk about *old*. The woman had to be eighty, eighty-five. I wasn't sure she was still alive, even. They trot her out for the fashion-award dinners like you bring out an antique Chanel dress. Belle Rosner. Maybe she's related to Golda Meir, she looks like her. That silly thought calmed her a little.

'She's Jewish, for one thing,' said Sternn. 'She's been running some big exchange program for American and

Israeli designers that works, works very well, apparently. Remember she wrote that op-ed thing in the *Times* about how when a grandmother visits Israel there isn't even a good kid's dress that's been made there, when every tailor in Europe has emigrated and is busy working right there in Tel Aviv? Well, the guys at the agency saw that, and there you are.'

And there I am, rubbing makeup stains out of fancy fabrics until I shrivel up and die.

'Okay, Jake darling,' she said miserably. 'I do thank you for trying. I love you a lot, you know?'

He stood up then to give her a good hug, and Maran thought how ridiculous they would look to anyone who came in, the small man and the woman a whole head taller. She kissed the top of his silver gray curls, feeling as if she were his mother.

While she went mechanically through the rest of her work, packing, folding, Maran's mind rattled furiously over and over the same ground. It's not final. They haven't announced it yet. Israel. What do I really know about Israel? Should I forget the whole thing and look around for something else like it? But there isn't anything else like it. Israel always sounded so sandy. Egypt, yes, five times for fashion shots at the Sphinx, but who shoots in Israel? Somebody told me it looks like Queens Boulevard. Fuck it, that's where you want to work, that's where you're going to work. I could have a sudden religious conversion. Baby, if that's what it takes, that's what's going to be. No one, certainly no old hag, is getting that job away from me.

Maran could feel her stomach gathering into a knot. All the way back in the cab her mind whirled on.

Domina, she thought, I'll get her moving. She'll talk to the right people, tell them I can tower above Belle Rosner. The Israel Trade Center, they'll have information I can put together to sound smart. The Fashion Group? They'll certainly have a list of Israeli designers. Sternn will help me, if I really get to him, remind him how that old bitch will want all the publicity for herself. And she'll keep yammering at him about Horst and Steichen and all the other dead photographers she knew. He'll hate it. She probably worked with Daguerre when he was inventing the tin-type. Maybe she'll die. Did they ever think of that, her dying in the middle of the job?

In the apartment Maran was greeted by a cheerful warm smell of furniture polish, onion soup, and good perfume, in a happy blend. Bill, with a dish towel around his middle, emerged from the little kitchen. 'Hi, baby,' he said, folding her up in his big arms. Baby. How good that sounded.

She returned the hug, feeling strength flood through her, feeling little ideas pop and sizzle along the wires of her brain.

Darling Bill. Whatever he didn't do, like bring home money, there were things he did do that she was grateful for. She never came home to an empty house, never had to shop or fix things or mess around in the kitchen getting her hands any worse than they were already. And best of all, Bill kept the peace with her difficult daughter, Dawn, who, thank God, no longer lived at home.

'Bill, darling,' she said, pulling back a little and looking her husband in the eye. 'How much do you know about Israel? How much could you find out for me, fast, really fast? You were a newspaperman, you know lots of people. I need to know *everything* about the fashion potential there in about fifteen minutes, and you've got to get out and snoop for me. Will you?'

Bill held Maran at arm's length for a moment, observed her flushed excitement, felt the bones in her shoulders under the soft fabric of her shirt. He wished she'd stop wearing those damned sunglasses in the house. They hid half her face. He liked to look at her face, into her eyes. She worried so goddamned much about her looks, her age. And she had nothing to worry about, he thought. She'd certainly never get fat, like other women. She'd always walk like a real empress holding court. Silly, he thought, women can be so silly. Look at her Dawn. Now it's a new guy, a jazz musician. Probably her best source of coke, that's all. He'd keep an eye on her. For Maran, beautiful, worried Maran.

'What's it all about, honey?' he asked.

'Bill. I'm about to go on the biggest, bloodthirstiest hunt

for a job the fashion world has ever seen,' said Maran with some heat.

And while the words came out, while her mind was racing ahead to all the things she might do, Maran began to realize that she was filling up with an old emotion, a young emotion. The same emotion that had bubbled up in her when she sat for Sternn for the first time, so long so. Suddenly she felt straighter, lovelier, younger, floating down a long runway in clouds of chiffon, an audience all around her, applauding softly, admiring her in the warm spotlight. Her old smile responded to the excitement in her mind, making her glow again, radiant in the rush of anticipation.

Belle

PLEASE COPY EXACTLY

Bella Rosner Karp
14 Sutton Place East
New York, N.Y. 10022
555-5680

Belle Rosner needs no introduction to the fashion world.
Founding member of the Fashion Fair, trustee of the
World Costume Collection in Paris, US delegate to the
World Economic Recovery Conference, Thailand, 1958,
author of *In My Fashion* and an autobiography, *I Made It
Myself*, her creative merchandising flair has increased
revenues for underdeveloped nations, countless retail
stores, and hundreds of individuals throughout the world.
Now in her eighties, Miss Rosner meets weekly with store
executives as chairwoman of the Retail Store Executives
Council, coordinating promotional activities. A native
New Yorker who never finished high school, Miss
Rosner's career began at Gimbels, covered most major
network stores, included travel throughout the world and
was climaxed in 1965 when she was named President's
delegate to the Commission for Underdeveloped
Countries. She also found time to marry and bring up two
daughters.

With the terrace doors open to the soft, spring morning, Belle Rosner sat at her desk wrapping Christmas presents.

Three a day was her rule. And three it would be even today, when her hands were shaking and she felt a little short of breath.

Control yourself, she thought. You're not rescued from retirement yet. You won't know positively until you meet this young man. So stop acting like a young girl waiting for her first job interview.

Belle opened the large box that held her ribbon, tape, string, cards, colored pens, and the collection of beautiful papers from all over the world. She set precisely what she would be needing this morning.

Three packages, she told herself. For people who may be able to help when you get the work. Who can bring in the right designers and manufacturers. Christmas presents to help you get away from this ridiculous retirement business.

Retirement. The very word was so repellent. It meant withdrawal, retreat. What had these words to do with Bella Rosner Karp, who had always attacked, directed, led the way. After all, it was only because she was always a step ahead of everyone else that she had chosen to retire, before others could even suggest such a thing.

She thought back to the beautiful luncheons, plaques from the stores, magazine articles about her career. And why not? Who had achieved what she had, who in the entire world of fashion? Edna Chase, Tobe, Estelle Hamburger, Carmel Snow, Mary Lewis, Diana Vreeland? She had known them all, was equal to any of them.

Still, most of them hadn't had to go through this idleness. Dreadful, when your mail was simply a pile of junk. And the telephone didn't ring. And you sat at fashion meetings listening to inferior speakers saying nonsense. Like the *Harper's Bazaar* editor who introduced a designer as one of Chanel's two right arms. And the commentator who had utterly botched the facts, confusing Lanvin with Poiret as she discussed the designers of the twenties. Belle had looked around, waiting for the laughter and the corrections. And there had been none. How could you sit still when you knew so much more, so much better? Retirement.

Well, she had managed her retirement as adeptly as she had managed everything else in her life. The reading program, The courses at the Metropolitan Museum. Her will. Her obituary typed in triplicate and ready for the press. The lists of all her marvelous possessions, and where they were to be sent. At least *they* wouldn't need Christmas wrapping.

Belle forced herself to concentrate on the job at hand. It would calm her, as work always had. She looked carefully at the three objects she had chosen to wrap this morning. A silver inkwell. A needlepoint belt. And the magnificent bolt of brocade, wound around a paper core, as she had brought it from Hong Kong so long ago. The three things made a fascinating still-life composition against the smooth wood grain of her table. How clearly she could still sense the beauty of shape and form! Even when the body was tired, how sharp her senses, how clear her mind! She simply must get this new work.

She glanced at the French crystal clock which dominated her desk. Still plenty of time. The appointment was for eleven. Though her hands had stopped shaking, Belle could feel a quivering in her heart, a flutter in her stomach. Ridiculous, no need for nerves. If she got the bus at the corner by ten-fifteen, she would arrive in good time. Everything was ready. She had checked over all the material last night.

Belle picked up the heavy silver inkwell. Art Nouveau, perfect for any of the magazine editors. She might be needing one of those editors. The inkwell had been bought in Paris, years before, one of her trips to the fashion collections. Belle used to dash out to the flea markets between showings, making every instant count. It had cost about four dollars, she remembered. Now you couldn't buy such a thing for under two hundred. How wonderful to *have* things, instead of buying them at today's outrageous prices.

Belle wrapped, using clouds of tissue, pressing creases firmly, tying each package with exactly enough ribbon to create a pretty bow.

The belt she had made herself, that time in the hospital when she had yearned for something to keep her hands busy. It would be good for the little woman at the Government of Israel Trade Center. She could be a tremendous help if the promotion took hold.

The brocade would go to Sternn. He would know its quality. Poor man, having to photograph the polyesters they made now, without drape or luster or weight to them. It would say all the right things to him, she thought. Remind him that she had been buying beautiful things when he was just a child with a box camera. That she understood beauty as no one else did. That her standards were the highest. She had found the brocade on her first trip to the Orient, in one of those fantastic shops. The owner had been tall and thin. He had used an odd instrument, as long and thin as he, with a hook on top, to reach rolls of cloth stored on high shelves. With her buyer's eye Belle had known that the best would be out of reach, up under the roof. She had insisted and pointed, and finally he had hooked it down. The moment she had unrolled the lustrous purple shot with heavy gold thread, Belle had known it was a marvel. Sternn would know too. After all, by Christmas, if all went well, they would be photographing together. She could almost see the shots, fashions shown against the crumbling walls and modern sculpture of Jerusalem. She could steer him to wonderful locations, suggest and cajole as she knew so well how to do.

Belle slipped each package into a plastic bag, stretching the sticky film tight so that it too would look neat and smooth. Then she took the wastebasket out to the incinerator. She liked the incinerator. It was final, decisive, to let your garbage drop twenty stories to a smoldering fire. No loose ends.

Belle put the wrapped packages into the closet with the rest of the completed presents. The whole Christmas business would be finished by summer. Well, she thought, I've always lived a season ahead. Bathing suits in spring. Winter coats in August. Christmas complete by Halloween. That was merchandising.

Belle tidied herself, patting down the black suit from Chanel, fluffing her silver hair, running a cloth over her handmade shoes, testing the safety clasp on her emerald pin. An imposing figure, she thought. She picked up the heavy briefcase, polished to its usual glow, and glanced inside. The folders were all in order. And there was her book, her autobiography, *I Made It Myself*, a present for Mr Rossen. With a purpose. If he glanced at it, he would get an excellent notion of precisely who she was. If he read it, surely the work would be hers. She double-locked the front door and walked majestically to the bus at the corner.

Belle sat, large, plump, and proper, at a window and watched the streets for a moment. She was early, of course, but that was fine. She opened the briefcase and took out her own book. She loved the book. Such a solid achievement, such a lesson for the young people today. She opened it at the beginning, admired the title page, and was instantly back in time, sixteen, chubby in blue serge, on a bus going to Gimbels to try for her first job, a real job of her very own.

Bella Rosner had got that job, over the objections of her parents, owners of their own small tailoring shop, who had never understood their driving, eager, ambitious daughter. Bella might have spent her time with the neighborhood girls, dainty in white muslin and black stockings, giggling. But she wanted a job, longed for the independence only work could give her. She got one, started that very day selling gloves on the huge main floor. Those gloves! Buttons all the way, a selling method, elbow on the counter, pull, stretch, buttonhook, admire, sell. Six dollars for creamy French kid opera gloves!

Bella adored the store from the first, poked and wandered through all of it, looked, listened, studied Gimbels' merchandise. Soon she had a personal triumph. When dress sales were slowing badly, as men went off to World War I, she realized that women without men have little need for fashion. Bella, who now worked in the advertising department, decided to send the fashion where the men were. She cajoled the buyer on the main floor into setting up a small photographic studio. Then she wrote a bold ad. 'Be the Girl of His Dreams in the Trenches. You Buy the Dress, We Photograph You in It.' Dresses, photographs, and frames marched out of the store. And management began to notice the large young woman who arrived long before the opening bell, stayed late night after night, spoke so excitely of new ideas and new combinations of merchandise. Bella felt her confidence soaring.

Just when her parents had resigned themselves to having an old maid for a daughter, had learned to count on the fifteen dollars a week Bella gave them from the unbelievable fifty dollars she earned, Johnny Karp came into the advertising office. He smelled of cigars and fresh air, he spoke of France and Belgium and England, he asked her tea-dancing at the Plaza. In two months they were married, living with her parents, rocking her tiny bed. The arrangement left Bella free of housekeeping and cooking, free to work just as hard as before she had married. And she loved working hard.

Her girls were born, each returning from the hospital with a nurse, as if Bella had borne both baby and nurse together.

When she moved into store management, Bella moved the family from Lenox Avenue to Fifth. At the same time, she shortened her name to Belle, one syllable being more efficient than two. Privately she thought Belle more suitable, more French. France was the only country where real fashion was created.

One afternoon when Belle was on Seventh Avenue worming secrets out of a rainwear manufacturer, a call came from her office. Johnny, struck by a car, dead by the time an ambulance could get him to the hospital.

To her own horror, Belle's first emotion was relief. Now she could manage everything, use her time exactly as she wanted. Old Mr Rosenzweig had looked closely at her. 'Bella,' he'd said, 'don't make a mistake now. Forget the store, forget working for other people now. No husband, you'll have it all your way. You've got the moxie. Go into business yourself. The girls will find you a taxi home.'

All during the arrangements, the funeral, she'd thought it out. Her own business. She would give stores everywhere the kind of advice and ideas she had given one store. She would show them how to advertise, arrange their displays, set up their departments.

For her own business Belle worked seven days a week, ten hours a day. Her older daughter's wedding was sandwiched between a visit from a new French designer and a Toiletries Association dinner. Her younger daughter's nervous breakdown took more time away from Belle's busy working life. She flew with the girl to a hospital in Chicago that specialized in nervous disorders. At the last, her daughter had raged at her, torn her clothes. Again, Belle had been astounded at her own feelings. She had wanted to smack her distraught daughter, to fend her off. Belle went home and buried her emotions in work.

Years later she was still working at top speed, keeping three secretaries busy, and then the blackout spells came. Belle would wake with her cheek pressed into the carpet, and no memory of how she had fallen. Once she fell in the street, waking to see a circle of faces staring at her, like a pearl necklace on sale for $19.95. Enough, she had thought. Even Belle Rosner cannot go on forever.

But today, she thought, if there is anyone who can, I can.

I'm rested, and I feel quite well, really. My weight hasn't risen much, my clothes fit perfectly, the doctors are amazed at my stamina. I need very little sleep, I never catch colds. I speak without a tremor. If I pace myself carefully, I can handle this Israeli promotion with ease and grace and style.

I'm so bored. I must get this work.

Belle got off the bus heavily and walked into the office building. She knew Mr Rossen was on thirty-eight, but she checked anyway, on the big index in the lobby. What a great number of people worked at Potter Jackson! Did they all contribute? Roe Rossen, there, Account Management, thirty-eighth. She entered an elevator, stood properly back from the doors. The elevator filled with a rush of noisy young people. Outlandish clothes, both boys and girls in blue jeans and T-shirts. And their feet! They all seemed to be wearing hobnailed boots. Inappropriate. Ugly. Belle chuckled to herself, remembering how young girls had always shown an extraordinary desire to wear hideous shoes. Black button boots, saddle shoes, spectator pumps, ballet flats, espadrilles, now hiking boots. Somehow they knew that ugly shoes by contrast make the most of slim, lovely young legs. A fascinating magazine article, she thought. It showed how much the right perspective could mean in the fashion business. One could guess which styles would sell. Her ears felt the pressure as the elevator rose.

'Mr Rossen's secretary will be out in just a moment,' said the receptionist. 'Won't you sit down.'

Belle chose one of the leather chairs, perching on its edge, ready to get to her feet without taking an old woman's time.

A girl came for her.

A long walk, a turn, and they were in front of a wooden grille. Through the gate and into a waiting room with desk, couches and a telephone with many buttons. The girl kept on going, so Belle did, too.

She had time only for an impression before he was on his feet, coming toward her with his hand out. Tall. Strong face. Large dark eyes. Lined skin, good teeth. Beautiful jacket, certainly Harris tweed, excellent with the flannel trousers. Shoelace untied. Warm hand, dry and comfortable, firm touch.

'I'm so pleased,' said Mr Rossen, 'so pleased to meet you at last.'

That was quite right. Belle smiled encouragement at him. She let him settle her in a chair between two of the windows, and she put her briefcase carefully on the polished coffee table.

'My father came back from Thailand talking of nothing but you,' said Mr Rossen. 'He said the only person in the whole operation that made any sense, or got anything moving, was you.'

'How is your dear father?' said Belle. 'Such a magnificent man, you know.'

'Well, he's getting on,' said Mr Rossen. 'Gave up the lithography last year, but he still keeps an eye on what goes on. He's near ninety, you know, but he remembers to ask about every account. Still a bit disappointed I didn't join him, I think.'

'But you have such a wonderful position here,' said Belle. 'In charge of such an important venture.'

She felt more settled, and she could look him over more carefully. Certainly an impressive young man. Looked right at you. Good voice, strong, educated, the way she liked voices to be. He seemed to be larger than the chair he sat in, bigger even than the office, somehow. A man who filled a room. She felt the force he projected.

'It *is* an important venture,' said Mr Rossen. 'First work of this kind we've ever attempted in this agency, and everyone will be watching to see how we do.'

Well, of course, Belle thought. And you don't know how to get started. All right, young man, watch this.

'Israel,' said Belle. 'The promise. The hope of every ghetto child in Europe for centuries. The laborers of Poland, Rumania, Russia, Germany, skilled and certain of their trades, people from sixty-five countries pouring into the desert, seeking work for their hands. The miracle for knitters, cutters, tailors, seamstresses. But what designs do they use? Where does this fantastic workmanship go?'

She was launched, beginning to work the magic that she had practiced so often.

Roe knew she was winding up for the pitch, and he relaxed, waiting to see the ball move. A big woman, he thought, in a lot of ways. My God, that voice – she'll come across like Golda herself. Her emerald. Haven't seen anything like it outside a lithograph of Queen Victoria. She doesn't talk, she sermonizes: Israel, the promise, for God's sake. But it's right, what they want to hear, it'll go. And I've got to make this go.

God, she is still on her first paragraph. I have met a woman who speaks paragraphs. I better get in there and get to the point.

'Absolutely,' said Roe. 'You put it beautifully.'

Belle thought: now for the material, before I lose the lead. She reached for her briefcase.

'So I've gathered a few things for you to see,' she said smoothly. 'A few plans and lists. May I use this table?'

She was using it already. Her plump hands moved swiftly into the polished Hermès briefcase, taking out papers, unfolding maps, spreading out what looked like battle plans.

'This is where we must begin,' she said, and began, opening the neatly typed drafts of the overall schedule.

Roe listened. She knows her way, he thought. It's all there, plan to send American designers one by one over there to teach. Quickie courses on the American market, yes. Which designers, right. Students back over here in return, what they should see here, where they should go, yes. Contest for the best designs, terrific. Funding? No, she's wrong there, missed a point, but I can handle that here in the agency. She hasn't got all the facts, but she's found plenty, facts I didn't have. Manufacturers. Who she can get. Everybody, probably.

Belle was through the papers, having moved each of them neatly from the pile on the left to another pile on the right, as she had used each one for a talking point. She stacked all the papers and slid them back into her briefcase. She sensed that Mr Rossen would have liked to keep them to look over, and that, of course, was why she was so firmly removing them. Love my paperwork, love me, she thought, as she had so many times before. But there was something to leave with him.

She smiled dazzlingly and removed her book from her case.

'I've used too much of your time,' she said modestly. 'But I did want to bring you a small piece of reading matter. My own book. It describes so many of my methods, you may find it useful. Perhaps you'll want to pass it along to your dear father after you've looked at it.'

She looked closely at Mr Rossen. Why, he had a small cowlick at the back of his beautifully barbered hair. She rather wanted to reach over and pat it back in its place. He was smiling at her.

'You're very kind,' said Roe. That was nice of her, he thought. Dad would probably be touched. Might even read it. *I Made It Myself*. Yes, his father would appreciate a title like that. Monroe Rossen had made it himself, working up from garbage boy in the print room. When he retired, the network of printing plants stretched from San Diego to Brooklyn. He and this Rosner woman were two of a kind, and a kind that wasn't available much anymore. Better grab her while he could.

No. Wait just a little. Simmer. You never lose by waiting just a little.

'I'm delighted to have your book, and I'm in luck to have found you,' said Roe. 'We'll settle this by next week, I'm sure. Thanks for all the thought you've put in. It's a stunning sample.'

A sample. Belle looked at him. Surely her sample was equal to anyone else's finished product. And who else could there be?

He was rising from his chair now, and he wanted her to go.

'This is sketchy, of course,' she said, with a little chill in her voice. 'But it will give you an idea of how I should handle the problem.'

'A very good idea, Miss Rosner,' said Roe. 'Thank you so much for coming in to see me. Right now we're getting our own personnel sorted out for this job. Our creative director, Mr Godwin, is putting our top woman on it. That's Domina Drexler – you may know her work, Boutique Bonnell? I haven't worked with her, but he says she's a natural for this. We'd want to put a woman on it, of course.'

'Naturally,' said Belle. Domina who?

'I'll reach you at your home, either way, the first of the week. And thanks again for coming in.'

Belle liked to leave the last word behind, but this young man was too quick. He had turned away a little and was picking up the phone by the end of the sentence. She had no choice but to smile and go with the secretary who was waiting to show her out. As they walked back together, a little faster than she liked to walk, Belle's heart began to thud, her breath in little gasps. When the reception room was in sight, she dismissed the girl with a smile. Then she went to one of the less prominent chairs in the wide room and sat down to collect herself.

Nice office, she thought. Clean, no cigarettes in these ashtrays. There, I'm settling down now. First of the week? Why not now? Who else could he possibly talk to? There isn't a soul alive who can bring in what I have in this briefcase.

The click of high heels on the polished marble penetrated Belle's thoughts. She turned her head. Someone was coming fast along the corridor. A handsome girl, Belle thought, deplorably dressed for an office, but handsome. The pants fit perfectly, the hair was lovely, coiled high into a pretty knot. Why, this girl was crying! In an office! She was quite pink in the face, and Belle could see tears on her cheek as she went by. We never did, Belle thought. If absolutely necessary, we got to the ladies' rest room and got it over with there. Not in the halls. Belle straightened her back. She had better get home.

I know, she thought as she walked to the elevators. I shall simply ignore him and keep working. I could have twice as much ready when he calls again. If he says no, I can say there's much more for him to consider. If he says yes, I'll be that much farther along. Must be fifty people I could talk to between now and next week. No harm to let word get around that the work is mine. Harder for them to give it to someone else.

Belle smiled to herself as she opened her purse and took out a token to tuck in her glove, ready for the bus ride home.

Brady Godwin

Who's Who in American Business

GODWIN, BRADY LEVERETT, b. 1918, Newport
Beach, R.I., ed. Lawrenceville 1935, Princeton
University, 1939. US Army, 1942–1944.
M. Priscilla Whitman Pond, 1941, i. John Pond
Godwin, 1943, William Whitman Godwin, 1945,
Barbara Leverett Godwin, 1951. Bus. advtg.,
The Potter Jackson Co., 8 E 40th St, New York,
N.Y. Member Princeton University, N.Y.
Athletic clubs. Director Lincoln Bank,
Consolidated Foods, Inc. Home address
withheld.

Brady Godwin stood at a window in his office watching the new building rising across Fifth Avenue.

For years his office had overlooked a neat row of small brownstones and shops, pleasant to look at, satisfying as an eighteenth-century engraving was satisfying. But four months ago the blasting had begun, and the houses had suddenly become a huge square pit filled with rubbish, machinery, and strange pieces of twisted metal. A wooden fence with peepholes had screened the construction from the sidewalk. But from the thirty-eighth floor Godwin could oversee the work. For months the explosions had sent jolting tremors through his walls, the whine of the concrete mixers had come menacingly closer, the building seemed higher day by day. Soon there would be a massive, faceless wall across the street, dimming the cheerful sunlight in his office, blocking his sweeping view. In the three years to go until he could retire properly, the building would fill with people, the sidewalks crowd up worse than ever, the traffic become more tangled. He hated the building, loathed being elbowed aside by the beefy construction men in their silly helmets, and he was reminded of his rage all day long in his office, which had stopped being a peaceful retreat and become a window on change and disorganization. Why hadn't they waited just a little longer to build, just three more years?

Well, he thought, I'll have to rise above it for three years. Then I can get out of it all to an honorable retirement, a life well spent, a place where I can barricade myself against crowds and noise and change. Sell the big house, sell the Vermont place, calculate the profit-sharing, cash in on the stock options, and go. Hilton Head. Or Palm Springs with the Bensons, who used to live nearby in the country, and who had retired last year. Godwin had gone to the dinner for Harry Benson, listened to the speeches, admired the fine gifts. He'd had his secretary clip the fulsome articles in the trade press. And he had envied Harry for getting out intact, unsullied by any diminution of his powers. But Godwin's own turn was coming up soon. It would be like walking off a football field after a winning game, a rush of locker-room praise. The game was won honorably, one had emerged unscathed, everyone pleased, one had done one's best and finished the job properly. Well, Priscilla was looking at Scottsdale, San Diego, places like that. It would be golf, sun, martinis at eleven in the morning, private guards in closed communities, no surprises, no decisions, another job well done, with a scrapbook of clippings for proof. High time, too.

Time. Two minutes past ten already. Where was that Drexler girl? Woman. You simply couldn't call them girls anymore. Ridiculous. Soon a baby would be born in a hospital and they'd tell the waiting father, 'You've just had a six-pound woman.' Well, whatever you called them, could they never manage to arrive anywhere precisely on time?

Godwin moved to the wing chair. He had managed a good many successful interviews from that chair. The arms were set just right for a relaxed pose, the back was straight enough to give him a look of command. Today's young people sat on their spines, sprawled, wriggled. They wore informal clothes, and their shoes dangled from their feet. He looked down at his own shoes. London. Same pattern for fifteen years. The shoeshine boy polished them every weekday, moving from office to office, free to enter anywhere as long as he kept his head down, his mouth shut, and did his job. Which was all one could ask of anybody.

Godwin looked at his watch again. Four minutes late. Domina was paid, wait a minute, seventy-six it was now. Seventy-six thousand was more than fourteen hundred a week before taxes, two hundred and eighty or so a day, about thirty-five dollars an hour. Five minutes of Domina Drexler's time cost the company almost three dollars. Not to mention his own time, worth more than twice hers. Add them up, five minutes was nine dollars wasted while he waited for Mrs Drexler to get herself up to his office. She hadn't even been summoned. *She* had asked to see *him*. Whatever had happened to Mr Drexler? If the woman had managed her marriage properly, had a man to earn money for her, this whole interview would be unnecessary. And Domina was of Italian descent, he knew, unusual for those people to be divorced. Just typical of what one hired now, he thought. It had been quite different in the early days. Even though the Jews and Italians had found their way into advertising after the war, Jackson had not lowered its standards. There had been a few Irishmen, nice fellows with good jokes, and pictures on their desks with too many children in them, but good men. Now there were Jews, Italians all over the art department, an Indian in the production department. Negroes everywhere. Blacks. Black girls as secretaries everywhere. A lot of good maids lost forever, Godwin thought.

He took his pipe from the long rack, reached for the tobacco jar, and filled the smooth grained bowl, tamping down the loose shreds with his gold pencil. He would light the pipe at a difficult moment in their meeting, use the clouds of smoke to screen his face from her gaze. Domina had an unsettling way of looking straight at one.

Well, he would settle her. He had to get her out the door just as pleased *without* what she wanted as she would have been *with* it. He could do it, had done it a thousand times before. That was what managing creative people was all about. He had to handle this situation well. A lot of people would be watching.

No question that Domina was clever, and had a pretty good idea of her own worth to the company. She was not the sort, he knew, who could be diverted into waiting yet again for the good of the company, distracted with bonuses, persuaded to defer to wiser heads. The woman managed a good deal of profitable work, and the board would be dismayed – and annoyed at him – if she quit to work for a competitor. On the other hand, they had made it equally clear, they were not about to promote her to board membership. It was unthinkable. That little girl occupying one of those antique chairs in the boardroom.

Godwin shifted uneasily. This would take managing. He'd look like a weakling if the girl lost her temper and walked out of the agency. She'd be a fool to leave, of course, wouldn't find another job like hers in a hurry. But then, the woman might act like a fool if she became emotional.

Well, there was one new trick he could play, one that nearly always worked with creative people. Ask not what your agency can do for you, he thought, ask what you can do for your agency. A challenging piece of work, distracting work, with the chance of a golden reward. Flattery can get a lot of things, thought Godwin. We'll see where it can get me this morning.

'Mrs Drexler is here,' said his secretary from the doorway of the inner office.

'Ask her to wait just a moment,' said Godwin. What the hell, she'd kept him waiting long enough. In his day, when one had a meeting with a superior, one damned well got to it on time. Ahead of time.

His day. Godwin thought about the old days at Jackson, before the financial wizards had got into management and organized the agency into a communications center. Whatever that was. In the old days, after the war, when he had first come to work in the mail room, it was forty dollars a week for him, a veteran and a married man. Old Mr Knowles, the office manager, had explained everything when he was hired. 'Mail room is your freshman year, Godwin,' he'd said. 'Everyone starts there. Do your work and do it well. Soon learn your way, just like college. Then we'll know how to make use of you.' It had been an excellent system. First one served, then one knew how to command. Nobody had to waste time explaining things, one picked them up as one delivered the letters and memos to the big offices on each floor. Anyway, everyone in the mail room was Yale or Princeton or Dartmouth, under old Smitty, who seemed like all the football coaches he'd ever met. It didn't last long, and then one was on the ladder that led to an executive job.

The girls had a parallel ladder, one that did not reach quite so high. All the Vassar, Bryn Mawr, and Holyoke girls who passed the shorthand and typing tests were turned into secretaries. They needed a lot of secretaries in those days. Important people always had two, even three. No machines, no copiers, no telephones with buttons then. Memos had eight carbons. If one needed ten copies, the memos were typed twice. But the girls enjoyed the work. After all, they had come to meet boys. And when two people paired up, the girl would give notice and go home to keep house. Priscilla had once been a Jackson secretary. She had been able to follow his office talk ever since. The work had been excellent training for marriage. Priscilla followed her interests during the day, he followed his. She never expected to share everything with him, thank God. That was probably why their marriage had survived through so many years. Each of them stayed in his own territory.

No, there simply were no women like Domina in the old days. There was a ladies' division, made up of all the female writers and artists. They all had pretty offices with plants and pastels in one wing of the building, and they worked on suitable accounts, fashions and foods and cosmetics. Those women had pretty much given up on husbands and children. In those days one chose a career or a marriage, not a halfhearted try at both. Of course there had been a few widows and divorcees, sad little things, but they were never important. The executive ladies were formidable, like maiden-lady teachers. They expected to work hard, not to be handed rewards on silver platters. Every one of them would have retired rather than come into a creative director's office and beg for a title. Undignified and embarrassing, they'd have thought.

Those women were wonderful. Old Miss Janno, seventy if she was a day, with her strange hats and her dresses halfway to the ankle, walking about to supervise all her ladies with a notepad in her clawlike hand. She kept those women in line, all right. And a male executive could treat with her as one general to another. The dining room was off limits to the ladies in those days, too. But there were trays.

Godwin smiled as he recalled those trays. There were maids all over the office, in uniforms with aprons and frills on their heads, dusting, emptying ashtrays, polishing desks. At noontime the maids would serve delicate lunches to the ladies right in their offices, perhaps two together for a business discussion, each lady with her beautifully laid tray with Jackson's own china, pink and white, and with little teapots. The mail boys were always colliding with those trays, he remembered, as they ran around corners.

The ladies had had a special trainees' class, too. Each fall a competition among the secretaries, a copy test. The ten best were chosen by Miss Janno herself, and all the ladies took turns teaching the girls. Competition was rough, under a polite set of manners.

Well, it was all rather long ago, he thought. Almost forty years with the company. Priscilla had wanted him to retire at sixty-two, but he preferred to wait a little. Actually, spending time all through the day with Priscilla, when he faced the idea, seemed dull. And after all, 15-percent profit-sharing on his salary, added twenty-four thousand dollars a year to the amount already safely banked for him. And even the added social-security benefits waiting at sixty-five would be helpful. Sixty-five was the proper age to retire, and sixty-five it would be for him, as it had been for his father before him. And no little snip like Domina Drexler was going to make it tough.

Because most of it was so easy now. He had organized everything so the work practically managed itself, had hired good men to oversee everything and report to him. He simply went to pleasant meetings where he reviewed other people's work as it pleased him, made a speech here and there, announced agency news to subordinates. He even had a special place in the company dining room, where his secretary telephoned ahead and his drink was waiting for him. Godwin always sat at a quiet corner table which custom had reserved for the chairman of the board, old Croft, for Platt, the agency president, and for Godwin's opposite number on the business side of the agency, the manager of all the account executives. If one of them was out of town, they would invite one of the younger men to join them, and draw him out for office news and useful talk. Good system. One dropped a word about one's latest accomplishments, or put in a scunner about anybody one cared to. Mr Croft had an eye on that Rossen fellow. They all had an eye on Domina Drexler. But it happened in such delightful surroundings.

The company dining room was Godwin's favorite room, next to his own den at home. It was furnished with valuable French antiques from the eighteenth century. Simple burnished wood glowing with the patina of useful, gracious service over centuries. Beautiful molding in the airy room, brought from Normandy and reconstructed undetectably. Fresh flowers, heavy crystal, widely spaced tables at which a man could relax his body but keep his mind alert for the talk. The old waiters, greeting him by name, holding the bottle to mix his drinks as he entered, collecting the chits unobtrusively as he left. Once a week the dining room was turned over to the ladies in the agency – only the executives, of course – but given to them for a luncheon meeting. He understood they always had a speaker and polite questions afterward, and he approved. Priscilla belonged to cultural groups that did the same sort of thing. He was sorry that hers could not take place in such glorious surroundings. The Jackson dining room was special. By tacit consent, the executives never brought their wives, even for drinks before theater or dinner dates. It was a preserve for members only. He wondered if Domina attended the ladies' luncheons.

Domina. Godwin buzzed for his secretary.

'Ask Mrs Drexler to come in now,' he said. He stood up as she entered.

'Good morning, Domina,' he said. 'Don't you look fashionable this morning.'

He noticed that her dark eyes flickered at his words. What the hell. He was complimenting her, for God's sake.

'Now. You wanted to see me,' he said. No more, until he knew precisely where she was prepared to take the conversation.

'Brady,' said Domina, in her low, clear voice. 'You know what I'm going to ask you. It should be no surprise. I think it's time we made me a senior vice-president. What do you think?'

Godwin reached for a match and lit his pipe. He puffed generously until swirls of rich smoke floated in the space between them.

'Domina, I've told you before. There are some things that can't be hurried. This is one of them. You'll simply have to trust me.'

Domina was reaching into her pocket. Handkerchief? Already? No, thank God, one of her interminable cigarettes. Matches. No, the girl had lit it herself in one swift motion. Nowadays you couldn't even light their cigarettes.

He went on. 'You're being handsomely paid. You're in the most beautiful office we possess on the creative floor. You've decorated it beautifully, too, we all admire how you've put it together, and it suits you. Now. Your benefits are superior, vacations, bonuses, better than any other agency would give you. Of course, you've earned all this. No one questions your right to these things. In fact, no one questions your right to a senior vice-presidency. Ultimately.'

'Ultimately. I see,' said Domina. 'How ultimately? What is the holdup, Brady?'

'Actually, there's no holdup. The promotion is honestly in the making. It's been amply discussed. I don't do these things all alone, you know. We have a board of directors, you know most of them. Not outsiders, our own people. You've certainly met Mr Croft.'

'Brady. You told me about them last time we talked. Surely that board has met sometime in the last six months. Why didn't my title go through then?'

'It was discussed,' said Godwin. 'You see, there are a few people who need to know you a little better, need some reassurance before they add a pretty young woman to the board. We're still a bit stuffy, you know. But it will happen. And it won't be long.'

He knew it sounded false. But it was the truth, really. Why couldn't she understand? Why were they all so impatient? Didn't they realize they'd be here a good long time? She had another twenty years at least. You could almost feel sorry for the girl.

'Bullshit,' said Domina.

Godwin stiffened. He kept still for a moment, letting the word hang in the air like the smoke from his pipe, trying to convey by silence that anyone might be forgiven for not promoting a woman who used language like that. Or wore shoes like that. Potter Jackson does not have officers who dress like tarts, he thought.

'Domina, my dear, you must grow up. I would give the same advice to my own daughter. And you are a member of the Jackson family, a valuable member. Bear with me. Control yourself. It's going to happen. I'm going to see that it happens, you have my promise.'

'How?' Domina was wilting a little, pink moving up into her cheeks, eyes turing misty at the corners. Oh, God.

'We need proof positive,' said Godwin firmly.

She looked at him and stubbed her cigarette out in the crystal ashtray on the coffee table.

'Proof of what? That I deserve it? For heaven's sake, Brady, my record here is unbeatable, no one around can match it, everybody knows that. Who does the work I do every single day? Who writes like I write? The hours I put in, the letters from happy clients, what proof?'

'Oh, there's nothing to prove to me,' said Godwin. 'I run this department. I know exactly what my people are capable of doing. If it were up to me alone, well.'

'Phantoms,' said Domina. 'It's fighting shadows. Well, I think it's high time I proved something, Brady. I think it's time I proved I can get the hell out of this agency. I came today for an answer, and I don't like the answer.'

Godwin stirred in his chair. She had her nerve, he thought. What would it feel like to fire her on the spot? Satisfying, all right. Then let her cry. But a memory of the board meeting shot through his mind. 'We need that woman, Brady,' Croft had said. 'But we need her managing that business, not here in the boardroom. If you can't smooth your people down, well, we'll have to see.' Godwin had smiled easily, but had felt a spark of fear ignite in his belly and flame up. Three years to go. The spark twisted and burned again. Ulcer? Nonsense, not now, not after almost forty years. He was perfectly fit, squash at the club, once a year a visit to the Life Trend Medical Service, stress tests, everything. But there. Something was burning in his insides, as if he had swallowed Domina's cigarette. Keep talking.

'You want an answer, but you haven't heard my proposal yet,' he said. 'It's very simple, and it's all up to you. What you and I need to make this happen is one piece of work, one isolated example so good, so unassailable, and so directly your own that nobody could question your ability, nobody.'

'Who questions?'

'Domina, you know we're a team system. You have superb people helping you, hired most of them yourself. Incidentally, that little girl, the red-haired art girl, seems pretty promising. You know talent when you see it. That's why you're a good administrator. But that's just the trouble right now.'

'I guess I'm not following you,' said Domina.

'I know your group's work comes mostly from you, because I keep an eye on things,' said Godwin. 'I've helped you grow, and I think you'll agree I've taken good care of you through the years. But there are people on the board who don't know you quite as well as I do. And they are the ones who may question your ability to stand alone, to command the way officers of this company must.'

'Brady, what the hell are you talking about? Ask the Bonnell people. The other clients. They know where the ideas come from. They *watch* me have them,' said Domina.

'Domina, I know. I am not your problem. But now I'm going to tell you something in confidence. Are you ready to listen?'

There was no reply, but she was listening. Good.

'There's a piece of work coming up, fascinating job, worthy of your talents. I've wanted you for it right along, but it took some swinging. It means trips, publicity, news, attention. A lot of work, but worth doing. Handle it, and the board, everybody, will know you.'

'Proof,' said Domina. 'I see. And what's the job?'

'Something we, as an agency, have never attempted before. A kind of ground-breaking I believe the whole world will watch.'

Surprisingly, Domina laughed. 'Brady, you're a real advertising man,' she said. 'Go on.'

The girl was positively rude, he thought. Still, when they laugh they can't cry. He couldn't stand it when women cried. It seemed so dreadfully inappropriate, so embarrassing in an office. Imagine, if the woman wept at a board meeting. Better keep it moving.

'We have been approached by the government of the state of Israel.'

'Israel? Us? That *is* news.'

'Yes, it is. They have a special problem they feel we alone can solve. The country is filled, naturally, with refugees from Europe and the Iron Curtain countries. A good many of them are skilled garment workers. They know all the steps, patterns, and cutting and fitting and all that. We all know about Jewish tailors, even here.'

'Yes. We all know about that.'

'The problem is, they are putting that splendid workmanship into the wrong clothing. They make clothes that the American market will not buy. They have little knowledge of what we call today, our life-styles, or our buying public. And America is the best export market they could have. They don't understand American sizes, apparently. Rossen was telling me the other day. They make the wrong fashions, heavy tailoring, stiff coats, all that sort of thing. And no children's clothes. I have the preliminary report right here.'

'Where would we come in?'

Good question. He was getting her interest. It was going to be all right. The cigarette in his stomach was burning itself out, thought Godwin.

'A whole program culminating in an advertising campaign,' he said with all the force he could muster. 'Design help. Exchange programs, their workmen visiting here, our designers over there, all that. But the rest is open. A wardrobe plan? A fashion show? You would know best about that. It's your field, after all. By the way, we've already actually contracted with Sternn for pictures. The Israelis asked for him, and we agreed. The best. You would work with him. And you could go to Jerusalem, Tel Aviv, Milan, Paris, anywhere, for whatever help you need. The budget is high, especially for a fashion promotion. Bring back some things for your pretty office, for your wardrobe. Domina, it could be all yours.'

Domina watched him making the speech. The bastard, she thought. He thinks I'll jump for the glamor, lose my way, forget why I came. The old shell game. Which shell is my promotion under? Not here. Not there. Why, it's under the shell with the Israel promotion in it, right? Not on your life, Godwin, I'm a smart lady. I didn't make it falling for sales pitches. I'm the one who makes the sales pitches. She felt a great weight settling in her throat, her middle, as if she were swallowing a stone.

'Don't react right away,' said Godwin. 'Think about it a little. It's an exciting project.'

Domina thought. I think I'm going to spit in his navy-blue eye and walk out of this agency. I think they can blank my name out of the company phone books, add up my profit-sharing, scatter my group to the winds.

And then, the image of the bankbook. That, plus the profit-sharing, wouldn't get her through the summer. Remember, she thought, you promised yourself you wouldn't quit. You'll go, at your own speed. And don't cry about it, mother of God, don't cry now.

'Yes, I'll think about it,' Domina said stiffly.

'Do. You'd be working with Roe Rossen directly. He more or less asked for you, noticed your Bonnell work. I don't need to remind you, Domina, he's the newest member of the board. Strong voice, too.'

Roe Rossen. The good-looking one, young for the board, she thought. There'd been a lot of talk when he'd made it. Could he have forced his way a little? Fifty, at least – that passes for young around here. M.J. last week. Said he was the cutest thing around. How have I missed him so far?

'Is Roe handling this along with his other work?' she asked.

'Yes. He has competent help for the cars. Those are his

main responsibility, of course, but not competitive to this. If you accept, as we hope you will, we'd like you to do it full time. You would be the mainspring, you see. He'll simply smooth your path.'

Oh. They wanted her separated from her own clients. Dangerous. What did Godwin have in his devious mind? Well, what difference did it make? She was going to be devious, too. Get out of this room. Call Maran. Call the headhunters. Start typing résumés. Go. Before she burst out and called this man terrible names, swore at him. Before all the rage and frustration turned into tears and she showed him how hurt she was.

'Brady, I'm very disappointed. I'll have to think about it,' she said.

Godwin stood up abruptly. 'Domina,' he said. 'You know I'm doing the right thing. You do not want to be made an officer of this company over a lot of dead bodies. What you want is genuine acceptance. You have years ahead of you here, you're not forty yet. When you arrive at that promotion, we want everyone in this agency to cheer for you. And believe me, my dear, I shall be at the head of the cheering section.'

Domina thought: It's too much, too good an act. I can fight back when they oppose me, but this? I can't handle it when he gets fatherly, gentle. I can't ask nicely for my allowance. I always fought for things. I don't know how to coax and cajole, and I don't want to know!

'Right,' she said. 'Thank you for your time, Brady.'

The very act of speaking, of forcing polite words out of a mouth that wanted to shout, made it harder to hold back her tears. Bastard, she thought, supercilious bastard, you'll be at the head of my cheering section? This isn't football, goddammit. You think I fall for that rot? You think you fool me? How dare you take me for such an idiot.

She turned her head, but it was too late. The warmth rose up in her face, the tears spilled out of her eyes, ran down her cheeks, sank into the pattern on her sweater.

'Domina, my dear,' said Brady. 'Take my handkerchief. Don't upset yourself. It will all work out, you know. One day you'll look back on this with me, and we'll chuckle.'

Jesus on the Cross, thought Domina. He's going to say, 'There, there,' in a minute, which really will make me sob hysterically, and then I'll look totally ridiculous. Got to stop this. I can't let him get me going. I hate this son of a bitch, this sanctimonious Ivy League creep.

'Better?' said Brady. 'Good girl. Now, just listen to some of the notes I have here. If you'd get your mind into this, Domina, get busy, your promotion will simply take care of itself. And you'll do a sensational job with this work, I know.'

He picked up the report from the coffee table and opened it, beginning to read the introduction, letting the words roll out, using his best client voice to soothe her, calm her down.

Domina struggled to stop the tears, get herself together. She was thinking now, replacing misery with anger. Fury began to swell up inside her like air being pumped into a tire. It was pure anger, the kind she'd felt in Elkhart when the store people had tried to keep her off the Bonnell account. The same kind she'd felt when Santo Triano had wanted to worm out of giving her the partnership he'd promised. The same rage that had erupted inside her when she'd discovered that her husband had been sleeping with one of their neighbors. *That* rage had not subsided until her divorce decree was crackling in her hands.

What would make this rage subside?

The answer came into her head while Godwin read on, sounding like a faith healer, as if he thought he could mend her with his voice.

My own place, she thought. An agency of my own. Small. Perfect. Organized the way I can organize, managed my way. I'll take Bonnell, the old man will stick with me. I'll do beautiful commercials, win a hundred awards because they'll be written the way I want. Make lots of money. And I'll hire smart people, good people. And then, fuck you, Potter Jackson, and your board of directors, and most of all, fuck you, Brady Godwin.

Godwin watched her over the edge of the papers each time he turned a page.

Damn the woman, he thought. The burning sensation

71

was still in his gut, sharper than before. By God, when he was a younger man, if someone had offered him an opportunity to gallivant all over the world on company funds, to plan and spend and promote, he'd have snapped at it. They didn't offer us anything then, he thought, they told us what to do, and we did it. Little bitch. She looked at this moment like the girls who used to wait on table in the old Orange Tavern, the spaghetti joint in Princeton so long ago. Sallow. All that black hair. What did she know about working for forty dollars a week, about slow, steady progress toward a goal? She only understood jumping from job to job, weeping hysterically, demanding things. What if he lied, told the board she'd blown up completely and walked out? No. They would say he'd mismanaged the affair. He couldn't have that, not now, not with so little time before retirement. Damn the woman.

He looked again at her. She seemed quiet. The tears had stopped, although she still breathed too fast. Probably thinking the thing over. Was she listening at all? Not really. Well, he'd give her the report when he could get her out his door. And once she got wrapped up in the work, she'd be off his hands for a while. Not permanently, he suspected. She was too aggressive for a real retreat. She'd be back with more nagging; her kind always came back. But a lot might happen. After all, if she mismanaged this job, a promotion would be out of the question. If she handled it well, it would still take a lot of time. No arrangement this complex could take less than several months. More, probably. The board could even change their mind, if she did well. But he would be off the hook: the decision to promote her would be theirs. Best of all, this work would get her away, out of the office, traveling. She'd be a fool not to take it. And Domina Drexler was not a fool. Emotional, impossible, difficult, but not a fool. Whatever she might spend, he could justify to the board, since the agency would pass the costs on to the Israelis. And there was Rossen. He was tough. Let him manage her. Godwin began to feel more fit, more like himself. He stopped reading.

'You get the idea, I'm sure,' he said. 'Take it. It's your passport to the future, Domina. I sincerely believe that.'

'Brady,' said Domina, 'you probably do. I'm sure you think it will get my mind off what I deserve around here, keep me busy.'

Godwin winced at her tone, sharp, sarcastic, almost vicious, he thought.

'Well, we do pay you to keep busy, Domina. Just as I'm paid to keep you working. Taskmaster. That's my job, after all.'

'Taskmaster. I see,' said Domina. 'I could put another name to what you've done with me here this morning.'

Well, Brady thought, now she's acting like Priscilla does when she's losing an argument. Using little nips and hints with me, letting out her anger. But she won't go any farther, she's defused. I've done it.

'My dear,' he said. 'You're upset, and I'm sorry. But you're a trouper, a professional. And if we can't meet some mythical timetable that exists in your head, I know that now you'll be professional.'

'I'll see,' she said. 'Thank you.'

He smiled at her as she went quietly out the door.

Gone, thank God. It seemed to have been solved, for the moment. Godwin moved back to his desk, glanced at his calendar. He would recount his interview with her in the dining room today. Push her behavior a little to the bad, move his own cleverness a little to the good, and it would all sound fine. The sun still shone into his windows, the building opposite was not visible from his desk yet. He could manage to make everything work properly for himself, just as he'd planned.

'Mr Godwin? Have you a moment for Mr Rossen?'

He could practice his Domina story on Rossen right now.

But Rossen was in already, without being asked. Pushy, thought Godwin. Looks well. Good jacket. Brooks Brothers? J. Press? Where did the man buy his clothes? He'd ask one day. Perhaps a touch too smart, but good fabric. He didn't stay put together, though. Shirttail always coming out. Busy, of course, but still, appearances counted.

'Hi, Brady,' Rossen was saying. 'Listen. What did you do to the beautiful Mrs Drexler?'

73

Godwin looked at him in surprise. 'Talked to her. Told her about your Israelis. Invited her to join forces with you, old man.'

'Well, she didn't look too happy about it,' said Rossen. 'Seemed to be falling apart when I passed her a minute ago. I was going to introduce myself, say I'd enjoy working with her and all that, but it didn't seem exactly the right moment.'

God damn the woman, thought Godwin. Was she walking through the halls on the thirty-eighth floor, of all places, with tears running down her face? What on earth would that do to his story about managing her so well? The burning sensation flicked on in his stomach again, settling under his belt buckle, growing sharper.

He smiled broadly.

'Roe. Do you know why women behave as they do? Does anybody know? She probably has her period. The vapors. What the hell, she left here a minute ago, seemed perfectly pleased about the whole thing. Maybe she's all wrought up about the shopping she can get in when she's traveling. She'll settle in, she'll manage it for you, don't worry.'

'Maybe so,' said Roe. 'Can you eat today? I want to tell you about Belle Rosner, the stuff she's put together for us already. Now, there's some lady. I bet she never cried in her whole life.'

'Well, more power to her,' said Godwin. 'Hire the woman. Wait, I have a lunch date today. How about five o'clock in the dining room, will it hold until then?'

'I'll be out all this afternoon,' said Roe. 'Let's get together first thing tomorrow.'

As Rossen walked swiftly out of the office, Brady Godwin turned back to the window. Across the avenue the men were ambling about in what they called work. They were handing each other tools, clustering around little dump carts full of wet gray cement, one or two smoking cigarettes that surely were forbidden. The sounds of wood being nailed for the supports, the whine of the mixers, the clatter of metal on metal all droned on, an irritating, constant noise. Whatever happened to the old construction methods, steel girders, hot rivets, solid, sure structures?

74

Now it was all this makeshift stuff, rising too quickly, chaos to watch, ugly from the inside out. The building seemed somehow to be looming up closer, much nearer to him than it had been only an hour before.

Lolly

Laura L. Moss
Carroll Associates, Inc.
320 Lexington Avenue
New York, N.Y. 10016
555-9800, ext. 324, 326

Mrs William Harding Moss
34 East 81st St.
New York, N.Y. 10028
555-7582

Presently employed as confidential associate to
John Brinnin Carroll, president of the Carroll
Associates group, executive recruiting services
with offices in twenty countries. I have held this
position since 1977.

Formerly employed for three years as copywriter
at Potter Jackson, in the New York and Los
Angeles offices.

Educated at Bennington College, Bennington,
Vermont, and the Hockaday School for Girls.

Married William Harding Moss, Merrill Lynch,
Pierce, Fenner & Smith. Two children, four
and two.

In the hotel room, Lolly waited.

Roe was late this afternoon, later than he had ever been in the year they had been meeting. Usually he came first, as close to two as he could make it, to give them the whole afternoon. There was never enough time. Lolly had to be showered, dressed, and in a taxi for home by six at the latest. Then she could arrive home at the usual time. Any later, and she would find her nursemaid waiting impatiently in the foyer with her coat on. The kids would have finished supper, rolling around on the living-room floor in front of a blaring television. They would be all excited, Lolly would waste time calming them down before she could fix dinner, and Bill would come home to a mess, which irritated him. Bill liked to get there and find things peaceful. That made six o'clock Lolly's midnight, her hour for turning back again into a dreary little wife, for ending the magic-princess afternoons with Roe.

What was wrong today? She and Roe always arrived separately, just in case someone they knew was in the lobby, though over here on the West Side, it wasn't likely. Roe would call her at the office in the morning, as if it was business, asking for employment records on somebody or other, and in the conversation he would mention the number of the room he'd reserved. Lolly adored these calls, the excitement of a shared secret, a code no secretary listening at either end would ever understand.

Lolly could arrive and go straight through the lobby to the elevators unnoticed, Roe had taught her. It always worked. Once she was inside the room safely, whatever number it was, everything was in place, the same every time. Same wide bed, same heavy draperies to shut out the world, same awful paintings of Venice or Roman ruins to giggle about. Same bland furniture, glasses with their skins of plastic wrap, closet hangers bolted to the rod, so she always dropped the bottom half when she hung up her dress. Roe never hung up anything. His suits were always flung on a chair.

But there was always Roe as she opened the door, Roe with a bottle of wine on the bed table, the glasses ready, a cigarette in the ashtray. Each time she got there, he said the same thing: 'I thought you'd never come. I thought, this time you won't really come.' Lolly loved hearing that; it always made her feel like the most fascinating woman God ever made.

Today she didn't feel fascinating. Today had been different. She had knocked and knocked, checking and rechecking the number she had scribbled down. Then she had gone back to the lobby, thinking out what to do next. She had told the man at the desk that her husband had forgotten to give her the key for 746. She lingered over the word 'husband,' saying it a little too sharply, because she felt foolish. But the man had simply handed her a key from one of the cubbyholes behind him, and she had come back to let herself in.

Lolly felt impatience bubbling up inside her. It was damned hard for her to make the time for these afternoons. She paid for them. Every hour meant extra work at the office, extra hurry at home. Why the hell couldn't he be here for her? Roe never paid for his time. He was too important. They'd simply assume he was out on business.

She decided to get undressed, to be all ready for him the moment he came. But though she took as long about it as she could, tucking her pantyhose into her shoes, neatly smoothing the folds of her tweed coat, lining her shoes up toe to toe in the closet, when she had finished, he still was not there.

Lolly moved to the bathroom door and looked at her naked self in the long mirror.

Your hips. Your ass. Diet, she thought. That's what happens when you're a few years out of college and there's no regular exercise. When you sit at a desk all day. And drink gin all evening.

She pinched her waist the way the magazines said would test whether or not you were really fat. Was that an inch between her fingers? It was hard to tell. And how did you figure about thighs? Well, from the middle up she was still safe. Her rib bones still faintly ridged her body, her arms taut, her shoulders rounded and smooth. Her breasts were too small, Lolly thought, but then, small breasts looked right in clothes. All the clothes seemed to be designed for flat-chested girls. Lolly could see the marks of her bikini. The heritage of a California childhood, a bathing suit all year long, especially since her father had a heated swimming pool. Lolly smiled to herself, remembering how Roe loved to trace the lines of that invisible bathing suit with his finger when they made love.

She shivered. At home in Bel-Air there were always fresh terry robes on the backs of the bathroom doors. But then, everything in California was easy and comfortable. Most of it had been wasted on her, she realized, because she had been too young. In New York you grabbed your lovemaking, like you grabbed everything else.

Lolly wrapped herself in one of the hotel's skimpy towels, padded out to the bed, pulled back the spread, propped both pillows on one side, and got in to keep warm until Roe came. Or didn't come. She considered that possibility, shivering again. He had to come. Today was important. Last week his divorce had been made final, had ended the year his wife had made him wait. Every week Lolly had bitten her tongue to keep from talking about the future, the hope she felt rising up inside her.

Where *was* he, why couldn't he have called if he was going to be so late? She knew he was busy. Detroit and the car work, the new fashion project – there were dozens of things to keep him. He might have to travel somewhere. Once or twice Roe had come in with a leather duffel bag full of overnight things, and a plane ticket for early the next morning. Those nights Lolly had risked everything, called home to say she would be working very late, and for Bill not to wait up. How easy it was to cheat, how quickly you could get used to doing it, she thought.

There, thank God, the door was opening. The roughness

of his jacket scratched her face as she hugged him. He smelled of rich tobacco and the fresh wind outside. Darling Roe.

'Lolly, I'm sorry, so sorry. There's all kinds of stuff going on at the office, and the crosstown traffic was murder. I had one of those drivers who gets stuck behind every truck. You all right?'

'I'm fine, now you're here, just fine,' said Lolly.

She knew how he behaved in cabs, trapped, curbed, itching to take over the wheel. Roe drove like a racer, always in the right lane for the traffic, weaving from side to side, conversing to himself about the drivers he was trying to pass. 'You drive to get somewhere,' he said. 'Driving in New York isn't for sightseeing.' Slowness made him crazy. She kissed him hard. Clever darling, she thought, he takes regular cabs over here, no radio cabs to keep a record of where he is when he's with me.

'It's only three,' she said. Actually, it was twenty after. 'Plenty of time.'

'I feel like plenty of time,' he said. 'How are you really? How's the headhunting business? Who cares right now? I'm not hunting for heads today. I'm after other things.'

'Like what?'

'Like this,' he said, yanking back the covers, pulling away her towel, picking up her foot, and kissing her on the ankle.

Lolly giggled. She always shaved her legs before these afternoons. She never knew where Roe would kiss, what he would do next. She felt eagerness bubble up in her throat, caught her breath.

Roe pulled at his jacket and shirt, scattering a button, dropping his clothes, while Lolly helped unbuckle his belt, undo his trouser button. Roe did the rest fast, kicked out of his underclothes, slid his warmth on top of her.

She could feel the heat turning up in her body, feel her breasts each gathering up into little pointed peaks. He ran a finger gently around her nipples until she couldn't bear it, and reached for him, helping him inside her. His penis felt hard and hot and filling, as if it had been designed for her, as if his whole body had been molded just for her. Lolly

81

clutched at him, feeling him pound at her as if he would drive right through her. She felt his explosion, and then got lost in one of her own.

This first time was over quickly, as always. With Roe there was a frantic first rush, finished quickly. There was always more, always time for touch and kiss and nibble and stroke, before his next slow gathering up for more. Lolly lay back on the two pillows, basking in his nearness, the way she used to bask in the hot California sun on her father's beach.

Roe, surprisingly, had grown still. When she turned her head, Lolly realized he was lightly asleep. Poor Roe, she thought, how busy, how much he had to think about.

She lay quietly too, trying to match his breathing, trying not to disturb him. This could all be so simple now, she thought. Roe had his divorce. No kids, thank goodness. He'd told her how disappointed his father had been about that. His father sounded fascinating, like a tough old Santa Claus. His father had pushed him toward his wife, because she was the right kind of girl, he'd thought. Religion had been the most important thing. He had wanted Roe to marry a Jewish girl so blond and blue-eyed and cool, of such an old German-Jewish family, that no one would ever have believed she was really Jewish at all. Lolly was always astounded at the way Roe felt about religion. In Hollywood, where everyone her parents knew was Jewish except maybe the Mexican maids and the Japanese gardeners, she knew right away who was and who wasn't. In New York, Lolly could never quite tell. There were the creative Jews she met, who all looked alike, beards and jeans and boots, but whose only real uniformity seemed to be the way they ignored religion altogether. There had been a few Jewish girls at school who wore crosses around their necks on little gold chains. They were protective amulets against invitations from the Jewish girls' clubs, the ones that had awful girls in them. 'Nouveau riche,' Lolly had heard those girls called, for the first time, and she didn't want to be one of them, though her parents would have died if she'd worn a cross. Lolly began to grasp the idea that being Jewish put you in a special, undesirable class. She learned to wear an invisible cross, to drop little remarks early in a relationship that would assure others that she belonged where they did. But in all those different kind of Jews, there was never one like Roe. He was so removed from being Jewish, with his schools and his job at Jackson, that he could actually own up to it, even make it sound like something special and exclusive. Everyone at home had used Jewish words, told jokes about Jewish mothers, followed the main traditions like Passover dinner, even though they didn't believe. Roe did none of these things. He simply seemed to feel he had just one more blessing other people didn't. Lolly could never have put that over in a thousand years.

Lolly smiled, remembering a personnel manager, long ago, who had looked at her closely and asked her about what her religion was. Lolly had laughed and said 'California.'

Though she had changed from Laura to Lolly at Bennington, to fit in with the Buffies and Cissies and Maggies, she had not felt really safe until Bill changed the rest of her name. Then she was Lolly Moss, on stationery and checkbooks and luggage tags. And of course, once she had worked for Jackson, she had been secure about not being known as a Jewish girl. Mr Carroll's job helped even more. Lolly Moss was the girl you saw about junior-executive jobs, the cute blond. Sometimes Mr Carroll let her screen the men for senior jobs. That was how she had met Roe. He had been an instant astonishment, looks, talk, background, jokes, and later on, sex. But the fact that Roe was Jewish too, the way she was inside, numbered in invisible ink forever, like a concentration-camp person, made him perfect for her.

Roe. Where Bill was predictable, Roe was surprising. He held hands on a plane, caused tables to be set up for him in restaurants, knew whole books full of ideas she had never heard about. Where Bill was like all the other men of his age at Merrill Lynch, Roe had dark secrets that came out in bits, like the days when he was in the army in the war when they somehow *lost* the captured German soldiers they were taking back to prison camps, lost them so no one ever found them. Where Bill was rough, quick, a little furtive in bed,

Roe was heavenly, strong, tender, funny. She never knew when he would give her a shower, or put her shoes on for her, or curl all around her in his sleep. Bill slept on his back, and seemed to try to make love without touching her. When Roe held her, it was like being in a gentle hand, touched all over.

She had not compared the two of them until a year ago. Mr Carroll had asked her to travel to Detroit with an executive from Jackson who needed assistance in interviewing local people for junior account jobs at Ford. She had talked to Mr Rossen a lot on the phone, but had never spent time with him. On the trip she'd decided he was a terribly attractive guy, even for a girl who'd grown up among movie stars. He looked real, sort of tanned when everyone else looked pale, as if he had been filmed in Technicolor while everyone else was in black and white. On the plane Lolly watched how the stewardesses broke their necks to serve him. He carried her small bag, even when she protested, and took her after their work to a marvelous dinner at the Chop House, with crêpes suzettes, because he wanted her to enjoy the attention they always created, he told her. Later, when he took her back to her hotel room, Lolly couldn't wait to tumble into bed with him. The night had been a revelation.

Well, maybe today she could get a start on belonging to him for real. Maybe they could stop the sneaking, the stolen dinners in out-of-the-way places, the hotel rooms once a week. It was fun, even if she felt a little guilty when she went home, because Roe made her feel like a star, beautiful, sexy, wanted. Being so loved in the afternoon, she could go home quietly, be gracious, even nicer to Bill than ever before. But lately, she thought, a feeling of irritation with Bill was taking over. Why was he not Roe? Why did he not behave, speak, joke, screw like Roe? When she went home after Roe, she felt as if warning signs were all over her body. Her skin glowed from Roe's rough skin, her breasts were chafed from his hands, her hair was flattened out of its usual curl.

There, Roe was turning, opening his legs, looking across the bed at her. Then he was swinging his legs over the edge of the bed, sitting up, looking around.

'No wine,' he said. 'I was so damned late, I never thought, just to get to you. Want some water?'

Without waiting for an answer, he took one of the glasses into the bathroom, and she could hear the water run. He came back with two glasses full of cloudy New York water, and gulped thirstily.

'What was it about, why were you so late?' Lolly asked.

'Bunch of things. Godwin. Detroit. A funny old lady I talked to this morning who never stopped. And another thing.'

'What other thing?'

'A closing,' Roe said.

'A closing of what?'

'Congratulate me, Lolly. You have just made love to the owner of a handsome one-room penthouse on Sutton Place.'

Lolly felt her temperature drop. She could actually feel her hands and feet change from their pleasant Malibu glow to an icy New York winter chill.

'Owner?'

'I wanted a place of my own, you know, after Louise got the house. That was mostly hers, anyway. And you know I've never felt comfortable in that sublet, even though it was pretty grand. It's not like my own.'

Penthouse, Lolly thought, penthouse. But that's not the key word. One room. One room, that's the important thing. Where would she fit in a one-room apartment on Sutton Place? Why hadn't he talked it over, why hadn't he told her what he was doing, why?

She shivered, and pulled the covers up to her chin. He was talking. But there wasn't time, there was never enough time with him. Still, she tried to listen.

'Something, this Rosner woman. Well over eighty, my father worked with her on the Thailand economic thing. He told me she was something else, but I saw it for myself .his morning. I've been wondering how she'll mesh with our own big creative lady. They both look like they take handling, and I met them both for the first time this morning – that was part of the problem about being late.'

'What big creative lady?' asked Lolly, her personnel work taking over her emotions for a moment.

'Domina Drexler. You must have a lot of stuff on her, don't you?'

That bitch, thought Lolly.

When Lolly had first gone to work for Jackson in the Los Angeles office, her first job, she had heard about Domina Drexler. Hotshot from Chicago who'd brought the Bonnell account to New York with her. Old Mr Bonnell, one of the worst bastards in the whole fashion business, adored her. She'd made Bonnell monograms something wonderful, something rich women all over the country wanted to wear on their clothes and accessories. Lolly knew that Domina lived in a fabulous apartment somewhere, dressed like a combination of fashion model and movie star. That she'd done it all by herself.

When Lolly had talked her mother into letting her transfer East, she'd hoped to get a job in Domina Drexler's group. There had been a brief interview. Domina had been pleasant enough, but Lolly had seen right away that it wasn't going to work out. Domina had gone fast through her slim sample book, pausing only once to read carefully through an ad. Then she had said casually, 'Well, they're behind us on the Coast, you'll find much more creative freedom here. Welcome to New York.' That had ended the interview. The meeting had upset her. Domina's was the group to belong to in the Jackson New York office, for a girl. Lolly had settled for one of the men's groups, but soon found her way to personnel. Writing copy was too tough. Her words didn't come out fast enough, weren't original enough, she had to do every ad over and over. Lolly felt safer with records and lists, happier in interviews, where she did the asking and the job-seekers did the explaining. There had also been the problem of one brief fling with her boss, a terrible mistake. If you're going to screw around in your office, do it with your equal, never your superior. When your boss gets tired of you, or you of him, you're embarrassing to have around, and there goes your job. Right about then, though, her father had called up Mr Carroll, of Carroll Associates, best of all the headhunting places in the whole world, and she had found her career. Lolly adored her work, knew exciting things that ordinary people didn't, met new people, was able to distribute jobs almost the way her father had handed out tips in the Beverly Hills Hotel.

But she had never forgiven Domina. The interview had been like for a college. Important. She still remembered every minute of it, and she still resented Domina for making her feel so useless, untalented, so out-of-place in New York.

Now Domina would work with Roe, and now Roe had a new apartment. Lolly thought about her own apartment. It had been fine when she and Bill had moved in, Upper East Side, one big bedroom, one tiny one, living room, dining area, small kitchen. But the two kids in the small bedroom wasn't good. Katie kept the baby awake at night. Willie woke Katie up in the morning. Toys all over the living room, zwieback crumbs crusted like glue in the kitchen. The nurse was the nurse, not the maid, as she constantly announced to them. So Lolly was the maid, laundress, cook. Last night she had been on her hands and knees wiping tomato juice off the floor, while the nurse had read a bedtime story to the children. Lolly had felt a fury at the nurse, at her fate. Still, her own salary would rise, and by the time the children were at school, she would be home free. But that time seemed far away. Jesus, how wonderful to scoop up the children and move into an apartment with Roe.

Still, she did have her job. An office all mahogany and cream paint with never a fingerprint. The work exciting, full of secrets. Expensive lunches Bill would never have taken her to, interviews with fascinating people, and wonderful moments when she put the right man into the right job. And the agencies and companies liked her, because she was always cheerful and sunny, no matter how hard they drove her to find new people.

If I didn't work for Carroll, Lolly thought, I wouldn't be here now. It's given me a full-blown, gorgeous love affair. Bill was always talking about her quitting, staying home, taking care of the kids like his more successful friends' wives. I might as well quit living. My job is what makes me feel important. Outside it, husband, children, parents, apartment, thing always going wrong with them all.

Lolly often felt in the wrong: in the wrong house, wrong dress, wrong ideas. When her father had first taken them to Hollywood, Lolly, like Dorothy flying off to Oz on a cyclone, had been frightened. The new kids, so different from New York kids – they were handsome, brown, sure of themselves. When Lolly had a bike, they had horses. When she had a Vespa, they had cars. When she went East to Bennington, they went to UCLA, talking about grade-point averages and things she knew nothing about. And when she got East, it was worse. The private-school girls were always ahead of her, first sleeping with boys, then with other girls. By contrast, it had felt so serene to go to work.

Lolly loved her babies, but she loved them most of all when they were bathed and fed, rosy in their tiny bath-robes, and ready for sleep. Weekends with them were no picnic. Before she became a mother, Lolly had always washed her blond hair on Thursday nights, to be ready in case the weekend should turn out wonderful. Now she washed her hair on Sunday nights, ready for the office to take her away from screaming and dirty diapers.

With Roe, all that could change.

Roe had plenty of money for nurses and maids and houses in the Hamptons, even with the alimony he was paying now. Married to Roe, she could help him, tell him the Carroll secrets, be a model executive wife. Roe always said how he loved being able to talk business in bed, for a change.

Lolly looked at him. She could protect him, sew on his lost buttons. And pat down his hair. Roe did make her want to touch him.

Roe reached for her again. Lolly slid a look at the clock. She knew it was late, but she felt helpless. She wanted to stay.

Roe followed her look to the clock. 'Come on, let's get you home,' he said, spanking her once gently to get her moving. 'You first, okay?'

She was stunned. Then she actually bit her tongue,

holding it fast between her teeth. But she spoke anyway.

'Roe,' she said, bursting it out, 'Roe, when are you going to fix it so I don't have to do this?'

There was quiet. Her question seemed to hang in the air. 'Do what?'

'This. Rush like this, sneak like this, hide out.'

'Oh. I didn't know you felt quite like that about it.'

'Roe. I want to have dinner with you tonight, and lots of nights. I want to have breakfast with you, as a matter of fact. And you can do all that now, Roe. You're free.'

'But you're not,' he said quietly.

Oh, she thought, he thinks I could be free except that I couldn't leave Bill.

'Come on, Mrs Moss,' he said. 'Let's get you home to your brood.'

Yes, that's it, he's thinking about what's good for me, but he's got it all wrong. He's what's good for me.

'Wait,' she said. 'Listen. I love you. I'll never love anyone like this. You love me, you must. You got divorced, Roe. I thought that was for me.'

'Actually,' Roe said, 'that was for me.'

Lolly shivered. 'Listen, what did we just finish doing? What do you mean, for you? Don't you want me?'

Corny, she thought. What can I do to make him understand?

Roe smiled and put his arm around her shoulders. 'Of course I want you. You're my California baby and my Mata Hari in the business world. Come on, Lolly, we'll be late.'

'Fuck late,' Lolly said, feeling desperate. 'I thought we were building to something. Did you want to meet me once a week in this hotel forever? We're not getting anywhere.'

Silence.

'We got to San Francisco last month. Had a hell of a good time there, too – at least I did. Lolly, it's almost six.'

'Don't joke, don't joke with me now, Roe.'

She sat tense, nails hurting her palms, waiting.

Roe sat up beside her. 'Lolly. I just got out from under, for God's sake. I married young, never had a minute to do things like this without guilt. Just to laugh in bed is something brand new for me. Today every kid on the block does this, but for me it's new. I've always been the responsible one, the hardworking one. Don't press me now, don't make it sticky for us.'

Isn't it sticky for me? Has he given that one thought? Dammit, doesn't he have any idea about how I feel?

'I sneak out week after week, and you don't owe me a thing? Bottle of wine? You hire some guy and give me the commission? Is that what you think?'

Roe looked down at her, pink, teary, like a dewy plump rose. Somehow they all get here, he thought. They talk friends, sex without strings, want nothing, and somehow it always turns into going somewhere, ties, the works. Women. Nothing can be just itself. Has to turn into something more. Sure, they were that way when he was twenty, but today? When they're all so assertive and liberated? They can all say 'fuck,' jump into bed. But here he was, the same conversation he'd had a hundred years ago. The words never changed. She wants locks, clasps, keys.

'Lolly, I never promised you a thing, you know it. I thought you wanted a little extra fun, a little more out of everything, like me. I don't want to be expected to do things right now. Louise did enough expecting for a lifetime. Listen. I'll do anything I can to make you happy. I love being with you like this, making love to you, you're marvelous, Lolly. But I can't get involved again, not now, not like that. I'm sorry.'

He was sorry. As if he'd stepped on her toe. Oh, she'd been so wrong.

'Maybe you could get used to the idea,' she said miserably.

Her words had come out all wrong, she'd fucked it all up. Now he'd be warned off. She'd lose him entirely.

'I'm fifty-one, you're twenty-seven, twenty-eight? It's ridiculous, Lolly, leave it, forget it. I'm going to. Okay?'

Lolly felt a little better. Roe seemed at least to want to keep things as they were. She thought of so many mean, hurtful things to say to him. She bit her tongue until it really hurt.

Stiff, quiet, she got up and went into the bathroom, straight into the shower, turning the water on full. It trickled out in a cold stream. Why the hell was the water pressure in these dumb hotels so absolutely awful?

I sure blew that, she kept thinking. If I tell him off, I'll never see him again. No Roe? I'd kill myself. I'd better pretend that I was kind of kidding. He knows I meant it, but I'll lie, be terribly careful.

She came out of the bathroom naked, wet and smiling. She preened a little, the way the girls on the nude beaches at home preened when they came out of the ocean and knew everyone was sneaking a look at them.

'You marry anyone else and I'll murder you. I'll put big black marks against you in the computer, and I'll only send you the worst names to hire, and I'll tell people you can't get it up, the works.'

Roe took her around the middle, swung her up on the bed. 'I'm not marrying anyone else,' he said. 'And more to the point, since nobody gets married anymore, I won't fall for anyone else, Lolly Moss. I'll save all my magic for you alone. As long as you want, Lolly. Just let's have some laughs. We can both use them. All right?'

No, it's horribly wrong. Laughs. What's funny about tiptoeing into hotels, about my acting bright and cute when I'd like to handcuff you?

'All right,' she said.

Dried off now, from the sheets, she began to dress. And while she tugged on her pantyhose, she thought: Take it easy, now, easy. He'll get lonesome, he has to, a man who's been married all these years. Won't know what to do with himself on weekends in that fucking apartment. If he touches other girls, they'll have to remind him of me, he'll remember me all the time in bed. I was an idiot with all that talk. His mind is still on the divorce. And I'm not going anywhere. Bill will always be the same thing over and over. And Roe will always be the best person I could have. I've got to hang in.

She tugged her coat off the hanger and turned to face him. She pursed her mouth into a smile, making an effort, working to make her eyes wide and bright.

'What day next week?' she asked.

Roe Rossen

Inside Jackson

Each month we publish a profile of
an outstanding member of our team.
Get to know your fellow Jacksoners.
Meet Roe Rossen, executive vice-president.

Cool, craggy, captivating Roe Rossen is the
thirty-eighth floor's answer to how to get new
business for the agency. This newest executive
V.P., in charge of marketing and management for
our biggest account, Ford, is on a winning streak
that has brought eight new clients in this year
alone! Roe is a native New Yorker, but went to
Exeter School and Harvard. He enlisted and
served in a special unit in Germany during the
war. When peace was declared he traveled to far-
off places all over the world. Then he went back
to Harvard for his MBA and joined his father in
his lithography and printing empire. A love of
cars led him to submit a new wheel design to
Ford, which led him to work for us! His planning
on the Rodeo car resulted in the biggest
introduction in car history! Roe has recently
deserted Connecticut for the city. You can find
him on the tennis court early mornings, before
work. We're fortunate indeed to have executives
who work as hard and successfully as our own
Roe Rossen.

There was always a gauntlet to run in getting to see any Jackson executive. But Roe ignored the lineup of secretaries all along the way to Domina Drexler's office.

'Hi,' he said to the secretary whose desk was placed directly in front of Domina's door. 'I'm Roe Rossen, Mrs Drexler and I have an eleven o'clock.'

'I'll tell her you're here, Mr Rossen,' the girl said. But Roe was past her, knocking once hard on the heavy door before he pushed it inward. From the corner of his eye he saw a smashing redhead looking up from a nearby cubicle.

Domina was on the phone, sitting in the sunlit window. She looked up, but simply gestured toward a chair and kept on with her conversation. Roe sat. He would give her two minutes. An appointment was an appointment.

Anyway, it was a chance to get a good look at her, on her home ground, in the office he'd heard so much about.

Good-looking, he thought. Sits straight even in that floppy armchair. Blue jeans, funny, but good ones, fit snugly all the way down. Terrific legs. And silver shoes. That's odd. Little strips of silver with sky-high heels. How does she walk? How did she move so fast out of Godwin's office yesterday? Brooks Brothers shirt, like mine. Only pink, the kind I still hate seeing a man wear. Good for her, brightens her up. She's fantastically neat. Diamond earrings, in the office, and with jeans? But what the hell. Godwin said she was the one to manage this job, if I could manage her. Come on, lady, get off that phone.

Roe shifted in his chair, making his movements abrupt and impatient. She was still listening intently, not looking at him. One minute more.

He turned his head to get a look at the office. Special.

The decorators had knocked themselves out for her, or she had good taste. Country farmhouse. But the worn fruit-wood furniture had the patina of museum pieces. Rugs glowing, reds and pinks and brilliant oranges. Farmhouse on Fortieth Street, a million-dollar farmhouse. If management ever bankrupts us, we can have one hell of a garage sale. He saw that Domina had a huge pottery bowl of apricots and tangerines on her desk. Near it, a picture of two children, teenagers. They both had her black hair, but looked nothing like her otherwise. She didn't seem like a mother. And much too cool to imagine in a rumpled bed, too unassailable for a hug or a tumble.

A challenge?

He looked at his watch with a broad gesture. Still nothing from her. Well, Godwin sure had the temperamental types. Roe's own account executives, a parallel kingdom, were men who understood rank and structure. Not one of them would keep him waiting. Was this woman going to be a pain in the ass?

There, she was finally putting down the phone, turning to face him. She had enormous eyes, almost totally black, and they looked straight at him.

'Hello,' he said. 'I'm delighted we're finally working together. I've heard terrific things about you, but with my cars and your fashion stuff, we've never really met. You don't socialize much upstairs.'

Her smile was polite.

'No,' she said in her low voice. 'My fashion stuff keeps me quite busy. And I hate to waste time.'

You've just wasted five minutes of mine, Roe thought, but he didn't let his annoyance show. We've got to get along, no sense antagonizing her right off the bat.

'Okay. You've read the proposal? There's not much written yet, but I'm getting some more facts for you. This is going to be a fascinating project, Domina.'

'They're all fascinating, I think. I never had patience with the people who won't work on cigarettes or liquor or toilet-bowl cleaners. I don't legislate people's behavior, and anything they want to buy, I'll be glad to sell them.'

Did I ask for philosophy? thought Roe. Just do this job,

95

lady, and then sell any fucking thing you want.

'Right,' he said. 'Now. I've met a woman who's perfect for consulting on this work. Do you know Belle Rosner?'

'I've heard of her,' Domina said.

'She's something. Very old, over eighty, I think, but tough and smart. The way those old-timers always are when they last. Worked since she was born, practically. Knows retail like nobody else. Well, she's done a lot of research on this project already, has it all laid out for you. And she's spent a lot of time in Israel over the years, knows all their key people in fashion.'

He saw Domina hesitate.

'Have you actually hired her?'

Tact, he thought, be tactful.

'Well, I wanted you to do the hiring, so she'd know you were running the show. It's you she has to help. Why? Did you want to handle it some other way?'

'When you walked in just now, I was talking to a fashion expert I have tremendous trust in. She's fantastic, and I wanted to sound her out a little for this project, see what she thought. It's always good to work with people you can count on.'

Oh, Christ, is she going to object to every little thing? Let's put her in her place right now.

'I think Miss Rosner's record shows about a century of being dependable.'

'You say this woman is over eighty?' said Domina. 'What about her health? Her energy?'

Roe smiled in spite of his irritation, thinking of Belle Rosner and the trouble he'd had getting her out of his office. He felt a little sorry for Domina, facing the storm attack of Belle's approach to work.

'Who is the expert you had in mind?'

He noticed that she lifted her chin suddenly, as if she were squaring off for a fight.

'Maran Slade. Of Maran Slade Associates. I've worked with her a great deal, on very tough projects. She has the best fashion sense I've ever come across. And I've been at it a while.'

The name meant nothing to him. What did he know

about fashion experts? A wave of annoyance washed over him. Details. Women always got stuck on details. Get past this one quickly, he thought.

'Well, we can decide next week. But I would like you to meet Miss Rosner. I'll have my secretary set up a date for you two to get together, Monday, if you can. Perhaps your mind will change. My father worked with her a few years ago on a government commission. He's an excellent judge of people, and he thought her work was spectacular.'

'Your father,' repeated Domina flatly.

He could hear in her tone her denigration of the opinion of some elderly man. And it wasn't the moment to explain the brilliant moves and instincts that had taken Monroe Roszenski from Essex Street to Fifth Avenue with no help from anybody. This lady would have to take his word. It was about time that Domina got the message. The overall responsibility for this project was his. He stood up.

'How do you plan to get started?' he asked.

Domina stood up too, and became as tall as he, in her spike-heeled shoes. He wondered suddenly if that was why she wore shoes like that. She must be almost as tall as Godwin. He watched her pick up a folder from her desk.

'I've thought about it a lot since I spoke with Brady. Last night I made some notes.'

She opened the folder and began to read aloud.

'"Purpose. To increase the potential exports for Israeli manufacture. Target. The American market over the next three years." Is that the main idea as you see it?'

'Yes, exactly.'

'All right, problem analysis. These are just starters. You know, the things you do till you do what you're going to do. Figures we'll need for the export volume now. Estimates for what it could be. Problems with things they make now, and with how they sell it. Lack of design skills, the lopsided business of enormous manufacturing expertise and quality materials that get wasted on poor styles no American woman would want to wear. A list of people who've already solved this problem.'

'Are there people who've solved it?'

'There's a woman who makes bathing suits. Leah Gottlieb. Gottex bathing suits and play clothes. Ever seen them?'

'Domina, I wouldn't know a Gottex bathing suit if you showed me a delicious blond wearing one.'

He saw her mouth tighten for just an instant.

'Well, they're interesting. Little handfuls of stretch cloth, so they pull on and fit tight, smooth out women's figures. Brilliant colors. Cut beautifully, and just what the American woman wanted when she got tired of bikinis. A lot more comfortable and practical than bikinis, too.'

Roe's mind flashed to Lolly, with her bikini marks white against her honey skin. He still felt a pang, an irritation, when he thought about yesterday afternoon. How much longer would Lolly be content as a once-a-week girl? Big outbursts like yesterday's were usually just the tip of the iceberg.

He wrenched his mind back to the woman waiting quietly for him to say something. Domina had a lot of, he guessed you'd call it repose. Her face reminded him of the little stone virgins in the French churches. Domina – pretty name. Again he wondered about Mr Drexler.

'Never heard of Gottex, but don't go by me. Do they sell?'

'She caught the market at just the right time, the way we ought to. The suits are knockouts, heavenly colors, beautifully made. And Mrs Gottlieb's a smart woman. I've heard her speak at fashion meetings, whole family's in the business. It's good to have examples of people who know how to manage what's precisely our problem.'

Roe looked at her closely. Why, she's smart, he thought. She's had twenty-four hours, with all the rest of her work, but she has a folder and there's something in it, and she's gone right to the heart of the problem. Not like Belle Rosner, who simply covers every possible thing, and leaves you with a mass of stuff.

Domina went on.

'Goals,' she said. 'We'd better establish them, and I'll need to see the figures for that, juggle them around a little, because nobody's will be just right, and we'll have to average them out, don't you think?'

'Always do,' said Roe. This was a creative person? She sounded the way he wished his account executives would.

'Then I just put together some ways to get from the problem, once it's fully defined, to the answers. These are sort of random. I just brainstormed it for myself at home last night.'

Last night. What does a woman like this do with her nights? Silly question, he thought. She brainstorms ideas for the office? No. Too attractive to spend all her nights working. No husband. Is there a lover? Other women? Younger guys? Christ, what's the difference? It's her work I'm interested in.

Still. Those slim, long legs under mine? Cool arms lightly around my shoulders, not clutching, just touching? And that hair – for the love of God, how long is it, what would it feel like by the handful? How would you get her into bed, anyway? She's mighty sure of herself.

Domina watched Roe, leaning forward to catch everything she was saying. Good-looking, she was thinking. A bit rumpled, and his shoes need shining. But a lot better than Brady Godwin. Mr Esquire, circa 1950. Damn, I wish I could pay real attention to this project, this man. He could be fun. Not like all the cardboard cutouts in this agency, in this world. He catches on fast, and I haven't met a man who understands things, little things, in so long.

I'd like to put his tie straight.

She thought for a moment about her one office fling. When she'd first come to Jackson there had been an account man, tall, eager, adorable. He'd eyed her in every meeting, arranged moments alone with her, moved closer and closer as they worked together. Soon there had been drinks after work, long talks about their marriage partners, before he went home to the suburbs. And then they began to travel together on business, which always made sex simple. Hotel breakfasts in bed, slipping into rooms late at night, exchanging room keys. Quick breathless tumbles, slow early-morning lovemaking, all the excitement and flattery of someone wanting you so often, so much. When you spent days away from home waiting for television cameras to roll, listening to silly in-jokes and talk from actors and crews, eating marvelous dinners with studio people, how far from reality, how wonderful a climate for an affair. And when you had to fly back to the real world, how easy to go on, especially if the man had an apartment nearby and you could take long lunch hours.

The affair had strung itself out, little irritations mounting, to the point where Domina, in an airport parking lot, had watched the man slip his wedding ring out of his pocket and onto his finger, and then she had wrenched it from his grasp and thrown it as far as she could out among the parked cars. He'd almost hit her, and that had ended it, as she must have wanted to. Later she'd realized gradually that everyone in the office seemed to know. Feeling ridiculous, she had never become involved with anyone in the office since, and never would. Office love affairs, she'd learned, were artificial. The common ground for conversation added empathy, but a kind that stopped when you left the office and had nothing to talk about. You chose each other not freely, really, but because you'd been thrown together. It was simply having someone who adored you around all day long, Domina thought, and that's pretty unreal. Never again.

Roe coughed, and she realized he was waiting for her to go on. Her next page was a brief rundown on Maran Slade Associates. Skip it, she thought, we don't need a tug-of-war on Maran versus Belle, not till he learns to trust me. Go on to the next thing.

'It should end with a fashion show,' she said. 'And maybe we send a traveling show, a little one, to show them how Americans dress. For different occasions and places. Europeans think we dress like women in movies. They don't understand how mixed-up our fashion is these days.'

'Mixed-up? Like the way you dress?'

Domina looked at him. Is he teasing? Criticizing? Just play it straight, she thought.

'Yes. Ten years ago in Chicago, I wore a suit to work, pumps, stockings, black coat, like that. Nobody dresses that way now, even in Chicago, but go see a movie about an office, and there it all is, frozen. Hollywood doesn't know that secretaries all wear jeans, that men compete more over clothes than girls. Girls are feminists now, they act as if clothes were all frivolous. They spend hours embroidering jeans, but that doesn't count, they think.'

There, thought Domina, right back to business. I do love talking about fashion, clothes, attitudes. It's fascinating, and I understand it. Oh, if I had an agency, what I couldn't do with a good fashion account.

'We did a research project for lipsticks last week,' she went on. 'Teenage girls talking about health and looks, but the talk wandered.'

Domina loved research sessions at the agency. Jackson had a suite of conference rooms set up as kitchens, bathrooms, living rooms, even supermarket shelves. Almost every day groups of consumers were invited in to sit behind a one-way mirror and discuss agency products. The people who worked on the business could sit behind the mirror unseen, but seeing and hearing everything. Sometimes they would join the groups and show commercials and ads to these outsiders, for their opinions. Other times they would stare silently to note how women really handled products, how they measured, shook bottles, followed directions. Very good for copywriters and art directors to see and hear what people really did with things they advertised. Domina would always review remarks, and think about those research sessions when she went to parties and people attacked her for selling the public things they didn't need. If they only knew the hard work it takes to discover just what they did need.

She went on.

'One of the girls was making a big speech about how great it was to be young in this free generation, how you could be unique, and individual and do just what you felt like, sleep around, tell your mother off, things like that. Then she got around to clothes, and how you could dress just as you pleased. The interviewer asked how she'd feel about a girl who wore a tweed suit with a matching pocket-book and hat. They all squealed – square, dumb, gross, turkey, those words they use. Some individuals. Every one of them wore jeans. More uniform than when I went to Catholic school.'

'Got you,' said Roe. 'I never thought about it. Interesting.'

'There's more,' said Domina. 'But why don't I dictate it and send it up to your office? Brady wants me to leave my accounts while I do this, so I'm trying to cover everything and get people moved around to manage without me. It's not so easy. Like quitting your job on a whim.'

Mother of Christ, why did I come out with that? And he's the one who saw me holding back tears yesterday.

'I'm sure it's tough,' Roe was saying. 'Detroit is screaming for me now, too. That's this business. Always a scramble.'

Thank God, he'd passed right over her remark, she thought.

'What was your name before it was Drexler?' Roe said suddenly.

She was stunned. A personal question? Was he another Potter Jackson social snob?

'Di Santis. I was Domina di Santis. Of Elkhart, Indiana. Wrong side, too, literally across the tracks.'

'I know just where you mean. I used to travel there for my father's lithography business. Selling. Elkhart looks like a magazine cover. But when you stay there awhile, you realize. Every ethnic group neatly in its own separate section. Never mind, Domina, you look like you've managed to find the right side around here.'

She couldn't believe it. A Jackson executive who knew Elkhart? Really knew it? An interesting man, she thought, and it's been a while since I met an interesting man.

Roe looked straight at her and asked another question. 'What was bothering you in Brady's office yesterday?'

Sharp, she thought. Damn. I was hoping he hadn't noticed.

'You may not know that I'm the one creative head around here who isn't a senior vice-president. I find that shameful, and I mean to do something about it. I was telling that to Brady yesterday.'

'He evidently didn't get the message,' said Roe. 'He wasn't crying when I walked in. You were.'

Domina felt a stir of irritation. Roe Rossen obviously

was smart about work, but not about emotions. If it was *his* goddamned title, he'd be excited enough, she thought.

'It may have been foolish of me. Don't worry, it won't get in your way. I've put it back in its cage.'

There, she'd reassured him. Everyone cares only about his own problems.

'Can I help?'

Christ, was he being polite? Sure. He's on that board of directors. But would he help, really?

'Maybe. But right now, I want to make this fashion promotion work. You won't have any of my emotions to deal with, promise.'

'Let me tell you a story,' Roe said. 'A few years ago I was desperate to be a vice-president, there weren't so many of them then. I wanted the stationery with those big black engraved letters. Finally I got the promotion and ordered the stationery from office supplies. It came, eventually, the heaviest, creamiest writing paper you ever saw, beautiful. Also a bill for ninety-eight dollars and fifty-three cents. The company doesn't pay for that stationery. You do. It's considered a personal expense. I told my boss if I'd known that, I'd have ordered it years before, that now I wanted stationery that said I was chairman of the board. Why don't you just order the fucking stationery with any title you want? Use it, tell everyone you *are* a senior vice-president. This is a make-believe business. They'll swallow anything you want to tell them, just about. And what could Brady do, issue a denial in the company newsletter? Confiscate the stationery?'

Domina thought: he's making fun of me. He doesn't understand how torn up I feel, how important this is for me.

'What's keeping it from happening for you?' he asked.

'I have to believe it's because I'm a woman, and Jackson hasn't promoted a woman to that level. Yet.'

She saw the interest die on Roe's face.

'You ladies,' he said. 'Don't you ever let up?'

There, right out in the open. Just when I'd got to hoping I'd found a man who might be different.

'We can't afford to,' said Domina. 'Don't worry, it's my problem. Why don't you just go back to Israel?'

103

Roe sat straight up and stared at her. 'What does that mean?' he demanded.

'What should it mean? Let's finish up about the Israeli stuff,' she said.

She could see Roe relax, lean back again.

'You do know I'm Jewish?'

Domina felt color flood up into her face. Did he think she was retaliating with a reference to his being Jewish? The idea that he could misjudge her so made her cross.

'No, I didn't,' she said. 'Why? Is it something like being a feminist? Does it make you act defensive?'

'Not me,' said Roe. 'Now. You've been pretty aggressive about starting on this work. I like everything you have so far, it's going to be smooth, I'm sure. When I'm on the plane to Detroit, I'll figure out a timetable. With that, and the chance for you to go over Belle Rosner's material, we should be able to get rolling, let's see, end of next week.'

Not only was he misjudging her, Domina decided, he was ignoring her. Who did he think he was?

'Maran Slade has some work ready, too. That was a report from her on the phone. When you came walking in here.'

'I don't doubt that your friend is tops, Domina,' Roe said. 'But this is special work, and it needs a special person. There's more to do here than the ordinary fashion expert knows about.'

'Ordinary?' Domina was annoyed.

'All right, terrific maybe, but not for this job. Belle Rosner is truly knowledgeable, really capable. She's entirely out-of-the-ordinary. And I'd like you at least to meet with her. Then I'm sure you'll see.'

Domina decided. This man was not going to push her around.

'Maybe we'd better start straight,' she said quietly. 'Are you saying I must employ Belle Rosner?'

'I'm saying she's a find, the perfect person. What about keeping an open mind before you get excited?'

Look who's talking about an open mind.

'Well, I've never interviewed a woman of eighty before.'

'No problem,' said Roe. 'She does all the talking. You listen. You won't get a word in.'

'That could be what's bothering me,' said Domina, delighted to drive her point home. As she spoke, she could see Rossen's hands knot into fists quickly, then relax again.

'I'm sure you two ladies will get along just fine.' Roe had raised his voice a little.

Domina couldn't believe he'd said those words in that smug male tone. The irritation that had been simmering inside her began to seethe, boiling up into rage. *The same thing, over and over. They tell me I'm in charge. But there's one big joker, always. A male boss. Do it this way, not that way; hire this person, not that one. And the boss is always an idiot who doesn't understand the hard parts, who's busy chasing his own rainbows.*

'Let me understand. You're insisting I use Belle Rosner, is that it?'

'Look,' said Roe. 'I asked Godwin for someone to manage this, and he says you're it, you're terrific. I also asked people for a fashion expert, and everyone says she's it, she's terrific. So I want to put you two together. That's intelligent, isn't it? In fact, we call it management. You don't even know the woman, you can't have any genuine objection. What's wrong, exactly?'

Domina made one last try at suppressing her fury. She took a deep breath. 'What's wrong is, if I'm managing this, I choose my own experts. Isn't that intelligent?'

There. Quiet, sensible, spoken like a man. People often say I think just like a man. Jesus on the Cross, they think that's a compliment.

'Why don't you meet *my* expert?' she continued, controlling her voice. 'Maran is marvelous. She was a top model, you know, so she knows fashion from the inside. She's traveled everywhere, has branch offices in most big cities, so we'd have a whole organization going for us. You'll like her personally, I'm sure. She's handled some of the worst bastards in the business, so nothing's going to bother her. How about *my* setting up an interview?'

Take that, she thought. *Civilized, sensible, professional. Wait, you son of a bitch, till you start acting macho with*

105

Maran. She'll put you away. And she's taller than you are, not to mention smarter.

Roe was uncrossing his legs, getting ready to stand up. 'My secretary will let you know what time Monday to expect Miss Rosner. I'll be away, but first thing Tuesday I'll stop to see how you two get on. Then we can make the decision.'

Domina went white-hot. He was going on as if she hadn't spoken at all. How rotten, insulting, infuriating. She wanted to shout it all over again. She wanted to grab him by that little cowlick and shake him.

'Listen,' she said. 'You haven't learned how to listen. I'll say it again, loud and clear. If you force me to work with that old bitch, you can take this project and shove it. Either I run the show, the way Brady said, or you run it and I'll just keep doing my own job around here. But if you want it to be me, suppose you just get the fuck out of my way?'

She watched Roe stop getting up, stay awkwardly in a position between sitting and standing. Then he righted his body neatly, and sat back down in the chair again.

'Talk about overreacting,' he said with a smile. 'Domina. I'm here to help you. Of course, everybody wants you to run this. Calm down. I just asked you to meet the woman. You might even like her.'

Domina felt the heat die down inside her, felt the slight pang of fear that always followed when she had really spoken her mind. Would she be punished somehow? Suddenly she felt wretched. What's the use, she thought, why do I even try? He's had years of conditioning. Men give the orders, women follow through. How stupid to let him hear all that.

'All right,' she said. 'I ought to meet her, I suppose. Actually, I've wanted to meet her, I've heard her speak. I'll see her on Monday.'

Sure thing. She'd see Belle Rosner when hell froze, when the agency burned down, when Roe Rossen wore overalls to the office.

'Good,' said Roe, smiling at her now in approval. 'I'll fix it all up. And I'll be back first thing Tuesday to see if you feel better about her then. Thanks a lot, Domina.'

'Goou-bye,' she said stiffly. God, he was dense. Taking that cheerful tone. Didn't he have a glimmer of how angry she was? Yelling didn't seem to affect him. Sarcasm hadn't worked. She'd better think of something drastic, something to *make* him understand how she felt. Something nervy.

And by the time Roe's footsteps had died away, Domina had thought of something.

For Roe, the next days were busy with Detroit, cars, heavy men intent on getting the most of their money out of the agency. In the few quiet moments, Roe found that Domina flashed into his mind like a quick cut in a television commercial. The instant when she'd changed from a statue to a fury, suddenly, over nothing at all. He couldn't forget the way her eyes had narrowed and her skin had gone pink, all in an instant. Why? Why such a blowup? She had a terrific job. Beautiful office. She must make ninety, ninety-five thousand. Did she just have to have her own way? Was she bitchy about everything? No wonder she gave Godwin the pip. No wonder they talked about her so much in the dining room.

On the plane coming back from Michigan, Roe thought about Domina's other emotional tempest, the one he'd seen outside Godwin's office. Then she'd been weepy, not angry. But weepy with a difference from other women he'd known. Lolly? She cried like a little girl denied an ice-cream cone. Louise simply fell apart, turned to dull red, looked ten years older the moment she started to sob. But this lady swept into emotion like a heroine in a classic tragedy that would end with the stage carpeted in corpses. Whose corpses? Not mine, Roe decided. She'd hadn't been the first person to question his authority. He'd keep a rein on her.

He wondered why Domina hadn't responded to him the way most women did. In offices, at dinner parties, in vacation places, women everywhere almost always wanted to please him, exerted themselves to be charming. Even that old Rosner lady had tried to please him. Why hadn't he impressed Domina Drexler?

Roe remembered a talk with a friend when he'd first thought about divorcing Louise, a friend who adored women. He'd always said, 'Women? There is no bad. There's only good and better.' Roe had asked him how it was, being single now, with today's girls. The man had said, 'You know when we were in Cambridge, the Radcliffe girls? How they'd do your laundry, but they'd never go to bed with you? Today it's just the opposite. They'll all jump into bed, but not one of them will wash your dirty socks.' Was Domina like that, determined not to be subservient about anything? Should he have tried to charm *her*? Hell, this was business. He didn't need to charm a copywriter. Still, she looked interesting. Those taut thighs under the denim, those breasts pressing up under the tailored shirt, that controlled hair ready to spill out over her shoulders. Interesting. And now she probably had him lumped with Brady Godwin. Well, he could fix that. From here on, if he gave her pretty much her own way, it could settle into a smooth relationship. And what the hell, if she really hated Belle, once he'd made his point, he'd even take a look at her expert. He'd be nice about it.

As he got off the plane with the other first-class passengers, picked up the big carrying case with the top-secret car photographs, Roe made up his mind.

On Tuesday, he'd agree with Domina. A fascinating woman, most fascinating when she'd blown up, then settled down pleasantly and got on with the job. Good girl, he thought, just like a man. I'll make it up, take her to lunch somewhere nice, ask her more about her troubles with Godwin. He could sympathize. A guy like Godwin, if a situation hadn't happened at Princeton in 1920, would have no idea of how to deal with it. Roe, at Harvard, had mixed with rich guys, poor guys, soldiers, nuns, tailors, blacks, everybody. Had Domina gone to college? How had she made it to where she was?

Tuesday morning early, Roe took the elevator down to the creative floor. He smiled at all the secretaries, waved to a couple of guys he knew in the big outside offices. Again he noticed the cute redhead who sat near Domina, and again she clearly took note of where he was headed.

'Morning,' he said to the secretary. 'Mrs Drexler in? She's expecting me.'

He kept moving, reached to knock on the door, thinking about Belle Rosner. The old lady had called twice already, would surely call him again this morning. She wanted an answer.

And then Roe realized that the secretary had turned in her chair, was staring at him in surprise.

'Mr Rossen,' she said. 'Mrs Drexler isn't here. Didn't you know? She's already left, Mrs Drexler left.'

Roe felt a thud in his chest, as if a tennis ball had hit him.

'Not here?'

'No, sir, she's left on that project you're doing, the Israel job,' said the secretary patiently. 'She only just managed to get the first plane after your meeting last week. She didn't even go home, her maid brought a bag around to the office for her. She was going to Paris for the weekend, and then on to Tel Aviv. She had no hotel, but she said she'd call in as soon as she found a base there.'

The first plane. The first one after our meeting. The bitch. She never meant to do what she said. To see Belle Rosner. Damn her to hell. Tel Aviv. I can't even bawl her out over the phone, they don't know where she's staying.

'Can I help you at all? Do you want to talk to someone else in Mrs Drexler's group?'

I could throttle that damned woman, just put my hands around her neck and close in.

'No, thanks,' he said. 'Guess I forgot. I've been away myself. You let me know when she calls in, will you?'

He turned, feeling foolish, as if he were a cartoon figure still running while the rug was pulled out from beneath his feet. He wanted to get away from Domina's office before the warm anger in his chest swept up into his neck and ears, making him visibly furious. He'd been had. Domina had made a passing shot, gone off to do God knew what in Israel. With an expensive fling in Paris beforehand. He'd go after her. He'd fire her. Hell, he'd kill her when he caught up. What on earth could he tell Godwin? Progress report, old buddy: Mrs Drexler had stolen the problem and flown away with it. And what was he supposed to tell Belle

Rosner? That he hadn't decided yet? That he had no idea where her leader had gone off to? Well, he'd fix it, and fix Domina Drexler, too. He'd think of a move that would cream the girl. Such as? Such as hiring Belle now, today, and handing over the whole job to her. Such as getting someone else in the agency to run it, and leaving Domina the hell out. Such as running it himself. He had choices, power, force. So watch out, Domina di Santis Drexler.

The girl with red hair looked up from her drawing board as he thundered past her cubicle. She smiled, showing pretty white teeth and a tiny pink tongue, like a kitten's. He caught just a quick look as he went by, trying to decide what in hell to say when the next call came in from Belle Rosner.

M.J.

M.J. Kent
411 East 63rd St.
New York, N.Y.
555-7249

The Potter Jackson
Company
8 East 40th St.
New York, N.Y.

MY RÉSUMÉ
The Story

The True Story

1. Jackson's choice from 279 applicants for art training in New York. Now art director on Boutique Bonnell and food accounts.

I was *wild* to get myself away from Birmingham!

2. Grossman Brothers' choice from 1978 high-school grads for merchandising training in Birmingham, Ala.

I showed up to apply the night *before* graduation!

3. Birmingham Council's choice from all county schools for Elite Art Training.

The word 'elite' is kind of misunderstood in Alabama!

4. Cotton Council's choice from all state girls for Cotton Queen, 1977.

What more can I tell you?

5. Birmingham Ad Group's choice from Alabama schoolchildren for Red Cross poster contest.

I was only nine, but I could outdraw every kid in the state!

6. My own choice, still single. Have all skills, will travel.

That *is* the truth!

7. Present salary, $32,000 plus benefits.

Well, everyone fudges a little on this, right?

Sunday morning, early, with Dan sleeping like a farmhand, M.J. slipped quietly out of the apartment and walked to the office.

She showed her pass to a sleepy guard in the lobby near the crazy clock and took the one working elevator up. It felt strange in such stillness. The huge halls were dark in the gloomy light. The air felt heavy without the air conditioning, and the smell of disinfectant hung over the oddly clean desks. The rows of covered typewriters reminded her of crows lined up on a fence back home. M.J. felt like a thief, wary, tense, her breath coming fast and her stomach knotting up as she moved quickly through the echoing hall.

Once down the hall safely, she pushed open the heavy door to Domina's office. Better bolt it, she thought. Then if a guard comes by, I'll just say I forgot some work in here on Friday. It might be a little risky, but I can explain it, if I look like I'm not scared, not guilty about anything.

M.J. wasted no time on the drawers and cabinets she'd looked in other times. She went straight to Domina's desk. It had to be in there somewhere.

She knew that every half-year all Jackson supervisors wrote evaluations of their employees, brief paragraphs about progress, effort, attitudes, things like that, which determined raises and promotions. The evaluations were written, not even typed by the secretaries, so the word couldn't get around about them. Many younger employees didn't even know about them. They were supposed to go straight to Mr Godwin. A good one got you moving up. A bad one kept you where you were. A stinging comment could just get you fired, especially if billings were down and they needed to get rid of people.

113

M.J. knew that Domina had been writing her evaluations just before she'd left so suddenly. She also knew, by asking casual questions of Domina's secretary, that the evaluations hadn't been turned in yet. That could only mean they must be somewhere in Domina's office. The chance to get a look at her own, along with everyone else's, was just too good to pass up.

There was a special reason, too, why M.J. was anxious. Raises came at Jackson on a fixed schedule, summer and Christmastime. This summer M.J. would be desperate for money. She was deep into her Visa credit, late on her American Express bill, which they hated you to be, and she owed plenty to four Fifth Avenue stores. Worst of all, there was the sapphire.

A month earlier, poking around on Forty-seventh Street in the jewelry market during a lunch hour, M.J. had discovered a sapphire, blue as a cornflower, oval, sparkling within a ring of good-sized diamonds. It looked old, like a family jewel, exactly the kind that shone from the portraits of prewar Southern belles in the Birmingham Museum. With that on her finger she could tell people anything, that she came from a fine old family ruined in the Civil War, that she had been engaged to a rich man who'd been killed tragically, that her mother had saved one glorious thing for her from their family past. That ring would back up any story. M.J. had bought it on the spot. Three thousand dollars, a tenth of her yearly salary. She had written a check on her overdraft, money she was nowhere near having. So a raise was vital, and not just a small one. If her evaluation wasn't terrific, M.J. needed to know, to figure how else to get hold of some real money.

She flipped through Domina's calendar. Three whole weeks out of the office, and M.J. was simply dying to know how come. But the date book was no help. M.J. flipped fast through next month's pages to see if any homecoming time was noted. Again, nothing. Her curiosity itched irritatingly, like a big mosquito bite.

She remembered Domina that last day going around to the people in the group, saying she was going away, didn't know for how long. She'd expect a full report on their work

114

when she came back. M.J. could tell that Domina was excited inside her cool look. But M.J.'s most prying questions couldn't get at why. Nobody knew. Even M.J.'s two best sources were no good.

Dan would have told her right off if he could have, even though he adored Mr Rossen and never spied on him. Rossen had picked Dan out of a passel of trainees, and after that Dan thought everything his boss did was just wonderful. Dan knew only that Rossen had Domina working on some project about Israel. M.J. wasn't too sure where Israel was, except that Jewish people lived there and fought Arabs a lot. She admired fighting, if it got you what you wanted. Dan was no fighter. But he did come through with the rent and pay for the food. And that meant she could hang on to her salary, after those carpetbagger taxes, and buy glamorous things in the New York stores.

M.J.'s new beau, Mr David March Noble, didn't know what Domina was up to, either. David was the personnel director. She had met him when she came to be interviewed. Mr Noble had 'vice-president' written on his door and 'letch' written on his face. Secretaries and young creative applicants were his favorites, but M.J. knew she'd been special right away. She'd hit his office at four-thirty, gone off for a drink with him to discuss the right spot for her at five, and had been in the right spot for him at six. The spot was an apartment Mr Noble kept for private interviews.

M.J. had passed an employment test in that apartment, getting A for effort. David March Noble was used to getting girls relaxed with a second drink, mixed strong, and gradually moving closer on the couch to them, getting their blouses open and closing in. M.J. had recognized his style the minute she sipped her drink. But passive acceptance was not M.J.'s style, and besides, she wanted the job. She had put the drink firmly on the table, stood up and got out of her clothes, while Mr Noble sat stunned. She had then removed Mr Noble's clothes, opening the shirt buttons, unzipping the pants, giving his foot a promising little lick of her tongue as she got his shoes off. While he gaped at her, she eased him back on the soft couch, kneeling between his legs. With her orange hair flung out to tickle his belly and rubbery thighs, M.J. had taken his little jigger in between her lips and coaxed it back and forth into a respectable size, teasing and nibbling till she judged he wasn't going to wait a moment longer. Then she had lifted her head, swung lightly on top of him, and ridden him into a state of weakened pleasure she knew would leave him hot for more. But she didn't allow more. After that storm attack, delighted to learn that what worked in Alabama seemed to work just as well in the big city, she smiled demurely, put her clothes back on, and drank her drink, now watery from melted ice and no longer dangerous. By the time she left, she had David's eager promise to send her to Domina. And since her drawings were every bit as good as her fucking, she'd been hired right off.

She'd been delighted with the work right off, too. The first commercial she'd been assigned, the writer had said not to worry, it was just the usual two C's in an S. When M.J. had to ask what that meant, he'd been amazed. 'You know, two cunts in a supermarket.' M.J. had giggled, and begun to be an advertising art director.

From the start she'd been fascinated by Mrs Drexler. She admired the way Domina shaped people up, got the most out of them, made them laugh and still work hard. It would be a tough job to fool Domina. But that lady kept the key to everything M.J. wanted: money, a big office, people to boss. So she just had to keep a careful eye on her boss.

Right now, though, she couldn't. She was baffled. If even David, at their afternoon fucks, couldn't tell her where Domina was, how else could M.J. find out except by doing a little snooping?

She sat down in the little velvet chair that was the color of peach blossoms, took the top off the big glass cookie jar on Domina's table, and helped herself to some sugar almonds. Domina kept candy, but never touched it. Didn't want to get fat. But M.J. knew she could nibble all she liked and never gain a pound. She crackled the almond against her teeth, sucking the delicious sugar part before she crunched hard into the nut. A little stale. Three weeks since that jar had been filled. She'd better get busy.

The little drawer where Domina sometimes tucked special things was almost empty. Only an ivory hairpin, the kind Domina didn't like because they kept slipping out, with a card that said 'To Mom.' M.J. thought that Domina was silly to put her hair up. It was her prettiest feature. M.J. would never yank back her own hair. It was the first thing men noticed about her. Plenty of them had told her.

Now what? M.J. looked around. She'd sure give a lot to have this office. Her own little cubicle was a dump. Though her open wall helped her keep up. She always knew who went into Domina's office, how long they stayed, what layouts they brought out and what temper they were in when they came out, which was useful. If they were happy, Domina had approved the work. More often, they grumbled some. And when exciting things happened, like when Mr Rossen had come charging out, M.J. knew first off. He'd sure looked mad when he found out that Domina wasn't there. M.J. giggled to herself.

She ate another handful of almonds. The exercise she'd been getting lately, between Dan and David both, she could eat as she pleased.

M.J. checked the cabinets just to make sure there were no papers there, but found nothing. The top drawer just had personal stuff, a gold pencil, a lace hankie, a bronze award medal, a valentine marked 'To Mommy,' a clay figure one of Domina's kids must have made. They sure didn't have any art talent. She turned to the shelves. The rows of advertising awards and trophies in fake gold and silver took up all the spaces between reference books and picture files. M.J. had won an award in Birmingham, a bronze cup with a corny angel engraved on it. That angel had flown her all the way to New York. You'd think this many awards would take Domina straight to the Advertising Hall of Fame.

M.J. looked at her watch. Almost nine. Even on Sundays they patrolled. She'd better not stay too long. She could feel her breath coming a little shorter, her palms a little damp. She had to find her evaluation. It had to be in this room somewhere. Where?

With her next move, she knew. The corner cabinet was locked.

Domina never locked anything. This is the place, M.J. knew, her heart thumping, her hands growing hot. I've got it, but can I open it? And how, so they won't know later on? She thought hard.

Then she took hold of the wide leather belt around her middle, whisked it out, and took the little prong of the buckle in her fingertips. It was sharp. She poked gently at the inside of the lock, thinking it was good that art directors had such trained fingers. At first the prong just skidded around on the metal. Again she tried. This time she felt the lock shiver. With a soft click, it sprang.

Every time she poked into a locked place, M.J. was carried back to the first time, in the schoolhouse in Eufaula. Then, too, she had been frightened to death of what she was doing, but still more of what would happen if she couldn't get hold of what she needed.

The evening before, she had ambled home, a skinny six-year-old, with her first reading report tucked in her pocket. Like on any evening, she spied her father rocking on the porch after a day in the field. She'd gone up the steps thinking about how much time she'd have to play before she had to help her mother get supper, and handed over the report. Next thing she'd known, without a warning she'd been hauled over his knee. In another moment, her father's big hard hand had started spanking her bottom, rocking her so she could see the rough boards of the porch sway back and forth with every blow. She yelled and yelled in terror and pain. Then he'd set her on her feet and held her between his huge knees, waving the report at her. He'd said that was just a start, that if she brought him home any more marks like that, he'd take his belt to her, never mind a little spanking. By this time, her brothers had crowded around, and she could tell through her tears that nobody was sorry for her. She had stood pinned between those big shoes of his, hurt, ashamed, petrified. She knew the rest of her marks would be just as bad, maybe even worse. School was dumb. Arithmetic was a mess of chicken tracks on paper. The reading book meant nothing to her. And she'd never realized it mattered. M.J. shook when she thought about her reading test coming next day.

While she'd picked at her supper standing up, M.J.'s mind had worked furiously. By bedtime she'd made up her mind.

She'd waited hours till everyone was asleep. Then she'd reached past her next-oldest brother in the big bed for the jackknife he kept in his shirt pocket. Just before dawn, when she knew country people sleep soundest, she'd tiptoed out of the house and walked fast to school.

She always remembered how the hole in her raggedy jeans caught at a splinter in the low wooden sill, how the sound of the window going up seemed the loudest noise she had ever heard. Her heart had felt ready to jump out from under her shirt, and her hands had been slimy with sweat and the warm dew from the window. The schoolroom had seemed vast and fearful. She'd felt like a snake, slipping in, sliding toward the big desk where the teacher kept her things.

With shaky hands she'd opened the knife and used its tip to turn the lock in the center drawer. There they were, the papers they'd have to stand up and read out loud. Still shaking, she lifted them out. They seemed to rustle loud enough to call in the state troopers. She'd taken them to the girls' bathroom, and stayed there an hour at least, practicing all the hard words. Then she'd sneaked out the same way, getting home before sunup.

Jumping around in the schoolyard that morning, she'd kept herself awake enough to read out the piece she got, clearly and quickly. Afterward she stayed around till the other kids had gone off, and went in to the teacher. M.J. had made herself look as forlorn as she could, her hands politely clasped behind her over her bruised bottom, and asked for a note to her father. The teacher had obligingly given her a fine grade, patted her hand, and sent her on home.

This time M.J. had walked stolidly home, worn out with action and emotion, gone straight up to her father, and given him the big red 100. He'd stopped rocking, nodded his head in satisfaction, and shaken his big finger at her with

119

a warning to keep up that way, now she knew what was good for her. Sleepy, relieved, M.J. had gone in to supper, stuck her tongue out at all her brothers, and vowed to keep up just that way for the rest of her schooldays.

She quickly learned to open up desks and drawers at recesses and in late afternoons, easier times than the middle of the night. Once in a while she'd thought about actually doing the studying, but she couldn't take the time. She needed her spare time for the one thing she really cared about. Pictures.

She had loved making pictures ever since she could remember. First in the dust with a stick, outlines of the house, the trees. Then she'd found that a burned stick would work on old newspapers. Day after day she kept at it, a small girl with flaming hair, always on her knees, patiently recording what she saw around her. Her mother thought it was harmless enough, kept her quiet. Her dad wasn't so sure. But when M.J. began to draw good likenesses of the family, her father pocketed the pictures and showed them around town, boasting about his baby girl's gift. By the time she was eight, M.J. could draw accurately, redrawing and correcting till she got things perfect. People said her pictures were as good as snapshots. She drew flowers, birds, sketches of the church for her teachers, and of the ladies her mother cleaned house for. And when she was eight and a half, one of those ladies gave her a paint set.

M.J. never forgot that day. She remembered the exact second when she caught on about making the colors match what was there, just like she'd made the lines do. She colored the church its precise flat gray, the steeple gold, the grass green. Then she'd looked carefully at her work and realized she had a long way to go. She'd stretched that set of paints till the color blocks were specks in their little squares, always trying new effects. The feeling she got when her picture looked right was a wonder, joy sweeping up her whole body from her toes to her head, birds singing in her mind. She began thinking in colors, staring at objects to sort out the lights and darks. And once she could see it right, she could nearly always get it on paper.

By then, she'd learned how simple it was to pocket the paint sets in the dime store, so she'd never be without the materials she needed. Every time she opened a fresh set, she had a satisfaction she felt even today when the supply room delivered to her a new set of markers and water-colors.

The teacher announced that a contest for the best Red Cross poster designed by a school child would be held all over the state. M.J. decided she would do the best poster, and grimly went to work, biting her lip over sketch after sketch. Determined, resolving that she would beat every-one else, she drew for weeks until she had settled on what the poster would show. She created a family, ordinary, blue-jeaned, straw-hatted, smiling out from behind a huge ragged-edged red X. Outside the X were animals, in a snarling mass, trying to get at the family but held back by the red cross. The animals were terrible, savage creatures, repulsive, with extra legs and horrible teeth. Like every-thing M.J. was drawing by now, the picture had an idea. And anyone could see the idea right off.

She was certain that no one near her age in Alabama could do anything as clear, as haunting as her drawing. She was so resolutely sure that she waited the weeks of judging casually. They had said that an advertising agency would be the judge. M.J. had no idea what an advertising agency was, but she felt sure that people clever enough to live in the city would recognize her work immediately as superior. The calm feeling lasted all through the weeks as her teacher told her, with mounting excitement, that she had won in her district, then in her county, and finally, in the state. On that day, the whole school buzzing with envy and excitement, M.J. walked evenly home, straight to her father, and handed him the letter. He read it slowly and carefully. And somehow, when he smiled and patted her in congratula-tion, she had to hold herself back from punching him. She realized then how much she hated her father, who was an enemy, and how important it was to stay safe in this world by fighting your enemies.

In her new mood, she went with her father to Birming-ham. There were ice-cream sundaes, chicken lunches, elevator rides, all new and wonderful. But the most wonderful discovery had come when they took her to meet the judges of the contest.

When M.J. was walked through the advertising agency, when she saw the rows of drawing boards, the array of markers and brushes and colors, the T squares and Polaroid cameras and all the back-up equipment for the artists, she almost died of amazement right there on the spot. When she realized that the artists were grown-up, when she looked at their work, and saw that much of it was not as good as her own, right then, she came to, with a snap. By the time the tour was ending, M.J. had thought up a plan. She would stage a temper tantrum. She waited till her father was taken off for a beer by someone, tensing herself up for a show that she wasn't sure would turn out right. In her house nobody had temper tantrums. The results would have been far too painful.

M.J. fell first to her knees, then to the linoleum floor, which felt cold and strange as she lay on her back and kicked at it. She also produced a scream, followed by deep sobbing, ended by curling herself up and resisting all attempts to find out what was wrong. When M.J. got to her knees again, she sobbed out her story. She had no pencils, even, and here were all these beautiful things lying around. How she longed for brushes like these, and the paper! Stacks of smooth white paper just waiting for new pictures she could think up. Everyone crowded around the pretty little girl who cared so much about pictures, wiping away tears, promising help, piling things next to her on the floor.

She'd known from then on that you went for what you wanted with everything you had.

When M.J. got to high school, the work was harder but the help was easier. By then she'd grown full, pretty breasts and a round behind, and by then most of the teachers were men. And in high school, the big event of the year was the contest for Cotton Queen.

Among the other girls, only two were even close possibilities. With them, M.J. went for the first interviews with the talent scout sent from Birmingham. She'd practiced for a week fixing her hair in surprising ways, cutting her one good dress low in front, whitening her high heels that showed off her shapely legs.

The talent scout turned out to be a middle-aged man with watery eyes, who wore a seersucker jacket with half-moons of sweat under each arm. M.J. held back to let the other girls go in and talk with him first. She thought: Let him get hot on them, and finish off with me. When it was her turn, she moved slowly into the room. The man sat behind a teacher's desk, and the other girls had obviously taken the chair placed on the other side of it. M.J. went around to the man's side of the desk. She was a little shaky, because if her father heard about what she was doing, he'd probably just kill her like one of the chickens. She bit her lip just once, and plunged, putting herself plunk in the man's lap. Right away she could feel his response with her thigh, feel him hot and bulging out. M.J. managed that interview just as if she'd been sitting in the proper chair, saying all the right things, all the while moving back and forth on the man's lap. She breathed into his ear while she talked softly about how badly her daddy needed money for the farm, how cute she thought his hair was. When she thought he was ready, she got up and turned the key in the door. Then she walked slowly back, while the man stared at her, and lifted her skirt. She'd worn nothing under it, and while he looked at her in amazement, she unzipped his pants. The man went suddenly crazy, so that the whole sweaty thing was over in a moment.

Next day at school they told her she was county delegate to the contest.

But now she couldn't climb into the laps of all the judges. Something else would have to get her past the last fences. In the final round there would be a talent show. She knew most of the girls would play the piano or dance. Well, she had only one talent, besides fucking. The idea came to her while she was painting fast, trying to catch a troublesome sunset in watercolor, one that faded and changed no matter how quickly she worked.

When it came time for her turn on the big stage, M.J. walked out in her modest white formal gown, carrying an easel and a drawing pad. Choosing people one by one from the judges, the audience, she made swift one-minute sketches right there. She ripped each one off the pad with a flourish, presenting it graciously to the model and asking him to display it to the crowd. It went over like cider in July, the crowd clapping louder for each sketch. When they put the crown on her red curls, she felt half-faint with pure joy.

She could coax things out of men just by playing around with them a little. She could draw her way to Birmingham. And it came to M.J., in a burst of light like one of the flashbulbs around her, that she could do more.

Without a word to her family, she lost herself in the city. She found a job in the art department of a store, a night class in a local art school. She saved all her efforts for the classes, learning the new materials, acrylics and oils and markers, studying the tricks of light and line and perspective, welcoming the models, who stood still, unlike the animals and people at home.

When she finished the course, M.J. asked around for the names of the ten biggest advertising agencies in New York, and counted up the money she'd been squirreling away. Two hundred dollars. Not enough.

She went to have a chat with Mr Grossman, the store owner who'd been eyeing her up and down, and made him a proposition. One night for one hundred dollars. Mr Grossman had a notion of his own.

Saturday after closing time, M.J. stayed behind. She went up to Mr Grossman's office, where five men stood around. They stared at her, but she tried not to look at them. She needed this money, and that was all she would think about.

While she shucked her clothes, pretending to herself she was all alone, she said in her head over and over: It doesn't matter any. Has to be done. There's no better way. It doesn't matter any.

When Mr Grossman came in with Black Jim, who swept up in the store, she shuddered once, and then made herself still.

She lay down on the worn divan, closing her eyes tight. She worked away at the shame and fear she was feeling, pushing it back, saying over and over: It doesn't matter any. She knew it did matter. She loathed the idea of letting one finger of that black man's hand touch her.

They pushed the sweating black body at her, and she held her breath in, waiting for him to get at her. Then one of the men laughed, and she opened her eyes.

Jim was petrified, shaking, on top of her, with the life gone out of him. His body had no bones, she thought, his big thing limp over his thigh.

Fighting down nausea, she realized she'd have to help him get going.

M.J. touched him high, low, here and there, playing with him, teasing and coaxing, till she got some life back into him. Screwing her eyes shut again, she took him in her mouth, bobbing up and down. When she came up for air, she saw one of the men drooling out of the corner of his mouth, not troubling to wipe his chin. She was overwhelmed by the sickening smell, the sweating men near her, the writhing body beneath her hands. She made herself stand it all, until Jim came, noisily, heavily.

Mr Grossman got him out fast, came back and ushered out the men. She lay on the divan, motionless, tired, fighting the nausea that rose in her throat. It cleared when Mr Grossman handed her the money, two hundred and fifty dollars, while he stole a good long look at her body. She yanked on her clothes and made herself count every bill, promising herself she'd never again lie down with a black man, never.

Two days later in New York, she'd started her job hunt at the Potter Jackson Company.

Her only doubts since that day – whether or not she was really moving up – could be resolved right now. Domina's evaluations. Then she'd know. Another report card. They never stopped.

She shifted the open lock and looked into the cabinet. There were a bankbook, a big folio, and a notebook. She took them all out and went to sit in the comfortable chair. It was still good and early.

The bankbook, once she slipped it out of its case, showed a balance of three thousand dollars. The same as my sapphire, thought M.J., not the huge treasure she would have counted it a year ago. Probably only one of the bunch of bankbooks Domina had.

In the folio there were ads and TV photoboards. It looked like a gathering of the best work the group had done lately. Several things were there that M.J. had worked on in bits. How come? Was Domina reviewing all the group's work? Why?

In the notebook she found her answer.

Lists of all the New York agencies, their addresses, phone numbers, all in Domina's handwriting. Largest agencies first. Xerox copies of Domina's résumé, dozens of them, dated right up to the present.

M.J. was stunned, shaken. Domina thinking about a new job?

Why? Things were wonderful for Domina in this company. People as important as she didn't just go off and look for new jobs. What had happened? M.J. knew just how much money Domina made, thanks to David March Noble. And she knew something that Domina didn't – that it was less money than the other group heads got, the men. When David had told her that, M.J. had right off decided she'd never let that happen to her when she got big. Maybe Domina had finally discovered it too, and was now mad enough to quit? But why had she said she was taking a trip? Could she be hiding out at home, taking a rest before she went job-hunting? Boy, thought M.J. Fuck the evaluations, she may never have written them. This is news, big news. Wait till I drop a hint to David. But what will happen to me? – that's the most important. Who would they put me to work for, if Domina left?

She started to read the résumé carefully to see if Domina told the truth, or lied a little, like most people, and was halfway down the page when the door rattled.

M.J. sat like a stone, a pang in her heart. Holy Joe, she thought, who? How come anyone was around? Fear clutched at her insides while she sat, paralyzed.

The rattling turned into knocking, and the knocking to banging. Whoever was outside had tried a key and discovered that the door was bolted from inside. Guard? Cleaning woman? Police?

126

M.J.'s spell of fear cracked, and she scrambled. She swept everything back in the cabinet and slammed the door. While the knocking kept on, she turned the lock and made it safe. The slowest thing was getting her belt back through the loops.

She looked around once, and moved to open the door, yanking it back suddenly so whoever was there would be startled, and she'd have an extra second to think what to say.

She came face to face with Domina.

M.J.'s stomach lurched, flip-flopped inside her. Confess? Cry? Lie? What lie? Never knew I could feel so scared.

She had just time to notice the buttery leather duffel bag on the floor, the wrinkles set deep into Domina's chocolate satin safari suit. Oh, God, the worst person of all.

M.J. spoke first. 'Domina,' she said with as much of a wail as she could muster. 'I was wondering if you'd ever get yourself back here. It's been so awful.'

Domina's straight gaze never left M.J.'s face. 'What are you doing, M.J.? Why are you in here?'

Domina's eyes moved around then, sweeping the office. There wasn't a thing out of place, M.J. was positive.

'Come on, M.J., I want an answer.' Domina's voice was made of a silver art pencil, brittle, bright, glittery.

M.J. made her eyes go teary, but she waited a mite longer to talk.

'I'm waiting. Why are you in my office alone on a Sunday morning with the door locked? Just why?'

M.J. put the desperate plan she'd scrabbled together into action. She screwed up her face in misery and flung herself into Domina's arms. Domina smelled different, a tired, smoky smell. The satin of her shirt felt deliciously smooth and warm.

'It's been horrid,' M.J. wailed. 'Everything's been so wrong without you, the account men making us crazy, nothing like you wanted. We can't do it without you. I thought if I just came and sat quiet in your chair, the peach one like our tree at home, maybe I could kind of pretend I was you, make it come out right. Domina, I didn't do one thing you wouldn't like in here, I just sat and thought. See

127

how the cushion's all squashed, see?'

Domina pushed her away, shook the shoulder strap from her arm, and undid the top button of her jacket. She went slowly to her desk chair and sat down.

M.J. made her tears fall, hoping to snuff it had come out sounding all right. Southern voices could get away with a lot, she knew.

Domina's silence was stretching, getting long.

M.J. remembered her interview with Mr Godwin, when he'd given her a raise. He'd been like a grandfather, tall, handsome, quiet-spoken, asking how she was getting on. She'd gone Southern, saying how peachy-keen things were, how much she was learning, how she loved being able to send money home to her folks. M.J. had come out of that office with a seven-thousand-dollar raise. Men were easy.

Domina wasn't. Everything with her was straight, direct. She bossed. M.J. thought bossing should be like bed, not ordering people, but hinting, coaxing, feeling your way with your fingers and toes and tongue, getting the other person to do what you wanted.

When Domina finally spoke, her voice was frightening. 'You've got no business in here, M.J. You know it. You're not dumb and you're not straight. When you came, you were, but you've changed. You don't need to do things like this. You're good, your work is enough. It's terrific, fresh and exciting, everyone thinks so. So why do this? You're much too smart to creep around people's offices. I should fire you this minute.'

Relief began to flood through M.J. like a wave, building up and washing through her. Domina wouldn't have said any of that if she'd been ready to do anything awful. She was acting like a mother, reproving, but she wasn't going to be a terror.

'Domina, I've honestly been topsy-turvy with you gone,' said M.J., following Domina's mood. 'I need you. I've been here weekends working, wanting to please you, make you proud. I feel just dreadful about being here right now, upsetting you.'

'M.J. Kent, you're still not being honest. You wanted something in here. You don't think I'm stupid enough to

128

keep important things in the office, do you? Now, what were you after?'

M.J. lifted her eyes and looked straight at her boss. 'Honest. I swear. I just wanted to sit in your chair. I thought it could help me think more like you, be like you. That's not grown-up and liberated and all, but it's how I felt. I locked the door because that black cleaning woman's around, the one from Jamaica I always think is going to voodoo me.'

'That's another thing,' said Domina. 'You'd better start forgetting you're Southern, baby – that stuff doesn't wash anymore. Around me, especially.'

A little firecracker of triumph went off in M.J.'s head. She'd thrown that in for distraction, and it worked. Whatever Domina said, people could always be fooled.

'Now, you take yourself out of here. Get in the sun. Go up to the Met and look at pictures. You can find better things to do on Sunday than snooping. Tomorrow I'm coming in like a tornado, and the first bunch of work I want to see is yours. One night you come up to my house for supper, and we'll talk this out. You're starting to go wrong, M.J.'

M.J. felt a jolt of fright. What did Domina know? Dan? But lots of girls lived with people. David? Could Domina have heard about the afternoons when she said she was shooting commercials but was really with David? Or the raise, the story she'd given Godwin? Especially after she always told Domina how she wanted to be a modern girl, demanding her rights straight out.

'Domina,' she said, 'I'd love to talk. All I want in the world is to turn out like you.'

It was true in lots of ways. And it must have sounded true, because Domina did smile then.

'We'll work on it,' she said. 'Now, scoot.'

'I'm really sorry I scared you,' said M.J. She went slowly out of the office.

Walking back through the streets, she decided to get started right away figuring out what Domina could know, could do about it. She stopped at the gourmet shop at the corner, for props to get Dan thinking too and helping her. She bought three beautiful, flaky croissants, a fat pot of damson-plum jam, delicious butter all the way from Denmark wrapped in gorgeous silver foil, a pound can of bitter New Orleans coffee with chicory. She moved quickly, the tote bag banging her knee, to get home. She'd get him to help her hard.

Once up in the apartment, M.J. fixed the breakfast, taking a board from the bookcase for a tray, because Dan didn't own a tray. When she was ready, she slipped out of her clothes, leaving them on the kitchen floor.

She shook out her hair to get some fluff-up in it, picked up the board with the coffee steaming in its cup, the beautiful breakfast laid out in perfect order. Jiminy knows what'll happen to any raise of mine. Could be I'll need to coax Dan into lending me some of his bankbook money. And one of these days I should think about getting hold of a bankbook of my own.

She pushed open the bedroom door with her bare foot.

'Morning, Dan, honey,' she said sleepily, as if she'd just got up and out of bed herself and was dying to get back in. She walked, pink and naked and beautiful, toward Dan, opening his eyes in the big bed.

Domina

For Release May 15
Advertising Age
Please Copy

The first agency project on behalf of the fashion
industry of the government of Israel was
launched this week by The Potter Jackson
Company's New York office. The program will
develop export potential of Israeli fashions.
Agency personnel include Roe Rossen, executive
vice-president, and Domina Drexler, creative-
group-head vice-president. Outside consultant
Belle Rosner coordinates and plans. The agency
hopes to create new markets in America over the
next three-year period.

Domina pressed her way through the mob of chattering women, dotted by a man or two, into the giant ballroom of the Waldorf. She tried to find some sequence in the numbered cards displayed on the hundreds of tables, but all around her, people kept shoving, their shoulders and heads getting in her way. The more she had to struggle, the less she felt like pushing on and trying to find her own table. There was no system. Table 3 was next to table 19. Table 7 flanked table 81. Like my life right now, she thought, nothing making any sense. What am I doing here? I don't like Belle Rosner. I hate these big, slick shows. It's hot, the noise is dreadful. And there's no point. Nobody gives a damn anymore what I think about the Israel promotion.

There, thank God, the right number. Still empty, a round table, places for ten, a centerpiece of tired flowers, a huge pot of coffee already there. Just in time to sit and get totally cold even before the lunch. She felt listless, her head ringing with the sound of a thousand voices compressed into one room. She fervently hoped that the table would fill before Belle arrived, so there would be no possibility of their sitting together. Fat chance. That woman is the kind to make everyone get up and move around one place for her.

Domina had met Belle twice since she'd returned from her trip. She'd come back inside a gray cloud, a depression. Nothing had seemed to matter, not the fashion promotion, her job, not her battle with Roe. Domina had tried to jog herself out of her mood. She had telephoned Michael at Choate. The housemaster had assured her that her son was quite well, back at shortstop, and that she could speak to him after dinner at the proper hour for telephone calls.

Disappointed, she'd dialed Maria's dormitory at Brown. But even her daughter's welcome home, the girl's excitement about a child psychology course and about her super new boyfriend, didn't seem to reach her. Domina could focus only on Maria's apologetic request for her allowance check, forgotten when Domina had left so suddenly. Feeling guilty, far from both her children, Domina had half-regretted making the calls. Though she'd had better conversations with both of them a few days later, the guilt had persisted. Tired from traveling, worn out by the heat in Israel and the total lack of interest she'd met there, Domina had been wretched even before she was introduced to Belle. Roe had informed her, through a series of curt memos, that splendid progress had been made while she'd been away. Belle was managing beautifully. It had not been what Domina wanted to hear. She felt sorry she'd flown off so impulsively, ruining her chance to start the work off properly. Well, she'd expected some reprisal. Roe Rossen was not a man to be ignored. He'd found the perfect way to get back at her. Domina thought. He hadn't reported her defection to anyone. He'd initialed all the bills for her trip. He hadn't fired her off the project. He'd just continued to run the show, no longer demanding any contribution from her. Belle was his second in command, and was handling all of it.

Domina poured coffee from the heavy pot and sipped it from the thick hotel cup. Her napkin seemed damp, and it lay in her lap like a burden. A woman sat down on the far side of the table, elegant in black with a hat and gloves. She never looked at Domina. But Domina looked at her, and thought: Hat, for the love of God. Who wears a hat today? Don't they care at all what real people are doing? She looked around. More than half the women wore black. Practical, thought Domina, but fashion? Fashion should be light, fun, colorful, uplifting, geared to how people feel. Out in the street now, kids are skating on red wheels, in luminous shirts and cute kneepads. Old ladies are brightening their spirits by wearing rose and yellow and spring green. Working girls are swinging along in trim pants and tops. Who *are* these women dressed like funeral guests?

Editors and designers and reporters and manufacturers, the ones who dictate how real women ought to dress. But how can they know? What an absurd place for Belle to find ideas. Warmed-over Paris, crazy, out-of-touch, costly. The Israelis should do real clothes for real women. Caftans for our sun belt, our resorts. Tailored pants like their army girls wear. Those stunning shorts all the men have on. The things they know, that will fit in perfectly for us. God, I wish I could get out of here.

Domina had spent her first night at home with Maran. They had talked out the discouragement of the trip, the mess in Domina's office, the problem of getting back into command again. Domina still felt guilty because she hadn't managed to snag the work for Maran. The two of them could have worked together so wonderfully on this; laughed, made progress in tandem. Now she missed Maran's cool hand and sensible decisions. Giving up her friend for a woman with Belle's reputation was more than she could bear. One long evening's talk with Maran made it worse than ever.

She'd thought her stop in Paris would be marvelous. It had been hot, dusty, muggy, the city jammed with tourists – German, Japanese, Arab, American – the shops ridiculously expensive, the new Beaubourg museum filled with jeering spectators.

She'd thought it would be thrilling to see Israel. It had been hotter, dustier, muggier, the airport a crush of pushing men and women, the hotels makeshift, the streets of Tel Aviv impassable for the crowds. She'd had a terrible time phoning anyone she wanted to see at the Israel College of Fashion and Textile Technology at Ramat Gan. Most people she reached in business didn't want to make appointments with her, and one man hung up before she could get him to understand why she was there. She tried sightseeing, and found that everything outdoors was wonderful, but everything indoors was dreadful, phony, dressed-up, too new and jerry-built. The shops distressed her, dresses that looked like 1940, coats that seemed made of wood, thousands of wasted stitches in suits that turned supple leather into stiff cardboard.

The low point of the whole trip had been the wedding.

Domina told Maran she had finally made contact with a man from the Jerusalem *Post* who understood her project and promised to help her meet the important people who could move her forward. He had asked her if she would like to accompany him to a big wedding, the marriage of the daughter of a member of the Knesset, which would allow her to meet many fashionable people and see the best of Israel's fashion at one sweep. Domina had steamed out her long chiffon skirt and halter top, slipped on her jeweled sandals, and tipped the doorman in her hotel lavishly to find her a taxi.

When she'd opened the cab door, she'd thought the driver had made a mistake. The wedding was in a grubby hall, windowless, hot and filled with smoke from the smelly cigarettes the Israelis all smoked. Most of the women were wearing precisely what Domina had seen women wearing in the streets – slacks, three-quarter coats, limp sweaters. She'd felt grander than anyone else, twinkling in her best evening clothes, everyone staring at her. When one of the women stepped out from the crowd, and Domina realized that this was the bride, she noted that slacks and a plain shirt were to be the wedding clothes. Holy Mother of God, she'd thought in horror, if they dress like this for one of their weddings, how can they ever learn anything about clothes? She felt sure the work could only fail.

Maran had listened to every detail with sympathy, horror, and then had spoken words of encouragement. She had terrific ideas written down just waiting for Domina to read when she felt rested. Domina would fix it all, and Maran would help on the side. She also had delicious gossip about Belle. People thought the old woman was a bore. Some thought she was brilliant for conning the agency into paying her a lot of money. News of the work was all over town. Domina was going to be just fine, not to worry. Over a bottle of wine, they'd agreed that the project was stupid anyway, Rossen a shit, Belle an old bat, and Godwin the worst of all, because all the trouble had begun with him.

Next morning, tired to death and a little hung-over, Domina had forced herself to get to the office early. She couldn't bring herself to interrupt the work her group was busy doing, so she delayed any inspection. She didn't feel ready to tackle M.J., either. She knew she'd better get to the bottom of that, but she didn't feel up to it.

Summoned to Rossen's office, she had been introduced to Belle.

Her impression was instant. Dressmaker, she thought. This woman only needs pins in her lapel and a tape measure around her neck to be like every dressmaker I ever knew, fussy, chattering, pushing and pulling while you had to stand still and submit. Belle's hand felt unpleasantly dry to Domina's touch. Her black suit was too heavy for the season. The emerald in her lapel was far too big to seem real, looked as if Belle had bought it in Woolworth's. She smelled of French perfume too long in the bottle and of mothballs just out of the box when she leaned over to kiss Domina in greeting. Her words fluttered out as she announced her pleasure in meeting the unique Domina Drexler she'd always longed to work with. She looked older than anyone Domina had ever met in an office, older than anyone Domina had ever met as a working partner. Yet her energy crackled out with her words, in a strange contrast. Everything private and quiet in Domina was outraged by this large, noisy, chattering, over-bearing old woman.

Rossen had smiled politely at her when she had come in, then gone to sit at his desk. His eyes never left Belle, never met Domina's. He sat stolidly while Belle rambled on, bringing Domina up-to-date on her accomplishments. They were indeed solid accomplishments. The promotion was launched, press releases out, connections made with designers, Sternn planning his pictures, all under Belle's exhaustive direction.

When Domina tried to say how beautifully planned everything was, Roe leaned forward with a question and shut her remark off. When Domina began to discuss a part of the plan, he frowned a little and said he thought she should hear the entire plot before she tried to help them. Domina realized that there was nothing, would be nothing, for her to do. She sat, feeling sleepy, stupid, listening in dull silence to the catalog of accomplishments. She knew she ought to battle Roe's attitude, but it somehow didn't seem worth doing. She was too tired, and Belle was too far ahead.

A few days later she was asked to another meeting. She went to Roe's office in some dread, feeling that she would again be ignored, that he was making a fool of her now. Belle had a list of problems awaiting action. But Domina understood only half the story, had come in too late for a clear gasp of any of it. Belle spoke in a kind of code, she thought, and only Roe had the key. This time Domina felt almost invisible in the big office.

When the talk was over, Belle invited Domina to join her at the Fashion Group's American Ready-To-Wear show on the following day. She told Domina with her customary enthusiasm that the finest clothes in the United States would be shown, embodying the newest ideas. They could choose ideas for their own show, Belle thought, as well as presentation techniques. 'They execute these things brilliantly, my dear, we simply must be there,' she told Domina breathlessly. And Domina agreed. Why not? She had nothing much else to do. Her rebellion was crushed, her holiday mood over, her spirits low. She felt lazy at home, dreary in the office, a little weepy in the mornings before Leota came in. Somehow, she wasn't angry at Belle. The woman was doing her job. And Roe still gave no clue to his feelings. He wasn't angry, wasn't friendly. He simply acted as if Domina were another chair. She could do nothing but wait for the whole promotion to be over, add it to her résumé as experience, get back to her own problems.

So here she sat while the table filled and the rushing, perspiring waiters began to bring in platters of food. Fruit cups in scarred metal dishes dripping ice over their sides. Wilted salads dumped hastily on plates. Vast platters of greasy chicken plunked in front of the diners one by one. Tired vegetables jammed next to the chicken on each plate. And still Belle had not come. One empty seat now, one plate of food congealing as minutes passed. Domina tasted her chicken once, then put her fork down. Nobody tried to talk to her, nobody introduced himself. Everyone sat sullenly waiting for the show to start. That was why they had come, for a view of the dazzling new fashions. They were all desperate to be first with the actual details, to be able to steal ideas and outwit their competitors, to check on everything that they could borrow. Domina felt the heat rise in the room, smelled the garbage odor of the plate in front of her. She was running out of cigarettes, she noticed in dismay. And the waiters were coming around with an ice-cream dessert that seemed carved out of soap. She could feel a twist of nausea in the pit of her stomach.

Domina was almost never sick. Whenever a wave of nausea attacked her, she would remember dizzily the times she had been pregnant in the office. She'd worked straight through all the months with both children. She'd endured morning sickness in big ladies' rooms. She'd suffered the sidelong glances men gave her belly when they thought she wasn't looking. She'd answered all the questions about how long she planned to stay at work, when she would return, was she sure she was healthy. Once at a client meeting when she had risen to present ads, there had been a whispered conversation at the far end of the room. A blushing account executive had come over and asked her if she would mind turning over the work for him to present. When she'd stared at him in amazement, he'd leaned close and muttered, 'You've got to leave. He's embarrassed to death to have you here working.' Domina knew that the head client, who wanted her gone, had two children of his own. Nevertheless, she'd smiled and left, feeling idiotic, angry, helpless as she walked out of the roomful of men. And that was only sixteen years ago, Domina thought. How they hated being reminded every second that they were working with a woman. Ordinarily they can forget, but not when you bulge in front and walk heavily. And I was unusual then. All on my own. Now it's easier for the young girls; men are used to seeing them at work pregnant. Now they get paid leaves of absence and their jobs are guaranteed. Now there are day-care centers and pages of advice in all the magazines. Think of Belle Rosner, she had babies fifty years ago and worked. How did she do it? But of course, then there were a million nurses and maids, and a working woman could afford them.

Just as the last plates were being rushed noisily away, and Domina's head was clearing a little, she felt a large presence behind her. Belle, making her way to the table in a passage of whispers and kisses. She was being unobtrusive in the world's most obtrusive way. She's the kind who'd complain she was recognized everywhere, thought Domina, while she was doing everything she could to attract attention. The old fraud.

There, she was finally in a seat, and next to Domina, too. Who could object to moving for such an elderly lady? Belle leaned close to kiss Domina's cheek. The dizzy feeling came back for an instant.

'My dear, I'm so delighted to see you again,' said Belle in a noisy whisper. It kept Domina from hearing the first announcement from the runway, where an angular model danced forward in floating chiffon. Whose it was, Domina would never know. More words from the commentator were covered by Belle's rustling her notepad, digging for her glasses in her bag, uncapping her fountain pen. Fountain pen, thought Domina. She's in the Dark Ages. The fashion expert of the Dark Ages, Miss Belle Rosner. She wondered suddenly why Belle called herself Miss. Domina had become Mrs the day she married, at home and at work. So much simpler to have the same name everywhere. I guess they separated things more, those old ladies who worked, needed to be Miss like all the other single women in offices, but had to be Mrs at home for the butcher and the teacher. Funny, how today's girls are going back to it, keeping their own names for everything. My generation is all out-of-kilter.

The show went on above their heads on the broad runway, evening gowns, bathing suits, sun dresses. Belle scribbled rapidly, peering up, shaking her head, making little clucks with her tongue. It didn't seem to bother the others, but it annoyed Domina. She couldn't concentrate, not even on the stunning bridal gown that completed the show. The final applause seemed the nicest sound she'd heard since she entered the room. She put out her eleventh cigarette and pushed back her chair.

'Now I think we should talk together,' said Belle firmly,

gathering up her things and stuffing them into her enormous handbag. 'Where shall we go, dear? Not your office, it's too busy there. Will you come to my little place? It's quiet, and we can get so much done.'

'If you like,' said Domina. Why not? There was no place else she needed to be. All her regular work was flowing along smoothly, the group enjoying their new independence. Maybe they'd never need her anymore. Maybe she'd flown herself away from a job.

Resisting Domina's attempt at joining the crowd waiting for taxis at the hotel entrance, Belle plucked at her arm. 'The crosstown bus,' she said. 'Over there. A few minutes to go east, that's all.'

Domina hadn't climbed on a bus, if she could help it, since she reached twenty thousand dollars a year, but in her new, listless mood she followed Belle. She was aware that the old woman was chattering on, something about the history of the fashions they'd just viewed, but Domina felt trapped in a bubble, deaf, blind, oblivious of everything around her. She wondered vaguely why she had found herself in this spot, words pouring into her ear, people walking on her feet, bus lurching beneath her. It was better when they got off and walked into the small neat building by the river.

Belle turned two locks on her door and went briskly inside. Domina put her jacket on a chair in the little foyer, filled with fussy furniture and ornaments. Belle immediately picked it up and hung it carefully in the hall closet. Fuss, fuss, thought Domina; the woman is all movement and words. How soon can I get out of here?

'There, now,' said Belle triumphantly when they were seated in her living room. 'My dear, you look beautiful among all my most precious things. Against my coromandel screen. Your head. It's positively quattrocento.'

'I'm Italian,' said Domina. Did she have to listen to this drivel? How long, O Lord. Some of Belle's precious things were beautiful, but so many of them were crammed together in the small space. Domina noticed a crystal-ball clock, French for certain, very old. She wished the hands would turn faster, get her away more quickly.

'Yes, well, to work. Now I'd like your approval on these, because dear Mr Rossen says you must be kept up-to-date. And of course, I want to hear all the wonderful results of your busy trip, and how we can mesh your work with my own. I'm sure we can find room for your suggestions.'

Rossen has told her to get me working, Domina thought. She sure as hell doesn't want my suggestions. What's in his head, I wonder? Does he really dislike me now? Or is he just punishing me for taking off?

Belle was handing her masses of papers, neatly dated, neatly clipped together, neatly typed. None of them seemed to make any sense. The words kept jiggling about on the pages. Domina suddenly felt faint, a huge wave of green washing over her, her stomach turning to water. She looked up to see Belle's eyes only on the papers, not on her guest's face.

'Before we start, may I have some water?'

And as Belle bustled back with a goblet, Domina could sense a satisfaction on her face, pleasure that an old lady was so energetic, a young one so delicate.

She began to read the lists silently, forcing herself to pay attention, add up figures, read closely. And as she read, she relaxed a little. It was the first work anyone had asked her to do in almost a month, and work had always been balm for Domina. She could lose herself in ideas, spin out of her moods with new thoughts, spark to something on a page. She began to feel peace moving over her, smoothing out her frown, calming her irritation.

Belle chattered as she read, pulling out papers, changing the order of the pages on Domina's lap, pointing things out. But Domina was not distracted. She fell deeper into each page. The trip had had some purpose, after all. When Belle listed the fashion classes at the Israel College of Fashion, Domina could recall the stone building, the dressmakers' classes, the black heads bent over cutting tables. Where the Tel Aviv shops to be contacted were listed on a page. Domina could summon them up in her head, little dusty boutiques, undecorated, uninviting, uninteresting to be in. The name of the director of Israel's collective boutique leaped from one page. Domina had taken the man to lunch at the Tel Aviv Hilton. He had been fascinating, a trans-planted German with lots of merchandising ideas, interest-ing plans, a hearty laugh. Belle was right, he could help them.

It seemed complete. The classes were under way, the dates were set for the big press show, the buyers of the top US chains had accepted their invitations, the shipments were due. The show itself was planned, models hired, commentator set, even music arranged. Belle had decided on Israel's folk music, suggested a dance troupe, kosher catering, making the show an occasion to exhibit Israeli culture and history in its most pleasant form. 'Near East Meets Now West' was the theme, a Belle Rosner phrase, and the plan was to feature fashion for American activities of all kinds. The Gottex garments would lead, because American buyers knew them, knew they sold well. Beged-Or coats would follow, and the brilliant caftans of Roji Ben-Joseph. All was planned, down to the table decora-tions. It had been a good idea after all, thought Domina, to meet at that luncheon today. Belle was showing her, at least on paper, how familiar she was with the format, how much better her show would be than the one they'd seen, how much livelier and more dramatic her settings would be. Domina looked at the woman from behind the papers. Belle was glowing. She hadn't sat still all afternoon, obviously in her element with all this. Eighty and more, thought Domina. Imagine the energy, drive, stamina. What's the matter with me? Less than half her age, and I don't care anymore about this stuff. I don't even know what I do care about? The kids? They both seem so far away, independent. Work? Turned to ashes. I'm stuck, like a fly in honey. Nothing seems to matter. I'd be a mess on a new job. My own agency? Too much trouble. Easier to sit here.

'This is admirable work, Miss Rosner,' she said. It seemed the least she could say, seeing that the work was very competent indeed.

'Oh, my dear, when you've handled this sort of thing as often as I, it simply means moving in a straight line,' said Belle. 'This is my life, you know, working on things like this. Getting people together. Moving mountains. I do it, you know, from such long perspective. You must call me Belle, the whole world does. Have you read my little book? My story? I'd love to give you a copy for your own.'

'Actually,' said Domina. 'I have. When I was in school, in the library. I remember it quite well.'

'You'll find it fascinating, I think, with your interest and your fashion background,' said Belle.

Domina gave up again. The woman didn't hear anybody but herself.

'I'd like to take all these papers of yours home to read more carefully,' said Domina, trying to get herself out. 'May I? Have you copies?'

'That set is for you, and Mr Rossen already has his copies,' said Belle triumphantly. 'He reads so swiftly, grasps so clearly. Remarkable young man. He should go far, don't you agree?'

'Oh, yes,' said Domina. Wrong, she thought. I was the one who went far. Outsmarted myself, taking that trip.

She said good-bye, trying to stem the tide of talk as she and Belle walked to the elevator. Belle waited with her, waving a cheery farewell.

How quiet it seemed when the old lady's voice was left behind.

Domina hailed the first cab and rode home, sunk in gloom. There was a run in her stocking. It made a line along her leg, so she looked lopsided, she thought.

I have got to get out of this mood. I've never felt like this, just lumpy. I can't afford it. I'll be stuck at Potter Jackson forever. Or maybe even – Rossen could really have it in for me, just waiting for a better time, when he can get me fired and blame it on somebody else.

She let herself in, put Belle's papers on the hall table, and went past the pile of mail sitting there. Usually Domina rushed for her letters. She loved the mystery of sealed envelopes. Anything might be inside them, an invitation, a check, a letter from one of the children. But now even the mail wasn't tempting.

She mixed herself a strong drink to see if it would help her snap out of it, and sat down with Belle's papers. Read them, she thought. At least you'll get an idea of what's going on, maybe you can push in at the next meeting and take over a piece of the work. She slipped her shoes off, put her feet up on the cool chintz of the couch, leaned her head back on the plump cushions. One by one she took up Belle's heavy folders and read every word in each of them.

When she came to the last folder, she blinked once, and read a sentence over. Then she set down her drink, sat up straight, and read the sentence still again.

Domina felt a key turning in a door inside her, revealing a sunlit garden, flooded with music, alive with beautiful bird sounds. Hope zinged into her head like a beautiful bird swooping low on her hand.

It was the date of the invitation.

Belle had set in order the steps leading to the final show for the fashion collection they would have. Every detail was covered, every possibility allowed for. All through the folders, the show was set for July 29, the date was everywhere. It was a date early enough in the year to allow time to complete orders for Christmas, to let buyers plan for a dazzling collection next spring.

But on the engraved invitation, which was the last piece of paper in the last folder, bidding the whole world of fashion, New York VIP's, a beautiful people, top media personalities, to come together for a giant fashion show with an orchestra and a buffet supper, there was a date, too. July 19. It bulged from the paper, Domina thought, as if the numbers were heavier, larger, more important than anything else in all the folders.

Domina sat straighter than ever and considered carefully.

A mistake, glaring, obvious, big. That's what the old woman got for covering every stupid detail five times over and leaving something so simple unchecked. Imagine. Ten days before a show, nothing was ever ready. Bundles arrived up to the last second; models caught cold, fainted, forgot their datebooks, failed to show for rehearsals. Fashion shows were like opening nights in the theater, scrabbled together into lucky perfection at the last moment, traveling on adrenalin and emotion. What's more, food plans and musicians and room reservations took

144

months of planning to coordinate. Belle had probably wedged her date between other major events. Who knew what was scheduled the day before her show, or the day after? You had to nail down all those people months ahead. The invitations would go out and be listed on thousands of schedules for July 19, schedules of people who had dozens of invitations for every night. What would happen when they discovered the real show was on July 29? What was more, the wrong date came plunk in the middle of a summer weekend. Saturday the nineteenth, all those people would be in East Hampton, Greenwich, Paris, Athens, Peking. Gods knows where. Beautiful.

Domina went on thinking while she made herself another drink to celebrate. She could simply forget it, and hope that no one else would catch the mistake, though it didn't seem likely. Rossen hadn't noticed, but he was busy. But the people who did the scut work, the secretaries and flunkeys, would surely catch it. The more Domina let it go, the more trouble it would make for Belle and for Roe when it came to light.

She went back through the sheaves of papers to find out how many invitations had been ordered. The figure would be there. Belle was exquisitely tidy, kept records of everything in her large round handwriting. Finally Domina found it. On the engraver's bill, neatly attached to the written order. Three thousand invitations. Going all over the world, for a night ten days before there would be a theater, a dress, a plate of food. When Belle Rosner put her large foot wrong, she put it very wrong indeed.

Well, she could call Belle up and let her know first. And what then? Belle would cover it. She could say that she'd forgotten to correct the sample invitation, that she'd changed the dates on all the written plans, that Domina had misunderstood. Possibly she could be grateful, thank Domina, get it fixed before Rossen or anyone else noticed. Domina didn't think she'd do that.

Once, when she was younger, Domina had gone on a job interview and sat at a woman executive's desk waiting for her to get off the phone. While she waited, she couldn't help seeing an ad on the woman's desk, evidently waiting to be approved for the typesetters. For fine china dishes, with a large picture of a plate, and smaller square pictures of different serving pieces surrounding the plate. As the woman chattered on, Domina noticed with a start that beneath the cream-and-sugar set the caption read, 'Dainty Salad Plates.' She had glanced over at the salad-plate picture and instantly read upside down where she sat, 'Delicate Cream-and-Sugar Set.' When the woman finally had stopped talking on the phone, Domina had pointed out the error, thinking that the lady would be thankful for the correction. The woman had gone red in the face, snapped the proof off her desk, told Domina there was no time left for the interview, and dismissed her. From then on, Domina had known, nobody was grateful to you for pointing out his errors. Belle would respond in much the same way, she was sure. And anyway, why should she help Belle?

Domina downed her drink.

The way to handle it was to tell Roe. She would have to do it gently, so he wouldn't think she was trying to pay him back for ignoring her. She would have to be businesslike, so he wouldn't think she was after Belle. But do it she would.

And how would he take it? Wouldn't he *have* to be glad that someone had caught a dangerous error? Might he be glad *she* had caught it? He'd been interested in her at the beginning, she was positive. He'd looked her over, in her office that first day, and he'd been full of questions about her, and she knew there'd been more ready to come out. Was he big enough to accept a mistake from his expert? Oh, if he were! Wouldn't it be something, a man secure enough for that? She knew he was clever, attractive, able to laugh at himself, if you counted that story about the stationery. And strong, able to strike back at what he didn't like, like his dealing with her after she'd skipped out on him. Could he possibly also be kind, honest, forgiving? Were there men like that anymore?

Suddenly Domina realized that her spell had been broken. She felt alive, eager, the way she liked to feel. God damn, she thought, let them try doing without me. See what happens? I didn't get where I am for nothing.

She went to bed exhilarated. There was a soft breeze, and she lay naked, wanting to be free even of the lightest nightgown. She couldn't wait to tell Maran, first thing in the morning.

At nine on the dot Domina herself telephoned Roe's office. His secretary, after a pause, said that Mr Rossen couldn't come to the phone. Domina countered with: her call was urgent. Another pause and he was on the line. She asked if he could spare her a few minutes as soon as possible.

'I don't know when,' he said coolly. 'Is it about the work? Miss Rosner's due here in twenty minutes. Reports in every day, like the army. One of her methods. They work, though, don't you think?'

'Up to a point,' said Domina. 'I'll join you, all right?' Oh, Mr Rossen, will I enjoy joining you.

'Of course,' his voice came evenly over the phone. 'After all, this work is your responsibility.'

'Right. I've just found a place where I'd like to take some responsibility,' Domina returned. And hung up.

She spent fifteen minutes at her mirror, taking her hair down, smoothing it into perfection, powdering her nose, darkening her lashes all over again. This was going to be her show. She wanted to look great. She was filled with anticipation for Roe's reaction, and for Belle's. If she handled this right, she could put herself back in command in one stroke. At the least, Roe would have to acknowledge her help. At best, he'd welcome her back, realizing they couldn't do without her. Cross your fingers, she thought.

This time, Domina walked straight into Roe's office without waiting for a smile from his secretary. Belle was already there, early, of course. The woman had that old-fashioned female viewpoint. No woman could ever keep any man waiting.

Roe turned from where he stood at the window and sat down, pad in hand, all business. 'Good morning,' he said. 'Can we go fast today? I haven't much time.'

Belle opened her mouth and her folder simultaneously.

But Domina was ready for action today. She interrupted Belle's first words. 'I read over everything you've given me,

147

everything you've planned in my absence,' she said. 'I've found something, I think, you've both overlooked.'

Roe simply looked bored. Belle began to fuss with her handbag, the color flushing into her large face. Overlooked? Domina realized it was a fighting word.

'There's all this material,' she continued. 'Stacks of it, detail on detail.' She put the mound of folders on Roe's desk. 'And then there's this sample invitation to the fashion show.' She put that down, too, and it lay there, slim and small, next to the tremendous pile of papers.

Domina waited a moment, enjoying herself, but nobody spoke. Okay, friends, she thought, here we go.

'You've arranged everything beautifully, Belle, for the show on the twenty-ninth of July. But did either of you notice the date that's engraved on the actual invitation?'

She caught Roe's puzzled look as he reached over to pick up the heavy card. But Belle was quicker, and she snatched it up, holding it close to her face as she scanned it. Suddenly she turned scarlet, color surging into her plump cheeks and thick neck.

'Something wrong?' asked Roe.

'Why, no, not really,' said Belle rapidly. 'This is just a model, you see, to give you both an idea of the kind of invitation I planned. With an elegant, wedding sort of feeling to it, you know.'

Domina felt a tinge of pure hate for the woman. Couldn't Belle admit any error at all? All right, she thought, I'll say it plainly.

'No. I found the order in your files, which are so well-organized and clear. Three thousand invitations on order at Tiffany, the order dated last week. They probably have already engraved the plate. With the wrong date. It would be nice if we could stop it before they print. It's quite a large order, bigger than most weddings.'

Too bitchy, she wondered? No, the old woman had asked for it. Model indeed. That was a lie.

Belle sat back and waved her large linen handkerchief at her face. 'Such a rush, you know,' she said. 'So many details to cover. I'd have caught it, certainly. You've had such a good rest on your trip, dear, your eyes are fresh. Good thing you noticed, saves trouble. I'll phone them immediately, you can leave it to me.'

Still Roe said nothing. He looked at Belle, flustered, and at Domina, straight and quiet in her chair. Oh, she thought, please see it from my point of view, understand how I hated being pushed away, that I'm demonstrating something to you. Please realize I'm good, eager, for the work to go right. Please.

'All right, ladies,' he said. 'Glad we cleared that up. Could have been a problem. Think of that huge audience arriving ten days early. Now, if you'll excuse me, I've got some other problems this morning.'

He never once looked at Domina. He simply turned his back and picked up the telephone.

Domina's spirits plummeted. He was only ordinary, after all. He couldn't or wouldn't understand why she'd done it. He might even be annoyed at her for upsetting Belle. Well, she'd been right, and she'd have to settle for getting that across. Being right was a little lonely, she thought. Especially compared to sharing, with someone you liked, the satisfaction of a disaster averted. Her hopes had shot up higher than she'd realized. What's happening? I'm acting like a young girl disappointed in a boyfriend. But I did want him to be pleased.

The two women walked silently to the elevators, and Domina said good-bye in the foyer. Belle murmured something that didn't sound like her usual crisp sentences, and turned away. When Domina looked back, as the elevator clanged open, she caught Belle staring at her, eyes hard. I knew *she* wouldn't like it, thought Domina, but I did hope *he* would. Silly.

As she stepped into her office, the phone was ringing. Her secretary buzzed, and she picked up the intercom.

'Mr Rossen calling,' said the secretary.

Domina picked up the telephone. What now?

'Domina?' Roe's voice sounded strong, warm, with a lilt in it, almost a chuckle.

'Yes? I'm here,' she said.

'I'm delighted to hear it. I thought I should say thanks. It would have been laughable, grim, a mess. She's old. I'm busy. You're smart. You could even have been right about not choosing her. But here we are. Now, would you like to join me working on this promotion? I think we could make it sensational. Provided you stick around and we get some work done together. Okay?'

'Okay,' said Domina. Her heart soared, her head cleared, her spirits danced. What a nice phone call, she thought. And he even waited so he wouldn't destroy that woman's ego. He's human. He's special. Everything's going to be just fine.

'Can I buy you a lunch today?' his voice was saying.

Yes, she thought. Oh, yes, you can. What am I supposed to be doing for lunch? Who cares?

'Yes,' she said.

'Celebration,' said Roe. 'Return of the native. Return of the senses. Back on the ship. One o'clock?'

'I'd love it,' said Domina. And smiled dazzlingly at the telephone.

Maran

The Government of Israel
Represented by The Potter Jackson Company
cordially invites you
to attend
a Fashion Show and Buffet Dinner
for the Premier Showing
of a new collection
at Avery Fisher Hall
July 29
Eight P.M.

RSVP
Ms Domina Drexler
The Potter Jackson Company
8 East 40th Street
BLACK TIE   New York, N.Y. 10016

151

Maran worked on her face, smoothing liquid adhesive sparingly on her forehead and around her eyes. She could feel it pulling the skin taut, stretching out her wrinkles, helping her look a little younger. The sticky stuff smelled like nail-polish remover, sharp and overpowering. It made her eyes water. But it worked. Not that anyone would look closely at her tonight. She'd be a nobody. If only the damned adhesive could mask her expressions, too. She'd hate anyone to see the way she really felt about this show. Like attending your class graduation after you'd been kicked out of school.

She began covering the shiny film with makeup, peering into her magnifying glass. Face-lift time, she thought.

What have I done to have to sit through this, to applaud Belle Rosner's work? I'm going to despise every damn dress. I already hate those pricks from the agency. And when I meet Jake Sternn, I'll probably cry. If it weren't for Domina, nothing would get me there, nothing.

Maran got quickly into her uniform for summer evenings. Black silk skirt slit to the thigh, to show off her legs. Black lace top, high at the neck, long in the sleeve, to cover up her arms and throat.

Yes, I'll stand by my friend. She's stood by me often enough. And I'll get a good look at that Rossen guy she's starting to talk about. I'll watch the Jackson people being nice to the Jews. That alone could be a good show.

'You're gorgeous, honey,' Bill said in an automatic tone of voice coming in from the other room.

She smiled carefully, to keep the adhesive in place. Bill was repaying her for his keep, she thought, giving compliments. To bolster her up for tonight. Bless him.

In the taxi to Lincoln Center, she kept still, dreading the long evening ahead. Three thousand people. the mayor, city councilmen, judges, minor politicians. Embassy people, Israelis and American dignitaries. Washington was sending someone important, maybe the vice-president, or his wife. There would be movie stars, stage stars, beautiful people, the New York party crowd that seemed to move in a mass from event to event – Jackie Onassis, Donald Trump, Kitty Carlisle, those people. The head of the Israel College of Fashion would be speaking, and the chairman of Potter Jackson, and Roe Rossen, which meant she'd get a good look at the man in action. New designs from Tel Aviv would sweep across the huge stage of Avery Fisher Hall while music played, flashbulbs went off, buyers scribbled notes, people applauded. A computer actually was going to be tallying up the first set of orders, so sales could be announced later at the supper party in the lobby. Everyone was anticipating a dazzling evening. Except her. She'd be wretched.

Oh, well, she thought, Domina's got her troubles tonight, too. She shuddered, remembering how her friend had looked that morning.

They had met to take a look at the theater and check on the preparations for the private party. Maran had waited by the revolving door for Domina, who was terribly late. That was unusual enough. But finally, when Domina walked up the steps, Maran had felt her heart thump.

Domina had a cold, her nose crimson, her eyes liquid, her skin pale as white taffeta. Her hair seemed to have gone flat, as if she hadn't washed it in days, and one strand hung limply over her forehead. Maran had never seen her look worse. My God, her big night, her new guy watching, that heavenly dress I blackmailed Zoran to finish for her in time for tonight. I've got to do something.

She'd bundled Domina into the nearest taxi and headed for a doctor she knew who took care of theater people. Bullying the secretary into admitting them right away, she stood by in the examining room while he worked, throat spray, codeine, vitamin shot, antihistamine, all of it together. Domina had protested. She didn't believe in any

153

of this garbage, she'd croaked. But Maran, who believed fervently in grabbing all the help you could find, put her foot down. If opium could have helped a cold, Maran somehow would have found it.

Then they'd gone back to the theater and looked around.

A hundred little tables were being decorated in the lobbies, with pretty skirted cloths and fresh flowers. Boxes of favors were being assembled, hundreds of them. Caterers, musicians, florists, maids, stagehands swarmed and milled about. Backstage was worse. The models were being pushed and pulled by the director, already semihysterical. The dressers seemed frantic, opening boxes, moving dress bags, setting up ironing boards. The familiar confusion made Maran feel still more awful. She had no part in any of it. Her fingers itched to iron, stitch, shine, steam, unpack.

With Domina sniffling miserably at her side, she'd insisted on hunting up the Israeli uniform.

The uniform had been Maran's best idea for the show, of the dozens she'd turned over to Domina in the weeks of work on the promotion. Maran had suddenly thought of redesigning the Israeli women's army uniform, updating it in a chic styling of the heavy khaki twill, adding brilliant metal touches, circling the tunic with a wide belt of luscious leather. She didn't give a shit if the army bought the idea or not. She saw it as the rousing finale to the show, after the traditional wedding gowns, shown with gun and knife on a tall model saluting the audience. It would knock everyone out, Maran was sure.

Stepping over boxes and bundles, asking all the dressers, reading labels on packages, Maran managed to find the uniform. It lay limp in its box, wrinkled and crushed. The accessories were nowhere to be seen. Well, thought Maran, I can't run the world. I can't even run this show. I'd better make Domina go home and get some sleep. Maybe by night she'll look better. Sure couldn't look worse.

At eight o'clock Bill helped Maran out of the cab, and they walked through the crowds that lined the entrance to the theater. New York on a summer night had turned out to watch the beautiful people enter the theater. Kids ran shouting around the fountain, boys and girls held hands as they counted celebrities, shirtsleeved men and bare-shouldered women pressed forward to glimpse the stars getting out of their limousines. Maran put her head down, watched the tips of her shoes, as she hung on to Bill's arm. Couldn't be worse. But it couldn't be better for Domina. I'll make myself remember that.

As they went down the long aisle, Maran felt the crowdedness, the balconies full of heads, the excitement in the audience. The center rows halfway to the front, she knew, were reserved for buyers. Their actions would make or ruin the show, no matter what the press said later. Fashion is selling, no talk. She'd urged Domina to save the best seats for the people who counted. Belle had wanted the dignitaries up front. Dignitaries, thought Maran in disgust.

On both sides she caught flashes of familiar faces, beautiful women, handsome men, people she'd seen in newspapers and on the television news. Ed Koch, tall among the people who swarmed around him, looking strange in dinner jacket and bow tie. Former Mayor Lindsay, handsomer than ever, greeting friends with a wave. Everywhere a celebrated face. Bess Myerson. Lillian Gish. Senator Javits talking to her. My God, Luciano Pavarotti coming in now. Grey's Ed Meyer, Sandy, with Dick and Jane Karp. Lauren Bacall? Yes, looking heavenly. There's a woman who knows fashion. Caroline Kennedy, how tall she's grown. Could that be Rock Hudson? Look at the clothes these women are wearing. Little furs, adorable. Lots of glitter, more than I like, sequins, paillettes, rhinestones. There's Jeanne Harrison, in those smashing pants she always wears. And Roy Scheider, he's pretty smashing himself. Diana Vreeland. Must have come in from the country. And talking to none other than Belle Rosner. Why isn't Belle backstage? I'd never leave the clothes. Look at those two old women. Vreeland looks marvelous in that black. Belle? That's a Dior she's wearing, for God's sake, a twenty-year-old Dior. It should be in a costume museum. Hey! that's Cheryl Tiegs. Too gorgeous to be real. She's keeping her looks a lot longer than I did. She doesn't have adhesive all

over her face. And here comes the crowd from the agency.
Dowdy. Look at those wives. Grant Wood ladies in musty
evening gowns. Weather-beaten from all the tennis and
golf. The only fat women in this whole crowd. How I hate
women who don't work. So smug, so protected from
anything real. And they act like they're smarter than we
are, working. They never have anything to talk about but
kids and cookouts. That man must be Croft, Domina's
chairman. They're all kissing his ass. He's small, but he
looks tough. Wife is a string bean. Suburban ladies are
either too fat or too thin. Could that man be Roe Rossen?
He's alone. Looking around. For Domina? Holy shit,
where is Domina? She's not going to be late! She wouldn't
stay home just for a cold? God, could she have slept too
long with those pills? I should have called her. We should
have brought her. But she was hoping to come with Rossen.
That must be him, he's waiting for someone with a front-
row seat.

Bill shifted next to her. She knew that none of this
interested him much, that she'd probably have to step on
his foot later in the evening to keep his head from nodding.
Bill liked to stay close to home, a little beer, a sandwich, his
remote control for the television in his hand, his recliner.
He'd tell callers, 'We worked hard today,' the way non-
working husbands of hardworking wives always said 'we.'
Only time he moves is when he cooks something. You'd
think he'd welcome a little commotion at night. But he's a
nice man, she reminded herself quickly, nice. She shifted,
her knees just meeting the seat in front.

Could Domina really have kept away just because she
looked so awful? No. Maran might have, but never Domina. She'd want that Rossen man to see her at her worst,
Maran thought, because she was like that. Honest, she
called it. Maran knew Domina was getting interested in
him. Maran had suddenly begun to hear about Roe's looks,
his talk, his attitudes, his command at work. And after only
a lunch or two. Good, she thought. If her icy friend was
finally interested in a man, melting a little, Rossen sounded
right for her. Maran had always thought it was such a waste
that Domina, so beautiful and so special, should run

around town with old men and fags.

The fag contingent in New York certainly was out in force tonight. Young and gentle, old and waspish, creative in little ways, difficult in big ways, they swarmed over every job Maran did. They had infiltrated the whole fashion business, hiring their friends and lovers, firing their enemies and ex-lovers, talking about earth colors and dawn pinks till she wanted to swat them. Domina was a magnet for fags. They adored her strength and decisiveness, flapped about her apartment and her clothes, kissed Leota, brought around Godiva chocolates Domina wouldn't eat and porno books she wouldn't read. How swell if Roe Rossen blew them all away.

Could Domina be backstage? The idea hit her, and Maran instantly needed to know, or else she would get to a phone and see if her friend was still at home. Patting Bill's arm, she slipped out of her seat, excused her way to the wide aisle. She could feel heads turn as she moved swiftly back to the foyer. Well, she could always walk better than anybody alive, she thought with satisfaction. Sternn used to tell her she moved as if she were walking through eight feet of water.

Maran made a sharp turn and headed for the stage doors. Even before she wrenched the heavy panel open, she could hear a babble of sound from the back. That was wrong. By now, everyone should be in place, lined up, quiet, dressed, ready to go on. Trouble? What kind of trouble? A show this big, it could be almost anything.

The door open, Maran stepped into a madhouse.

Circled by models in various states of dress, a bathing suit here, a wedding gown there, a fur cloak dragging on the stage floor, the little director stood, furious, screeching. But everyone else was screaming, too, the noise spilling out through the soundproof wings threatening to leak out the crack in the heavy curtain. Maran saw Belle, waving her arm, shouting down the director's tantrum. She saw the Jackson chairman, ashen-faced, pinch-nosed, withdrawn from the tempest at the side of the stage. Domina? Nowhere.

'What's up?' Maran said crisply to one of the models near

her, lounging in neat shorts, tan makeup visible on her long legs and arms.

'Shoes,' the girl said in a nasal voice.

'Shoes? What about them?'

'There aren't any,' the girl said.

Maran digested that news and looked around the stage.

She had never seen so many bare feet at one time in all her life, even at the beach. Girls in evening gowns, furs, pants, coats, all marvelous from their heads to their ankles. But there wasn't a shoe on the stage. No, here and there a model was still in her own footgear, a hiking boot showing beneath an organdy skirt, a sneaker peeping out from a fur shawl. She couldn't hear herself think for the bedlam noise all around her.

'What happened to them?' She shook the girl's arm to make her hear the question.

'How the fuck should I know?'

Maran shoved her way nearer to Belle and the director. As she got closer, she could hear Belle's strong voice more clearly. 'Barefoot, that's the thing,' Belle was announcing. 'Desert sands. Eastern roots. Soil. Barefoot says it all. We'll make the most of it. We'll go on without shoes. It will be thrilling. Listen to me.'

Maran gave one last push and looked down at Belle, frantically trying to get some order into the chaos, screaming out her silly sentences.

'Barefoot, my ass,' said Maran in the loudest voice she'd ever mustered up. 'You. Belle Rosner. Go out there and talk to that audience. Ask them to wait fifteen minutes, maybe a little more. Come on, it's your big moment. Fifteen minutes. You can fill up that much time in two sentences.'

She didn't think Belle could hear her, because the woman had never once stopped talking. But someone at the back of the stage had noticed. The man pushed closer.

'What can you do?' he said into her ear.

'Capezio. Down the street. Know the owner. Telephone, quick,' said Maran.

'Right,' said the man. 'Over this way.'

While he pulled out of the crowd, he was reaching into

his dinner-jacket pocket. By the time they made it to the backstage telephone, he had a dime in his hand. Thank God, someone with a brain. Maran thought.

Flattening her left hand over her ear to block out some of the noise, Maran dialed 411, got the right number, repeated it to herself as she dialed. While the phone rang at the other end, she offered up a little prayer.

'Tony?' she shouted into the phone. 'Maran. Urgent. You've got to do something for me now, this minute. Biggest fucking emergency I ever had.'

'Shoot,' she heard at the other end. And she began to hope.

'Now listen,' she said. 'I'm backstage at Avery Fisher, just a few blocks uptown from you. Can you get a van? Open the store? I need, let me think, about a hundred ballet slippers in five minutes flat. Hundred and fifty. Mix up the colors and sizes. Bring the store, everything. It's a disaster if you don't. Can you?'

She heard a whistle at the other end. 'You got a flood up there or something?' his voice said. 'Dry feet? What goes on?'

'Haven't time,' said Maran. 'Tell you when you get here. With the shoes, for Christ's sake. Move, please. I'll owe you the moon, don't worry. Stage door, okay?'

'For you, baby,' the voice returned.

Maran put the receiver on the hook and turned to the man standing silently at her side.

'Who are you?' he asked.

'Maran Slade.'

The strangest look began to wash over the man's face, a mixture of amusement, dismay, wonder. Suddenly he started to laugh, a great big, warm, rollicking laugh that seemed to come up from his toes.

She stared at him. Then she figured it out. 'You're Roe Rossen, right?' she said.

He couldn't speak because he was laughing so hard, shoulders shaking, arms folded over his chest as he rocked back and forth.

She looked at him, surrounded by the flurry and bustle of the backstage mess. But he's darling, she thought, adorable. He's even sort of tall. He's got a cute, crumply face when he laughs like that, and he's younger-looking than fifty, and he's nice, he's got to be nice to roar like that in a scene like this. Domina, she remembered.

'Hey,' she said. 'Stop. Where's Domina?'

He quieted a little, a cheerful grin still on his face. Then he took a handkerchief out of his pocket. Linen, she saw right away, rolled edges, good. He blotted the corners of his eyes and crumpled the handkerchief back in his pocket again.

'Just got here, out front,' he said. 'Saw her through the peephole. Looks like the devil. Got a cold.'

'Don't I know,' said Maran. She looked closely at him to see if he was really disgusted or annoyed about the cold, but he seemed to have stated a fact, that was all. Good, again.

'Come on, then,' she said, and yanked at his hand.

She ran interference for them both, pushing wildly through the people to get to the outside door. At least the backstage signs at Lincoln Center were new and clear, not like signs in Broadway theaters, she thought as they made their way. Rossen put his shoulder to the iron door and pressed it open. The night air was heavenly after the backstage heat, filtering through Maran's lace in little breezes, clearing her head, settling her down. Rossen seemed to collect himself too, as they both stared out at the side street. The light was red, and nothing was moving. In the warm darkness and the quiet, they might have been miles away from a crowd of so many, a theater full of excitement and commotion.

Maran began to count. She always counted out horrible moments, like the dentist drilling, the electrologist sending buzzes of shock through her skin, the worst of her fucking situations. At the dentist she could make it up to slow sixty before she made faces and moans. Now, by the time she had said 'Forty-nine' to herself, they could see the van speeding toward them in the empty block. It screeched to a quick stop, and she could see Tony, blessed, beautiful, sixty-four-year-old Tony, in the driver's seat.

'Get help,' she said over her shoulder to Roe Rossen,

and ran to the back of the van, where Tony was already yanking open the big doors.

They pulled at the boxes in the van, piling them on the sidewalk. She was aware of a small crowd of stagehands, dressers, helpers picking up the boxes in clumps and taking them inside. Better get them in there, she thought, they'll need me for sizes, colors, they'll fuck it up if I let them.

She went back as fast as the slit in her skirt would let her, wrestling with the doors, shoving into the crowd. She found the director, grabbed his arm. 'Tell them,' she shouted. 'Get them in order. We'll do the first ones first, time after to get shoes on the rest. What's on first? Bathing suits? Fine. Use all the bright colors. Forget the smaller ones, they'll all have big feet.'

Order began to impose itself, quiet settled over them, lines started to form. The dressers, used to sudden emergencies, picked up where Maran left off, began weeding out large and small slippers. The soft, flat shoes seemed to be everywhere, lying on the stage floor, being held in girls' hands, being tugged onto feet, strings pulled to tighten them. Like Cinderella, thought Maran, beginning to laugh to herself, a garden of delight for foot fetishists. Silliest scene I ever saw. God help the dancer in this city who needs shoes tomorrow.

She made herself stop, put her hands up to smooth her hair, calmed herself down. She couldn't see Rossen anywhere, but the stage was clearing, the music starting out front again, the lineup snaking back through the wings. All God's children got shoes, thought Maran. And I did it.

She slipped quietly through the stage door to the theater.

As she edged her way back to her seat, she saw with relief that Domina was next to Bill. Like a marble statue, her eyes blank, absolutely contained. The drugs, thought Maran. Domina's in a fog, zonked. When she got close, she could hear Domina's breathing, raspy, thick. If Domina had been backstage, Maran decided, she'd have stopped breathing altogether. I hope later she sticks to Belle, gives that cold to her. Maybe it'll develop into pneumonia.

Up on the stage, the clothes danced, flirted, strutted, marched. Bathing suits, lots of applause, and whistles.

161

Tennis dresses, milder applause. Slacks, gorgeous, Maran realized, tailored to perfection. The crowd realized too, and the clapping swelled. Caftans, sweeping, full, stunning. Leisure suits, trim, neat. Suits, coats, leathers, the things from Beged-Or getting special applause, even bravos. The girl wearing the leather shawl came to the front of the stage, crumpled the silken skins in her hands and let them fall again, unwrinkled, beautiful. More applause. Long gowns now, scarlets, sky blues, mauves, silver and gold, straight, frilled, narrow, wide, every flattering silhouette in the designer's bag of tricks. Maran watched each outfit from the bottom up, anxiously scanning every foot. It was fine, she thought. Mostly the standard black flat slippers, with the drawstrings to make them fit. How ghastly if one of them slipped off! Did they yank those strings hard enough? Looked all right so far. Here and there, colors to go with fashions in color, pink for the pastels, gold and silver for the formal gowns, fine. The wedding dresses were set on top of white satin slippers, the caftans hovered over red ones, everything perfect, she thought. Maran began to relax, and relaxing, to feel absolutely triumphant, wonderful, shaking with excitement and joy. Where would they have been without me? she said to herself over and over. Where? Dirty feet, that's where, dusty soles, mottled toes with the dirt from the stage, making the clothes look ridiculous, a laughing stock. Hey, I'm the best there is, everybody. Next job, the world *has* to choose me.

Domina sniffled into a lacy handkerchief through the whole show. Next to her Michael sat stolidly, his hair amazingly neat, his black eyes on the stage but his hands fiddling with a tiny silver knife. Bored to death, Maran thought. What a good kid, to sit through a whole fashion show for the love of his mother. Domina's done a good job with Michael.

She couldn't wait to tell Domina what had gone on backstage. Jesus, she thought, we'll talk about this the rest of our lives. Belle shrieking about bare feet and desert sands, dumb. When the music changed to a martial beat and the Israeli uniform marched on stage complete with black ballet slippers, the noise in the theater was thunderous. Two thousand, seven hundred and forty-two pairs of hands clapping furiously. No, Maran thought, more, there's standing room three lines deep back there, more. Marvelous night, she exulted, marvelous party. If only all these people knew how she had made it a success.

Over the applause she whispered the story to Domina, who registered horror, then wonder, then total glee. She stood on tiptoe to hug Maran, then kissed Michael for coming, released him to go off to a party with his own friends.

The two women moved up the aisle together, Maran floating, Domina hurrying a little to keep up with her friend's long stride. They headed for the escalators, remembering to lift their long skirts just in time.

They coasted down to the brilliant scene, little tables filling, chairs moving, glasses clinking, waiters trying to make order in the buffet line.

'Bill,' said Maran. 'Can you get us champagne? Domina can't make it through that scene.'

Darling Bill, she thought. This was one of those places you just couldn't do without a man.

'Are you all right?' she asked Domina, who was sinking slowly into the chair next to hers.

Domina turned her large, dark eyes toward Maran's face. 'All right?' Her voice was a crow's voice, thick, croaking, alternately a whisper and a cough. 'All right? I've never felt so bloody marvelous in my whole long eventful life!'

And she started to laugh, as Rossen had laughed, with her whole slim body in her laughter, her hands to her face, the tears spilling over her beautiful dress. Incoherent, she rocked in the flimsy chair, unable to get more words to come from her mouth. Out of nowhere, Rossen appeared. He looked at them both and stared, appalled, at Domina, who was starting to attract attention from the people around at the other tables. Over her head, he looked at Maran.

'Let her laugh,' said Maran sweetly. 'She's entitled. Me, I should be crying, but Domina can laugh. Don't you think so?'

163

He looked sleepish for an instant, and then grinned. He reached across Domina's shaking body and took Maran's hand, pressed it firmly. Then he turned back to Domina and put his whole arm around her. The black cloth of his dinner jacket circled the whiteness of her beautiful arms, folding her in close to him. Maran watched while he held her steady, smoothed her hair with his free hand. When she was quieter, he reached for his handkerchief again, found it where he'd jammed it in the wrong pocket, dabbed at Domina's face with it gently. Thank God Bill came with a tray of goblets filled with yellowing fizzy champagne. Not the good stuff, but with so many people, you couldn't expect it. Maran tossed hers down in one thirsty gulp. The tables were filling now. She looked nervously at someone's plate going by at eye level. The food looked lovely, she saw with satisfaction, curry and rice and broccoli, fruit and cookies. Kosher, she remembered. Could curry be kosher? What the hell did she care? She was acting as if it had turned into her own work, this party. One slipper does not a stylist make, thought Maran.

Women kept coming over to congratulate and kiss Roe, to say hello to Domina, all kinds of people in the mixture of evening clothes women wore nowadays for big New York evenings. Gowns, pants, tailored evening suits, caftans, Mexican folk dresses, Guatemalan shifts, Indian gauzes. Well, thought Maran, now Israel can join the fashion race. Next year, if the computer ends up with the right numbers, Israel's designs will be in Houston, in Bel-Air, in Grosse Pointe, in Marin County. She kept smiling at people Domina introduced to her. Writers and art directors from the agency, from Domina's group. Domina stepped on her foot when one of them came over, a tiny girl with the most beautiful hair Maran had seen anywhere. Of course, she thought, this is the M.J. I've heard about. Funny. She's so open-looking, she manages to seem sly. Like the people you know are lying because they look you right in the eye.

More people, congratulating Roe and Domina, waving, smiling, kissing their hands and blowing greetings to their table. The director of the show arrived, all smiles and plump contentment now. He accepted an introduction to

Maran as if he'd never set eyes on her till this moment. So it goes, thought Maran. He should be kissing my feet. Or at least my shoes. A plump girl spoke to Roe, leaning over his shoulder, pretty in pink gauze and shoes that were dyed to match. Her escort stood patiently behind her, looking as bored as Bill, she thought. Lolly Something-or-other, she heard. Maran noticed that the girl's eyes scanned Roe's face anxiously, even during their brief conversation. Who's she?

There was a stir at the far end of the room, a rustle of the people seated there. What now? Maran saw a ripple through the crowd as people pushed their chairs back awkwardly and tried to stand up. Who? Oh, for Christ's sweet sake, Belle Rosner, clumping along in her black number like the queen at court. As Belle came closer, Maran could see she was giving a magnificent performance, nodding, smiling, moving slowly, accepting the congratulations of the crowd. Maran suddenly felt beaten, insignificant in this crowd. She remembered Tony, with a jump. Jesus, what had happened to him? She was as bad as the director. Tony had been the real hero, and she'd entirely forgotten him after that van had rolled up. Well, he'd probably gone home long since. First thing in the morning, Maran thought, a call from me, a case of cognac, and the address of Potter Jackson for the world's biggest shoe bill. Belle was on top of her now, they were moving a chair for her. She was going to sit right there with them. Everything happens to me, Maran thought. I even have to face her the rest of the night. Shit.

She watched silently while the old woman sank heavily into the chair, took up her glass with a slightly trembling hand. Reporters and fashion editors plucked at her sleeve, clustered close to hear anything she might say to them. Envy and rage rose in Maran's insides, making her own hand shake her glass, bringing a little buzz into her head. The old fraud, she thought. If they knew how she'd fucked up. What a story for *Women's Wear*. And I'll never be able to tell it to anyone who matters, never. For the love of Domina, I'll have to keep my mouth shut. She woke from her angry spell when she heard a reporter asking Belle about the ballet shoes. Why those with everything, he was asking, with even the army uniform? What did it mean? Was Belle pushing the manufacturers in Israel into slipper making?

If she's got any decency, Maran thought, she'll tell them the truth. She's a big enough woman to do it. She has a reputation I'll never live to match. What would it cost her to tell them, even to give me some credit? I'd do it.

She watched Belle put her glass down and turn to the reporter, smiling. 'My dear, you noticed the most important thing,' she said. 'The most perfect detail of the show, my own favorite detail of all. Ballet shoes. The steps of artists. The footgear of the talented. The soft, supple footprints of Pavlova and Taglioni and Makarova, borrowed for their link to the art of the dance. Because from this night on, Israel's fashion will *be* an art, an art to dance across the stage of the world. You'll see. Tonight was simply the overture.'

In the respectful silence that followed this pronouncement, Maran felt as if she'd been shot by a poisoned arrow, thud, and was experiencing the agonizing aftermath.

That old bitch, she thought wildly. I could pour this champagne right over her silver hair. I could yell out that Belle Rosner is full of shit. I should quit the business forever. I should tell them all it was me, and that if they had let me at it from the beginning, the show would have been twice as fantastic.

The table began to shake at her side, and she turned toward Roe and Domina. Slowly she absorbed what was happening. They were both starting to come apart, to rock with laughter, together, twice as noisily as each of them had laughed before separately. Maran looked across at Belle, staring, annoyed. Suddenly Maran's resentment dissolved. How ridiculous the whole thing really was. What a wonderful joke. Fashion, how silly. Emergencies. How dumb to call this an emergency. That old woman was past and gone, Maran had years ahead of her to stage and manage things. It would all be fine, the whole rest of her life. Roe knew the real story. Domina had always known how good she was. Now she ought to take it a little easier, try laughing at herself a little. Laugh? How the whole fashion world would laugh when they heard. And they'd hear. Tony would talk at Capezio. The dressers. There had been a lot of people on that stage, near that phone. The models. Everybody gossips in this business.

Once she began thinking about laughter, she was finished with self-control. The champagne egged on her excitement, the laughter next to her was as catching as Domina's cold.

While the whole table watched, while people at other tables turned to gape, Domina and Roe and Maran laughed. Freed from tension, responsibility, worry about the show, the three of them rocked with laughter. Over their heads the computer display was flashing, racking up the numbers of sales being made as buyers' orders came in. Around them waiters paused with their laden trays, wondering what on earth was causing the commotion among such an elegant crowd. And in the middle of it all, the three of them roared, wept, howled uproariously.

Domina

When will I see you again?

M.

Domina heard the telephone shrilling from her office as she walked along the hall.

Who would call before eight-thirty? The ringing echoed in the cold air. Every summer the office was freezing, the air conditioning turned up for men in jackets, to a point that left women sniffling and shivering. No wonder she'd had that cold. Domina kept shawls and cardigans in her closet, an afghan on her desk chair, especially for these early mornings.

She caught up the telephone.

'Hi,' said Roe's voice. 'Got a minute?'

She felt a little skip of her heart.

'Sure,' she said. 'What's up?'

'I've just got the last set of figures from the show. They want breakdowns fast, to start manufacture, get the orders moving. And I'll be locked in Detroit for the next two days. Could I come down now?'

Her heart slowed down.

'Roe, I don't see how. That'll be more than a minute. I'm early because Mr Bonnell decided to drop in at lunchtime. I've got to review everything my group has been doing for him. I won't get through it all, as it is. And he knows when you fake. Could we do it later?'

Silence. She'd never said no to Roe, either, not since they'd got going with the Israeli promotion.

'I'm jammed too. Screening this afternoon for Croft, all the commercials we're taking out tomorrow. Till six at least. Well, listen. Could you have an early dinner? Go over the figures then?'

Now Domina's heart started to flutter.

She thought furiously. Dinner. Restaurant tables. Small.

170

Crowded. Hovering waiters. And she'd been longing to ask him to dinner in her apartment. She wanted him to see her there, wearing something soft, pale, feminine, different from every day. Till now there hadn't been a good time to ask. And this August was too hot for entertaining, the muggy air turning the city into a steam bath. But now?

'Look,' she said. 'Why don't you come to my apartment when you're finished. I'll give you supper. We can spread out the papers, think about them. And finish early.'

A pause while the telephone crackled.

'Well,' he said. 'If you're sure. I couldn't get there till seven or so. Can you send out for Chinese food, something easy?'

Domina's heart speeded up again. 'No trouble,' she said. 'Come whenever you're done. One forty East Sixty-seventh, twelve-C. I'll look for you after seven.'

'Good. We'll make it quick. My plane's at the crack of dawn.'

When she'd hung up, Domina realized she felt like a schoolgirl who'd just asked a boy to a prom. Come on, she told herself, stop it, get busy.

She tapped the phone without hanging up, dialed home.

'Leota? Listen. Two for supper. Special. Turn the air conditioners on, leave them when you go, okay? And would you check the terrace, make sure it looks nice from the living room?'

'Special,' she heard Leota say. 'Special how? Business? Or a date?'

'Chocolate dessert,' said Domina.

'Date,' said Leota.

Domina hung up, thinking suddenly of the years when the phone calls to and from home had been so dreadful, when her children were small. A nurse complaining about a dog brought home from the park. Michael calling in the middle of a meeting in her office to say he'd never go back to school again. The doctor, when Maria had sledded through a fence in the snow, sliced open her forehead. Domina thought: I've earned Leota, earned her the hard way.

All through the day the idea of Roe in her apartment

171

sparkled at the back of her mind, keeping her smiling.

While she listened to Mr Bonnell screaming about the increased cost of goods, Domina thought about Roe looking at her books, her pictures, her petunias in their rows of pots.

While she reviewed Christmas ads, she considered what to wear. Something soft, clingy, sexy.

While she presented suggestions for new promotions, she imagined Roe at her white marble dining table, eating Leota's frozen mousse, drinking her strong coffee, relaxing over Cognac from one of the Baccarat glasses.

The moment Mr Bonnell went to the men's room, she called Maran.

'Send yourself flowers. A dozen roses,' Maran said.

'Don't be childish,' Domina returned.

But when Domina got home, after outrunning three people to grab a taxi, there were yellow roses on the hall table from Maran's florist. They stood suggestively in a tall cut-glass vase, a white card nestled among the ferns. 'When will I see you again? M.' the card asked in big block letters designed to be read clearly a foot away. Domina laughed, threw the card away, redid the flowers in a plain low bowl, ruthlessly chopping at the costly stems, sticking in petunias from the terrace.

Still before six. She poured straight perfume into a hot bath, floated in the soothing water thinking about clothes. Blue, pale blue. Slit skirt? Flat shoes, for a change, quieter on her polished floors, different from work. Chiffon shirt, filmy, touchable. Jesus, she thought, I really do want him to touch me. I'd better be careful. Remember that bastard account man I fell for, that was a mess. Well, Roe doesn't have a wedding ring for me to throw, that's some help.

As she dressed, she thought: I'm rushing things, I haven't a clue to what he thinks of me except at work. I'm acting like those awful girls who complain that men keep making passes at them while they do all they can to encourage passes. Working tonight, that's all.

She did her face and hair, leaving off the blushers she wore to combat the office fluorescent lights, pulling a few wisps of hair out of her knot to curl around her face. She settled, finally, for a plain long cotton skirt, a sleeveless blouse that showed her smooth arms.

When she could do no more about her looks, Domina went to the kitchen. Vichyssoise in a brown pottery bowl, cut chives on a plate ready to be sprinkled on the soup at the last second. A huge chef's salad, brimming with golden cheese, pink roast beef, firm white turkey, baked ham, salami bumpy with peppercorns, more of each than any restaurant would use. Tiny beat biscuits wrapped in plastic, on the counter. Butterballs in a glass dish. She peeked into the freezer at the chocolate mousse. Then the dining room. Leota had used a paisley cloth, heavy white pottery dishes. My God, Domina thought, I haven't fussed over a dinner like this in ages. But Roe has taste, he knows what's what. It's a production, really, like the fashion show. My damned generation again, the ones who have to be perfect at everything. Belle's bunch didn't bother – they went back to work in the bedroom after a quick dinner. M.J.'s opened beer cans, called out for pizza.

The house phone buzzed, the doorman shouted into it that Mr Boston was on his way up. Domina suddenly felt stricken, nervous as a girl.

Roe. Taller, because she had no heels on. His face looked tired, the lines etched deeply. And he's tried, too, she thought: his tie is straight, his cowlick is brushed down. I miss that little lock of hair.

'Hello,' he said. 'Hope I haven't kept you waiting. We had to fight the last batch of commercials through Croft. They're new and different, and you know how Jackson reacts to anything new and different. Domina, what a great apartment.'

He walked past the roses, headed for the most comfortable chair, sat down gratefully.

She made a strong drink for him, a weak one for herself, so she could stay in perfect control. And Roe talked, about his meeting, about which ideas had gone wrong, about how he'd helped put them right. Finally he asked her about her Bonnell meeting. She wondered: didn't he even *see* her beautiful room, her English chintzes, her Oriental rugs, her Frankenthaler painting? She'd spent two years paying for that painting. Well, she thought, he's all wound up about Ford, maybe later he'll relax. And Roe went on talking vigorously, striding up and down, refilling his glass.

When she went to put supper on the table, he followed her, still talking. Not a word about her fantastic kitchen, her copper pots, her greenhouse window. She gave up.

'Domina, what a terrific kitchen,' Roe said suddenly, pausing in the middle of a sentence. 'How long have you lived here?'

Congratulations, she thought, you noticed something.

'Since my kids were little.'

'I just got a new place,' Roe said. 'My wife kept the big house in Connecticut, and I've camped out since, but now I'm starting to think about fixing up an apartment. I got it for the view, the river.'

'That's something I'm missing,' said Domina, as they sat down. 'No views on Sixty-seventh Street.'

Roe ate. The soup disappeared, the salad vanished, the biscuits went one by one.

'This is sensational, Domina,' he said. 'Who does it all?'

'I have a marvelous maid,' she said. Roe, she noticed, had somehow come apart during dinner, his tie loosened, his jacket off, his cuffs turned back. When they got up, she could see one sock crumpled around his ankle. She thought: He's the kind who can't stay put together, gestures too big, concentration on ideas too strong, not a man for clothes. I'm too used to fag art directors who coo over everything in the apartment, they look like dress dummies at two in the morning. There hasn't been a man here for a long time, a real man. He'd be so good for Michael.

Domina closed the door on the dirty dishes, cleared her coffee table for the papers. While Roe rummaged in his attaché case, she watched him. He isn't even one of the walking wounded that newly divorced men usually are. Who tell you how their wives just didn't grow with them. That always made her think of a tiny little wife, one you could hold on the palm of your hand.

When they looked at the figures, Domina forgot herself

in the work. Surprises. Orders for the uniform, of all things, probably the military trend that had made Army & Navy Stores so popular. The bridal gown, of course, mountains of orders for that. And the jumpsuits. Domina got her calculator out, to match the one Roe carried. They listed the priorities for Israeli manufacturers.

They worked for more than an hour. Domina was suddenly tired; she'd been keyed up all day, and here they were. And the dishes still had to go in the machine. Domina couldn't leave dirty dishes for Leota; the thought would keep her from sleeping.

She offered him brandy, her best, a big one for each of them.

Roe looked around for his shoes, which had come off altogether as they worked. But he made no move to put them on. Instead, his feet went up on her coffee table, his back sank into the cushions of the couch.

Domina tucked her feet up, too, the brandy trickling warmth all through her.

'Do you know Detroit, Domina?'

Of course, his mind was on his Ford commercials.

'Certainly. I come from the Midwest, remember?'

'I remember. I never asked you, what got you out?'

'Advertising,' she said.

'Tell me.'

'The usual story. I worked in Elkhart's finest emporium while I was in school. You know, the kind of place with glass counters for dry goods, and little scarves tied around the necks of the dummies. I stood behind one of those counters and sold. Until I discovered that in the back of the store people were writing ads for the local paper. I hung around whenever I could, and when they got busy, I picked up a pencil. And here I am.'

'Slower,' said Roe. 'You left out a little.'

'Well,' said Domina, 'one of the writers was an old lady, former mistress of Mr Trimble, the owner. She had a heart attack at her typewriter one day. I abandoned my pencil for her typewriter. Then I wrote some hot copy, did some things that hadn't been tried before, and more people started coming into the store. Terrific training. The ad ran in the morning paper, either crowds came in or they didn't, you knew right away if an ad was good. And one afternoon, a merchandising genius named Bonnell, formerly Bernstein, came in, too.'

'The ogre?'

'Right. But I didn't know that. I'd never heard of him. He was franchising his boutiques all over the West, grandson of a peddler, and he wanted to move East. Noticed my ads. Said he'd put a boutique in our store if I'd handle the operation. I began to study what he did, how he did it, and found a lot of holes. I did some fliers for his merchandise, thought up a Bonnell Club, a newsletter on fashion. It was a start. I was taking care of my mother, and every cent counted. Mr Bonnell paid me extra.'

'Didn't anyone ever take care of you?'

More personal questions? Doesn't ask about the apartment, but he does want to know about me.

'Mr Bonnell did. Until he had a fight with Mr Trimble, yanked the boutique, took up with a bigger store in Chicago. Asked me to go along and write full-time for him. Mr Trimble suddenly realized I was indispensable, and I felt wonderful, fought over. But I went to Chicago.'

'And your mother?'

Domina thought about her mother, how she'd tried to get through her mother's alcoholic haze that day to explain about Chicago.

'No,' she said. 'I found a neighbor to take care of her. She was pretty sick at the time.'

She thought a moment. For God's sake, it was long ago, tell it right.

'My mother was a drinker. She'd been in a fog for years, since I was little. My father'd gone long before – I never knew him.'

The old pain descended as she said it, the mixture of anger and shame and pity and resentment. Even that day she'd seen how pretty her mother must once have been, her black hair luxuriant, her dark eyes misty. Well, Sister Nina had said that everybody had some sadness, not just Domina, and that she owed it to her mother not to be ashamed.

'I see,' said Roe. 'So then Chicago.'

Domina wrenched her mind back to the story.

'Then, a whole big city, museums, theaters, concerts, and fashion, what seemed to me real fashion, expensive, exciting. Once I made it clear to Mr Bonnell that I wasn't writing ads sitting in his lap, he gave me a lot to do. We christened all the stores Boutique Bonnell. I did everything, fliers, booklets, charge-account stuffers, even some designs. Got another account too, a crazy thing called Dial-A-Maid. And I wrote a book about Bonnell, people began to know who I was.'

That's modest, she thought.

'Slow down again,' Roe said. 'Tell me about the book.'

He poured another brandy, nestled back in the cushions again.

She thought he looked very much at home. The lines had softened in his face, the soft light made him look younger. Domina hoped it did as much for her.

Does he really want to know all this? Is he paying me back for dinner by listening? The nuns always said talk about others, not yourself.

'How did you find time to write the book?' he asked.

Nuns, thought Domina. Why should they know anything about men, anyway?

'I was pregnant, so I didn't go out much. The book was called *How to Begin the Boutique*, the story of Bonnell, only told funny. It sold, wound up in a magazine, too. Mr Bonnell adored it, he was a celebrity. It got me a great job offer, too.'

'Pregnant. And your husband?'

She remembered Stephen during that grim summer, sitting at the window of the airless bedroom holding a bottle for Maria while he read the newspaper. And while she got dressed for work, in one of those terrible maternity skirts with a hole in front for her stomach to poke through. She had awakened on those suffocating mornings feelings as if giant fish were nibbling at her flesh. Stephen. Maria. The new baby inside her. Chicago in summer. How wretched she'd been.

'He was writing magazine articles,' she said.

177

Anyway, that's what I told people, she thought. All those husbands of working women, writing books, consulting, painting, teaching, freelancing, that's what women say when their husbands do nothing, earn nothing.

'How old were you?'

'Twenty-two.'

'My God,' said Roe.

'I felt very old, responsible. My mother in Elkhart, my husband, my two-year-old, and the baby coming. None of them earned much, either.'

'Not even the two-year-old?'

'Especially. She's my daughter, Maria. She's at Brown. But the book saved us, and the new job.'

This is like confession, she thought. That summer. Stephen, complaining about the hot apartment while she worked in a cool office. Maria, into everything, always a mess. Each morning, she'd left, tired, cross, heavy with the new baby, making herself smile for the office. And then, in one wild week, everything had changed. The first check from the book. A medium-size agency had offered her a job to work on national accounts. Her mother had died. Domina had wept all through one sultry night, while Stephen slept. Then in the morning she'd gone to an agency, hired a nursemaid. And to a department store, for chic maternity clothes, baby clothes, things for the apartment. And a beautiful electric shaver for Stephen, the best they had. When she'd got home, he'd been furious at her extravagance, slammed the new shaver on the kitchen floor. Domina, furious, for the first time had broken through her Catholic upbringing to shout at her husband.

She turned back to Roe, sipping his brandy, watching her. Jesus, she thought, I'll scare him to death.

'Then everything got better fast. My first New York job, then a better one, finally Jackson. And here I am.'

Roe leaned over close, suddenly. But he was only reaching for more brandy. Don't get your hopes up, she thought.

'Did you get to college?'

She had wanted to stop talking about herself.

'Only to a Harvard Management Seminar, thanks to

Brady Godwin, after I came to Jackson. I loved your Harvard.'

Okay, nuns, now we'll talk about him. Sister Nina, how was that for a change of subject?

'Twenty-two,' Roe said. 'When I was twenty-two I was battling my father for my life. He knew just how I should live it. We didn't agree then on anything.'

He looked at Domina, flushed, beautiful, swirling her brandy in the big glass. She certainly got herself to the right side of the tracks. Some story. At least she knows what she's working for, doesn't have to wonder if this is the right way to spend her life. She seems so sure. I wonder at least once a week why I'm involved in an agency, why I don't move to something bigger, more important. Why don't I move right now, next to her? Take her toes in my hand, move my hand up, keep it there awhile. Or trace the line of that beautiful bone from her neck to her shoulder. Clavicle. End up untying the string on that blouse. What kind of a shit did she marry? How does she feel about men after that?

He leaned back, enjoying the relief from his tense high of the afternoon. Croft always keyed him up, brought out the competitor in him, made him want to shine. Sharp old bastard, he thought. Probably as anti-Semitic as they come, too. Too smart to show it, not like Godwin, with his little extras. Jewish, but good family. A Jewish lawyer. Jews separate from the human race. Well, when I wonder why I'm there, remember that. To show them they're wrong, partly. And to show myself I'm right.

He remembered his father when the announcement broke about Roe's going to Jackson, leaving the lithography business. 'They're not your kind,' his father had said, driving him wild, because his father had never brought him up as any 'kind,' anything but a guy who went to Exeter, to Harvard, to deb parties, to Christmas parties, clubs, everywhere. Well, he'd held fast, taken the Jackson job. In a year he'd built up a small electronics account, moved over to Ford, headed that in just a few years. Now he'd made it to the board. If a Jew could do that, he could head up the whole agency, too. Do the company good. Had his father sent Belle along to stir him up again, get him out? She'd hinted that there were bigger things, politics, government. Had that come from his father? Roe wanted to run Jackson right, run it as it would have been if the guys from Grey and Norman Craig and Doyle Dane had been allowed in from the start.

But how much easier he'd had it than this girl, in her perfect room, with that serene expression. Domina was the kind you longed to mess up a little, longed to test and see if the coolness could mask something exciting, fiery. Could she use that strength to kiss, to cling? What did she do, say, in someone's arms, what was the quiet mouth capable of when you got close to it?

Suddenly he had to know.

He moved, swung his feet down, stood up. He moved his arms to imprison her, curled in the corner of her chair.

'Domina Drexler,' he said. 'You're something.' He leaned down to start finding out the answers.

But she put a hand on his shirtfront, pressed him away gently.

'That's okay,' she said. 'Too much brandy and story-telling. You have a plane. Crack of dawn, you said.'

Looking down at her, smelling her fresh fragrance, Roe felt the heat rise in his body, the urgency grow.

'Domina,' he said.

Domina felt his breath on her cheek, looking down, saw the brown firmness of his arms where his shirt cuffs were turned back. His hand moved to take her chin, and she could see the shiny gray of his tennis callus on the palm.

Why not? she thought. Why the hell not? It's been so long since somebody held me, warmed me, loved me, and I'm cold, nobody's touched my hair, smoothed my face, cradled me, for so long.

And then: no. Where can it go? What happens when he gets tired of me, steers work away from me, when I see him having a drink with one of the secretaries? Don't let it get to that.

She moved away, held the brandy glass in front of her. 'You'll be dead tomorrow, dead for Ford,' she said.

'That,' he said, 'is six hours away. I can sleep on the plane.'

'Roe. It's not a good idea.'

'I think it's a sensational idea.'

Sensational. The word seemed to fill her ears with delicious whispers, her mind with happiness. She wanted to let her head fall back, her shoulders loosen, to open her mouth, arms, her whole body to him, let him reach, touch, stroke, move in, take over.

Wait, she forced herself to think, *wait*. Sit straight, clear your head, wait. Don't be easy. Don't be like other women. Don't let him think you asked him here for this.

But Roe was very close, very warm. Her hands wanted to reach for him, to pull him closer, to take his hands and guide them to her breasts, her thighs. She felt herself turning to him the way a plant does to light.

'Not now, Roe,' she managed. 'Too soon. Too pat. We both have to get up in the morning, be wonderful for Jackson.'

There was a long silence. Roe seemed to be holding his breath.

Then he stood up, put his hands to his hair, making a complete mess of whatever neatness he'd had left. She knew he was trying for control, watched him put his head down, come up calmly.

'Right,' he said. 'First date and all. Absolutely right. I shouldn't have started. But you wait. Be warned. I usually get what I'm after.'

'So do I,' said Domina. 'We come from the same school. I like my own way, too.'

'Then we both better want the same thing,' Roe said.

He straightened up, smiled his nice, crinkly smile.

And got out fast, cramming the papers in his case, picking up his coat from the hall chair, passing the roses, glorious, eye-catching, fragrant, as if they didn't exist.

Domina left the dishes for Leota, walked slowly into her bedroom, and left her clothes where they fell. She thought, why must I always be so damned neat, so damned controlled? Why can't I be different for once?

She got into bed. Tired as she was, she couldn't find a comfortable position, a restful place for her heavy head. The bed felt wider, emptier than ever before.

Lolly

ATTENTION YOU COCKSUCKERS IN
CARROLL ASSOCIATES AT ELEVEN
TODAY A BOMB WILL DESTROY YOUR
ENTIRE OFFICE ESPECIALLY YOUR
FILES THAT KEEP DECENT MEN FROM
DECENT JOBS YOUR DIRTY WORK IS
FINISHED AND YOUR MONEY WILL BURN

The bells began clanging, a loud warning that rang right through Lolly's temples and throbbed in her cheekbones. Annoyed, she turned off her electric typewriter. Another bomb scare. Becoming commonplace. Everyone inside an office seemed to have someone outside who hated him. People who'd been fired hated their bosses. Wives who'd been cheated hated their husbands. Terrorists hated big international organizations. Easy enough to send a note through the mail. Nobody even needed to plant a bomb. The warning was enough. Everyone would file out while the police searched. The warnings couldn't be ignored. The very one you didn't pay attention to could just be the one that some nut had actually planted.

This bomb scare had come at a particularly irritating moment.

Lolly had a lunch date with Roe, and a mountain of files to get through beforehand. She wanted to leave the afternoon free, just in case, though he'd only said lunch. Now the interruption would put her off.

The hell with it, she thought. She hadn't seen Roe in five weeks. That damn Israeli thing. He'd been awfully distant at the show itself, too. She was dying to be with him now. She was all ready, best underwear, best perfume, best appetite. Hungry, she thought, I'm actually hungry for him. I'll leave now, and if I have to, I'll tell Mr Carroll that the bomb scare kept me from finishing the files.

The files. Confidential, tidy, fascinating little cards. John Brinnin Carroll had built an international business out of a small search company with just those files. His edge was his method of going out after executives and persuading them to move to another company before they'd even thought

184

about it. Lolly kept files on thousands of executives. Researched from news stories, business records, alumni magazines, company newsletters, even restaurant talk and elevator gossip. The cards were valuable, insured for a lot of money, kept under locks in a room only three people entered. And Lolly was one!

The information brought in huge fees for Mr Carroll, often as much as thirty percent of an employee's annual salary, sometimes a retainer from a large company, occasionally a special fee from an executive who needed extra effort, like the cured alcoholics who wanted to get back into top jobs. All the executives she met would have loved a peek at the files on their own organizations. The information was amazing. Even records of jokes about people, phrases and tags that stuck through the years. Lolly loved looking at the cards at random, familiarizing herself with names, companies, especially the jokes. One man's card said, 'Kidded about joining the board of directors on an athletic scholarship.' Mr Carroll had warned Lolly never to discuss the files, or any of his systems. The systems were tabs. Little bits of metal in different colors. Red for really hot prospects, people ready to move quietly to better jobs at higher salaries. Green for hot prospects unwilling to move at all. Those were the ones Mr Carroll most liked to sell. Everyone has his price, he always told her. Enough salary, incentives, insurance, bonuses, stock options, percentage guarantees after retirement, and there you were. A green tab turned into a red one. Wonderful, Lolly thought.

The tabs came in other colors, too. Blue meant female, black meant black, so you could pick out minorities right away. There were other colors for Jews, handicapped people, people over forty-five. Lolly could make the system work in seconds. She loved the idea that Union Carbide or Colgate or Procter & Gamble or AT&T would give a lot to look at her information. It made her feel like a beautiful spy in a war movie.

The bell kept on clanging. Lolly picked up her handbag, looked at her watch. Dammit. There wasn't time to get fixed up perfectly for Roe.

185

Lolly put the files inside her desk drawer, turned the key, and put it in her wallet. By now the wardens were shouting.

Stairs, she thought, so I won't risk meeting Mr Carroll in the elevator.

Once through the heavy iron fire doors at the lobby level, Lolly headed to the edge of the crowd gathering in the street. Her calves ached from walking down the twelve flights, and she wondered if she was perspiring. The crowd was growing, standing around while the bomb squads, like men from Mars in their masks and asbestos shirts, hurried inside the building. Everyone was having a fine time in the sun, she noticed. The Sabrett man was selling hot dogs at the curb, the cookie wagon was doing a terrific business, and a Good Humor cart was hastening down the avenue to cash in. Boys were talking to secretaries, girls were flirting with executives, everyone was standing close to the build-ing to see if anything really might happen. If a bomb went off, Lolly thought, half this crowd would probably get hurt. What a great way to revenge yourself, she decided, one dime invested in a phone call would cost somebody's company thousands of dollars in lost time.

At the edge of the crowd now, Lolly turned the corner and waved at a cab.

Early as she was, when she got to the restaurant, Roe was sitting in a booth. He had a glass in front of him, so he'd been there a little while, which surprised her. Why was he early?

'Hi there,' she said with a big smile.

He bobbed up, in the only gesture of politeness possible for a man trapped in a booth. He's adorable, thought Lolly, so different from all the young guys. Roe always held coats and lit cigarettes. It had been ages since her husband bothered with things like that.

'Drink?'

'Sure. I'd like a nice big martini.'

He turned to get the waiter, who seemed to materialize out of nowhere. Roe always got things done so well. He ordered her drink the way she liked it, and asked for another of his own. Then he turned and faced her. 'How are you? How's work?'

'Fine. As ever. You've been busy. I haven't seen you in so long,' she said.

He cleared his throat. 'Lolly. I've got to talk to you.'

She felt a peculiar sound in her head at his voice, his tone. Talk? Why?

'There's no good way to say this, so I'll just say it straight,' he said.

The sound in her head increased its hum, like a warning. What is it? Please don't let him tell me that. No. He's got to go away awhile, or he's a little sick, or he's quitting his job, anything but that.

'Lolly, I think it's time we stopped,' Roe said.

The sound in Lolly's head became a bell, like the one in her office. It trilled, sending pain through her head. Getting louder every moment.

'It's no good doing this on the side.'

The bell was so loud, Lolly felt surprised that Roe didn't seem to hear it. A bomb will go off soon, she thought. This is a bomb warning. Something's about to blow up.

She held her drink up, just to put something between them, something physical.

'I could say I'm thinking about you, but honestly, I'm thinking about myself, too. This isn't any good, Lolly. I'd like to be as kind as I can, to spare you misery. You're such a good kid, Lolly. You've been a revelation, believe me.'

The drink was wobbling in her hand, so Lolly set it down. Why, it's an earthquake before the bomb, she thought, a California earthquake. Once in Bel-Air there'd been just a tremor of earthquake, enough to make pictures fall from the walls, crack some plaster, over in an instant. Lolly had been astounded how she'd known immediately that it really *was* an earthquake. This was an earthquake, too. Goodness, was she going to cry?

'Lolly. Listen to me. May I tell you why? I think it might make things a little better. Don't cry. Listen to me.'

Her tears were spilling over, falling, spattering the paper place mat in front of her. The little teardrops sank slowly into the paper, making a pretty pattern, Lolly thought. She felt shaken to bits, bits of tears flying like pieces of her. She had been happy. Now she would be miserable. It had all been Roe. He alone had made life seem marvelous, made her job seem exciting, her home bearable, even her children like a gift she could bring to him. Everything was related to him. And now he would not be there. She'd be just like everyone else. Worse. She'd always been worse off than other girls. The plump ones, the ones they chose last on teams, the Jewish girl with the dressy clothes. Now what will I do? she thought. Alone.

'Lolly. Say something. Please.'

What could she say? He'd said it all. No. A piece was missing from what he'd told her. She couldn't quite think what it was.

'Something is happening to me,' Roe went on. 'I feel different. It's as if I'd finished a whole piece of my life, and I need to get on with a new part. Lolly, I realize now I felt kind of hopeless about everything but work. And now that's changing.'

Now we're getting to it, Lolly thought. Now he'll say why it's changed. No, don't. Her place mat was drying now, little puckers showing where her tears had fallen. The tears were drying inside her head, too. A different feeling was gathering up behind her eyes, replacing the misery. She tried to get the sadness back. I'll never see him again, she thought. I'll never sit across a table with him. Those hands will never touch me again, those nice hands. But the new hot feeling grew. The sadness floated away. Anger came.

'Lolly, I'm making you discontent with your husband, your home. Taking your attention from work, from your kids. You're too young, too vulnerable, and I'm a shit for doing it, it's all breaking over me now. Lolly. I'll always feel bad about doing this to you. But I'd feel worse doing it any longer.'

The bomb was materializing in Lolly's head, a bomb she could almost see, a homemade can with nails and ugly twisted pieces of metal, with dynamite. It was ticking in her head. I've been warned, she thought. I have the message, but there's more. There's something in that bomb that hasn't gone off yet. I'm waiting to hear about it, and you haven't set if off yet. And when you do, I'll blow up in a million pieces.

'You've met somebody else,' she said, thinking: why did the corniest words always express the biggest ideas?

'I think I have,' said Roe.

And the bomb went off, spattering pointed nails and black metal and fire sparks in Lolly's head. It went off so surely that she put her hands over her ears, surprised that her head was still intact.

'You think. What does that mean? You *have*. Who?'

He didn't answer, but there was no quiet. Rockets kept bursting, little explosions following the big one, light flashing behind her eyes, the way scenes lit up in her father's war movies in night explosions.

'Lolly, what difference does it make?'

The flashes suddenly lit up a scene for Lolly, a picture. A crowd, a round table. Roe was there in black, with a crumpled hankie spilling out of his breast pocket, and his arm around a woman, a familiar woman. He and the woman were laughing. She could see their heads thrown back, and the long, white throat of the woman. Lolly understood. Roe was in love with Domina Drexler. He'd laughed like that with her because they were in love, wild and crazy and not caring about anybody else, about her. Roe in love with that old bitch. And it wasn't even a surprise. She'd known it ever since that evening, really, felt it somehow.

'Domina Drexler.' It came out of her mouth like spit, the D's noisy and wet and disgusting.

'Maybe,' said Roe.

'Maybe? Why maybe?'

'Maybe just because she's appropriate, right, Lolly. Nearer my age. Grown children. No strings, no cheating. Baby, I know you'll never understand, it's got nothing to do with you, it's all what's happening to me. Let's talk about you. I want to know how you really feel about your husband. I've been taking you away from him – is that something you can fix? Because if you can't, I think you should face it, instead of passing the time with me, fix it and make something good happen for you, for your children. Your problem isn't me, Lolly, it's you. If you could fall in love with me, then there's something wrong at home,

189

there's not enough for you at home.'

The explosion was dying down in Lolly's head now, and the last bits were settling into a rumbling earth. He was shifting the blame, of course, heading her away from Domina Drexler, where the real pain was, back toward herself, where there was nothing. Handing her life back, and she didn't want it. Bill? Something wrong? What shit. She could handle Bill and more, nothing was wrong. She was just sexier, greedier than other girls, she wanted a husband and a lover too, and she wanted Roe. She wanted it all, and she had just lost the best part, because of Domina Drexler. Domina Drexler was making this happen, making Roe talk this way to her.

And the last time they were together he'd said he would belong to her forever. She remembered just how he'd said it. Liar. Bastard.

'You told me,' she said. 'You told me you'd stay as long as I wanted, you promised.'

Roe looked at her, crumpled, her pretty face mournful, streaked where the tears had been. Oh, God, he thought, this is just as awful as I thought it would be. She has no defenses. Jesus, I always fuck up. I fucked up a marriage, I'm fucking up her life. What could I have done? Told her more gently? Just faded out? Kept it up whatever else I did with other women? Well, she'll hate me, that's all. Christ, there's no way to have this conversation. Why don't I just go and get a plane ticket to Cairo? How did I get myself here? Christ, I'm almost twice her age. I'd had my biggest crisis, with my father, before she was even born. Poor baby.

For something to do, to break the tension, he waved at the waiter, ordered two bacon-and-cheeseburgers, rare, the way she liked them. She was young enough to be hungry, maybe it would distract her. And I know how it goes, the pain fades. The day comes when she'll think: what did I see in that old man? Did I cry over a stiff like him?

'Sweetheart, you said yourself you hated sneaking around, you knew it was wrong. Think a little. Why? You know you didn't want more of that. We were winding down, Lolly. Later on you'll see, it's better to stop.'

She was staring at him. 'I hated sneaking, that's right. I

190

hate you for making me sneak, when you were free, when you could have made it right, sure. I'll always hate you for that, Roe. You've got nerve, lecturing me now. You're something. All you're really interested in is sneaking around Domina Drexler, right? Will you take her to our hotel room. How is she in the sack? She looks like a bag of bones to me, what do you think?'

Roe felt as if she'd thrown her glass at him.

He reached over the table for her hand, but she pulled away.

'Go on, tell me,' she said. 'Tell me the whole thing. How long have you been fucking her? Where do you go? What do you do about her kids, don't they live with her anymore? Where's that ex-husband of hers, the no-good one they used to talk about? Are you helping her get a better job? Is that why she wants you? Tell me, Roe, tell me all about it.'

'Come on, Lolly,' Roe said wearily. 'Don't give me all this to remember, just let it go, okay? Let's have the good parts to think about, not all this stuff, it's not like you. It's not the way I want to remember you.'

'Tough shit,' said Lolly. 'You haven't started remembering me, yet. I'm still here, right here. Come on, Roe, tell me about Domina Drexler.'

'Let's go,' he said.

Lolly ignored him, her eyes blazing now, mouth set in a straight line.

'Finish the story,' she said furiously. 'Are you getting married? Does the company know? How does she feel about your being a Jew, or didn't you tell her?'

Roe stood up, loomed over her. 'I'm going now,' he said. 'You can get up and walk out that door with me like a lady, like someone I'll always be fond of. Or you can stay here and eat that hamburger. But I'm going now, before you say more things you'll be sorry I heard.'

'Oh, you're listening, are you? Well, I haven't started to say things, I'm just beginning.'

Roe put his hand on her shoulder lightly, and turned away, walking evenly out of the restaurant. He felt like a criminal walking away from a rape. Every eye in the room seemed to burn into his back. At the door, he felt the guilt.

He'd hurt her, and she'd never done anything but what he wanted. He'd hurt her badly, and she was a good kid. He'd hurt her in the worst way short of physical damage, and he'd live with that. And if he saw her ever, unexpectedly, it would wash over him again, shameful and ugly. But the thing was over.

Lolly watched him go. She sat, waiting for the devastation to settle in her mind, so she could leave, too. She never wanted to see this place again, ever. She imagined rocks, glass shards, bits of furniture, the whole room in smithereens around her. The way of her life would be from now on.

Were people looking at her? She glanced around, but no one seemed interested. Well, why would they be? No one ever noticed her except when she was with Roe.

Holy shit, and tonight I have to go home. I'll kill myself. Oh, wow, I've seen too many movies. I've seen this movie I'm in right now, sobbed all through it. Bette Davis was in this movie, and Joan Crawford, and Judy Garland sang all through it. And Domina's the other woman, but the heroine gets back at her before the end.

Lolly opened her purse and took out her compact. Surprisingly, her face looked the same way it always did. How peculiar, she thought, I expected to look wrecked, ruined, older, thinner, even.

She got up as smoothly as she could and went out. It was still lunch hour, and the crowds were hard to get through. Black kids on swift bicycles, with shrill whistles in their mouths, swooped the wrong way down the avenue. Horns tooted. She winced at a pair of kids in jeans holding hands as they walked. She felt empty, blank, like a sleepwalker. She moved along as fast as she could through all the people. Sidewalk vendors held up cheap shoes for her attention. The man selling falafel at her corner called out to her. Ordinary. Normal. Everything was the same. But she wasn't the same.

Back at her desk, a new stack of letters and memos. She glanced at the top one. Carroll Children's Day, a week away. Usually she looked forward to that.

Everyone brought their kids in the afternoon, and they

192

had a little party with balloons and games and ice cream. Mr Carroll wandered about like an old Santa Claus, patting the shining little heads and ignoring temper tantrums the best he could. Mostly it was fathers who brought in kids, and Lolly was pleased to be one of the few office mothers with attractive children to display. She always felt superior to the single girls, as if the children proved how well she could manage two jobs, how womanly she really was inside, despite her efficiency in the office.

Lolly also liked showing the children where Mommy worked, letting them poke at the big typewriter, make pictures with her pencils. Katie was old enough this year to ask questions, curtsey, be a credit to her. Katie, she thought. Would Katie grow up and have love affairs and end up feeling like this? Well, if she did, she'd have a mother who understood. Before I could tell my mother this, I'd have to kill myself. My mother couldn't even understand why I wanted a job. When I first told her about working, she said, 'But will you have to work in the summer, too?'

She opened the files again. At least that way, if anyone came by, she'd look industrious.

Staring down at them, still feeling drained, as if she'd dieted too long, Lolly saw all the little tabs dancing before her eyes. Red for hot, she thought. Blue for women. Women. Domina Drexler. She flipped to the D's, feeling a surge of misery.

There it was. A long paragraph. Schools. Courses. Children. Book. Bonnell, her reference, he loved her. Top-notch. Excellent prospect. Has changed positions, may change again.

Could Roe change again? Could he miss her and come back? If something went wrong between him and Domina? Could Lolly help make something go wrong?

She looked again at the card. It dawned on her slowly, deliciously. Roe and Domina worked in the same office. Jackson was one of Carroll's best accounts, agencies hired and fired a lot, always had people moving in and out. Old Mr Godwin talked to Mr Carroll all the time about new people, about placing people the agency wanted to get rid of quietly. The two men lunched often at some club or other.

She stared at the card, at all the little tabs.

Then she picked off a red tab from a card, the hot-prospect tab, and clipped it to Domina's card, nestled it neatly next to the blue tab. Red and blue glinted up at her, catching the light from her desk lamp because her hand was shaking a little. Changing the Carroll files. Immoral. She felt like a traitor.

For a moment she thought of adding the tab that would designate Domina as a drinker. No. Everyone knew the drinkers. In an office, the big brothers watched, but the real watchers were the people under you. Nobody fooled secretaries for long. She wished there was something more to do to Domina, though.

Lolly sat with the cards in her hand. Soon they'd all be back from lunch, she'd have to put the files away and go on to some other work. Hurry, she thought, do something.

What was left to look forward to? She'd go home on the lurching bus. It'd be filthy. Some of the passengers would talk to themselves, which depressed her terribly. So much misery in New York, millions of wretched people rattling home on gray nights to gray apartments. And she couldn't do a thing, even to hurt her true enemy, Domina Drexler.

She looked again at Domina's card. There was something.

She took the tabs off the card. Then she rolled the stiff oblong into her typewriter, centering it carefully so the line she was going to add would look exactly like the rest. Everything on the cards was current, and almost all of it was correct. Mr Carroll didn't make money on mistaken information. He said so, all the time.

Lolly switched on the typewriter and listened to it buzz. The sound seemed menacing, as if a wasp had flown into the room. Carefully she began.

'Contact complete. Urgently requests referrals. Willing inquiries at present position. Direct Brady Godwin, Creative Director, Jackson-NY. Will accept lower salary if necessary. Soonest.'

Exactly correct. The same words were on many of the cards with red tabs.

Lolly pulled it out and checked to make absolutely sure it looked right. Then she clipped the two little tabs back on top and slipped the card in its place in the huge Carroll files.

But she didn't feel better. In fact, she decided, she felt a lot worse. She'd adored her job, and now how could she look at these files again, ever, and feel proud, clever, knowledgeable? She'd remember cheating on them for her own selfish reasons. Nothing left to be happy about, she thought, and a huge, tough surfing wave of misery broke over her. She was drowning, underwater in misery.

Then as if a life jacket had been flung at her, had hit her body, Roe's words in the restaurant hit her: fix things at home. Make something happen for yourself, Lolly.

What could she do?

Well, people got divorced and started all over again. She wasn't terribly old. Roe had thought she was pretty, had loved her in bed. Maybe somebody else might think she was worth loving. But it was one idea to get a divorce for Roe. To get a divorce for nobody? Be alone with two babies? Manage everything? I couldn't.

Except, I manage now, don't I? I take care of everything for the kids, the apartment. Divorced, I could go home on a night like this and cuddle up in an old nightgown with the kids, watch late television, the old movies Bill hates because he wants to fuck and I won't come to bed. I could do whatever I wanted. No shirts to take to the laundry. No big meals to bother with. No evenings with his dumb friends.

And if I did get a divorce, and I stopped pretending, sneaking, then maybe I'd find someone else. If Roe came back then, I wouldn't have to sneak. I'd be all ready for him. I could go to a health club and get skinny, beautiful.

She closed her eyes and saw, in her mind, a card with her name on it, with lots of little tabs stuck on top. 'Urgent,' the card said. 'Will accept referrals, less money if necessary. Wants freedom to move. Soonest.'

Could she handle it? Lolly wondered. Oh, could she?

Domina

Meeting Detroit Rouge Plant Sept. 26
introductory planning Blossom, 9:30
A.M. Mrs Drexler, Mr Rossen for
Jackson, Brand Group for Ford.

Domina watched the chauffeur lift the flat black carrying case with the ads out of the limousine while Roe gave their plane tickets to the waiting porter. They went through the automatic doors to the terminal. Domina felt, crazily, that Roe should have picked her up, carried her through the doors like a bride. A beginning, she thought, her first trip to Detroit, their first trip together.

She settled for the touch of his hand on her elbow as he guided her toward the gate. It was, of course, the farthest gate, the way it always seemed to be. I don't care, she thought. I'm on my way to Detroit, to Ford, with Roe Rossen, to a car account all my own. The Blossom. Beautiful. Not a woman on Madison Avenue who supervises a car. Except me. And with Roe? Marvelous.

It was so early that the bookshops and gift shops were just opening. Even the groups of kids with crew-cut hair who handed out religious literature were still lumped together in the lounges, half-asleep. Outside the huge La Guardia windows the sun was coming up fast. The sharp glare illuminated every stray cigarette butt and scrap of paper on the terrazzo floor. Who cares, thought Domina. I'm going to Dearborn, with Roe Rossen. Right now I don't even care about coffee.

'Coffee?' said Roe, as if he'd read her mind.

'There'll be some on the plane.'

'Sure. But you can have some now, too. My treat.'

By now he knew she drank twelve cups a day, felt lost without coffee in her hand – in paper, plastic, or china. But Domina knew it would slow their trip to the gate, and she also knew how eager he was to get moving.

'I'll wait,' she said.

They passed through the electronic security, walking the long path to their plane. All the way, Domina's heart sang. Her own car. Everyone knew how Detroit felt about women. For years, out of Ford had come ads showing languorous beauties draped seductively across the hoods of cars. Copy told women how to choose the color of car upholstery. Commercials showed glamorous men driving lovely girls along coast roads in California. Never any ads that showed women at the wheel, or changing tires, or driving a carload of kids. Never even the suggestion that a woman might actually pay for her own car. Showed how the ad men in Detroit looked at women. But now, change.

When Roe had told her, after the Israeli promotion far exceeded all estimates for sales, that he wanted her on his account, she had felt herself relax into a vast happiness. Even the grapevine around the agency – that they were forcing a woman onto the Ford account, not for her competence, but because the government was querying racist and sexist hiring – didn't bother her. For once, she thought, the government's helping *me*. And if Roe wanted her near him at work, if he trusted her to handle one of his precious cars, who cared who had caused it?

They sat in the waiting space at the gate, Roe checking his case. Domina watching him. He looked terrific, she thought happily. The soft, heathery tweed jacket was different from the blazers on all the other men sitting with their newspapers open. The khaki pants made him look like a college boy, and so did his loafers, not the Guccis everyone else wore, but real penny loafers like the ones her own boy always chose. His face seemed to have lost some of its lines in the past few weeks, she thought. But then, Roe, when he was pleased looked utterly different from Roe displeased. She'd never known anyone whose feelings so completely affected his looks. When she'd first worked with him on the Israel promotion, he'd seemed older, stern, lines gathering around his eyes. Now, she thought, his face looks bright, alert, ready for pleasure. Is it the cars? I know he loves Detroit.

But can some of it be me? In a few months of lunches and dinners, have I erased a line or two? Heaven knows he makes me feel younger, better, softer. Not prettier. I've never been pretty. Beautiful for a few, chic for a lot of people, but never what they call pretty. Pretty is snub noses and blond curls. Pretty is M.J. And my own Maria, now that she's discovered boys at school, she's prettier each time she comes home. Even Leota's said so.

Roe frowned a few more lines into his face as he scanned the financial pages. Domina wondered if Maria would like him, if Roe would get on with her. College sophomores could be dreadful in conversations with businessmen. Especially economics majors. And Roe had no kids. He could turn out to be a severe judge, and Maria was never the girl to sidestep a battle of ideas. Well, Domina thought, let's get through this trip, and then I'll worry about my kids liking him.

Funny, she thought suddenly, I don't worry about whether he'll get on with Michael. I know he'd be terrific with Michael. Why? He's easy to talk to. A little sports news, film talk, vacation plans, a cinch. Maria is so intense about everything. At least she's not like Maran's daughter. Abortions, drug busts, and Maran feeling horribly guilty. Maria's a darling. I just wish she'd grow up past the point where she hates having a mother in advertising. She'd like me a lot better if I lived among lepers, Navahos, mental patients. But she'll change, I understand. Could Roe understand?

The ticket agent called for the first-class passengers, and Roe folded his paper in one neat gesture. They walked through to the last row of the first compartment, where she could smoke. She could give up coffee to let Roe keep moving ahead, but cigarettes, never.

To her disappointment, they worked almost all the way, Roe showing her figures, lists of names, organization charts she'd have to understand. They worked even over their breakfast trays. Pancakes that seemed carved out of flannel. Fake maple syrup in sticky cartons. Whipped butter that clung to the insides of paper wrappers. Domina sighed and reached for her coffeecup. Weak as tea. Leota had spoiled her forever.

By the time she'd finished, the no-smoking sign blinked

on, then the seat-belt warning. As she reached for her clasp, she touched Roe's hand for an instant. It felt warm, dry, a little rough. She concentrated on the clasp, looking down at it in case she was pink in the face. For heaven's sake, she thought, get a hold of yourself. When you wanted him to stop, he stopped. Now you want him to start, and he's not playing. Get your timing right.

The plane swooped down, bumped, and settled into a slow roll toward the gate. When it came to a stop, all the first-class passengers were crowding the door, in spite of the best efforts of the stewardesses. Business, thought Domina. Nobody gets in its way.

Roe reached past a fat man to get at his carrying case, took Domina's arm firmly. He knew the Detroit airport perfectly, all the shortcuts for cabs, car rentals, hotels.

He watched Domina's long legs climb the steps toward the exit as he moved just in back of her. What nice legs, he thought. No wonder she looks so good in pants, but a shame to hide legs like that. Glad she wore a skirt out here. Better for the guys at Ford. Old-fashioned. They're probably expecting to see her dressed in black suit, sensible shoes, glasses. You'll never catch this lady in sensible shoes. I'd like to catch her. Put my hand on that ankle and hold on. Wish I could get out of this crowd. I'd take her through that passageway to the airport hotel, right up to a room on the top, quiet, spend the afternoon there with her in bed. Take those high heels off her feet very slowly. And all the rest of her things.

Forget it. Not now. She's got to be a hit, now. Ford and Domina Drexler, got to make sure it works.

Into a taxi. While they drove the ugly highway out to Dearborn, he gave her a schedule for the day, a warning about the toughest traps. She'd be given a chance to drive the prototype of the Blossom, probably over Ford's test track. The prototype would be made of fiberglass, delicate, unique, hideously expensive. All the engineers would be standing around watching a woman handle their precious model. The track would have obstacles, high rises, pits, gravel, zigzag patches, and she must take the car around that track smoothly. She would be the first woman who ever

201

drove it. She must appear to grasp the diagrams they would show her, blueprints, plans, whether she understood the technical talk or not. She must speak out in a good, strong voice, especially in the big presentation room, where the long U-shaped table made it difficult to be heard. She must eat lunch in the executive dining room, where women never penetrated, alone among all men, without embarrassment. Roe poured it all out while the cab sped past the used-car lots.

Domina listened carefully, her dark eyes wide with concentration.

God, he thought, how beautiful she is.

They reached the Rouge, a place Roe loved. The heart of American industry, he always thought when he arrived. Reginald Marsh could have drawn the scene. They drove past the carriers, unloading limestone from Michigan, coal from Pennsylvania, iron ore from Minnesota. They turned to look at the wall of fire that was the blast furnace, where steel was changed into slabs of metal that would become cars. The Rouge was a city, built to make Model A Fords in 1929, converted to an assembly plant for submarine chasers during the Second War, converted back into a complex of machines that created more than a thousand cars every day. He watched it all, looking past Domina's elegant profile as she drank it all in. Will she see what I see? he wondered. The energy, the magic in this place?

Domina looked serene enough, he thought. She hadn't stopped for the ladies' room, powdered her nose, fussed at the end of a trip, like other women. How different she is, he thought.

As the car slowed, Domina began to feel the fear.

There was always terror at moments like this. There had to be. Everything that would happen now would be important. A silly remark, a laugh in the wrong place, a stupid question, could start the whole relationship with the client off badly. She would be on display. And this time, she would represent not just her agency, but her tribe, the whole world of women's work. Terror. A thickening of the throat, an urge to blink too often, a weakness in the knees, a knot in the stomach. And nobody must catch one glimpse.

Well, Roe's here, she thought. But somehow that makes this even more frightening. I want to do wonderfully for him.

Receptionists. Passes. Elevators. Introductions, hand-shakes. Men in neat suits, men with sharp blue eyes, men with gleaming shoes. 'Howdy,' they said, and, 'Pleased to meet you.' She smiled and smiled, shook hands firmly, looked straight into all the blue eyes. Jesus on the Cross, she thought, do they get these guys from the Jackson television casting department? They all look exactly the way I'd imagined. It isn't possible they're real.

One of the men turned to Roe, slapped him on the rear like a football player. 'Change for you, old buddy,' he said. 'Shift in our lineup today. Switch play at the top. Foster's going over to trucks. We're getting Barber.'

She watched Roe absorb this news, frowning a little. What was wrong? Foster, Barber, who cared? All these men seemed interchangeable, like car parts.

'Never met him,' she heard Roe say. 'Sorry to lose Tom, he'd have liked our creative lady, here. Barber's first name is, wait a minute. Harrow? Harrell?'

Domina thought: he's good, a great account man. That was exactly right. A bow to the old guy. A bead on the new one. Even the slip for his name, to show he doesn't grind away at his job, just stays on top of Ford executive charts naturally. Harrell Barber? Good Christ, another backward name? Another management creep?

Now they were all walking in a group, evidently toward a conference room. Roe turned his head toward her, fixed her eye with his. He wanted to tell her something, was that it? She tried to read his mind, but couldn't. Well, they couldn't confer privately now. Let it go. She made con-versation with the man next to her about the trip out.

In the room, a medium-sized one, they settled in around a long table. The table held ashtrays at each place, she was glad to see, and a block of yellow paper next to each one. No pencils? Ford men are probably wired to their pencils, she thought, nobody'd dare come in here without one of his own. Her own gold pen was in its proper pocket in her handbag. Score one, she thought.

The chair at the head of the table was left empty. Presumably, for Harrell Barber. He's the most important, the one we all wait for, we don't start without. She saw one of the men setting up an easel. Charts? Drawings? What went on in a new-car introductory meeting, anyway? Roe had never told her, he'd been so busy getting the names straight for her, the procedures.

The door opened and all the heads turned, the conversation stopped abruptly.

Harrell Barber was not like the rest of the men, she saw immediately. He was black. Tall, black and handsome, she thought quickly, surprised. His navy-blue suit fit to perfection, his wedding ring was chased gold and matched his small tie pin, his white collar seemed made of paper, it was starched into such stiff splendor. Well, well, there's something Roe didn't tell me. A black man for a Ford client. Now, what would Brady Godwin think about that?

Roe shot her a look while Harrell Barber turned around to shut the door, but the look was gone by the time Barber approached his seat. Domina was primed. She looked directly at her new client and smiled. Her curiosity was boiling up. Who was he? How had he made it up so high in such a conservative organization? He could be a token black, of course, his looks were certainly right. He could be a fighter, too, extra clever to get where he was. Well, she would soon find out.

She heard Roe saying the words to introduce her, and reached across the broad table to shake hands. Mr Barber's black hand felt cool and hard. His smile was nice, and his voice fascinating, deep, unaccented, even. This is going to be one fascinating account, she thought. These men and this boss? A woman and a black for these fellows to contend with, both at the same time? Minorities of the world, unite.

Harrell looked at the agency team across the table. The woman was interesting. Different from agency ladies he'd read about in trade magazines. Those women had looked grim. Perhaps it had just been the way photographers pictured them. Come to think of it, every photographer he'd ever met was a man. This lady reminded him of the few girls who had been in the Business School, smart, alert, attractive. He supposed all those girls had gone on to jobs like Domina Drexler's, good, high-paying ones. Funny, he hadn't thought about those girls at all once he'd left school. Women at Ford were almost as out-of-place as blacks. His own immediate superior, whose office was precisely one-third larger than Harrell's, and who was given a new car four times a year to Harrell's twice, kept a book on the coffee table in his office. *Everything I Know About Women* was the title, and the whole book consisted of blank pages. Harrell felt a wave of sympathy for this woman.

Roe he'd heard about when he'd worked in the truck division. All the guys said he was good. Well, he'd have a surprise for Roe Rossen this afternoon, after these prelimi-naries. A little test for an agency man's devotion, to see if Roe really was right for this spot. Harrell had developed a habit of making one unreasonable demand early in a relationship. The reaction to that demand determined his first opinions. If Roe should be unnerved, negative, Harrell would know from the start. But if Roe took the demand in stride, and managed his creative person easily too, then he'd know this was a promising team. Harrell needed to have the sense of these people as early as possible. This move to luxury cars was the break he'd been waiting for. A man could go only so high in trucks. Top-line cars were the focus of the company. They were driven by top manage-ment, for one thing. Received the most exciting advertising – not mass, but class space. Harrell wanted the best on this first campaign. He hadn't made many mistakes in his career so far. There weren't going to be any now, if he could head them off. A black man has to produce more than other people, he believed. He'd managed his life that way, and he wasn't about to change. If the Blossom turned out to be a success, it would mean promotion, raises, the heights.

Domina listened intently as the meeting began. Charts. Figures. Sketches of the car. The idea behind the car, explained to her in simple terms. Total luxury in an Amer-ican car. Features hitherto found only in European models. A car women would adore. Small turning radius. Easy steering. Automatic everything. Designer interiors. Easy-access doors. Foldaway wheel. Sun roof. Domina began to understand why they'd allowed her to work on this car. It had been designed with women in mind, for once, she thought. Or fags. They'd like all these frills, too. Not exactly a macho truck, she thought, but we all have to begin somewhere. So I've been brought out to handle a female car. The way Thunderbird used to be called a fat man's fat car. Okay. But no power on earth is going to get me to do ads with girls in evening gowns lying across windshields. She suddenly remembered how scared she'd been. Silly. Nothing to worry about. No errors yet, no false steps, just an open road.

She'd always felt advertising was marvelous work for women. We learn young how to manipulate, coax, push without seeming to. Clients, who pay the bills and want action, are all like men, used to being obeyed. We treat our clients like old-fashioned husbands and fathers, and it works perfectly. And we know how to juggle everything, the way women know. Men want one thing to handle at a time; we know how to put down the baby and pick up the pots, separate the fighting kids, and get dinner on the table. It's terrific training.

She thought about the Potter Jackson management. They'd like to be treated like clients, like husbands and fathers, too, she realized suddenly. That's my trouble, I can't do it inside the agency. Somehow I get demanding, tough, what they always call masculine, ballsy. What a mess. Men act the way they feel, and succeed. Women have to hide the way they feel to get anywhere. Will it ever change?

Now they were all getting up, pushing back their chairs. Oh, yes, the test drive, the tour. Roe had said they test-crashed one car every day at Ford. Please God she wasn't going to crash anything. Harrell was leading the way to the front of the building. Good-byes to some of the faces. Now there were only five of them – a carload, she realized. We're going for a ride.

Into a van at the door, lurching on the rough roads toward an enormous oval track. Out of the van. Domina looked at the track, appalled.

Of all she'd feared, the track for testing cars was the worst. It looked like an endless road, with terrible obstacles set every fifty feet. The most terrifying was a steep little mountain for a car to climb up, slide down. But equally dreadful was a wide gravel patch. A zigzag track. A muddy place. A watery pit. A sharp turn, a loop. Holy Mother of God, thought Domina, I can't get into a car and ride around that.

Fear came bubbling up into her throat. This meant exposure to a secret she'd kept, even from Roe. Especially from Roe.

Domina couldn't drive.

In Elkhart, her family had been too poor even for a secondhand car. In Chicago they'd had a jalopy of Stephen's, jealously guarded by him. And then, in New York, there had been no question of a car. People in New York hired limos, took cabs.

When the invitation to work on Ford had come through, Domina had quietly telephoned a driving school. But she couldn't get the knack. The instructors had been dismayed. Her kids had been thunderstruck. Something Mom couldn't handle, when she handled so much, so easily. Every lesson worse. After she'd nearly driven the instructor into the side of a building, Domina gave up. I can't do everything, she decided. The hell with it.

Not for anything would she have admitted to the Ford people her terror, her ineptitude. Ford people drove cars the way most people breathed. She'd have died if they'd known how petrified she was. Roe had said an engineer would probably take them around, though there was a chance she'd be asked to handle the car. Fiberglass. Did that mean it was actually made of glass?

Inevitably, like her worst panic coming true, she felt Harrell turn toward her. 'Want to take her around?'

Holy shit, thought Domina. I'll kill myself. I'll smash it. They'll kill me.

They all watched her. One of the men grinned, which decided her. 'Love to,' she said, a little too loudly.

Here goes nothing, she thought, and got into the car. The engineer leaped into the passenger seat. Straight ahead loomed the artificial mountain. Up. Down. Oh, my God.

'Take it nice and slow, we all do,' said the young man in the jumpsuit. 'This one has no emergency brake. Just put your foot down, turn her on, and she'll go.'

Domina did as she was told. As the car moved slowly forward, everything seemed to blur, dissolve in front of her. Steer, she thought, you only have to steer, there's no traffic, no competition – that was your biggest problem. Steer straight, that's all. She felt horror at the steep angle, her back pressed hard against the seat, her head in the air, as they went up, for what felt like miles. What would happen at the top. Roller coaster, she thought wildly, that awful moment when you hit the top and plunge sickeningly, horribly down. Holy Mary, Mother of God.

Down was a relief, not as ghastly as she'd thought. Ahead of down lay flat roads, normal levels. Domina moved none of the knobs or pedals, kept it at the same speed, clung rigidly to the wheel, holding it straight. She could feel a trickle of perspiration from the back of her neck, dripping. She thought in a flash: it won't show in what I'm wearing, they won't know.

Then they were on the zigzag.

The car shimmied frantically, but Domina hung on.

'You steer with it, Mrs Drexler,' said the engineer patiently. 'You wouldn't know, of course, just steer with the pattern.'

Domina had no idea what she'd done, was doing, but the rattles and bumps ended suddenly. Gravel and mud and water? No, the worst is over, she thought, it must be. I got down that fucking mountain.

The turns and loops, thank God, were at the far end, yards and yards away from the little crowd watching her go around. Once or twice the engineer steadied the wheel for her. She was sure no one could see what he'd done to help her.

She came down the straightaway to the beginning. Inside her clothes, she was sopping. Her fingers hurt from their grip on the wheel. She felt exhausted, drained, relieved. She wanted to get out and lie down on the soft green grass around the track. Idiot's luck, she thought. I'm alive, he's alive, the car is, too. If they make me president of a car company, I'll never, never do that again.

Roe smiled at her, as she leaned against the hood, pretending to admire the lines, steadying her legs.

'Fantastic,' Domina said to him as loudly as she could, for the clump of men to hear. It's me that's fantastic, she thought. Hot stuff, racing driver, that's me. Wait till I tell Maran, she'll laugh for years. No joke. What would she do without her best friend? She'd be sorry if I crumpled to death test-driving a model car.

They all got back in the van, waited while Roe took the car around. Domina leaned her head on the leatherette back of her seat. She didn't even watch. She resisted drowsiness. The men all joined her in the van. Roe was enthusiastic about the car, gesturing happily to Harrell.

They drove – on level ground, smooth ground, thought Domina – to the plant. It seemed vast, incredibly noisy, unbelievably busy and buzzing. Foremen in goggles riding bikes or on roller skates to cover the huge area. Fires. Machines. Assembly lines. Ropes of wire stretched overhead, crisscrossing the enormous ceiling. Domina accepted a pair of heavy goggles, stretched their elastic over her head. They made her feel idiotic, like a frogman. Well, she thought, nobody would expect conversation from her in this hubbub.

They walked. Up iron stairs to a catwalk over a gas furnace. Steel glowing vermilion, enormous slabs radiating heat. Rollers sliding the slabs through clouds of steam, magically spinning out to a steel ribbon. Down the steps. Leave the goggles. Back in the van.

Assembly plant now. Harrell leaned forward to say something. She caught a whiff of lavender as he came close. His wife puts lavender in the bureau with his shirts, she thought. Figures. Concentrate, he was telling her figures. Twenty-eight hundred pieces to assemble. Parts gliding along nine miles of assembly line. Converging at the end, she'd see, he said. Thank God she'd worn comfortable clothes. Suppose I need a bathroom? she thought. Well, I can't, that's all. Anyway, there are women here, there'd have to be a ladies' room. Women in overalls and boots.

Sisters, thought Domina. Thank God I typed my way, out of Elkhart, away from a job like this.

When they got to the final assembly line, she stopped, transfixed.

Domina had toured dozens of factories. Advertising copy always began with a trip to the plant. She'd seen cookies coated by rivers of chocolate. Lipsticks creamed in huge vats, looking like rosy soup. Drugs handled by workers in surgical masks and rubber gloves. She'd seen hand lotion blended, coffee roasted in huge ovens, cereal puffed up by blasts of air. She'd always been intrigued, fascinated by the way things were made – simple, ordinary, taken-for-granted things.

But this? Who could have imagined that cars were made like this? Who could have pictured it? Was there a sight like this anywhere else in the world?

Way up over her head, what seemed to be millions of car parts journeyed slowly to a central place, like parts of a star joining together. Red, blue, silver, copper, black. Fenders, tops, hoods, radiators. All gliding majestically toward the middle and crashing together perfectly. No chance for a red fender on a black car, a white door on a green body. This was computerized perfection. Domina thought: computers in banks seem to go wrong all the time, at least with my checking statements they do. Why not here? She watched, but the cars fitted together perfectly, in endless succession.

The finished cars floated down to the floor, where workers seemed to attack them, like meat-cutters on a large animal. Welders, men with wrenches, men loading in dashboards and seats, women with hoses squirting fuel and coolant. Harrell explained, shouting, told her about the spare parts and the keys placed in each trunk by the very last worker. After that, men took turns driving the cars away, to alignment tests, engine tests, car washes. Every fifty-four seconds, another car. Fantastic, she thought.

Outside the air was welcome. So was the quiet. Roe was deep in talk with Harrell. She saw Roe nod. He came close to her. 'Can you stay overnight? He wants to do the rest tomorrow. Has a lot of stuff to finish from his old desk. He'd like you to stay, okay?'

'Overnight? I haven't any clothes. But if that's what the client wants, fine.'

Her head still rang with the noise. Mesmerizing, she thought, that slow floating of parts to the center, that crash of the joining.

More good-byes, handshakes, and they were alone, heading back to the reception area. Someone had called another taxi. Someone had called the Dearborn Inn. Domina leaned back in her seat, feeling hammered, blasted, rolled out, exhausted.

The inn was beautiful, even before she saw the front door. Like Williamsburg, she thought, an old-hotel look, columns and porches, beautiful. The door was amazing, red, fat, welcoming. In the lobby a buzz of guests, more navy-blue suits, more car men at the bar. Stairs, wide and carpeted. Tremendous room. Fireplace. Four-poster bed. Cream heirloom quilt. The world's thickest towels.

'Listen,' Roe said. 'It's not five yet. Call your favorite Detroit store, get them to send you what you need for tonight, tomorrow. Jackson will take care of it, it's client business. Why don't you get a rest, and I'll take you into town for dinner, the Chop House. Or would you rather stay here?'

'The Chop House,' said Domina. She could see he liked the idea, probably wanted a big steak. The food here was bound to be kind of colonial, relishes in trays, creamy desserts.

She closed her door, went to the phone, and did as he'd said, ordering expansively. Nightgown, a Pucci. Toothbrush, toothpaste, hairbrush, comb, Chanel cologne and soap. Skirt, a Calvin Klein she'd tried in New York and knew would fit. The matching blouse in two sizes, eight and ten, because she wasn't sure which would be right. Pantyhose. Messenger out to the inn by eight o'clock. Bill included. She gave her New York charge number at Saks, her American Express card. It all took fifteen minutes. Would every suggestion Roe Rossen made be as efficient, as simple to carry out?

She took a bath, floating in the hot water, feeling the assembly-line noises recede from her mind, the suggestion of a delicious evening taking over. She had to get back into her clothes to open the door for the messenger, but by seven-thirty she was as ready as she'd have been at home. She called his room. He was starving.

Still another cab, now the taller buildings in town looming ahead of them against the evening sky. Empty streets in mid-Detroit. Closed doors, blank windows, a few people scurrying fast to their homes. A dead city, she thought. Roe told her everyone lived out of town, all the car people they worked with. The new hotel showed some lights and life, but everywhere else seemed unusually quiet to a New Yorker.

The restaurant was lively, after the dark streets. Around the walls hung framed awards, just like her own ad awards, Domina thought. Roe was happy. He ordered for them. Vodka martinis. Thick steaks. Baked potatoes. Creamed onions. A huge pot of coffee. They didn't talk much, just relaxed in the noisy room, cutting, buttering, sipping. Domina was so warmed from her drink, she floated hazily through the rest of the food, eating one bite for every three of Roe's.

'We can have a brandy when we go back,' he said, when all the coffee from the second pot had been emptied. He signed a check, patted a waiter's shoulder, and they were gone again. What a life, Domina thought. How wonderful not to be a lady welder. How terrific not to be a housewife. How marvelous to float along in the half-dark toward that four-poster bed, like part of a car along a pre-destined path to a central spot. Roe's floating too, she thought. And I'm a little drunk. In love with his beautiful hands and unruly hair and special voice and his untied shoe.

When they reached the red door she stumbled a little on the step, and Roe put out his arm. She could feel the muscle in his shoulder, smell the freshness of his heathery tweed coat. Then she realized he had not let go. She turned to look at his face, straight into his eyes.

Like the assembly line, she thought, as he moved with her up the stairs, we're gliding toward the one place in the world we both want to be this minute.

When he'd shot the bolt on her door, they came together

on the wide bed, with the same thundering sound in Domina's head she'd heard all afternoon in the plant.

She knew he was freeing her from her clothes, but his hands moved so gently and slowly that she relaxed, closed her eyes. Cold air on her neck, her shoulders, then her breasts, made her shiver a little. Then his hands were at her feet, easing off her shoes, kneading, stroking her legs. How had he known how tired she'd felt? Now he moved his warm hand slowly up her body. Somehow she was out of her skirt, and the touching went on, sending electric shocks out of her hands and toes. When he stopped for an instant, moving to sweep her clothes off the bed, she suddenly felt hungry, desolate, cold.

When she forced her eyes to open, there was Roe getting out of his clothes like a fireman on fire. He yanked, pulled, unbuttoned, dropped his shirt, kicked out of his shoes. He was back at her side quickly, his body burning.

He reached for her hair, his fingers searching out the pins that held it. One by one she felt them slip out, taking her control with them, leaving her feeling as light and free as her own dark hair brushing against her breasts. Roe picked up great fistfuls of her hair, buried his face in it as if he'd wanted to for a long, long time. Domina felt her breath catch, the shivering take over her body.

After what seemed an age of stroking, smoothing, touching her everywhere, his fingers moved to explore her inside. Now he was circling, rubbing gently, caressing, making her back arch closer to him. Her arms and legs seemed to melt away as she focused on the urgent sensations where his hand moved. She stretched upward, moved to rub all of her against the length of his body, lifted her hands to fondle the back of his neck, feel all down his spine, clutch him closer.

The first marvelous times with Stephen came into her mind, the wonder of being the only two people in the world. She had loved his athlete's body and hard hands. But Stephen had been rough, boyish, not like this, not like Roe, now.

And when she couldn't bear it, Domina stretched away from him, sat up straight, eager, desperately impatient.

'Now,' she said. 'Please. Now.'

As if he'd been unleashed. Roe covered her with all his body, thrust deep inside her. She felt him filling her, barreling into her as if he would drive straight through her back. Above her his face frowned, strained with urgency, tension. She wrapped her arms and legs around him, helping him, easing him.

And Domina began to burn, to soar, grew hotter and brighter like a Catherine wheel whirling and bursting in the night sky, scattering drops of fire into the dark air. She felt all blazing light, blue and green and orange, white-hot and dazzling over the whole world.

When she came back to sense she wondered how long, how late, what next. Clothes. Alarm clock. Early meeting.

But when she turned her head cautiously to look at Roe, he reached for her again, holding her close, tight, as if he never wanted to let her go.

Warmed, fulfilled, complete, Domina snuggled into the welcome of his body, curled into the haven of his arm.

Harrell

John Harrell Barber
Ford Division
Ford Motor Company
Rouge Plant
Dearborn, Michigan

> Vice-president, marketing associate in truck line.
> Employed since 1970.
> Born Montgomery, Alabama, 1946. Educated
> Andover Academy, Mass., Yale College, magna
> cum laude, 1967. Harvard Business School, 1970.
>
> Married Christine Chase 1972. Children: Samuel
> Johnson Barber 1974, James Boswell Barber 1976.
> Home address unlisted, confidential.
>
> Notes: Top ratings each year except 1973,
> second-place runner-up to top performance.
> Winner George Washington Carver Medal,
> scholarship, Montgomery 1961. Salary 1978
> $90,000, total compensation $131,000 including
> deferred compensation, insurance, car privileges,
> profit-sharing, management-incentive plan,
> stock-option plan, bonus. Highest
> recommendation any marketing opening.
>
> Contact refused. Never interviewed by Carroll
> direct. No interest in move to date.

Harrell walked into The Potter Jackson Company's conference room ahead of his two assistants. All the agency people were already there, and all of them stood up.

I wish my father had lived to see this, he thought.

Introductions. He concentrated on the faces. Domina Drexler again, with her staff this time. A young man in shirtsleeves, the writer. Another young man with a beard, the art director. A stunning tiny girl with pumpkin-colored hair, the art assistant. They were all on the far side of the table, where easels and bulletin boards were ready to show the ads. The account men moved around the room to shake hands, greet him more formally. Rossen, of course. His second-in-command, Dan Trueman, freckled, pleasant, alert. Another, younger account man, a junior. Harrell knew that big agencies always hired one account executive for each client. That way, equals worked with each other. An important client never dealt with an agency assistant. A young, inexperienced client never made stupid demands on top agency personnel. Interesting system, he thought, but expensive for the agency. Well, they make plenty on us. Fifteen percent of Ford advertising. Probably their most profitable account, millions. Budget for the Blossom is eight million, and that's small for us.

The table was filled now. At its head sat Brady Godwin, the man Roe had introduced as the agency's overall creative director. Familiar type, Harrell decided, a lot like management men at Ford, big, handsome, expressionless. He was pleased that Godwin was at the meeting, though. Showed how the agency felt about the account, that a top executive had come to kick the meeting off formally. Different from the agency I used in Detroit for the trucks, he thought. An antique cart with coffee and stuff, and so help me, here comes a man in a white coat to serve it.

While the coffee was being handed around. Harrell looked at the room. Beautiful. The whole place paneled with carved mahogany, even the ceiling. Twin brass chandeliers hung over the huge table, polished until they looked as if they were wet. There were actually candles in the chandeliers, not light bulbs. One whole wall of the room was cabinet-work, with corkboard beautifully fitted into the moldings. The chairs looked like Chippendale, carved open backs and padded seats covered in heavy satin. Satin for a business meeting, he thought, imagine that. He'd heard that Jackson owned a fortune in antiques. All very well, but I want to see what the ads look like.

The ads for his car, his Blossom, had to be the best in the history of the automobile. Hard work on trucks had taken him this far in the company. But no truck got the attention that a luxury car would, especially this luxury car. He'd felt his hands get damp with excitement when he'd first seen the prototype. Every car magazine, every engineering trade paper, every financial-newspaper editor would pay attention to this car. The Blossom looked different from most American cars, longer, sleeker, rounder than anything since the twenties. Great gas mileage, too. And if he made the Blossom sell, the Blossom would make him a top man in the industry. Probably the best-known black man in the business. It had happened to a handful of car people. McNamara, Iacocca, right back to Henry Ford. Started with a car model and wound up multimillionaires.

He stopped dreaming, because Roe was on his feet getting ready to start. Everyone had coffee, most of them halfway through plump doughnuts and crullers. Funny, how they'd all asked for Sweet'n Low and then wolfed down all those calories. Harrell had accepted only black coffee. He'd missed his morning run, and he wasn't taking a chance on gaining weight. No fat men in top management, he thought, amused. Someone did a study on it, and after that, every ambitious man in America joined a gym.

'I think we can start,' Roe was saying. 'There's a lot of stuff to show you today, so I'll just explain how we'd like to

217

handle the meeting. Domina's going to present the ads, and we'll pin everything up as we go along. Then, when you've seen it all, I'll come back to give you our recommendation. But first, I've asked Dan here to do a quick review of the sales objectives and strategy. Dan?'

Harrell felt himself tense, his back straightening away from his chair. Now we'll see. Those first meetings out in Detroit were preliminaries, getting to know them. He'd liked Roe and Domina, but it would be their work that would count. Roe talked straight, anyway. So many ad men talked bullshit. And both Roe and Domina got to the point fast. Furthermore, they'd passed his little test, his asking them to stay in Detroit an extra day, and they'd been quick and alert through all the long meetings. He looked at Roe across the conference table. Someone had said Roe was Jewish, last thing Harrell would have guessed. Not that he gave a damn. He'd spent his life being the one dark face in every crowd; maybe Rossen had done the same. And there's Domina, different, too. *Vive la différence*, he thought, and began to listen hard. Dan Trueman had covered the sales objectives quickly, but that wasn't what Harrell had come to hear. He knew those objectives better than anyone else. What he wasn't sure about was how to advertise the Blossom, how to do a campaign that would make everyone in America want his car. But Harrell was sure he'd know the right campaign when he saw it. He hoped desperately that he'd see it this morning.

The room was quiet now. Harrell noticed that Roe's eyes were on Dan. But Brady Godwin's eyes were everywhere, checking out clients' expressions. Management men at Ford did that, got ready to smile when the boss smiled, jump when the boss jumped. Well, he's old, thought Harrell, and he hasn't lasted in this business without second-guessing his clients.

Now the art director was pinning up a sketch. There on the wall were the sleek lines and luscious curves of the Blossom.

Domina was getting up now. Her writer fellow was producing a big pile of layouts from under the table.

218

Domina put a hand on top of the pile and looked straight at Harrell.

'Harrell, we've got four basic campaign ideas. Each is executed in several ways, so there's a lot of material here. We wanted to offer you a choice of advertising at this stage, rather than put all our thoughts into just one campaign.'

Either she works hard or she's just churning up a lot of action to impress me, Harrell thought.

'I'll present the overall campaigns, and Davy here will read you the headlines and rough copy for each one. Mark, our head art director, and M.J., his assistant, will explain the visuals if you have questions. When you've seen it all, I'll give our recommendation. And it's a work session, so interrupt whenever you want.'

Organized, thought Harrell. Good.

'Go ahead,' he said.

Suddenly, startlingly, the young girl shoved back her chair. It squeaked loudly, the sound of old wood and stiff joints shrill in the quiet room. Her hand on the table flashed a sparkle of diamonds from a big ring.

She spoke, though it clearly wasn't her moment.

'Mark, honey? Just let me get this old chair out of your way, so you can be comfortable? If I scrunch back here by the wall, then you can get nice and close to the bulletin board, okay?'

Like the stab of an electric shock, her voice shot through Harrell's mind, jolting him out of this time and place. Her tone seemed totally familiar and totally unexpected, both at the same time. Her pronunciation was out of his child-hood, but out-of-place in this room, among these people. A soft, slurred purr, every note as purely Alabama as if it had been delivered from the State House steps. Good Lord, I knocked myself out for ten years so I wouldn't sound like that anymore, Harrell thought. She makes me feel fifteen again, as if I shouldn't look straight at her because she's a white girl.

Domina was speaking about the first campaign now, and he could get what she was saying, even while his mind clung to that other voice, that accent. Harrell thought suddenly of a split-screen commercial on television, two pictures at one time, each showing something different, but understandable as a whole. He felt split himself, one part in this room listening attentively, one part back in Montgomery.

That little redhead looked like the prettiest girls in school, the white girls who'd never looked at him, and whom he'd never looked full in the face.

His father, tall, bony, silver-haired, dressed always in the stiff black suits he wore in the pulpit, had cautioned him about white girls. His father had been old when Harrell was born, come from a time when things had been tough in Alabama, really tough. Nobody'd been lynched, his father had said, but plenty of black boys had done jail time just because they looked too long at pretty white girls. Harrell hadn't worried about it much. His father's views on white girls were about as old-fashioned as his views on almost everything. Harrell had been born to a different time, a time of opportunity for black people. But the stories stuck in his head somehow. So he'd never really eyed a white classmate the way he'd looked at the black girls. Not in Montgomery, not in college, not anywhere.

Funny, how much he was thinking about the old man today, in the midst of a meeting his father would not have understood at all. Samuel Barber had been a businessman, though, all week long, when he sold insurance to the blacks in Montgomery. Sundays he preached the sermons that took hours, that people traveled far to hear. Most blacks in town knew Reverend Barber by sight at least, and Harrell had been proud to be his son.

In the parlor in winter, on the porch in summer, Samuel Barber had sat with his children and told them about their proud heritage. Harrell's younger brothers had interrupted with questions, his sister had complained about hearing that old stuff again and again. But Harrell, skinny and solemn, had loved every word.

'You are all descended from a famous man,' his father would always begin, 'a man in history people still read about today.' And Harrell would say, 'Go on, Father, tell the whole of it.' Half the time he didn't really listen, since he knew the story so well. But the words had seeped into his bones, he thought.

'Francis Barber left Jamaica when he was just a little older than you, John Harrell. He wasn't a slave, even way back in the eighteenth century when he lived, when most black men were slaves. Not him. He'd worked for the sailors in the English navy, and one of those sailors took him all the way to England on a sailing trip. That would have taken months, that trip.'

Harrell's sister would close her eyes, wrinkle her nose, but the boys were always lulled by the story.

'When he got to London, down and out, the greatest man of the day, Samuel Johnson, found him and hired him to be a servant. Not a slave, a paid servant. The whole tale is in a famous book, a book scholars read now, always will. That Samuel Johnson was an important writer, had many friends. He valued education. So he sent Francis to school, gave him good clothes, and never asked him to do anything in the house that was low or undignified. Samuel Johnson used to go out to market himself to buy oysters for his cat, Hodge. Told his friends he didn't want Francis to wait upon the convenience of a quadruped.' Harrell's father would always chuckle over the phrase. He'd explained the words so often, they all understood.

'Then, after Samuel Johnson died, he left some money for Francis, enough so he could marry an English lady. Her name was Betsey. It's all in the book. And they became the parents of a boy who grew up to be a famous Methodist preacher in England, in that time. And he had boys of his own, and they had boys, too, all the way down to me, and you.' Here his sister would squirm. All the kids knew that girls didn't count in this story, because they didn't pass the family name along.

His father would invariably end the story with an admonition for them all to remember who they were, so they would always make the most of their chances in life, the way Francis Barber had. Well, thought Harrell, all of them had. One of his brothers was an architect in Phila-delphia, the other a doctor in San Francisco. His sister was principal of a school in Boston. Not bad for a poor family. It amused him, since he'd gone to work for Ford, that he alone of them all was busy waiting upon the

221

convenience of a quadruped, if you could consider a car a quadruped. But he earned for it well over a hundred thousand dollars a year, more than his father had dreamed a Negro could earn. And I'm only beginning, if the Blossom takes off. Salaries in automobiles soared up into the two-, four-, eight-hundred-thousand-dollar range. There wasn't a reason in the world why he shouldn't move on up there.

He knew how to move up, after all. As a kid he'd always had top grades. Always read every book around, easy or difficult. Always worked after school, helped with church affairs when he was old enough, busy while the neighborhood boys loafed around. He'd learned to save his money, too, while the other kids were dripping ice-cream cones in the steaming summers, sharing a bottle of cheap wine out of sight of the grown-ups. If Harrell hadn't turned out tall and strong, with a hard fist that came from so many heavy jobs, he'd have been the target of every bully in the neighborhood. But he'd had buddies, too, and guys mostly listened to him, took his counsel. Everyone knew he was one smart black boy.

All Montgomery knew it when he was fifteen and won the George Washington Carver Scholarship, founded by Montgomery's rich families, the chance to go to a private school anywhere, South or North. His father, blazing with pride, made him listen to the advice of every teacher, black or white, in his school. The principal steered him toward Andover, in Massachusetts. He'd get the most modern, solid, valuable education in and out of books at Andover, the principal had told Harrell's father. And the boy, standing tall, his wrists and ankles already sticking out from a suit just a month old, ready for adventure like his ancestor Francis Barber, took the endless bus ride North.

He'd expected everything to be different, part of him frightened silly at such a jump. But he'd found school life not so different, libraries bigger, classes smaller, kids smarter than home, but not the other planet he'd expected. The white kids were friendlier, except the Southern ones, who kept as far from him as possible without looking rude enough for a teacher to notice. Harrell played football, learned to cope with guys who threw dirt in his eyes when the coach looked the other way. He learned to keep cool when he approached a lunch table and conversation stopped for a moment before he was welcomed a touch too heartily. He learned to handle the effusive friendship some of the boys offered, often as hurtful as the outright nastiness had been at home. But Harrell had long training from his father in 'rising above it.' That meant never hearing, never seeing, never responding to prejudice in its smaller forms. It took practice. But by the time Harrell had won early acceptance to Yale, he felt as if he'd won high honors in rising above things.

Almost the first weekend in New Haven he'd met Christine at a dance. She'd come down from Smith to date a black guy Harrell knew slightly. The guy had been drinking, and it was easy to rescue Chris. They'd liked each other instantly. She'd seemed to him the first person he'd ever met who felt about being black just as he did. Christine was rich, had gone to Dalton in New York, almost never faced outright prejudice in any violent form. But she knew all about the subtle kinds they practiced up North. The two of them discovered that they could kid about all of it. The whites who fawned on them to show their liberal attitudes. The blacks who sneered at them for acting too white. The conservatives who ignored them. Bitter jokes, perhaps, but shared now, not buried in each of them alone any longer. Rising above it with Chris was a hell of a lot better than going it alone.

When Harrell went on to the Business School, Chris came up to Radcliffe for extra credits. In Cambridge, released from dormitories and restrictions, they indulged their physical hunger for each other. Harrell had thought it astounding that the more they made love, the hungrier he got. In those days he had only to look down at Christine's mocha arms, slim and shapely, against a white pillow, to feel himself get hard, hot, ready. The day his Ford job came through, they told her parents they were going to marry. It had seemed to Harrell that Christine's father was relieved. It hadn't dawned on him till then that her family had worried that she might choose a white classmate or a militant black.

Once that was settled, he'd taken Chris down home.

She had never seen a city like Montgomery, never imagined how it felt to be black in the South even in modern times. Harrell watched her noticing how many blacks still passed to the backs of the buses out of the habits of their lifetime. He saw her looking at groups of little kids playing in schoolyards, as segregated by color as if they'd been sorted out. During the whole visit he'd watched her rising above it, with a dryness in his throat and a ringing in his ears, he wanted so to protect her from this ugliness. They clung together at night in his bedroom at home, shutting out the world till morning. Chris spent hours listening to his father, hearing about Francis Barber. She had been several times to London, had visited Dr Johnson's house off Fleet Street. His father just couldn't get over it, that she'd actually been in the very house the first Barber had worked in.

Their wedding in New York made the society page at a time when the editors had finally allowed a few black social notes to creep into print. Chris hadn't used her teaching license, because the boys had come along fairly soon. In the family tradition, he'd named them Samuel Johnson and James Boswell. When Chris had asked what on earth they'd call another boy, he'd said, 'Honey, we've run out. We'll have to stop here.' She replied gently, 'Oh, I don't know. I'd like a Betsey.'

When he told his boys that being black didn't make much difference anymore, he tried to say it with conviction. He never considered telling them anything else. They'd find out the rest for themselves.

He did not tell them about the Southern guys at Ford who kept as far from him as possible. He never talked about the time in Detroit traffic police had stopped him for no reason, given him a rough time at the station house. He'd never told them how many maids, black and white, their mother had interviewed before she'd found one who'd work for them. Those were tiny things, and they'd either stop happening as time passed, or the boys would learn to cope, as he'd done. Harrell knew that the best protection was being better than anyone else at your work. He also knew that two-, four-, eight-hundred-thousand-dollar salaries bought a lot of safety. Sometimes he almost saw the cash stacked into a wall, surrounding Chris and the kids.

So, why, thought Harrell, while Domina went on explaining her ads, why the shock when that Alabama girl spoke up?

And while Domina presented layouts, and the art director took them from her and pinned them up, Harrell dug into his head for an answer.

What about that girl troubled him so? Not her looks. Too pretty to remind him of anyone back home. Not her voice. He'd come across plenty of Southern talk in his job world, even Alabama talk. And she hadn't said anything remarkable, just about getting in the way. So what was it exactly that bothered him?

Harrell let his eyes move from the layout Domina was displaying. He glanced at the redhead, as she sat slightly hidden by the bulk of the man who was pinning up the ads. Mark Something. 'Mark, honey,' she'd called him.

'Mark, honey' turned suddenly to reach for a pushpin, and Harrell got a clear look at the expression on the girl's face. When he did, the feeling of shock shot through him again, as startling as before.

She was glaring at him. Her eyes were cat slits, her stare as diamond-hard as the light from her huge ring, her mouth pinched. Her pretty face had turned to stone.

And he remembered. Ellie Ann Hutchinson. Hadn't thought about her in years.

When he'd been twelve and first noticing girls, Ellie Ann had been far and away the prettiest girl in his class. She'd had white-blond hair and bright blue eyes. She'd come to school every day in tight sweaters and swingy skirts, belted in tight. All the boys were crazy for her, the white boys, and all the girls jealous. In the lunchroom he'd noticed the black kids stealing looks her way when they carried their trays past the white kids to the corner tables.

One brilliant spring noontime Harrell had seen one of the handsomer, smarter white kids move in on the table full of giggling girls. As Harrell approached, carrying his tray, he heard the boy mention last night's fight in Chicago.

Sugar Ray Robinson had won the middleweight title for the fifth time, he'd been saying. As Harrell got closer, his eyes turned down to his tray, Ellie Ann had suddenly pushed back her chair, crashing into him. The chair had made the same creaking sound he had just heard in this room.

While he'd righted the jiggling tray, Ellie Ann had said loudly, 'Dick, honey, let me just tell you, my daddy says those nigger boys shouldn't compete with white folks, they're all muscle and no brain to hold them back.'

It had been beamed straight at him, top student in the class. And her expression had been just like this girl's now, pure, straight hate, and no mistake. Funny. He and this redhead came from the same state, the same kind of school, probably. Their accents were the same, or would have been if he hadn't taught himself to talk like a radio announcer. Their work was shared, their objective, their concentration, on the same thing at this moment. And there she was, glaring at him. Like Ellie Ann, who by this time was probably an alcoholic housewife in Montgomery. Well, one more piece of his life he wouldn't be telling his boys about.

Once he'd located the source of his feelings, Harrell snapped to. He'd managed the situation in the lunchroom, moving on as if he'd heard nothing. And there was nothing to be done now. He forced his mind to stop its split-screen action, made himself listen to Domina.

The ads were good, he thought. The first campaign had made him feel nervous. Too fancy. He wanted the ads for the Blossom to be low-key, quietly intrusive. 'Less is more,' he'd learned, and he wanted simple words, accurate pictures. The second campaign had been sensational, however, just what he'd hoped for. The work Domina was showing now seemed excellent, too. He knew his bosses, the management committee at Ford, would approve, because this set of ads was in the Ford tradition, all big pictures, and short selling copy. But Harrell decided he'd press for the campaign he liked best himself, unusual, striking, a breakthrough like the car itself. I'll dump the first one, he decided, and tell them to get the rest ready for the committee.

That Drexler woman is good. And Rossen, he's straight,

too. They don't know my taste yet, had to bring in a campaign like that first one to see how I'd respond. But they did show it first. The last stuff they show is usually what they want to sell. Better than I'd hoped, he thought.

He allowed a silence when Domina finished, to keep all of them on their toes. Then he moved his gaze from Domina and looked around the table. Godwin's eyes were on his yellow pad. Rossen's were straight at Harrell. The art director was turning back from the bulletin board. The writer looked anguished, waiting for the client's verdict. Domina kept quite still, looked directly at Harrell, too. Behind her the red-headed girl raised her eyebrows, as if she expected Harrell to say something country, stupid.

He cleared his throat. 'I have to thank you. You haven't had much time, and you've done very interesting work. What's more, it's all right on target. The right things come through, the right sales points are featured. And the whole look of the ads is right, what I wanted for our top luxury car.'

He saw Godwin's head come up now, a slight smile start to form, as if he'd known all along the reaction would be good. Roe kept quite still, and so did Domina. They were waiting for a sentence that began with a 'but.' He knew they'd heard negative sentences right after praise like his, plenty of times.

Domina watched Harrell, noting every flick of his eyelids, every move of his hand. This was the critical instant. Yes or no. Will he or won't he? He loves me, he loves me not. And now, it's more vital than ever. If he hates everything I've done, it splits me off from Roe. We'd never work together, everything would change. We could see each other, but it wouldn't be as good, I'd have failed him. But if Harrell likes what I do, maybe a lot, heaven. I could forget Brady's nonsense. They'd have to pay attention. God, the biggest account in the house. These men respect that. Not the fashion supervisor anymore. Jesus, I'd get that title fast. And Roe, darling Roe. A champion. I've never had a champion. All the men I ever knew held my coat while I fought, even my husband. Especially my husband. Harrell Barber, say what I want, please.

The weeks since Detroit had been strange. Ford all day. Ideas, sketches, engineers, blueprints, words, arguments. Roe all night. Hamburgers, wine, his bed looking out over the beautiful river lights, her bed with her best Italian linen sheets, magic. She'd had to plan for time to do the simplest things, like washing her hair, until she learned one night that Roe found her beautiful even with a towel turbaned around her head.

Harrell somehow had become part of the magic, too. She knew he'd had to struggle, just the way she had. Which is tougher, she'd wondered, black or female? Shirley Chisholm had said that being a woman was much more trouble than being black. The remark had been taken up by NOW and the other feminist groups. No, thought Domina, not when being a woman means nights like mine with Roe.

She waited for Harrell. The right words would make up for a million miseries. The silly masculine barriers she'd had to push through, even since she'd begun on Ford. The other supervisors on the account, the ones who regularly handled the big models, hadn't welcomed her, by any means. In the brief time she'd been learning the account, Domina had been busy catching up to meetings these guys forgot to invite her to, struggling through lunches filled with the sports talk men use to shut women out, ignoring the snickers that erupted when she asked a question about anything technical. She'd been the first female admitted to an exclusive club, car-advertising experts, and no one had been about to make it easy. The hardest thing had been their language. In meetings, the guys loved saying 'fuck,' 'shit,' 'balls,' then turning to her to apologize. Domina had considered using words like those herself, or going the other way and blushing. In the end she'd simply decided not to hear them, rising above the talk as if it hadn't happened. Jesus, men are little boys.

Harrell Barber was not a little boy. He looked as if he'd learned to ignore any number of slights. His hands, his eyes, his body, gave few clues to his thoughts, and he'd obviously taught himself containment. Well, it's the best defense, she knew, no clues to the weak places in you for your enemies to press and use against you. They always say

I'm cool, quiet, calm. He's much better at it than I am. Even I can't guess what he's thinking. Could he see me as an ally? Or will he want to get away from me, to cling to all the establishment people so he can move ahead faster? Come on, Harrell Barber, love my work, love me.

'I think we can pass on the first campaign,' said Harrell. 'It's elaborate, complicated for my taste. The Blossom is a simple car. The thing that makes it special is, its simplicity comes from the best materials and advanced design features we could find. But still, plain, clean, unadorned.'

Domina's throat seemed to thicken, her brain to shrink. He'd sounded terribly cool, dreadfully negative. She forced herself to stay quite still, holding herself in a pose of pleasant interest. Come on, Harrell, she thought fervently, come on.

'The last campaign is excellent, right in the tradition of our company advertising. I'm sure it would sell a lot of cars for us. And I want to let my management-review committee see it for themselves.'

Domina couldn't breathe. He was zeroing in on the right campaign, her favorite, the best of them all, the riskiest. When Godwin had reviewed the work, he'd shaken his head over it. Only Roe had managed to save it from destruction, to keep the work unchanged for this meeting.

The campaign was revolutionary for automobile advertising. No headlines, no display type, no extras on the page of any kind. Only an outline picture of the Blossom at the top of the page, with large, simple type balancing the picture all the way down the page. The layout was like a page from a child's primer. The copy was primer, too. 'Ford says Blossom. Ideas Blossom. Personalities Blossom. Affairs Blossom. You Blossom.' Over and over, every possible combination of the car name with idea words, ending always, 'Buy Blossom.' Domina had pored over competitive car ads for days, put files together of everything the agency possessed from years past, noting the dreary similarities of most car advertising. She'd seen how Volkswagen leaped out of the crowd with the famous 'Lemon' headline and modest attitude. She'd compiled lists of the usual adjectives in car ads, the longs, leans, lows, cleans, words like 'luxury' used again and again. She'd seen the use of abstractions like 'impressive elegance' and 'move up to quality,' and she'd determined to keep all these clichés out. Roe had coaxed her into putting some of the ordinary words and phrases back in, mostly because who knew what Harrell would be expecting, he'd said. But the primer campaign, free of every tired picture, word, and thought, was far and away her favorite. Was Harrell possibly going to agree? Was he going to be the perfect client, the one she'd waited for all her life?

'This campaign, I think, is the right one,' said Harrell, as if she'd programmed him. 'It's simple. It's different, people can't fail to notice it. It's easy to take, like the Blossom. Some of the words are a little far-out, but that's easy to fix. I'd like to take stats of all your work back to Detroit and go over it carefully with my staff. But this is the campaign you should keep going on, I think. Congratulations, Domina, Roe, all of you. This is an excellent show.'

This is what it's all about, Domina thought, this business, just this moment. She could feel the tension ease, the breath exhale, the heartbeats slow down to normal in all the agency people around the table. Get Godwin, she thought, trying to look as if he invented the whole presentation, beaming at me as if I were his daughter. Look at Roe, he's going to get up and kiss me if I don't frown at him.

She frowned at him.

Roe was on his feet, walking around the table to her side. He reached his hand down for her chin, kissed her on the cheek. Everyone smiled at them.

'You don't mind if I congratulate the lady on her first car campaign, do you, Harrell?' he said pleasantly.

'I congratulate her myself,' said Harrell from where he sat.

And Domina thought she would explode with joy, right there in that room, right in front of them all. She smiled over at Harrell, at his assistants, who'd never opened their mouths. Ford men, she thought, thank the Lord Jesus I've got this unusual black guy. He takes chances, he's smart, thank God.

They were all standing now, picking up the papers, opening and closing briefcases, getting ready to move out of the room, with its overflowing ashtrays and dirty coffee-cups. The clients were all moving in a group toward the door, starting to shake hands, saying good-byes. Roe stood with Dan, arranging for the shipment of photostats of the ads to be placed on the afternoon plane to Detroit.

Domina turned to smile her thanks at her own team, moving them toward the door with her. She walked first, past where Harrell and the other clients stood, getting ready to leave.

'Harrell, thank you for listening,' she said, 'and for your nice words. You make it very easy to work hard on this advertising.'

She smiled her best smile and shook his hand for a good-bye.

Following her lead, Mark and Davy shook hands too, moving up the row from the youngest assistant to Harrell to the threshold. Thanks were being said all over the room.

M.J. came last, hanging back a little, as the youngest member of the agency team should. When it was her turn, she put her tiny hand into the hand of the assistant client, smiling prettily, murmuring some polite phrase that Domina couldn't quite hear. Then she lingered a little with the second young assistant, leaving her hand in his.

When she moved on to Harrell, Domina turned her head back to see what was taking M.J. so long to get out of the room. That was why she had a full view, though the other agency people didn't, of what M.J. did next.

As she came up to Harrell, the smile rippled off M.J.'s face. It was replaced with a hard, stony stare. Then she slowly, deliberately, put both her hands behind her back and clasped them there firmly. Chin up, without a word to him, she marched straight out of the room, past Harrell, past Domina, past all the others. She began to walk smoothly, slowly down the corridor.

Domina felt nauseous. She saw Harrell react. He only blinked once fast, while he angled his outstretched hand smoothly to meet his jacket pocket, so it wouldn't look to anyone as if he'd been passed over. The whole incident was over in a moment.

Domina turned toward Harrell in dismay, but Roe was there ahead of her. Had he seen? Domina wasn't sure. Roe had been apart from the group, talking about the plans for shipping out the ads. What was he saying to Harrell?

'Got time for a quick drink? Come on, you've got time before your plane.'

By the end of the sentence he had Harrell and the two helpers headed for the elevators. Domina couldn't be sure whether he was being marvelously tactful or whether he just hadn't seen.

That little bitch, always rotten to black people. Like that cleaning lady. But to a client? Impossible. And he's been so darling, such a lamb, and he's my white hope. Jesus God, listen to me, I'm thinking like a racist myself. Well, that's it for M.J. Now she goes.

'M.J. Kent,' she called, stepping forward to catch that innocent-looking little figure moving away, her hands still clasped behind her back, like a good child.

M.J. stopped and waited for Domina to catch up.

'Okay, baby. You can go downstairs and start clearing out your desk. I've never seen anything so rotten in all my life. How could you do that?'

'Do what?' said M.J.

Domina felt turned to stone.

'Come on, M.J. You can fool a lot of the guys around here, maybe, but you haven't got a prayer with me. I saw the whole thing. I never want to see anything like that again, especially from someone who works for me. Do you understand? I'm firing you. Now.'

M.J. looked up at her. Domina could almost see the indecision on her face. The girl was wondering whether to continue to pretend she'd done nothing, or whether to come up with an excuse. Giving M.J. no chance to do either, Domina turned away from her and went back toward the conference room, where Brady Godwin was chatting with her writer and art director.

She broke into the group urgently. 'Brady,' she said, 'I need to talk to you right now. I'm coming back to your office with you, okay? Davy? Give Mark a hand with the layouts, Dan will be waiting for them to get them ready for the plane. And thanks, you two. It was a terrific show. We've got work to do, but we couldn't have had a better response. Thanks.'

Brady was watching her carefully, his face absolutely empty of expression.

'There's a meeting waiting in my office, another meeting,' he said.

'All right, let's talk right here,' she said, and walked past him back into the cluttered conference room. 'Brady, please call David Noble. Now. I want M.J. Kent out. That was a ghastly thing she did just now.'

Without waiting for his reaction, she went herself to the phone in the corner, dialed, asked the secretary at the other end of the line if Mr Noble would step around and join her and Mr Godwin in the conference room immediately.

Brady sat down again. From his breast pocket he took a flat leather tobacco pouch and a pipe. He set them on the table and searched his pockets for a match. After several moments of silence Domina reached into her handbag and tossed her own book of matches across the table to him. She threw it harder than she'd intended, and it landed near his hand like a small missile.

David March Noble walked through the door.

Domina turned around to ask him to close the door behind him and sit down. She found that he wasn't looking at her, but beyond, to Brady Godwin, with a worried expression.

'Emergency?' said David.

'You bet,' said Domina. 'We've just had a little episode in here that puts the final touch on something I've been thinking about for quite a while. M.J. Kent. You know, the little redhead in my group, who seemed so good, so promising? She's not promising. She's a very peculiar little girl.'

David March Noble sat down heavily at the table opposite Godwin. He seemed to collapse and crumble, Domina noticed in surprise, and his face began to look wary. Oh, God, she thought, they never know what I'm going to come up with next, these two. Now they're waiting for me to do something else unusual, unexpected, female, capricious. I'd better explain, slowly.

'David,' she said pleasantly, 'M.J. Kent is Southern, from some tiny town in Alabama, and she has a real thing about black people. She can't stand them, has almost a physical reaction, even to the cleaning people on our floor. She hasn't been in New York, in the North, all that long. She may very well get over it after a while. But not on my time, I've decided. Just now we've presented the first ads for the Blossom, for my new car account. Nothing could be more important in my group, my life, right now. It's important for the whole agency, really. And you may have heard from someone, there was a last-minute switch at the client, at Ford, and our man, our top client, is black.'

To her surprise, she saw relief flood into David's face. How odd, she thought. Why should that be? You'd think a story that began like this would start upsetting him. Godwin was puffing at his pipe, still looking blank. She took a breath and went on.

'Just now, at the close of a terrific meeting, when everyone was feeling fine, when he'd been marvelous to us, M.J. deliberately insulted the man, wouldn't shake hands with him. It wasn't a small gesture, either. She could have slipped past him, but she didn't. She insulted him on a grand scale, made it obvious to him that she wasn't going to touch him. He saw it, he got it, he's a bright guy. It's dreadful. Now, I want her out of this agency, there's no room for her, for anyone who insults a client. None at all.'

She saw David look at Godwin, who kept silent. Finally, stuck with making a decision, David cleared his throat. His eyes didn't meet hers. 'Domina, you're always so impulsive,' he said. 'This is a terrible accusation you're making.'

'You bet,' she interrupted. Anger began to stir inside her. Impulsive? Men are decisive, women are impulsive. 'You bet it is.'

'We would all have to be sure, very sure. Were you standing where you could actually see the whole incident? Could you possibly have misjudged? I find it hard to believe that any young person in this agency would deliberately

234

insult a client. All our people know that clients are ours to serve, that they control our livelihood.'

'I'm very, very sure. I saw the whole thing clearly. That wasn't all, come to think of it. Brady was in the room when she interrupted the meeting with some silly remark at an important moment. She spoke out at her most Southern, for no reason at all. She's poison, that little girl, particularly in this situation. Who knows what other kinds of people she doesn't like?'

Her anger was growing, righteous, burning. Why the hell weren't they as shocked as she? Maybe you couldn't expect these two to worry about a black man, but a black *client*? Brady would go to a disco, dance a jig, vote Democratic if a client wanted him to.

'Well,' said David. 'This is all very difficult. Perhaps we should end this discussion now, think it over very carefully, get together later on when we've cooled off.'

'Brady,' said Domina, getting hotter by the moment. 'Tell him. You heard her. Explain, please. I don't seem to be getting through.'

Brady puffed another smoke cloud across the table. 'Domina. If you could have your way right now, this very minute, what would you like to see happen?'

She felt the blood riding up into her face, the heat turning up in her body.

'What would I like to see happen? I'd like to see what any decent, modern business person would like to see happen. I'd like that girl out of this agency in about an hour. Fired. Finished. Look, it's probably partly my fault, I chose her, and she does do good work, but that's not everything. We can't have young art directors delivering racial statements to clients or anyone else around here. Get rid of her before there's real trouble. I still have no idea how the client felt about it. He could be sore as hell. It could change his whole attitude about the work, for God's sake. Get her out. What else is there?'

'I understand you perfectly, Domina,' said Brady. 'And in a great many ways, you're absolutely correct. Certainly we can't have trouble like that. The error was really in allowing her to come to the meeting. She's too young, too inexperienced. You should probably have managed the presentation without her.'

Holy Mother of Christ, this bastard can dump trouble in my lap faster than anyone I've ever known.

'I probably should,' she said. 'But some of the work was hers, and I like to let the younger kids see what happens to their work in big meetings. It's the only way they get experience in the real selling. This meeting, you're damned right I should have left her out. On the other hand, now we know about her. It could be worse another time.'

'I applaud your leadership. It's the reason you always have such a happy group, you're easy with the younger people. That's why I'm surprised that you should want to fire one of them so summarily,' said Godwin smoothly.

Domina stood up abruptly. He was lawyering with her, turning her words against her. Her fury bubbled up to the brim, her controls felt about to blow.

'That's right, Domina,' said David quickly. 'I thought M.J. was a real find, a truly talented natural artist. She's done well in a short time, made a lot of progress. Perhaps if we put her in another group?'

While Domina turned to stare at him, Brady picked up that solution like a football and ran with it. 'Good idea, David,' he said. 'I certainly don't feel that Domina should have anyone under her command who doesn't respond, doesn't measure up to her values. We need an art assistant over on the toy account right now. This little girl would be fine, she's still almost a child herself. I think you're right. We'll move her immediately. Why don't you take care of it this afternoon?'

Domina found that she was lifting her hand, flattening her arm as if it were a weapon. Amazed at herself for an instant, she realized why, just what she wanted to do with that hand. She banged her stiffened fist on the beautiful wooden table, sending a thunderclap through the room.

For the first time, both men looked at her directly.

'Listen, Brady Godwin, listen, David Noble,' she said. 'Listen to me. I've taken a lot of shit in this agency, for a lot of years. Most of it, I've swallowed and I've held on. But you made me a group head, and you put me in charge of a

236

bunch of people. You screen them for me and for everyone else, but I hire them, just me alone. And now I'm going to fire one of them, for good cause. And you're going to back me up. Why, if that had been a young man, or even a slightly less talented girl, you'd have been with me. That's it, that's how it's going to be.'

David was looking down at the table again. Domina thought he was taking this very strangely. Brady always wanted to do the opposite of what she asked. But David was a stickler for the rules. Why the hell didn't he want to throw M.J. into the street? True, David had been singing her praises since his first interview with the girl. Jesus, Domina wondered, what went on in that interview? What does this precise little man, with his picture of his wife and kids on his desk, ask of all the young girls he hires? Does he have them all do a tryout in bed? Nonsense. I'm imagining. I'm so fucking mad, I'm going off the deep end.

'Domina, dear,' said Brady with a warm chuckle. 'You're very hot today, aren't you, simply explosive. It's your success at the meeting, of course, you've worked hard and you've just released a lot of tension. We understand. Calm yourself down. You're not behaving very nicely for a lady right now yourself, you know.'

She began to tremble a little, not quite believing what she had heard. Too much, she thought, one thing too much to take. Quit, that's all. Tell them off and quit, the only thing left. Turn around and walk. Away from these men, these shitheads.

But the bankbook. The kids. The bills. Go, but say nothing. Go home and call Maran, call Roe. Roe. You can't quit and leave Roe. Tell him, he'll help. He'll believe what happened with M.J. He'll fix it up with Harrell, too. Just take it easy.

When she spoke, she almost spat the words across the table, straight at the two of them.

'All right. I get your message, it's quite clear. Listen, now. It's going to be me or M.J. Kent, it's that simple. If you won't fire that girl, I'm finished. All the promises and the words full of lies from you are finished.'

Good, let them chew on that, wonder what I'll do about

237

it. Those two rotten, bigoted, lying shits. And they're the company. I can't get back at this whole place, too big. But I don't have to stay. Let them worry about my work, about when the ads will get done. Let them try to find someone else to make the fixes Harrell wants. Their black client. They probably can't stand him either. Shits.

She picked up her handbag, her cigarettes, her notes.

I've backed down for Brady before, and he thinks I'll do it now. They think they've got me. My job is too good to blow. A nice Catholic lady who'll knuckle under. I *must* show them I mean business, that I can be just as tough as any man.

The words bubbled up through her anger, the words she wanted to shout across the table.

'Brady? David? You two aren't worth a rat fuck. There isn't one ball between the two of you. And as managers, as human beings, you know what I think? You both suck.'

She stayed just long enough to make sure her words were sinking in, to watch their expressions change from bland to angry, and got herself out of the conference room.

M.J.

JACKSON EMPLOYEE MANUAL
TELEPHONE PROCEDURES   page 38

NY OFFICE/PARIS NIGHT RATE

$12.10	first 3 minutes
2.10	every minute thereafter
	tax 2%

M.J. shot the bolt on the ladies'-room cubicle and sat down. Outside in the lounge there was only one girl fixing her face, and she'd been almost done when M.J. had dashed through. She'd be pretty much alone for a while. She looked down at her wonderful ring. Lately, that ring had been reminding her of just how broke she was getting. Her credit repayments seemed to come around faster all the time. If she sold it? Not yet, she thought. I'll wait till everything else fails.

Anyway, now I'll be out of Domina's group. But it was fun. That nigger bastard, sitting there in his navy-blue monkey suit with everyone kissing his black ass. Now we'll see. Domina said right out she'd fire me. She sure thinks she can. Bet if one of the men supervisors fired someone, they'd stay fired. But with Domina? Well, we'll just see. Brady Godwin thinks I'm a honey child, I've fixed that, I think. And David? He's not about to let me out of his hands now.

She shifted a little uneasily on the uncomfortable toilet top. Just suppose she did find herself fired? Oh, for heaven's sake, I've got a place to live and a man to feed me, and give me some cash, too, if I ask pretty. And I've got my work, everyone says it's fantastic. Proofs of everything I ever worked on, and a few things I didn't work on, borrowed from people in the group. I've got a television reel, even, a little one, but good enough for someone my age. Bet I could land another job in a day. Three days. And there's always unemployment insurance.

She felt one twinge of fear in her bones, but put it away firmly. Dumb to worry till she knew what would happen now. Chances were they'd stick her into someone else's group. Sure hope it's a man boss, easier to handle. Dumb, getting caught in Domina's office. Never been quite the same since. Well, Dan is starting that finance course in January, that's going to give me two nights a week free. Maybe time to move. I hear tell that Mr Roe Rossen has a mighty nice place over by the river. Looks like he's been getting sweet on Domina lately. Kissing her right in that meeting. I could have died. She looked like an old tabby cat somebody's just fed cream. He's cute, though. It'd be nice to get him on my side.

She heard the outer door close, and felt silence in the marble walls of the ladies' room. She'd never dreamed there were rooms like this one before she got to Potter Jackson. Ladies' rooms with showers? Pink towels? Huge mirrors and makeup shelves, lockers, the nicest soaps and colognes set out fresh almost every day? I'll never leave Jackson if I can help it, she thought suddenly, never. Let old Domina leave. I'm staying right here.

She leaned back against the cold wall and thought about her supper at Domina's house. She hadn't been able to get the image of Domina's glorious apartment out of her head. Even in the glossy magazines Jackson sent around free every month, she'd never in her life dreamed of a lady alone in a place like that. The whole building was elegant, elevator men in white gloves taking you up, fresh flowers in the hall. Just two apartments on each floor, and even the foyers had pretty wicker furniture. Domina's living room had stunned her, with all its color and glow, had made her want to grab for a paintbox and set it all down to remember right. And the bedroom was even better, those beautiful fans on the wall, and reds and pinks all mixed up together. And the bed. What I couldn't do with a bed like that, M.J. had thought. What a waste for a dried-up old thing like Domina.

Dried up is right, she thought now. Domina had talked to her like a teacher, an old-maid school principal. While she'd served the pretty supper her colored maid had left ready, wonderful hot chili with big bits of steak in it, and beat biscuits like M.J. was used to from home, and icy martinis like she wasn't used to anywhere, Domina had talked. Guessing a little too much, closing in now, like one of M.J.'s pa's hounds. For one thing, Domina had asked about the afternoons off, the ones M.J. had been spending with David. M.J. had said she'd been up at the museum. For another thing, Domina seemed to know all about her living with Dan. And while she'd gone on praising M.J.'s work to the skies, she sure had said a lot about fudging the truth, learning to talk honestly.

M.J. had come home to Dan feeling it was time to get out. Another group to start fresh in, make hay in, see what she could learn in a different part of the agency. It was a big place. She could get herself on another floor, where she'd hardly set eyes on Domina again. But then she'd decided to wait, look for a chance to get Domina good and mad. It had to be something Domina couldn't come down too hard on, something people might think two ways about, so M.J. would have a side she could stick to. Meantime she'd make sure that David knew how miserable she felt, how tough Domina was on her and on the other pretty young girls in the group. David was plenty ready to hear bad news about Domina. He'd never liked her, said she'd always been trouble, trouble for management. When David spoke about management, he made it sound like something holy, perfect, unquestionable. It was easy to drop little hints about Domina's moods, her unreasonable demands, her hours out of the office, let things roll across the pillow into David's ear. David. If he ever thought she'd leave, he'd turn handsprings to keep her close, M.J. was positive.

Well, she'd done it today, and settled an old score of her own besides. Hadn't planned it, but just the sight of that black man sitting so tall and sure of himself had inspired her. And now what? Bound to be an explosion. He was a client; they were sacred, she knew. What could David do for her? What had Brady Godwin seen? Most of all, what exactly had Domina told them, how had she handled it when M.J. had walked off down the hall? Well, now there was a wonderful new way to find out things. M.J. had just figured it out, had tried it only once before. Now would be a perfect time to try again.

She giggled, relaxed against the wall, which was warming

up with the heat of her body against it.

Domina's office had three telephone extensions, it was so large. One on the desk, one near her chair, one at the side of the couch. The phone system at Jackson was old, and the sound was crackling sometimes, just like the phones in the stores at home. So if you could pick up an extension outside Domina's office, the one on her secretary's desk, or safer still, the one at reception far down the hall and out of Domina's sight altogether, no one could tell where the crackling came from. M.J. already had run a test. She'd got an old lady receptionist to let her listen in one time on Domina's phone, by saying she needed to hear where the meeting was going to be, she'd forgotten. It had worked like magic. So then, early one morning when she'd come in just after Domina, she tried it out.

Domina had been talking to Mr Rossen.

They weren't stupid. But even allowing for their caution on an office phone, M.J. had known something was sure going on. He'd been gentler than when people were around, and Domina had sounded entirely different. So that's what she's up to, M.J. had thought, exulting, and that old lady doesn't think I should play around? Bitch.

She heard some girls coming in, their heels tapping on the floor, chatter bouncing off the walls. Time to get going, she thought, and flushed the toilet, waited a moment, unlocked the cubicle, and stepped out.

She'd been exactly right. As she turned the corner to her part of the floor, M.J. saw Domina's door tight shut. Her secretary was gone. The light on her phone was on, so Domina was in there talking on one of her lines. Whatever she was saying, it was bound to tell M.J. something. Would she be talking to Roe Rossen? That would be the best of all.

The office was clearing, almost nobody left in the corridor. Still, better safe than sorry. This phone thing is too good to blow. In spite of her eagerness to snatch up the receiver, she made herself go back down the long hall to the reception desk.

A big square white phone, this one, with lots of lights and buttons. Perfect. She'd know just when Domina was hanging up, have plenty of time to clear out before Domina came out. And she'd look innocent enough sitting there, after hours, helping somebody on the telephone. No one would ever think what she was up to. Perfect.

M.J. sat down at the reception desk, tidied now for the night, and carefully pressed the button to come in on Domina's line. She lifted the receiver lightly and slowly, holding her hand over the mouthpiece, so nobody'd even hear her breathing.

Damn. A woman's voice at the other end. Not Roe Rossen. Shit. Who's this she's talking to? Why so much noise on the line? Long distance?

'Good for you,' the thin voice was saying. 'You finally told the pricks. How do you feel?'

M.J. heard Domina's low voice. This was terrific. Excitement stirred in her middle, her heart began to bump.

'Determined. Furious. Petrified, all those things, together. Jesus, I'm glad I found you. What time is it there?'

That's funny, thought M.J. She must be talking to California.

'It's fine, we just got back from dinner. Lucas Carton, great, but the prices. I had *fraises*, stuffed myself. We've got all the time in the world, keep going.'

'Your office is terrific, they knew just where to get you. How's the hotel?'

'Domina, you're being polite. Forget it, tell me what's next. What does Roe say? Talked to him yet?'

Here we go, thought M.J.

'First tell me about the hotel. I could just be coming over to join you. I could use a holiday. What's it like at the Abbey?'

M.J. heard a laugh at the far end.

'Adorable. They read a book about quaint Paris hotels, copied everything. All the help comes from Balzac. Big iron pot-au-feu in the front hall. Come anytime, I've got a suite. No, don't. You better hang around and get things straight, Dommie. What are you doing next?'

Paris, thought M.J. France. On the telephone? My, my. That would cost Jackson something terrific. She'd always thought people who talked long distance hurried up, said only the important things. And Paris was long, long distance. Dommie? That other lady must sure know Domina well. M.J. thought she had to hand it to Domina, making calls like that on Jackson's money. It was one thing to take home paper clips, markers, pads, things like that. M.J. had always loved getting those extras. And most people did the same, she knew, using the office copier for recipes and clippings, taking home typing paper and pencils for their kids. But she'd never thought about the telephone. Her father would have a fit if she telephoned the store in Eufaula and asked them to get hold of him. Not that she'd do such a thing, ever.

'I'm thinking,' she heard Domina go on. 'I have to get with Roe, find out how he feels. He's been stuck with the client ever since, Maran, took him out to the airport, sort of gave a little extra. I'm dying to know how that man took the whole scene. That damned girl. She's a throwback.'

Me, thought M.J. Little me, causing all this. She felt a thrill go through her, felt the excitement of making things happen, big things.

'I'm glad you're getting out of there, Domina. You're too good for that place, those people. We'll find you a better one, don't fret.'

'Maran, it's not another job, I think this is the time for putting everything together,' Domina said.

What would that mean? wondered M.J.

The next sentences told her. 'I'm going to do what I said, what I've wanted for a long time. I'm going to try to start a place. My own. Look at that Belle Rosner. She's got her own business, really, even if it's just consulting. She made a fortune on that Israeli thing, a fortune you should have had. If she can run her show, at her age, I can.'

Wow, thought M.J., her own advertising agency? That would be a piece of news to have before anyone else. Hey, this phone thing is heaven. The best I've ever done.

'Of course you can. And I'll help. But Belle Rosner? Dommie. I get mad every time I hear that name, that old fraud.'

'Well.' M.J. heard a hesitation in Domina's voice. 'Look.

245

She isn't all that terrible, you know. I had a lunch with her last week, and we talked.'

'She talked, you listened. You had lunch? Why did you have lunch with her? Traitor!'

'Never. She asked me, invited me to Windows on the World. And when she got through explaining New York to me through the glass, which took till about the main course came, she got sort of nice. She wants something of course. She wants to get back into the real world, she said. The promotion convinced her she still could hack it. She loved it all, the commotion, the reporters, everything.'

'It didn't convince me,' said the far voice.

M.J. wished they'd get back to the plans. This was just a side trail, leading nowhere, she thought.

'Well, she wants to be friends, actually talked to me about her daughters. They've disappointed her. Didn't turn out like her at all, one's a housewife, even.'

'You make it sound like one's a criminal,' said the voice.

'She almost thinks that,' said Domina. 'Almost said she'd have loved a daughter like me.'

'Oh, fuck,' said the voice.

M.J. couldn't have agreed more. Get back to the real stuff, to what I need to hear.

'Well, don't worry, it's not just me she's after. She's interested in Roe. Thinks he's political material. Talked about his father, who wants him to be a senator or a governor or something. She thinks she could help him do it, like Benton, Bowles, even Haldeman. And she wants to help him run his show, so she'll be big stuff, too.'

'My God, how they latch on, those leech people,' said the far voice. 'Where do you fit in that beautiful picture?'

'Well, we weren't talking about me. She thinks I have a fine future here.'

'I'm sure you weren't talking about you. That woman never talked about anything but herself in her whole endless life.'

'Maran, be fair. It isn't as if she's nothing. She planned almost that whole promotion. Even on the stage, you said she had an answer. Bare feet, remember? I mean, she didn't absolutely flip, go blank or anything. She had a way to pull it out. It's just your way was better.'

'Fucking A, my way was better,' said the voice.

M.J. heard Domina laugh. Damn, she thought, get back to yourself.

'Listen. Nobody is you, nobody. But think about it. If I did get started on my own, I'd need someone like Belle, too. She's got heaps of prestige. Knows everyone from her era, just like you know all the right people in ours. She's right about Roe, too. He'd be a fantastic politician, bigger work would be great for him. And listen, Maran. She isn't interested in money. She's got plenty. I could get her for almost nothing, have her name on letterheads, that kind of stuff. You wouldn't really mind? She's so sad at times, with that family to look back on. And she's got plenty of bounce left. Suppose you couldn't work? Ask Bill for money? Fill up your days with junk? Especially if you still thought you knew more than anybody. Come on, Maran.'

'I will never retire,' said the voice.

'She wasn't going to, either. It crept up on her. And she was good about it, didn't want to lower her standards, so she stopped. Hates it. By the way, she madly admires everything you've got for me. There, one stylist admiring another's taste.'

'That's the best thing you've said about her.'

'Oh, Maran. If anything ever happened to you, if you needed help, it would be a credit to you to have Belle Rosner as a backup.'

'Nothing will happen to me,' said the voice of Maran. 'She'll dress you in black silk, pearls, you know. Ruin your image.'

'My own agency, maybe it's time,' said Domina.

M.J. could hear her laugh a little.

'Look,' said Maran's voice. 'Get moving. I think your best bet now is Roe. Talk to him, find him. For one thing, he's got pots of money. He could stake you. You're going to need backing. Offices, people, machines, it all costs. Talk to him, just ask him straight out.'

M.J. was pressing the phone so close to her ear, she could almost feel a pink circle forming on her skin.

'I could get a bank,' Domina said. 'I've got a reputation,

a lot of background. Those headhunters call me all the time, big jobs. Maybe they'd help – they put people together to start agencies. Maybe there's an account man somewhere who'd join, or a couple of clients who'd back me.'

'Talk to Roe. Why don't you want to talk to Roe?'

M.J. heard the wires hum, as Domina thought. Gracious goodness, this call must be costing a mint. They sound like they're chatting over the back fence. And I thought *I* was getting away with murder around here.

'Oh, Maran, I hate asking people for things. I like doing them myself.'

'Domina, Roe Rossen isn't people. He's your lover. He adores you, anyone can see it. He's got money to spare, and brains besides. He could sell you to people, give you contacts, all that. It's time you asked a man for something. They aren't all shits, you know.'

Lover, rejoiced M.J. He's her lover. Thanks, telephone.

'Yours have all been,' said Domina. 'So have most of mine. Why should any of them turn out decent, it's never happened to either of us.'

'It's happening to you now,' Maran's voice said firmly. 'At least try. If he won't help, he's a shit, too. My guess is better. He's solid, Domina. He'll help. And he knows the score with you and that agency you're in. Even better, he was on the spot when that little slut acted up.'

Up yours, thought M.J. Who's a slut? Someday I'll meet you, lady, and I'll remember that.

'Well,' said Domina. 'Maybe I don't want to know what he'd do. He's the nicest man I've met in years. Ever. Sometimes I think how great he'd be with Michael, for Michael to look up to. Sometimes I think about baking bread for him, sewing his buttons on. I don't *want* to find out he's a bastard. Ever. Silly isn't it. But I'll talk to him. When I find him. Wonder where he went after the airport. Maybe the Detroit plane didn't get off – I could call the Admiral Club. You know, Maran, I'm not even positive he saw what M.J. did. Can't remember where he was standing. I was so excited they'd liked the ads, you know? And then for that kid to get me to blow up. Well, it wasn't all M.J. It

248

was Brady, really. It's been coming for a long time.'

'Domina, they've made you crazy for ages, it's high time you talked back. You're so fucking Catholic, you think if you're good, they'll notice and reward you. It doesn't work. You're good, they step on you some more. Wake up. Be glad it happened.'

'What's your schedule tomorrow? Where can I find you when I know something?'

'There's, wait a minute till I look at my book, a show at Beged-Or, lunch with Ziva, and by the way, she asked me the real story on the shoes at the fashion show, imagine that. I knew the real word would get around. Then I'm going to the atelier to see the basics, how they treat the leathers. Listen. The office has a number for each place, they'll find me. Call me. Call every ten minutes. I want to know what's happening to you. Why the fuck am I always somewhere else when things happen to you?'

'Maran. You're always there when I need you, always. You're the best. So long, take care. Bring me back something Early American.'

'Me,' said Maran's voice. 'I'm getting pretty Early American. Even Payot can't do much for my skin this trip. Got you something, though, you'll love it.'

'Well. What?'

'You'll see when I get back. I want to be there when you open it. It's to wear with Roe, at night. Guaranteed to drive him insane. The prices are twice as high as last year. Breakfast was seventeen dollars at the Plaza Athenée, and I mean a croissant and coffee. Served by six dishonest serving men. It's crazy here. Wish you were around.'

'Well, if things keep going like this, I will be,' Domina's voice said. 'Be good, now.'

'Talk to Roe. Don't worry about me, I'm shopping. If working girls don't buy stuff for themselves, who's going to? Talk to you tomorrow.'

M.J. waited for both phones to click off before she replaced the receiver. Now to get away, fast.

Wow, she thought, fantastic. Better than she'd ever dreamed. What a lot in one easy phone call.

M.J.'s heart bounced up and down, just like her breasts,

as she ran for the fire door and the back stairs, to get herself out of sight until Domina came out and took the elevator down. Roe was her lover. her lover. She wanted her own agency. Amazing. M.J. knew she'd never have guessed about that. A real stroke of luck. And she wants help from Roe. Wonder if Roe knows that. Wonder how he'll like Domina asking him for a loan, a big one. Or maybe a present.

M.J. stood breathlessly behind the iron door as she heard the tap of Domina's heels growing louder out in the corridor. They tapped past where she was standing, then grew fainter. She could hear the heavy roll of the elevator doors as they opened and closed again. Safe to come out.

For absolute security, M.J. walked down a floor and peeked out carefully before she entered the foyer. Nobody around, thank goodness. She rang for the elevator, stirring her brains around with all their new information, letting it all sift together like flour, waiting for the best ideas to powder down, leaving the lumps of silly, impractical notions caught in the strainer.

Standing alone on the echoing marble floor, tapping her foot impatiently, M.J. suddenly realized that one piece of information was better than all the rest.

Roe Rossen might not have seen what she'd done to Harrell.

Domina hadn't been sure. M.J. racked her brain to remember where Roe had been standing. Hadn't he gone on ahead? Couldn't she get her version of the story to him before Domina did? It might solve a hell of a lot of problems. Be fun, too.

And as the elevator doors opened for her, she knew exactly what to do next.

Roe

Roe watched the Ford men go through the gate to the Detroit plane.

As soon as the last blue suit disappeared, he turned and dashed back to the terminal entrance.

God, he thought, the fog, the waiting around. Thought they'd never get that bloody plane off the ground. Three hours, seven beers, and all I wanted was to get to a phone alone, to talk to Domina.

He slipped into the first booth along the passageway. The phone was out of order. In one swoop he was in the one next door. This time the telephone accepted his dime, and he dialed for a taxi.

'Roe Rossen, Potter Jackson Company, La Guardia across from the parking lot. Hurry it up, all right?'

He waited impatiently, while the phone went dead and the canned music came on the line. He didn't want to wait one minute on the taxi line outside. He wanted to get back to Domina.

The meeting had been a smash, he thought, right out of his dreams. Everything he'd wanted for her, guided her toward, had worked right. Harrell had been delighted. He'd said so straight out in the Admiral Club, and even those anonymous assistants had said pleasant things. Harrell hadn't liked the one campaign, but what the hell, they'd had to prepare that one, for tradition's sake. He *had* liked Domina's campaign. Must have thrilled her. What's more, Harrell had liked Domina as a person. He'd asked Roe a lot of questions about her, where she'd come from, what else she worked on. A lot of bridges had been crossed in that one meeting. The work was coming along. The client relationship was, too. And Domina's future in the agency would be working out just fine.

Where the hell was Domina? He'd tried her once from the club, but she hadn't come back to her office. The instant he got the number of a cab, he'd try again, unless they had one for him right away. Domina, he thought, while the unctuous, smarmy music slurred on the phone line. Beautiful. Brave. Independent. Doesn't need reassurance every ten minutes, doesn't lean all over me, isn't after what I can do for her. She does it herself, whether it's managing an apartment, giving a dinner party, running a copy group, thinking up an advertising campaign. Tough and pliable, her own person and mine, and, she's something more when I've got her all alone and that cool comes apart and warms for me. My love.

'Rossen? Car 182 in three minutes. Going back to the office?'

'I'll tell the driver where, I'm not sure yet,' said Roe.

He hung up quickly and dialed Domina's apartment. After three rings, he gave up. She always got to the phone fast or not at all. He'd never seen a woman who could let the phone ring on, unanswered, the way she could. 'I wouldn't let a person barge in here when I'm busy,' she told him, 'so why should I let a telephone do it? If it's important, they'll call back.' Sensible, but how many women were sensible?

He ran for his cab, found it, slammed inside, and leaned back in the worn seat.

'Go on into the city,' he said to the driver, 'and I'll tell you the exact address when I see how fast we get in.'

They slid out into the airport traffic, picked up speed heading for the Triboro Bridge. Roe was glad. The driver was adept at weaving in and out of the crowded lanes.

Harrell's some guy, he thought, willing the car to go faster. Doesn't talk much about himself, doesn't brag about past triumphs, what worked for him last year. But the Blossom is for next year. A new product, and eighty percent of every year's new products are failures. People think they want catsup in low, fat jars so it'll come out faster. Make it, and it's not the catsup they're used to. The Blossom looks sensational, but who really knows? Somebody thought the Edsel looked great, too. I'd like to see

Harrell Barber make a hit with this, find out how far in that company a black man can go. He was acting a little strange back there in the Admiral Club. Doesn't like drinking? Something bother him about our meeting? God, I'm dead. Just let me get to Domina.

He could see her so clearly. Glowing naked in his bed, her beautiful hair spread out on his pillow. Working on the ads, chewing a pencil and frowning. Sipping wine across his table, tipping her head back, her lovely neck gleaming in candlelight. Domina.

The car radio blared, repeating names for new pickups, hurrying individual drivers to various addresses. More and more, advertising people were depending on radio cabs, as the regular street taxis in New York got creakier. Jackson had a company charge account, and all the top executives signed chits for their rides. We run on cabs, thought Roe, as well as planes. Always in a hurry. Never enough time in this business.

When they reached the sharp curve of the bridge into the city, where zebra stripes warn motorists to slow down, which they never do, the driver angled his head toward the back seat. 'Where to, Mr Rossen? I'll be downtown in five minutes.'

Like hell you will, Roe thought, looking ahead to the crowded highway along the East River. Home, he decided. Shower, drink, fresh clothes. Then I'll find her and we'll eat. Celebrate.

'Sutton Place,' he said. 'Corner of Fifty-fourth, you know.'

The driver nodded. When the next call came screaming through the mike, he picked it up and gave the number of his cab. 'Ten minutes,' he said into the mike.

Exactly fourteen minutes later, after a slowdown at the Ninety-sixth Street exit and an accident that stopped movement near the New York Hospital, Roe swung out of the cab. He handed the driver a bill, even though you weren't supposed to tip. He wanted these guys liking him, coming to get his calls fast, anytime, anywhere.

He went quickly through his lobby and into the elevator, pressing the top button. Speed, he wanted speed. Get to the phone, try Domina at home once more before the shower. Where the devil is she? She wouldn't celebrate without him. There wasn't any other account right now to hang her up. Emergency? But she'd leave word for him somehow. Well, if she still didn't answer at home, he'd call the office night line, see if there was any message.

The elevator door opened at last. Roe went for his door, key in hand. And stopped cold.

On the floor, her back to his front door, her arms clasped around her knees, sat M.J. Kent.

The last person in the world he had on his mind. Before he had an instant to wonder what she was doing curled up against his door, she smiled up at him. 'Hi,' she said.

Her voice was full of breath. M.J. exhales words, Roe thought.

'Well, hi. How'd you get here? Did the doorman let you up? He's not supposed to.'

'I have a way with doormen,' M.J. said lightly. 'You going to ask me in?'

'Not till you tell me why you're here. I wasn't even supposed to be here. How long were you going to wait?'

She smiled wider, and got herself up from the door. Graceful, he noticed, which most girls wouldn't be. When she stood up, the top of her head didn't quite reach as high as his chin. Doll, he thought suddenly, she's like a fragile, tiny doll.

'I knew you'd be right along,' she said. 'Just so happened, I was in a cab going home. They kept saying your name, waiting to see where you were headed from the airport. When you said here, I just came right along, too.'

Roe reached past her to open the front door, walked into his apartment, and turned around to face her again. 'Do you usually drop in uninvited on Jackson executives?' he said. He put as much chill into his voice as he had left after a tough day.

'There's a reason. Please ask me inside?'

Roe was tired. He'd been watching every word all day long. He wanted to handle this right; he knew this little girl was trouble. All sorts of thoughts zinged through his mind. She does work for Domina, for Jackson, she's not a strange hooker just showing up at my door. But she's too pretty to be here. Too sly to talk to here. Fuck it, I can handle this.

'Look, M.J., you want to talk to me, see me in my office tomorrow. I can't imagine what we'd have to talk about, anyway. You just go home, and we'll forget about this, okay?'

She walked past him, dipping under his outstretched arm as he leaned to block her.

'Domina Drexler,' she said. 'How's that for a reason?'

Roe felt a trickle of fear at the back of his neck, a heartbeat skip. A little blackmail? Office gossip? She wanted something, but what? All right, he thought, let's get to it, see how bad it's going to be.

He walked through to the living room and turned on the lights, putting his jacket on a chair, loosening his tie. Without speaking, he went on into the little kitchenette. Ice cubes, glass, Scotch, water, one drink, his. When he'd fixed it, he turned back into the living room and sat down in an armchair. M.J. was perched on the threshold of his terrace, looking out at the river without a sound.

Roe shivered, he couldn't help it. 'Okay,' he said. 'Talk.'

'I will.'

She came around and sat primly in a straight chair, with her back to the river. With her hands in her lap, her feet set straight and together, M.J. in her best pink jeans and top made a pretty sight. He caught himself. Pretty is as pretty does – the words kept going through his head.

'Roe. I wouldn't be here if I wasn't just in the most terrible trouble. You left too fast this afternoon after the meeting. You don't know what happened after?'

Was she going to appeal to him? Ask him for something? Jesus, he'd been sure she was about to threaten to tell Brady Godwin he was screwing her boss, or tell him Domina was going back to her husband, or something just as grim. Had something happened to Domina?

'What was it? What bothered you enough to come here to my apartment at night? Keep going, M.J.'

The girl looked surprised, glanced around the room quickly, as if she'd noticed for the first time that it was night. When she looked back at him, tears were starting in the corners of her eyes.

'The most awful thing,' she said. 'Domina's furious at me. She knows I heard about something you won't like. She picked a whole fight with me over it. And after you left, she turned on me like a witch and said I was fired. She called Mr Godwin and everyone, and told me to get out, just like that. And, Roe, I don't know what I'm going to do, you've just got to help convince her for me.'

Just another office mess, he thought, relaxing a little. Something anyone else would have waited till tomorrow for, but she's young, doesn't know how to wait.

'Take it from the top,' he said. 'Why is Domina angry? We had a great meeting, the client was happy. What did you do?'

'It's not what I did,' said M.J., the tears beginning to spill over out of her violet eyes. Tears turned those eyes a deeper purple, Roe saw, made them look like dewy flowers. 'It's what I heard, I'm telling you.'

Tears always got to Roe. Louise had cried, Lolly, now another girl starting to weep. Even Domina, he remembered suddenly; the first time he'd really looked at her, she'd been teary, too. Women, all do the same damned things. Then he realized he was betraying Domina even in a quick thought, and he put the thought away fast, to concentrate on M.J.

'You see, I was in her office right after the wonderful meeting, so excited, so keyed up with everything going so well. And she had this phone call, Roe, from somewhere in Europe, someone she seemed to know real well, who knew enough to call and ask her how the meeting went.'

Who? A man? Where the hell was this conversation going?

'I was right there, tidying up the layouts to give Dan, you know, for the shipping. I couldn't help hear. She acted like I wasn't there, she was so anxious to talk to whoever it was. And that was when I heard.'

M.J. paused, reaching her small hand up to her cheek to wipe away the tears that were spilling out now, over her pink T-shirt, into her lap. Those little water drops, somehow, Roe thought, emphasized her breasts, brought his eye toward her crotch, outlined in her tight pants as she sat in his Queen Anne chair.

'Roe, she's going to leave Jackson. I don't know what to do,' said M.J.

That was madness. But still he began to pay attention.

'Leave Jackson? Now? M.J., you don't know what you're talking about. You've got something mixed up. Why would she leave now, when everything's going so fine?'

A vast relief was stealing over him now, he could understand what this conversation was all about, where it was going. M.J. had listened, must have said something, annoyed Domina, that was all. The girl had been scared. Just a baby, really. Everyone knew she adored Domina – that had been plain all through the car work. Every time she'd been in the room with her boss, M.J. had been alert, responsive, eager to please. He'd get to the bottom of it, give her a drink maybe, send her on home.

His relief ended with M.J.'s next words.

'Because she's going to start her own agency,' she said.

Roe felt stunned. 'She said that?'

'That's what I'm telling you. I heard her talking about it on the telephone. She said this was the time, now when everything was going right. And whoever she was talking to, she said she was ready to ask you for help.'

He felt as if she'd dealt him a karate blow. Domina? Who'd never asked him for a flower, an extra moment of his time in the office? Who'd even put him off about helping her with her title?

'What kind of help?'

'I don't rightly know,' said M.J., 'and I don't care. What I care about is, she was real mad at me for being there. And, Roe, I couldn't help it, you have to help, tell her that. She was so excited with who she was talking to. And then she turned on me! I didn't think Domina could ever talk like that. I got a whole different look at her.'

Jesus, another one of those damned female quarrels, like Louise used to have with her friends, and I'm smack in the middle of this, somehow. It's late. I'm dead tired. I've got to get this kid out of here, and she can't go downstairs crying through my lobby, either.

He got up and went to the phone in the foyer, dialed Domina's number. It rang, once, twice, three times. He hung up.

'You can help me, Roe, please,' said M.J., calm now. 'I want to stay at Jackson, I love it there. It's everything I ever wanted, that art department, those nice folks, you, Mr Godwin, Domina. Well, now not Domina, I guess. Not anymore.'

Her face began to screw up again with her tears, he saw. Head them off, he thought.

'Okay, baby, listen,' he said. 'For heaven's sake, stop crying, it doesn't help anything. I've got your message. You come on in the kitchen, I'll give you a Coke.'

Not for anything was he going to give this kid a drink. Who could tell how she reacted to liquor? OUT. He wanted her out of his apartment. She sure was upset, though. Always pretty calm before, during all the late-night meetings, the frantic pace they'd worked at to get the Ford stuff ready. Something had knocked her out. What had she heard?

'Domina was sore at you?' he asked.

'Oh, Roe, I can't begin to tell you. She hollered. Reamed me out for being there at all, and ended up telling me I'm fired. Fired. I'll have to go back home. Be poor all over again, and I'm dead good and tired of being poor,' M.J. said, burying her pretty face in her little hands, her whole body tense with anguish.

'Come on, M.J.,' Roe said comfortingly. 'Nobody's going to fire you, your work's too good. People don't get fired for being in the wrong room at the wrong time.'

While he was saying it, he knew it wasn't so. People got fired for exactly a reason like that. When he'd first gone to work, Roe had assumed that people got ahead if they worked hard, helped their bosses rise, responded well to pressure, things like that. It had taken him a while to learn that all those things could go askew. Sometimes pleasing your boss was the wrong thing, if management disliked your boss. Then they'd dislike you, too. Sometimes working hard wasn't wanted; taking the client out for golf was. People got fired for being one too many in a group, for being the last person hired during a recession time. People got fired in advertising for making jokes at the wrong moment, for wearing the wrong clothes, even. If this girl had been in Domina's office, overhearing something Domina wanted kept private, she could easily get fired.

'Why me?' he said. 'Why didn't you wait till morning and go talk to Mr Godwin? He's the creative director, he's supposed to straighten out things like this for people. Why come to me? And at night, in my apartment? I could get all sorts of wrong ideas about you, M.J.'

He smiled, to show her he was joking a little.

She stood up suddenly, took her hands from her face, came closer to him as he stood in the kitchenette at the refrigerator.

In the doorway she looked twelve years old, her head just measuring up to the top of the fridge. Pink in the face from her tears, orange curls spilling over her back, one strand of orange hair threaded across her cheek where it was wet, M.J. glowed against the lights from the terrace. Christ, she's a beauty, he thought, even a woman like Domina would probably want to kill her, one time or another. She's a beauty even in this city, where beautiful women are ten to a block, at every restaurant table, in every other seat at the theater. A beauty.

'I wouldn't dare bother Mr Godwin,' she was saying quietly. 'He's too grand, too big, I'd be scared to pieces to tell him. You're different. Not stuffy, and you're so much younger and all, and you've seen me work. I kind of trusted you, Roe. I thought you'd help me with old Domina. At least, it came to me that way in the taxi. I had no mind to come here at all when I left the office. Just wanted to get home, think it all out, figure what I did wrong. And then, when they said your name on the radio thing, I thought it was like fate, you know, telling me where to go. I never thought before where you lived. But they said where on the radio. Honest, that's how it was.'

Made sense, he thought. Port in a storm, that was all.

He opened the fridge, flipped up a can of Coca-Cola. He poured the dark, sparkling liquid into a glass and handed it to her.

M.J. took the glass, dipped her face to it, sipped gratefully, like a little girl holding a glass of milk carefully with two hands.

'Drink up,' he said, as if to a child. 'Then we'll call you one more cab and send you home. Don't fret. As soon as I can catch up with Domina, I'll see what's what.'

Old Domina, M.J. had said. Well, this kid was just out of her teens. Guess she would think of Domina as old. And I seem all that much younger than Godwin to her. Funny. Only ten years or so between me and Brady. Just that he's so old-guard. But Roe was pleased at the comparison.

'Oh, Roe. I knew you'd help. Please make them let me stay, whatever she does. I could work hard in another group. And I love the cars. Couldn't you get me on one of the big ones? In one of your other groups? Couldn't you?'

'I'll give it a try, honey,' he said.

He felt great now, somehow, expansive, helpful, powerful. She was such a pretty little thing.

She was looking up at him with a smile starting on the corners of her pink mouth. It wasn't every girl that looked up at him, he thought suddenly, at his height. Kind of nice, he realized. This little thing he could pick up like a child, carry.

Get hold of yourself, he thought, and went resolutely to the phone. He dialed the cab company again, gave his name, waited.

'Car 42, seven minutes? Fine. The lady will tell you where.'

'Roe?' said M.J. over the top of her glass.

'You better get downstairs now, M.J. The doorman will put you in the taxi, car 42. Don't worry, we'll see how things go in the morning. I'm sure there's some simple reason Domina acted the way she did. She was probably keyed up, getting the ads back in order, getting things straight: There's no telling who she was talking to when you heard her. And I'm sure you've got it wrong about her leaving.'

'Roe,' said M.J., 'thank you. Really, thank you. Forgive me coming here and all, I was really beside myself. She never acted like that before, ever. It was like something you know all about suddenly turning into something else, some-

261

thing horrible and scary. She scared me. I didn't know she could do that.'

A child, Roe thought, just a child. Forget all this now, get her home.

In spite of himself, in spite of knowing better, he felt the pull of her enough to lean down and touch her cheek, to smooth away the strand of hair that was out of place.

Somehow M.J. suddenly was curled in his arms, pressed against his body.

He could feel the swelling of her breasts against his chest, smell the warm fragrance of her skin. As he looked down at her, the amazing color of her hair filled his eyes with fire and sunlight and excitement. His body stirred, his cock warmed and swelled, starting to strain upward.

Jesus, he thought, and he pressed her away with his hands, held her by the shoulders, moving her to arm's length. Jesus Christ, I'm acting like an idiot, a dirty old man. A hungry kid. She's even younger than Lolly, for God's sake. What the fuck am I doing?

'Okay, baby,' he said. His voice strained, he thought, the words coming out peculiarly.

'Thanks,' she said. And smiled dazzlingly, moving away.

When he'd put her out the door, Roe mopped his neck with his shirt sleeve and headed for another Scotch.

Nuts, he thought, I'm nuts. But she's some little dish, anyone would react to that kid, that's a sex kitten like nothing I've seen before.

What the hell went on after that meeting? That's nuts, too. I'm tired, or I wouldn't be so nuts.

He picked the telephone up and carried it to his couch, the long cord trailing behind him. Again he dialed Domina's number. Where in the name of God was Domina? It was late now. She should be home, even if she'd stopped off somewhere. Why didn't she answer?

He lay back on the cushions and looked out over the terrace. The lights moved along the river, boats going by, cars streaking along the highway, planes soaring upward. New York, he thought, out of this world. God, I'm tired.

The telephone awakened him, shrill next to his knee,

where he'd set it on the couch. He had it in one ring, jolted alert.

Domina.

'Domina. Where were you? I've called you, I don't know how many times. You home?'

'Roe, darling, listen. This has been some day, I have a million things to tell you.'

His heart seemed to pump relief, serenity, through his veins, circulate relief all through his body. She was there. Her voice cool, low, quiet. She had a million things to tell him. Nothing was amiss. She was there, at the other end.

'I want to see you,' he said. 'I don't care how late it is, I have to see you. Now. Will you come? Or shall I?'

'I can't,' said Domina.

Everything stopped in his head, his body. He felt dazed, confused.

'What do you mean? Why not?'

'It's a whole long story,' she said. 'Right now, I just can't, Roe. It's been one long mess since right after the meeting. Trouble. I couldn't reach you, tried at the airport, the apartment, and then I got stuck where I couldn't call at all. I was going to say, could we meet for breakfast?'

She sounded different, peculiar. Why?

'Fuck breakfast,' he said. 'Either you come over here now, or I'm coming over there. Right away.'

He heard her hesitate. What the hell was going on?

'My son is home,' she said. 'Some trouble. He was driving home with a bunch of kids, and they had some trouble on the road in Connecticut. I had to go get him. Police station.'

Son. Driving. Police station. God, he thought, what's going on today? She'd never had trouble with her kids before, not that he knew about. Her son was home, at her house. She couldn't let Roe come over, that's what she was saying, and she couldn't just walk out in the middle of the night and leave the boy there, either. Shit.

'So you see,' she was saying. He could hear the pleading. She wanted him to understand, to wait for her.

'I see,' said Roe. It was a whole different picture he saw, suddenly. Till now, she'd been his, all his. There hadn't been anyone else in their lives. Now her son was home.

'If you say so,' he went on. 'Breakfast where? I need you.'

'Meet at, let's see, the Yale Club. Dining room. As early as you like, Roe. Seven? Seven-thirty?'

'The Yale Club,' Roe said. 'You belong to the Yale Club?'

He heard Domina start to laugh. 'Roe, everybody belongs to the Yale Club,' she said. 'It's like everybody's playing polo.'

He was startled for an instant, then remembered. In the twenties, when George Washington Hill had controlled Lucky Strike advertising and blanketed the radio with his own versions of commercials, he'd once refused to let his agency put on a radio broadcast. Sunday afternoons. 'Sunday afternoons, everybody's playing polo,' he'd told the agency men.

'Seven,' he told her. 'It's sooner.'

He looked at his watch. It was two in the morning. He could last, he thought, last until seven to see her.

'Seven,' she said. 'There's a lot. I need your help, Roe. I really need you to help me now. Tell you tomorrow. Good night.'

He held the phone to his ear for a few moments after she hung up. He felt stung. Help. M.J. had said that Domina would ask for help, and he hadn't believed her. What else had M.J. said? Domina wanted to leave Jackson. Well, she didn't need his help for that, she could do that on her own. Though why she'd want to right now was more than he could fathom. But there'd been something else M.J. had said. Domina wanted to start her own agency. There's where she'd need help.

Roe stood up. His shirt was sticking to him, his pants were a handful of wrinkles, his fingers were sticky from Scotch and Coke and sweat. His stomach felt jumpy, and his head, which had started to thud when the phone had rung, was really throbbing now. Something was eluding him still, something M.J. had hinted. He had to discount some of her talk, maybe all, because she'd battled with Domina. But still, what was the last piece of information?

He shucked his clothes, left them for the cleaning lady to get straight in the morning, headed for his bedroom.

Had M.J. tried to tell him that Domina was using him? The girl hadn't really said that, he was certain. So where had the idea come from? Was it his own? Had he been waiting, without knowing it, for Domina to ask, need him for something? Well, didn't most men want women to ask, to need?

The longing to see her close, to get it all straight, to touch her cool skin and bury his face in her glorious hair, overwhelmed him suddenly. Why the hell shouldn't he help her? She was the woman he'd spent his life looking for, he thought. She was the woman who matched his idea of what women ought to be, who fitted into his checklists as he'd never dreamed anyone really would.

Roe yanked the down comforter from the foot of the bed up around his naked body and curled himself in it. The wind was rattling the panes, letting the fall-night chill seep into the bedroom. The lights from the river slid across his ceiling, breaking up the darkness. Tired as he was, he longed for Domina in his arms, and he felt his cock throb.

Why the hell shouldn't he help her? He'd been touched all along by the way she'd done it all herself. Who else had managed life like Domina? Who else had taken care of everybody all along the line? Why wasn't it time somebody took a little care of her?

Roe sat up, pulled the comforter around him like an Indian blanket. He was charged up now, filled with energy and excitement. Why shouldn't he let her ask him for something? He'd feel like a powerhouse, a woman like that having to turn to him. Needing his help. He'd feel like Superman. Jesus, he thought, Domina Drexler needs *me*.

And I need her. Only, not the way she thinks. Not with her flying all over the country, out late with clients, knocking herself out. I need what she can give me. She'd understand everything I do, the perfect backup. With her, instead of a woman like Louise, I could take on anything.

No. There were better things for her. It was time he fought the bastards off for her, got her the hell out.

Hurry, morning, thought Roe. Hurry.

Domina

May we suggest our very own
French Strawberry Omelet?

Farm-fresh country Grade A eggs
whipped with heavy cream, filled
with rosy berries, and glazed with
brown sugar under our broilers.

Domina saw him waiting in the lobby of the Yale Club, pacing. She felt warmed by the sight of him, as if the sun had just come out.

She waved once from the revolving door, went to him, kissed him.

They took the elevator up to the big dining room, walked with the headwaiter past the big bouquet of fresh flowers, past the businessmen eating their giant breakfasts on expense-account money, past the elderly gentlemen who lived at the club, in their worn tweeds and gray flannels, to a table by the window.

Roe, she thought. He actually makes me glow, as if I were basking in hot sun. I can practically feel the side of me that's near him warm up, just as if he were the sun.

He'd been quiet in the lobby, remote all the way up in the elevator, but when they reached the table, he kissed her. Domina was glad she'd waited to put her perfume on till she was in the cab, happy to feel his mouth brush hers again, radiant at the feel of his hand on her arm.

'Order something,' Roe said abruptly. 'We have a lot to talk about.'

'You do it, I don't care.'

He smiled a little, picked up a card set next to the salt and pepper.

'Waiter? Bring us two of these. And coffee now, right now.'

'Orange juice,' Domina said. She was as thirsty as if she were in the sun. Thirsty for Roe, she thought.

'Now,' he said. 'Begin at the beginning. Or tell me about your son. Which?'

'Beginning,' she said. 'Did anyone tell you about M.J.?'

'You tell me,' he said.

She took a deep breath.

'Right after you left, I guess. Saying good-bye to the Ford guys. I didn't know if you'd seen her or not, but she was absolutely horrible to Harrell. Shook hands all along the line with the other men, and when she got to him, put her hands right behind her back and glared. You may have missed it, but Harrell certainly didn't.'

Roe looked down at the table. He put out a hand and moved the salt shaker. He didn't even start to say anything.

Domina was so surprised, she blinked at him. The news hadn't done any of the things she'd thought it would. He was just sitting there looking peculiar. Surprised? No, suspicious. Well, maybe she hadn't explained very clearly.

'Don't you see? It's the last straw for me with that girl. Partly my fault, I shouldn't have let her anywhere near a black guy. She can't stand blacks, she's even wary of the nice black cleaning ladies in the office, but I thought she'd knock it off for a client. Especially Harrell. He's so Ivy League.'

Their orange juice came, little skinny glasses in silver dishes filled with shaved ice. When she tasted hers, somehow it was warm, anyway. And Roe still didn't seem to be understanding her.

'I blew my stack, told her she was fired. Then I got Brady and David Noble right away. And then the trouble started. They won't do it, Roe. They won't let me fire M.J. Kent. Both those bastards stuck up for that kid as if I were the Wicked Witch of the North. It's their reaction to me, of course. They always want to do the opposite of anything I want. But it was the last thing I could take, especially after that meeting. They should have been falling all over me, doing everything I say. So I told them both to go fuck themselves. In actually those words.'

When she looked up at Roe, he was still blank, still different from what she expected.

Suddenly Domina felt weary, stiff, drained. She hadn't slept well. At her age, the lack of sleep showed. There was a lot of light in this breakfast room, she realized, and her face must look exhausted.

'Roe, don't you understand what I'm saying? Forget

M.J., it's what I've done about me. I couldn't stay at Jackson now if I wanted to, I don't think. It can't be smoothed over, it was all-out war from me. And I don't want to stay. I don't mean I want to leave you, leave the Blossom, all that. But I can't stand their damned hypocrisy anymore. Not even to be with you.'

The waiter was bringing the serving cart. Proudly he whisked the covers off the dishes, handed them over with a flourish.

Roe was thinking hard, thinking: what's the truth of this, what really happened after I left, for Christ's sake? I can't turn my back on any of them, even Domina, without something going screwy. Wait, that's disloyal as hell. Why would I listen to M.J. Kent's side of anything? Especially against Domina. Why? Because M.J.'s story made sense, that's why. And it'll make more sense if Domina goes on to talk about getting out. Wait. Let's see.

'What happened next?'

Neither of them lifted a fork.

'Next I wanted you. Called the airport, but you weren't anywhere. And just then, Leota called from home. Beside herself, I could hardly understand what she was saying. The police had my Michael in Naugatuck. She got them to promise to call back in half an hour, wanted me to come straight home. I flew up there. Imagine, Roe, I had no idea what he'd done, why they were holding him. I nearly went mad. He's only sixteen. And I couldn't do a thing till they called again. I got a car and a driver and just waited by the phone, dying.'

'What was it all about?'

'He was coming down to the city from school in a car with a bunch of kids. The police pulled them over for something small, looked around. Somebody had dope in a backpack. They took all of them in, called the parents.'

She said it lightly enough, but it hadn't felt light. Domina kept remembering her terror. Michael, her Michael, she'd thought him safe in the common room at Choate. Instead, he'd been slumped on a bench in a grubby police station.

The ride up had been pure horror. The car had lurched

horribly over the rough highways, the lights flashing by had pierced her eyes. Domina's nervousness had made her smoke one cigarette after another, and her shaking hands had sent burning sparks into her lap. Stray pieces of the day whirled in her mind, the meeting, Harrell, Roe, M.J., but always the fear of Michael beat at her. Why? Because he'd had no father? Because she'd been busy working? She'd remembered Michael held down by the heavy leg cast, imagined him locked in by handcuffs and bars.

Domina had been the first parent to get there, followed by two men. Fathers. The officer had avoided her eye, spoken to the men. The boys, he had explained, had agreed to plead guilty, could pay fines, then go home.

Michael had come through a door with the other boys, looking so young, ashamed, vulnerable, Domina had almost moved to put her arms around him, feeling a rush of protective strength. But Michael had pressed her away, embarrassed in front of the others. She'd felt another great wave of misery and guilt.

Then outside, when Michael had caught sight of the limousine, the uniformed chauffeur, near the two fathers' cars, he'd hung his head. Domina had known he was hating the richness of the big car, feeling ashamed of a mother who couldn't even drive herself anywhere.

Once in the car, he had turned away from her, stared into the moving darkness. Domina had felt totally shut out, unable to reach him. She couldn't bear it, her failure to reach him. She wanted desperately to pull him toward her, soothe him as if he were still a small boy. Only Michael wasn't a small boy anymore.

'Waiter,' said Roe, as she sat thinking how she adored Michael, how she would beat at his captors with her hands if she had to.

'Bring us two more of these,' he said. 'We let them get cold, sorry.'

Domina suddenly felt hunger like a huge hole in her stomach, remembering she'd eaten nothing since yesterday morning. Maybe she would feel better, look better once she'd eaten.

'Anyway, then I got to you,' she said, wrenching herself

back to this moment, this sullen male figure. 'Now. Tell me. Did Harrell say anything about M.J.?'

'No,' said Roe. 'Not a word.'

Damn. If Harrell had complained everybody would be on her side. M.J. would sail right out the door. But then, nothing would change what Domina had said herself to Brady and David. They'd never forget.

'Look,' said Roe. 'Is it all settled about Michael?'

'Yes. He went back up to Connecticut on the bus this morning. My lawyer says it happens a lot, police look for kids on the road, they've no right to search cars, but they do. There's nothing against Michael. He's even been a little grateful, admitted he was glad I came. And that he was scared. That's a lot from a sixteen-year-old boy.'

Roe thought: I'd like to scare him, belt him one. That's all Domina needs, a drug rap to handle.

The omelets came. This time they both ate, Roe finishing first, but Domina not far behind. The eggs were delicious, creamy on the bottom, crunchy on the top, sweet on the tongue. The waiter poured more coffee. Roe looked at Domina's cup. Jesus, she drank that stuff by the gallon, and without a drop of cream. No wonder she got all nerved up, blew her stack with Brady.

'Let's talk about the office, then,' he said. 'What do you want to do?'

'I could look for another job,' Domina said wearily. 'It's the standard move. It wouldn't be too hard. Getting to the end of the year when everybody moves, after bonus time, and profit-sharing. And I get calls from headhunters all the time. But I think I have a better idea.'

Now, Roe thought, now she's going to say it.

'I want to start my own agency,' Domina said.

Yes, M.J. did hear her. But was it Domina? Or did the girl really insult Harrell and make that up to cover herself? I'd bet on Domina. M.J. looks like a born liar.

'I think I could swing it,' Domina was saying. 'Ford is out, I suppose. But Bonnell should come, he's followed me before. I'd find space, hire a writer, an art director. Or farm the work out – there are plenty of freelance people. Roe, I've had it with big agencies, stuffed shirts, management

272

guys who think women are lucky to work at all. I'm sick of fighting my own bosses. And I really think I can make it work on my own.'

Roe cleared his throat, the way he did before any sales pitch. 'Domina,' he said firmly. 'You're out of your mind.'

She looked as if he'd socked her one.

'You're dreaming,' he pressed on. 'You're like Michael, you haven't any idea what you're talking about.'

She tried to say something, but he wasn't going to let her.

'Wake up. This isn't moving from Elkhart, Indiana, to Chicago with a two-bit account you stole from a store. This is taking on The Potter Jackson Company. They've got the biggest law firm in Wall Street to handle people like you who fight them. They'll sue you for more money than you've made in your whole life, put together. Did that occur to you? You think they're sore now? Wait till you flounce out the door with some of their business. See how they act then. And how they'll go after you.'

Domina looked at him in amazement. 'Flounce?' she said.

'Don't pick at words.' Roe went on. Hit her hard, he thought, then you can pick her up again once she's down. 'All you women pick at words. It's actions you should be worried about, it doesn't matter what they say about you, for Christ's sake, it's what they *do* to you. Can't you get that in your head? Jesus, I could really kill you, if I didn't love you. Why would I want to see you walk out of my life? And you'd *be* out, if you had an agency. Have you the foggiest idea what it's like? You wouldn't have a minute of your own. Agency presidents are the original workaholics. Around the clock, day, night, Sunday, keeping every little client happy because God forbid one of them should walk out, there'd go a month's profits. That's another thing, Domina. You're talking little stuff.'

He could see her swallow.

'Little stuff?'

'Yes. Small, picayune, two-bit advertising. Haven't you learned anything at Jackson? You've handled the best. The government of a country. Cars, the center of the whole American economy. That's television, four-color magazine ads, expensive production, research, top clients. Where the action is. You know what you'd get in your own agency? Local stores. Dress manufacturers. Mrs Nobody's pies. Matchbook covers. Subway cards. Radio, if you were really lucky.'

Now she was silent. Good.

'Christ, I don't know where to start telling you. Have you any idea who the people are who start agencies?'

No answer. Better.

'Losers, that's who. No-goods, people who couldn't make it in big places. Creative geniuses who feel stepped on. People who couldn't take the politics, the rejection, the hard work. People who got fired. They look for a job, their unemployment insurance runs out, and pow, great idea, they'll start an agency. And they fail. Fast. For the same reason you'd fail. Because they haven't a clue how to do it. They can't pay bills or factor money or do projections of business. They can't even arrange to keep the office clean. They don't understand the shit work in running an agency, they've been living too big in agencies where whole departments do that stuff.'

The waiter came around again, because Roe had let his voice rise.

'You're talking like a wife who wants to go back to work after a lifetime of kids,' he said in a lower tone. 'Wants to open a tea-shop. Or a bookshop. Sees herself in a hostess outfit handing out brownies to her friends, or discussing Proust with a young poet. But that isn't what happens. She gets bills, waiters who have knife fights with chefs, dishwashing machines that won't pass sanitary inspections. Or she gets a mountain of books to dust, crazy order forms, cartons to open. It's the same thing. You see yourself as Madam President, no Brady Godwin, no board of directors, no stuffed shirts bossing you, doing beautiful creative work your own way. What you'd get is drudgery, scramble, a battle for accounts, hiring troubles, lawsuits, the works. For that you'd leave Jackson? Not to mention leaving me. I wouldn't see you once a week. You'd be exhausted, drained, broke all the time, worried sick. Knock it off, Domina. You're talking like a small-town girl.'

Enough, he thought.

'I see you don't think I should start an agency,' Domina said.

He glared at her.

'Well, what *do* you think I should do? Apologize to Brady? Say I was sick? Menopausal? Insane? Tell them I'm lucky to have that cute Southern girl working for me? That I'm thrilled to have men of their experience bossing me? Not to mention men of *your* experience. What?'

'If you loved me at all, you wouldn't want to do this,' said Roe.

Domina thought: my God, it always comes down to that. Men. If you really loved them, you'd do every last thing they said, right or not.

'Jesus,' she said. 'What shit. What corn. I mean, it *has* been done, you know. People have taken accounts and started great agencies. Colwell. Backer. Jordan. Della Femina. For God's sake, Roe, what was *your* idea of what I'd do if I loved you at all?'

He put both hands to his tie, yanking it loose. 'I have it all figured out,' he said. And grinned. 'Now that I've softened you up, I have it all figured out.'

Domina felt terribly confused, terribly cold. She'd never dreamed he would feel so superior to people who wanted to be out on their own. To her. Did he really mean all that? Did he just want her near him? Would he brush her whole working life aside just to have her nearby?

'I think you should forget about running your own show,' Roe said. 'I'd hoped you'd start thinking about running mine. I could do with your brains and spirit helping me, Domina. And I'd do a lot for you in return. Listen. I never expected to say this to anyone again, but I'm saying it to you. Marry me. I'll take care of you, we'll be terrific. I'll be good for your kids, we'll be a family. Domina, let me take you away from all this.'

The cold dissolved. He loves me, Domina thought. He wants to take care of me, nobody ever wanted that. I'm getting warm again. I'm coming into sunlight and heat and it's marvelous. Roe Rossen wants me to marry him.

275

Her pulse began to speed, and little stray thoughts popped into her head, beating time with it. Mrs Roe Rossen. Mr and Mrs Forever and ever. Night after night. Same bed. Same house. Traveling. Growing old.

Then her heartbeats all seemed to flutter together, and she thought, Michael's graduation and we'll both be there, Maria's wedding and he'll give her away, I can let go, rest, lean on him. Marry.

She imagined all of it. Waking with Roe, Leota bringing breakfast for both of them, pancakes, warm syrup, crisp bacon. No, he'd hate breakfast in bed. Too restless. But dinners, company dinners. Roe at one end of a long table, white damask, gleaming silver, Roe carving. And summers, beaches with Roe, sailing with Roe, the steep rise and fall of a deck under their feet, the salt spray in their eyes, the gulls swirling in their wake. Heaven, she thought.

She focused on him, across the table. His palms were down beside his plate, his eyes looked straight at her, he leaned a little forward. Just the way he did in meetings, waiting for the client's verdict. His face was ready for a client, too. He looked calm, sure of himself, ready for action. She'd seen that look work with clients after he'd presented the agency viewpoint, when clients gave up some silly notion and capitulated, agreed to do things his way. Roe was selling. Astounded, she realized that she recognized selling so clearly because she could sell, too. She was every bit as good at it as he. And now he wanted her to stop doing it. To marry him and stop working. If she agreed, she would never sell a client anything again, ever.

The thought was so shocking, like agreeing never to walk again, that words bubbled up to explain it to him.

'Roe, darling. I love you, you know it. There's never been anyone like you, there could never be. But I don't want anyone to take me away from all this, this work. I want to be let loose on it. I want to see how far I can go. To run my own show. To try for something better. You should understand, it's just what you want for yourself.'

Even while she spoke, the dizzying idea of marrying Roe was fluttering in her head. Think what Maran would say. She'd say grab him, then go design my wedding dress.

Think what Brady would do. Probably have a heart attack. Tempting thought, turning over everything to Roe's steady leadership. But then what? How would she fill the days? Wait for Roe to come home at night? Wait for Roe to come back from a trip? Wait for Roe to tell her what Ford had said to him? When she'd just begun working along with him, being there for everything, keeping up with him?

'Domina, this is the right time,' Roe said, as if he could hear her thoughts. 'You've had the best job in the business. All the extras, trips, expense accounts, power, luxury. You've proved yourself a hundred times. Try something new. You've never had a husband who was somebody. Who went places, did things, took you on up with him. Why not try that? You'd be fantastic. We'd be fantastic. Think. We could do anything, go anywhere, share everything. What more do you want?'

Domina thought: even Freud asked that question. What more is there? What do women want? Freud should have known, Roe should know, men should all know. We just want the same things they do. I want to know how good I can be. How far I can go on my own. How much I can handle. I'm only thirty-seven, I've got years. He makes marriage sound like honorable retirement. Who retires at thirty-seven? I've got energy and talent and push.

The waiter was back again, holding the big silver pot in a spotless napkin. 'More coffee?' he asked them.

Domina nodded. He poured out the steaming coffee carefully.

Roe looked over at her, then down at the coffeecup. He made a little face, a small gesture of disapproval. 'Christ, at least put in some cream,' he said. 'It's not good for you, all that black coffee, you'll get all nerved up. Here.'

He picked up the cream jug and poured generously, before she could stop him. He kept pouring, ruining with the thick, greasy, cloying cream the good, strong, bitter coffee she wanted.

Suddenly she felt exhausted. Why couldn't Roe just help her with an agency the way she'd asked? Why did he have to offer a counterproposal? He thinks he knows it all, that I haven't really thought it out. He's forgotten that I was

277

smarter than he was about Maran versus Belle, that I found the flaw in that stupid invitation. Can't he realize I've thought about my own agency for a couple of years, I know all that junk he's talking about? Does he think what I'd be like if I didn't work? I could turn into somebody he wouldn't like. I love the routine, the gossip of an office, the small-village life of an agency, who's doing what to whom, a place where they need me every day. Jesus, men retire and go mad with boredom, have heart attacks in Florida, start hitting their wives. Why doesn't he realize I could go mad waiting around for him? He's thinking about himself, what I could do to make life glorious for him. Sure, I'd be a good wife, better than some suburban lady who doesn't understand what he's talking about. But for how long?

And then she was angry, not just at Roe, but at herself.

What's wrong with me, she thought, why do I think so much? Why can't I just relax, stop planning, guessing about the future? Why isn't it enough just to please him? Am I greedy? Selfish? Crazy?

She looked at him, angry, adorable. He looked so loveable, she put her head down, away from his eyes. There was her coffee. Cream was curling lazily into the black liquid, turning the hot bitterness into something sweet, thick, heavy. Not what she wanted. What Roe thought she ought to want. Domina began feeling hot. The pleasant glow was warming up now, making her a little dizzy.

'Roe,' she said carefully. 'I know you want to save me misery. But I don't want to be saved. I want to take that misery and turn it around, make it into something I'm proud of. Do you understand? Can you possibly understand?'

She looked up. Roe seemed to be shimmering in a haze of heat.

'I understand,' he said. 'I understand I've just asked you to marry me, and it doesn't interest you much. I understand you've turned on a little girl who got wind of your plans a bit too soon. I understand, Domina, you've used me up. Now you want to chase rainbows, get your own fucking advertising agency, that's all.'

It was as if he'd reached over and slapped her. Her cheek

actually burned. Little girl. Was that M.J.? Rainbows. Used him up. Holy God.

'You've got all the answers, Domina, the hell with anyone else's ideas, feelings. Everyone should obey, Jackson, M.J., your own son. And me. First of all, me. What I want doesn't matter. You're so positive you're right, no wonder you make men furious at you.'

Domina could feel the marks of his fingers burning on her face, feel tears spring up. Her head rang. Her throat closed and she began to breathe hard, trying to get air, trying to hold back the sob she knew was gathering in her lungs.

She looked at Roe through tears, his face dissolving. And she turned, left her chair, moved fast to the front of the room.

Domina

Mrs Drexler:
Don't forget your massage,
Elizabeth Arden, 9th floor,
Tuesday, 3:30.
                    Leota

Wrapped in heated towels, lulled by absolute silence, Domina lay under a velvety blanket on the massage table. Rich fragrances from open pots of cream and bottles of lotion swirled in the air. Shadowy darkness loomed all around. There was no earthly way a woman could feel more cosseted. But there she lay, rigid with tension, neck hurting, back aching.

Usually a massage made her look and feel five years younger, sent blushes into her face, sparkle into her eyes, smoothed away the week's problems.

Today, all the comfort served only to focus her on everything that was wrong with her life.

She hadn't heard from Roe in six days.

At first she'd been sure he'd call when he calmed down. After a whole day of waiting, she thought perhaps he'd call at night. But in six days and nights he'd never tried to reach her. Every time she answered the telephone, she'd composed her voice only for him, but the voice at the other end had never been his.

The phone had been ringing a lot. Her secretary. Where was she? When was she coming in? What should be said to people who asked for her? People in her group. Could they help? What should they be doing about the work? The headhunters. Was the gossip right? Was she going to leave Jackson? Would she come in to talk?

Sick with disappointment at every call that wasn't Roe's call, Domina fielded all the questions, gently put off all the answers.

Domina shifted uneasily. The masseuse finished polishing one arm into a smooth glow, tucked it back under the blanket. Obediently Domina shook her other arm free, gave it to the woman.

In those six days she'd felt herself slumping into a mood like the one after Israel. But this one was tougher, more intense, somehow.

Domina felt as if she didn't belong in her body. As if she were a spirit watching her real self go through the motions of living.

Look, there is Domina telephoning every prospective client she can think of, saying all the right words, smiling into the phone like an idiot.

See, there is Domina at a desk that looks like a battlefield, a strategic-operations center. Plans, lists, résumés, stationery, old engagement books, phone directories, all tools in the search for new clients, office space, money to make an agency happen. At the desk, Domina sits staring into the air.

Watch, there is Domina dressing for the theater with friends, slipping her gold ram's-head earrings into her pierced lobes, how pretty they look.

There goes Domina, wrapped in a pink towel at Elizabeth Arden, weighing herself on the fancy digital scale, getting lighter, thinner every day.

And there is Domina again, walking on Fifth Avenue, looking at all the faces to find one face that isn't there. Hear Domina cry, cry in the street, all alone in the snow at dark twilight, without one New Yorker turning to ask if she needs help. Watch Domina alone, all alone, among the couples walking in their matched pairs. Like seeing a film of herself, she thought, feeling misery for the woman in the film, at the same time feeling remote and disconnected from that woman.

She had never, even at her most wretched, felt this disembodied misery.

When Stephen had said an apologetic, weak good-bye, leaving her with the children and a flood of bills, then there had been so much, such fear, that she'd worked her misery away. Even while she had ached with every breath, awakened each morning to dull sadness, she had been present, inside her own body. She had managed everything, work, kids, creditors, separation agreement, apartment, nurse, worked so hard that she had slept exhausted through the nights. Now, nothing let her sleep, not Seconal, not Valium, not Scotch, nor warm milk. She needed Roe now, for sleep.

The arm was finished. The masseuse tapped her shoulder gently. Domina obligingly turned on her stomach. Now, at least, the woman would smooth her aching neck. Perhaps the massage would help. She needed help now. Six o'clock was Harrell Barber. If she could only look better, get her spirit inside her body, say it all properly, then Harrell might help her, and maybe things would all fall back into place.

As the strong fingers kneaded her shoulders, Domina calculated for the thousandth time. Bonnell. He hadn't been overjoyed that she wanted to leave Jackson. Mr Bonnell was getting older, settled. While he adored her, he liked being a client at a big, elegant agency, too. She'd get him to move, eventually. And with him, she would have an agency. Little. Struggling. But an agency with real ads to do, a real routine to pull her out of her mood. I *must* coax him around, she thought. That was why Harrell was so important. If Ford would give her business, Mr Bonnell would be impressed into anything she wanted.

If only I felt up to this, she thought. Why is losing a lover worse than losing a husband? Stephen. The handsomest boy in Elkhart. A triumph to catch him. After Stephen she had never trusted handsome men. Always stuck on themselves. Stephen, she remembered, watching a football game on television and complaining that her sewing machine was too noisy, as she finished a dress for Maria. Stephen, out of work, watching race riots on television, putting her down because she'd been working and didn't know the details. When Stephen walked out, blaming her for being more involved with her work than with him, she'd said, 'But if I hadn't worked? Where would we be?' And he'd answered bitterly, 'But you didn't have to do it so well. And enjoy it so much.'

Well, there wasn't any more Stephen. He'd gone out to San Francisco, found an older woman to support him in style. How lucky I was to raise the kids myself, without all those fights.

Maria had come down for the holiday, and Domina

hadn't been able to get at the telephone since she'd stumbled in with backpack, clogs, bundles, and shopping bags. Boys called five times an hour, and girls filled in the rest. Correction, thought Domina, call them men and women now. Michael, his escapade with the police over, was plunging into New York, biking everywhere, coming to dinner with news of SoHo and Tribeca, the old guys he'd talked to in Washington Square Park. Like anybody's kids, like a stay-home mother's kids, she always rejoiced. How I worried all those years about depriving them. But maybe I wasn't on their backs, maybe that was better.

The masseuse tapped *her* back. Finished. Domina stretched her neck. It still hurt. Well, the trouble was not in her bones. It was her spirit. No massages for the spirit, no quick unkinking of hurt places in the soul.

She pulled herself up, slipped the pink paper slippers on her feet, reached for her handbag to give the masseuse a five-dollar bill. Then she wearily went off to shower, to begin the long process of getting herself together to face Harrell. An hour; she had an hour to move through washing, drying, dressing, painting her face, steeling her mind for the meeting. It had to work. If Harrell broke off a piece of the Blossom for her, she could show the world. Even Roe would take notice.

But the odd feeling of watching herself persisted. It was as if she sat quietly in the dressing room, seeing a familiar woman pull on her clothes, brush through her long hair, linger over lipstick. The woman looked nice, efficient, neat, fashionably dressed.

Domina got a cab, checked the address of the restaurant. She had thought a long time about where to ask Harrell for this drink. No club. She didn't want anyone she knew to see her with a Jackson client. But she didn't feel it was businesslike to invite him to her apartment, either. Finally she'd chosen a place off the advertising track, an elegant restaurant people went to for dinner, not just drinks. At six, it would be empty, quiet. By eight, when fashionable couples came to eat, Harrell would be leaving for his plane.

As she walked into Toscana, Domina saw that she had guessed right.

Among the tailcoated waiters folding menus, the bus-boys arranging pastries and fruits on stands, Harrell sat alone. In the white-and-gold brilliance of the room, his dark face seemed darker than ever. Her heart skipped a beat. He's so important to me now, she thought. Wish I felt up to persuading him. Wish I'd waited to do this till I felt better.

He stood, smiled as she slipped into the seat opposite him.

Every important episode of my life takes place at some table with food on it, Domina thought. All omelets and demands, salt and questions, coffee and anger. I *must* stop thinking nonsense.

He looked neat and trim, as always, in a pinstripe suit, a white shirt. The shirt disturbed her, suddenly.

Can I sell an oddball idea to a man in a white shirt? Can I fit into his plans for himself? I've got to get it in his head that if he had a small agency absolutely at his command, he could shape his own future.

With her shadowy extra self watching, Domina went to work.

Harrell made it easy to begin, because he said again how much he'd liked her advertising, enjoyed meetings with her, looked forward to more.

'I'm very glad you like my work. There's nothing in the world I'd rather handle than cars. They've been my dream for years, Harrell. You know what they give women in agencies. Fashion. Food. Cosmetics. Never cars. And cars are where the big money is, the attention.'

'Never thought about it,' Harrell said. 'Naturally, when I worked on trucks, we expected men – men copywriters and artists. It's big driving, hard stuff to handle. But of course, that's why we thought about a woman for the Blossom. She's got a small turning radius, easy handling, smooth parking.'

Domina decided to plunge.

'Harrell,' she said, 'what kind of car does your wife drive?'

He looked surprised. 'Station wagon. Kids to school, shopping, all that sort of thing.'

'Right,' said Domina. 'So what about the small turning radius and the easy parking? Station wagons are almost as big as vans.'

Harrell looked at her. Then he laughed. 'Okay,' he said. 'You're absolutely right, Domina. The gospel according to Ford isn't gospel at all.'

The waiter brought their drinks, glanced curiously at the black man seated with her so intimately.

Good, Domina thought. Make him feel black, make him feel different. So he has to feel something for me. I'm different, too.

'The gospel according to Jackson isn't always right, either,' she said resolutely. 'That's why I asked you to come talk to me.'

Harrell's eyelids lowered a little.

Well, he's not stupid, he knows I want something, that this is irregular, this meeting.

'I'm planning to get out of Jackson,' she said.

Harrell shifted his glass a little.

Just like Roe playing with the damned salt, she thought. Oh, Roe, how I wish you were here, helping me, helping me feel like myself again.

Finally Harrell spoke. 'I'm very sorry to learn that. I've enjoyed working with you from the beginning. You know what you're doing. You don't make a fuss, like a lot of creative people do. And the ads look to be terrific.'

'Thank you,' Domina said.

'Is something wrong we could help with? What's behind your decision? Is it a final decision?'

She took a deep breath. 'Well, it's not a sudden one, if that's what you mean. It's been coming for me a long time. I'm behind on promotions, money, things like that. Jackson management is the world's most conservative, you know, they can't seem to realize that women are here to stay. So it's a considered decision.'

'Where are you going? Another agency with a different kind of management?'

'I can't find one,' Domina said. 'Those agencies are all alike, Harrell. What I thought I'd do is make one. Build an agency. The way I think agencies ought to be.'

Harrell looked up at her. 'Tall order, isn't it?' he said. 'Times are tight. Recession, clients pull in their horns. Do you have any clients?'

Now it was Domina's turn to move her drink around. She was getting to the heart of things, and beginning to feel a little frightened. This man understood quickly, seemed sensitive to people's feelings. She mustn't look scared.

'One, but a good one. I've moved it from a couple of places already – they wouldn't dream of leaving me. Built their business, over a lot of years.'

'Boutique Bonnell,' said Harrell.

Now it was Domina's turn to be surprised. He knew that much about her? Harrell Barber did his homework.

'Yes,' she said, trying not to remember Mr Bonnell's mealy-mouthed answers when they'd met.

'Is that enough to start on?'

'It's enough,' said Domina. 'Lots of small agencies exist on billing like Bonnell. But I had something bigger in mind.'

Harrell smiled, took a big pull at his drink. 'I see,' he said. 'And you hoped I'd be able to help you.'

'Right again,' Domina said lightly. She didn't feel light. Her neck ached as if she'd never had a massage in her life.

'Tall order,' Harrell said.

'Well, there are all kinds of help.'

'What kind did you have in mind?'

'Harrell,' said Domina, 'the Blossom is probably the most unconventional car Ford has brought out in years. Every indication you've given tells me you want equally unconventional advertising. And yet, you're in the most conventional agency the world ever produced. If your car had gone to one of the usual Ford group heads, you'd never have seen a campaign like mine.'

Harrell sat back. 'I've come all this way getting unconventional decisions out of conventional people. Gotten pretty good at it.'

Not promising, Domina thought.

'But think how it would be if you didn't have to battle. Didn't have to add the standard campaign to the one you really want to sell. Had somebody with you who pushed for the oddball advertising your car needs. And let's face it, Harrell, that *you* need. You want to rise at Ford, jump over a few bodies out there. They have to notice you, for that.'

Harrell smiled. 'You don't think they notice me, Domina? I'm a little different from most of them, I think.'

'So am I, and it hasn't helped me. They're scared to death of me because I'm different, they watch me because of it.'

'Me, too, but I pay no attention,' Harrell said. 'Cars need big agencies, Domina. There's too much work for a little place.'

'Not always,' she said. 'A little place, poised, aimed to move fast in new directions, that might be just right for a special Ford man. Most agencies are Jackson, in one size or another. None of them are daring. Wouldn't it be great to have your own agency, ready to jump with you, fly you to the moon?'

'Domina,' Harrell said, 'nobody could say you don't have guts. You want a car account? The Blossom? We've worked together for what is it, two months? Three?'

'Come on, Harrell,' she said. 'How long does it take? You know a lot about me. Just the fact that I got where I am tells you a lot. I know the same about you.'

'Women don't succeed on car accounts,' said Harrell. But he smiled as he said it.

'Women drive small cars with small turning radiuses. Radii.'

'Radii?' Harrell started to laugh.

'Suppose you could show management some work,' she said, glad for his laugh. At least he wasn't sore at her. 'Speculative work. Brilliant, imaginative stuff that Jackson wouldn't come up with in a million years. Harrell, you should have seen what got away from your presentation, what they wouldn't let me show you because they were scared, it was so radical. And there's more where that came from.'

Harrell waved for the waiter, got them two more drinks.

'Look, Domina,' he said. 'I wouldn't put you through showing them. It's impossible. I know what you want. I even think you could do it, manage a car account. But I'm in no position to do anything about it now. Moving the

Blossom is too much for me to manage by myself. Jackson does all the new-car development, always has. The stuff that gets away from them is tiny stuff, new-idea cars, vans, harvesting machines, maybe a luxury model or two at a high price. Those things are small enough to move somewhere else. But the Blossom? How many people would you need to handle an eight-million-dollar account, Domina?'

'I'd sure as hell like to find out and hire them,' Domina said resolutely. She didn't feel resolute.

'I have a maybe better idea,' Harrell said firmly. 'Why can't I help where you are? Talk to someone. Spell it out for them. I know Jackson would move if I spoke to them about you. What about Roe Rossen? He's on your side, isn't he?'

Domina felt sick to her stomach.

'He was,' she said, 'but even he can't move this for me, make them promote me. Anyway, it's too late. I've made up my mind.'

Harrell looked at her closely. She thought he looked concerned. But what difference did it make? If he won't even let me try for the Blossom.

'Funny crew you have there at that agency,' he said. 'I can see why some of them might get you down. That creative director? And your little Southern belle? Both fairly depressing, I thought.'

Domina stared at him. He *did* notice, I wasn't imagining. M.J. did make him feel horrible. Goddammit, I was right. To fire her. To yell at Brady. To be angry at Roe, for not believing me, not understanding how rotten they all are.

Harrell watched her face change, set, her mouth press into a firm expression.

Handsome lady, he thought. Built like my Chris, long, elegant, smooth-moving. But in a battle with her management. No good. Individuals who fought companies had to fail. Companies could do terrible things to people. People could do very little to companies. Women less than most people.

Still, probably right for her to get out of there. She could build herself a nice little agency, her brains and looks, history in the business. Bonnell was a good, solid account, he knew. And just the kind she ought to have, as a female agency president. But she wanted more.

Did she really think he could move the Blossom to another agency? He hadn't picked Jackson, Ford had. Not a chance, especially now the work was launched. He wasn't beating his head against any stone walls. He hardly knew this woman. But then, he liked what he did know. Special, he thought. And if that Godwin character on top of her, that little racist bitch underneath, were examples of what she had to put up with at Jackson, why not help her?

Except, how the devil could he? He ran one car line. Hadn't even made a success with that, yet. Pity. In a few years, he'd maybe be able to move accounts around for people he believed in. But not yet. Too soon.

He looked at his watch.

'Domina, I'd better run for that plane. Listen. I kind of know what you're going through, deciding all this. I wish I could do more about it, but I don't see how. But I'd like to keep you on my business, and that's something I can try to do. Let me work on it, okay? And things will happen for you. I'm about to start coming down heavier on Jackson, anyway, now I've had my first big meeting. Pretty soon your ads will go to our management committee. Why don't you wait, see what happens there? If the committee likes the ads as much as I do, you'll have something to go on with your management. What do you say?'

Domina tried to rally herself. He was, after all, being terribly nice, behaving better than a lot of clients would. She could think of dozens of guys in Harrell's position who'd have turned pale at the idea of sitting in a restaurant talking treason with an agency executive. Anyway, Harrell couldn't turn pale, wrong color.

She stood up with him, put her hand out, and smiled, the best smile she could muster. 'I do thank you for listening to me. If I cut the tie, I'll talk to you before I really leave Jackson. Harrell, thank you, really. You're going to make quite a trail at Ford. Don't let the bastards get you.'

He looked for a split second as if he wanted to lean down and kiss her. Then he shook her hand, gave it back to her, asked for the check.

She knew she should try to pay for the drinks. Agency people always paid. But her spirit floated listlessly with her to the door. She'd known it would fail. Too big a demand, too uncertain for Harrell. If she'd had an agency all set up, had Bonnell with her, waited till then to ask him, it might have been different. But she couldn't set up anything till she had business. There's no way to move this, she thought, no clue to the first step.

She seemed to watch herself leaving the restaurant, as couples were coming in for dinner, laughing and talking.

See Domina looking for a taxi, alone, with nowhere to go but home, where she will be alone. She will eat something or other, alone, get into her beautiful bed, alone.

Harrell can't help me, she thought, Bonnell isn't sure he'll come with me, Roe doesn't call, I have three thousand dollars in the bank. And I'm shivering, my neck still aches, I'm miserable all over. I've never felt so hopeless in all my life.

When a taxi finally stopped for her, she pulled a cigarette out and began to light it. The driver turned in his seat to swear at her for not noticing his No Smoking sign.

Domina crushed the cigarette back in her bag and began to cry.

Domina

. . . surprises from Slade Associates as
glamorous Maran Slade wings off to Florence,
Italy, for some special shopping. When Slade
shops in Italy, she's not buying pasta.
Rumor has it that Janie Hitch, gospel girl
extraordinary, is about to change her style
again. We all know joyous Janie won't buy a
hairpin without Maran's okay. We're waiting
breathlessly, Maran doll . . .

293

Domina walked along the corridor of Doctors Hospital, following numbers to find Maran's room. She felt annoyed, by the lack of help at the hospital in finding the right hall, impatient at the slowness of the hospital elevators.

The drink cart was heading toward her down the hall, with its uniformed maid tapping politely at each door to ask if anyone inside wanted a cocktail.

Domina wondered if any other hospital in the world sent drinks around every afternoon. If I'm ever sick, which I refuse to be, this is where I'm coming, she decided.

She tapped once at the door with Maran's name typed on the little card in the brass frame.

The room was empty. It looked unused. The bed was neatly made, the water glass wrapped in tissue, the charts at the foot of the bed blank.

Jesus Christ, she thought, one more thing I can't manage right. They've told me the wrong room. I'll have to go all the way back to the nurses' desk at the far end of that corridor.

I wish to God Maran hadn't picked now for getting her face fixed. She's so peculiar about her looks. Well, she lived so long on her beautiful face. Sees every wrinkle as a vicious enemy.

Maran had been fretting since summer, finding lines in her forehead nobody else could see, pinching her chin line, weeping about her eyelids. Bill had tried reassuring her. Domina had told her she was nuts, only eight years since her last face lift, all the doctors said wait longer than that. None of it made any difference to Maran. To her, mirrors never lied. In fact, Domina thought, mirrors were all Maran really trusted. So when she'd found a way to schedule a couple of weeks between jobs, and to cover her absence with a story planted in the trade press about a trip abroad, Maran had nagged her plastic surgeon into making room for her. And she'd begged until he'd agreed to tighten up her jawline, lift her drooping eyelids, stretch back the skin over her cheekbones, to iron out the lines around her mouth. 'Three days in the hospital,' she'd told Domina jubilantly. 'Sunglasses, a turban, for a week or so, that's all. Nobody will even guess. I'll just look good and rested. But only you and Bill know. In the whole world, just you and Bill.'

Domina almost smiled as she walked, admiring the way Maran had made it all happen. The two of them so alike in wanting their own way. Maran had even talked the surgeon into using general anesthesia. He'd said all that had changed since her last operation, everybody used locals now. Better for recovery, for keeping your natural expression, because you smiled, frowned, talking during the cutting and stitching. Maran had been appalled. 'Awake during that?' she'd said to Domina. 'No way. Last time I went to sleep a hag and woke up looking thirty. I didn't mind that a bit, except afterward when they bandaged my ears tight. Fuck my expression. I just want my face back the way it was in photographs.' Domina had listened with sympathy, wishing that somebody could operate on her mind, smooth it out, cut away the bad places, leave it untroubled and beautiful as Maran's operation would leave her face. And where the hell was Maran?

Domina had no time for socializing now. She felt impatient, all this wandering around hallways. Time. Between her work and her own life, she'd never had time. Long ago she'd learned to dovetail everything, read in taxis, do her nails watching television, shop for shoes on the way to the dentist. It was one reason she loved Maran so. When they talked, their conversation was a blend of business and fun, never time out from Domina's real world. Now she needed every second. Looking for new business was harder work than any job would ever be.

She reached the desk. A black nurse in a white pantsuit sat behind it writing in a large book. A glass of milk stood perilously close to the book. Domina wondered if the glass held only milk, whether or not the drink cart had added a dollop of vodka.

'Excuse me,' she finally said, since the nurse wouldn't look up. 'Isn't Mrs Slade in 368? The room's empty.'

The nurse looked irritated. 'Just a moment,' she said.

She went on writing, shaping letters in a large, clear hand. Domina realized that writing was a total activity, did not come easily for this woman. Ordinarily Domina would have said something sharp, something to get the nurse moving. But these days, still in her strange listlessness, she just waited.

After what felt like a long time, the nurse lifted her head. 'You said?'

Domina repeated her question, with far more than her ordinary patience.

The nurse consulted a chart. 'Mrs Slade is up in intensive care. That's on another floor.' She put her head down again.

Domina thought: dumb bitch, she's got it all screwed up. Intensive care? Maran's had a face lift, for God's sake. Right after the operation, maybe, but that was yesterday.

'What floor?' Domina said, her voice picking up some of its usual authority.

'Intensive care is on the fourth and fifth floors,' the nurse said, as if to an idiot. 'Go to four and ask at the desk.'

Saints give me patience, thought Domina, and turned without a thank-you. She pressed the elevator button, longing for the old-fashioned buttons she could lean on, make noise with, to bring the car faster.

See Domina waiting for the elevator to take her to her friend, she thought.

She couldn't shake the feeling of being two people, one watching, one doing things. Would she ever again feel like herself, get back into her own body?

The elevator came, floated her up to the fourth floor.

Suppose I died now, right in this elevator, she thought. Who would care? Might be more help to her kids dead, her Jackson insurance good still to the end of the year. Be worth a hell of a lot more dead than alive, if this double-image thing I'm living through is even alive.

For a wonder, the desk was immediately opposite the elevator, and there was an alert nurse behind it.

'I'm looking for Maran Slade,' Domina said. 'They told me on her floor she was in intensive care.'

The nurse nodded.

'Didn't she have the operation yesterday? How long would you keep her in intensive care?'

'Are you a relative?'

Domina began to feel a stir of irritation, wanted to say she was Maran's grandmother, for heaven's sake.

'No. A friend.'

'I'm sorry, then,' the nurse said. 'Her husband is with her now. The rule is one at a time. He won't be long, I'm sure. You could go in when he comes out.'

Well, Maran must be just out of the operation room, must have delayed a day. But could anything be really wrong? Impossible. She's got energy, health, for five working women. I'm so distracted, got the day wrong. Thought it would be the perfect visiting time, twenty-four hours after. Last time, she was in great shape by then.

Last time, Domina had walked in to find Maran lazing among her own blue silk sheets and tiny pillows, her head swathed in bandages, face stitched with black threads, looking like a Raggedy Ann doll. 'Isn't it beautiful?' she'd said. 'Look at my neck, Dommie, see how smooth? And all the lines in my forehead gone?'

And now? Well, Maran would reach that stage tomorrow. Maybe Domina could run back up here between chasing clients.

She sat down on a bench and waited for Bill.

This evening's shot, she thought, and I wanted to get things in order for a last try with Mr Bonnell. Supposed to be my sure thing, my start, and he's carrying on about why do I want an agency of my own. Actually, Mr Bonnell sounded just like Roe, asking if she really knew how hard it was going to be, did she really want to work day and night, would she watch over his business, while chasing other clients? He was coming around, but it had been a hell of a lot more difficult than she'd anticipated.

Just when she was considering the ladies' room to smoke in, because she was going to explode if she couldn't have a cigarette, Bill came out into the corridor.

He looked drunk. His step was uneven, his eyes hooded, his hand shaking as he reached to her. God, thought Domina, she leaves him alone for two days, and he starts right in drinking. The man needs a keeper.

'Hi,' she said. 'How is she, Bill?'

To her enormous surprise, Bill plunked down on the bench next to her and put his head in his hands.

He's really gone, Domina thought, like my mother used to be, unconscious. Imagine coming to the hospital like that, full of gin, probably. What the hell, I'll get in there and get out.

The nurse had vanished. When Domina stepped inside the doorway, there was quiet, broken only by the electronic beeps and buzzes from a wall of monitors. They looked just like the control room of any tape studio. Green lines wriggled up and down on the screens. Prettier than most commercials, she thought, and went past.

'Sorry, you can't come in here,' a voice said. Doctor, finally. Doctors Hospital, and she'd finally found a doctor.

'I'm looking for a friend. The nurse said I could come in when her husband came out. And he's out.'

Another nurse appeared out of nowhere, took Domina's arm. 'It's okay, Steve,' she said. 'I'll take care of this.'

A pang shot through Domina, impatience, worry, and something more. Fear. What the hell was going on? Why were they all acting as if Maran had suddenly died, surrounding her with electronic gimmicks and surly doctors? Nobody dies of a face lift. Why are they carrying on?

'I'm terribly sorry,' said the nurse, as if Domina had caused her to say the words, written them out for her to repeat. 'I know this will be a shock to you.'

Domina's heart began to beat faster. Quick, get it out, get it over with, what shock, what now?

'Mrs Slade has upset us all,' the nurse said. 'The whole hospital is disturbed. She didn't survive the surgery. We rushed her here, intensive care, but it was no good. It's been dreadful for everybody concerned, her doctor is beside himself.'

'You're kidding,' said Domina. And saw the amazement on the nurse's face.

'I'm so sorry to be the one to tell you,' the nurse said. 'We're all very upset here.'

Domina's shadowy extra self, the one that had stood near her for days watching her body go through motions, slipped easily out and watched what she did now.

The pretty lady who was Domina screwed up her face in concern, confusion. She opened her mouth and words came out.

'How?' the lady said to the nurse, as the shadow watched, listened. 'How could she? She was having her face lifted.'

'Heart,' said the nurse. 'The anesthesia wasn't good for her heart. She's not young, wasn't young, you know, though we don't have her precise age, she wouldn't give it exactly.'

Right, she'd never give you her age. What the hell, I don't know how old she is, and I know every last thing about her, including how she fakes orgasms, but not how old she is.

'It's a lengthy operation, you see,' the nurse went on. 'Hours on the table. It wasn't anyone's fault, the best surgeon, best anesthetist. Her heart just wasn't strong enough for being under so long. It's terribly rare, this, one in thousands. I'm so sorry to have to tell you.'

The pretty lady stood and looked stupid, while the nurse kept on explaining.

After a short space in which nothing happened at all, the nurse took the lady's arm and steered her back into the corridor.

Bill still sat on the bench. When she realized that he was weeping, Domina slid back into her body, stopped observing herself, fast. Bill. Stolid, uninteresting, patient Bill. Actually crying, crying for Maran. If I were in that room, would anybody cry for me? The kids, sure, but any man? Bill is nice, I didn't know that, but he's nice to cry for Maran. I was wrong about him all along. Wrong. Jesus, could I be wrong about Roe a little? Could it be he's really trying to save me trouble? Help me?

Her mouth suddenly grew dry, her heart began to pound. Panic. Have I pushed Roe away? When he was trying to get me to see danger?

The nurse was pulling at her, shaking her arm.

'I need your name. Who are you?'

Domina swallowed, moistened her lips with her tongue.

'My name is Domina di Santis,' she said. 'I'm Maran's best friend. And she's mine.'

The idea came to her that if she explained carefully enough, spoke politely and patiently enough, the nurse would relent, take her hand and lead her to Maran's bed, where Maran would be lying on silk pillows, her head wrapped in bandages, smiling her glorious, magnificent, unforgettable smile.

But the nurse was turning away, leaving her standing alone in the corridor. Her steps echoed on the hard floor. Domina looked down at it and blinked against the hard brightness of its clean finish.

'Aren't you Domina Drexler?' somebody said.

A very small man in jeans and a silk shirt, sneakers. She knew who. Jake Sternn. She's seen enough pictures of him at galleries, theaters, fashion shows. Maran's friend, of course. How had he gotten here, now?

Sternn pushed her down on the bench beside Bill, stood protectively over her. Their faces were almost level. Short. He's so short, she thought, no wonder Maran always felt so tall.

Tall. Wrinkled. Suddenly Maran's death hit Domina like a smack. Maran was gone. She had died on an operating table, died because she had wrinkles in her face, hated her looks, didn't feel young and beautiful anymore. Jesus on the Cross, what a stupid thing, a horror, to die of wrinkles.

Domina felt as if hands were at her throat, choking her, bruising her neck. She tried to say something, felt a sob burst past the squeezing hands.

Sternn was looking at her with concern.

'Terrible,' he said. 'Terrible. She insisted on doing this, kept yearning over the old pictures. I feel guilty as hell, isn't

300

that crazy? Guilty about my beautiful pictures of her. Terrible.'

Domina put her hands to her neck, trying to break the stranglehold.

'No,' she whispered. 'Never. She loved you, loved your pictures. You *made* her.'

'You all right?' Sternn peered across at her.

'Yes. No one's fault. Nobody could talk her out of this, not you, not me, nobody.'

'Come on,' Sternn said. 'Drink. Let's get something to drink.'

He yanked at her arm, pressed her into an elevator. She looked back, wondering about Bill, but he had disappeared. Papers to sign? Doctors? Bodies, she thought with a chill, undertakers, funerals.

Surprised, she discovered she was crossing herself.

Sternn's Mercedes, black and dazzling, stood right across the front door. His driver leaped for them, settled them in the back, jumped to the wheel. Before the car had started up, Sternn had opened a little cabinet, picked up two small silver cups. He gave both to Domina, reached again for a bottle of Chivas, poured some sloppily into each cup. Some of the amber liquid spilled on her skirt. The rich smell of the alcohol floated in the still air of the big car.

'Take you home,' said Sternn. 'Where?'

She stammered out the address, looked once at the beautiful heavy cup in her hand and drank. It seemed impossible to swallow. She looked stupidly in the cup, wondering why.

'Terrible,' Sternn was still saying. 'She was stubborn, terrible. I'll miss her.'

He poured out more liquor for himself.

Domina sipped at her drink, let the warmth trickle past the constriction in her throat. It didn't seem to relax the terrible tightness.

She was aware that Sternn was calming down. He was leaning back, settling into the comfortable seat.

'Heard you were thinking about starting an agency,' he said. 'Big job. Tough today.'

Domina shook her head, trying to free herself from the

301

strangling feeling. She couldn't seem to speak.

Sternn turned in his seat, tucked one leg under himself. The position made him look exactly like a gnome.

'Bitch of a job,' he said. 'Not like the sixties. Everybody got away with it then. What's wrong with your place? I hear all the time what a good thing you've got there. That Israel promotion? Made a big splash. Can't you just hang in there? Relax, take it easy, enjoy it?'

Oh Christ Jesus, Domina thought, even here, now, while I'm so full of pain. If I have to hear this from one more person, I'm jumping out a window.

'You're Maran's friend, all right,' Sternn went on. 'Just like her. No one can tell you girls anything. Stubborn. Look at her. Hellbent to look thirty again. You. Hellbent to throw away a terrific job. What the world needs is not more advertising agencies.'

The hands closed tight on Domina's throat. It was hard to breathe at all.

'Here,' she said.

She could have let the driver stop at her door, but she was terrified to stay another second in the suffocating car, reeking of Chivas, despair, hopelessness.

Domina turned the beautiful door handle, fled from the car.

Roe

Ford Detroit:
Meeting Report
Confidential

Advertising for the Blossom was presented in agency
rough form. Work was approved in general for further
refinement. Next due date subject to Christmas-holiday
schedules, to be determined as soon as possible. The
committee urged all possible speed for agency to return
with final copy and layout.

'Listen,' said Harrell. 'Didn't they tell you you're supposed to let the client win?'

'Only in front of the committee,' said Roe. 'Not on the tennis court.'

They gathered their yellow tennis balls and reached for towels, warmup jackets, racket covers. Together they walked through the canvas bubble past the other courts, where men were taking healthy swats at more tennis balls.

Roe thought: a great way to take the edge off, to get your feelings out. This forehand's for you, Mr So-and-so, and this slam is for you, Mr Somebody, and if I could punch you in the mouth the way I itch to, maybe I wouldn't have to play this game so often.

Harrell played well, better than most clients. For one thing, he was lanky, slim. For another, he had good wind, ran every morning, he'd said, which sure helped on a tennis court. Harrell was younger, by a good ten years, too. That was why Roe couldn't help putting on the pressure, working hard as he could to win, client or no client. There was a particular joy in beating a younger guy. Roe had once beaten a kid who was Ohio State's number-one player before he'd come to Ford. The kid had been sore, had thrown his racket crashing to the locker-room floor. From then on, he'd sabotaged Roe's advertising in every way he could. They'd moved him into some marketing department a year later, thank God. But every time Roe saw the guy in the dining room, he would smile broadly, and the guy would look irritated. Hope *he* doesn't wind up on the Ford management committee, Roe thought. What the hell, he wasn't paid to lose at tennis, whatever people said about account men currying favor.

Besides, one great thing about tennis is that you can't deliberately lose without showing that you're trying to lose. All out in the open. Every shot, your opponent can tell what you did wrong, where your wrist turned, your eye strayed, your stroke pulled short. Do it on purpose, and anyone can see. No client, even a psychotic, wants to know you're throwing the game. He wants to believe he really beat you. Golf is the game for losing deliberately. Easy to aim a little wrong, check your swing a trifle, edge a ball a shade off. You can lose a golf game on strokes, come just over a guy's score, give him a close match, and not even your caddy will know. Roe hated golf.

He'd had a good match with Harrell, learned a little more about the man. Anyone who keeps his temper on a court, never stretches a call, plays as hard as he can on every point, Roe thought, he's just got to be a terrific client. Things were going damned well on the account so far. Ought to stay that way. Now that the first big Ford meeting was past, there weren't likely to be any surprises for a while. The Jackson team would finish up the ads, mount them on board, and come back out to Detroit for another review.

Roe had flown out early in the morning for the crucial Ford management meeting. Not that he was invited to attend. The agency never penetrated to meetings on this level. But he'd come to sit in Harrell's office while the meeting took place, to hear the news as fast as an agency man possibly could. If management hated anything, Roe would be ready like a shot to start more work going back in New York. He'd told the agency supervisors to stick around, be within call during the noon hour. And if Ford approved the campaign as planned, fine. He'd have shown Harrell and his guys that this agency cared, cared enough to hang in there for the word from the top. It was Harrell's ass now, as well as his own. Harrell had approved everything that went to the committee. Roe thought the man might maybe appreciate a little friendly companionship during the nervous hours.

Amazingly, the meeting had been over quickly. Harrell had been back in his office, the ads under his arm, a smile on his face, after only an hour. He'd called in his people, broken out a bottle of bourbon, rounded up paper cups, and they'd all toasted each other raucously. Roe knew that the committee could always flip-flop later on, just by saying that the refinements hadn't worked out the way they'd anticipated. He'd been through it all so often. But meanwhile, everyone was delighted. If the public knew, he thought, if anyone dreamed of the sweat a lot of men put into making ads, they'd never believe it.

A lot of men. And one woman. These were Domina's ads.

Fuck that, he thought, I'm not going to think about that. If she'd cared, she'd have stuck around those ads. And me.

Roe shook his head, as if it would help shake his thoughts out of his mind.

The tennis bubble was halfway between the Rouge and the airport. The courts were adequate, but not up to club standards in Connecticut or New York. He wondered where Harrell played regularly. Dumb, he thought, this guy could join a club in Grosse Pointe if he wanted. They'd be delighted to have him, fill their token allotment of blacks. His wife is probably a winner, too, though the girls fuss more about blacks in locker rooms than men do. Louise had never failed to mention at dinner that one of the black members had been in the locker room with her, back East. Louise, he thought, what else did she ever have to mention? Not like Domina. Always conversation, never enough time to finish talking, with Domina. Good Christ, he thought, forget her.

He looked at his watch. Either he moved fast now, or waited a few hours for the plane after next.

'You in a hurry?' he asked Harrell, who was popping open a soda.

'Not specially. I'll ride you over when we're dressed. Have a beer.'

They shucked their wet clothes at adjoining lockers, walked the ugly carpeting to the showers together. He's not circumcised, Roe thought; that's getting more unusual these days. Wonder if it really makes a difference in how you feel, screwing. I've been a little out of it in that department lately. Under the shower, Harrell's brown skin was the color of coffee with a drop of cream. Roe thought about putting cream in Domina's coffee. Damn.

He drenched his head, let the hot water fill his eyes and ears.

Clean, a little tired, feeling revved up and lazy at the same time, Roe pulled on his clothes. He was buckling his belt while Harrell still was buttoning his white shirt. The shirt looked as if it had just come out of a bureau drawer. Well, Harrell gave a shit about clothes, and he didn't, that was all. Roe bought good clothes only because they'd endure whatever he did to them better than cheap ones. His father had taught him that a long time ago.

At the front desk he stepped in before Harrell could, paid for court, lockers, sodas. Agency men pay. Immutable rule. From tennis to hookers, agency men pay. But they get their money back one way or another.

They slid into Harrell's car, which looked as if it had come off the line that morning. Roe wondered how often Harrell's cars were changed by the company now.

At the airport they headed toward the hotel bar, passing the crowded drinking places in the airport itself. The hotel was quieter; all the smart money knew that. And Roe had been coming out this way a long time.

They ordered Coors. The waitress, in a miniskirt out of fashion, brought peanuts in the shell, cardboard coasters. Roe was suddenly starving. He began on the peanuts, enjoying the thick, velvety crunchiness. The good, bitter beer tasted the way television commercials tried to tell you all beers did, icy, tingling, sensational.

'Tell me about Domina Drexler,' Harrell said unexpectedly.

Christ. He'd just gotten her out of his mind.

'What about her?' Roe said.

When he lifted his head, Harrell was watching him steadily.

'Shove that,' Harrell said. 'What happened?'

Now what? Tell him she wanted to fire a sexpot teenager because she thought you'd been insulted? Or because that sexpot overheard Domina's plans. I'll never know which?

No. Tell him I love her, loved her, and she wouldn't love me back like I wanted and quit?

'Domina has plans of her own,' Roe said.

And that's the truth. Dumb plans, but her own.

'What are they? A better job? I thought she had a pretty good one,' Harrell said. 'She seemed to have a real feel for the car. To enjoy working on it. And you – she seemed to enjoy you.'

Roe looked at him sharply. Dammit, tough to read a black face. And this one is good at staying poker blank. How much does he mean by that?

'She always wanted to start her own agency,' Roe answered flatly.

Harrell seemed to consider that idea. 'I see,' he said. 'Tough proposition these days, isn't it? She got any business?'

'Well, she came to us with an account. Boutique Bonnell, she's been with it for years, started with it in the Midwest. There's an old guy, maybe you've read about him, a real bastard, likes her a lot. The billing is way up, too, over the last few years. I guess she thinks he'll follow her, whatever. That'd be one. I don't know about anything else.'

'But that account's been around with her for a while, right?' Harrell said. 'So why now? Why would she pick just now to want to start an agency?'

The miniskirt came by, and they ordered more Coors.

Could say I don't know why. What the hell. He's been straight with me, so far.

'She's been battling with our management for quite a while,' he said. 'Wants things they don't feel she's ready for. Domina is quite a pusher, you know. And our management is pretty conservative. Some of those guys are just starting to get used to girls in any kind of a big job. They're not quite ready to give her the key to the men's room.'

Harrell was quiet for a while. Then he leaned back and looked straight at Roe. 'Had a few problems like that myself.'

'Yes. I imagine.'

While he said it, it suddenly dawned on him to wonder why the questions. Harrell wouldn't have had time to miss

Domina, no creative people ever came out anywhere near management committee meetings. Who had told him anything? Jesus, had Domina spoken to Harrell?

They fingered through the shells for peanuts, but there weren't any more. Roe turned to find the girl, asked for another bowl, two more beers. He had plenty of time, and the food on the plane would suck.

'Where'd you hear about Domina?' he asked straight out.

'Around,' Harrell said. 'Who's going to work on the car, if she goes?'

Sure, Roe thought, I guess there's talk. Good thing he asked; he ought to hear it from me, not some news peddler. Every client wants to know who's handling his stuff. And they all hate losing anyone they think is good.

'I'm not sure yet. Domina's plans aren't hard. She hasn't left, officially, that is, or I'd have told you about it. She's taking some time off, thinking it over. Christmas, you know. She has kids, did you know that?'

'Mentioned them,' said Harrell. 'Said once her boy would flip for the Blossom.'

'So you see,' said Roe.

He tried to think of another subject, something less difficult. He didn't feel resentful, hurt exactly, when Domina's image came up. He just wanted to keep it from coming up. Sensible, knowing enough not to look for trouble, wallow around in pain. Christ, there are millions of women. Like streetcars, the guys used to say in college, another one along every minute. But he couldn't think of anything else to talk about.

'I thought she was one in a million,' said Harrell, as if he'd been reading Roe's thoughts. 'No complaining. No feminine shit. Not to mention talent. She got the idea of the car like a shot, saw it right – at least, saw it the way I do. Got it down in the ads. I've worked with creative people who talk a great game. Then they can't deliver ads. Or the other way round. She did both. She listens well, lots of ad people can't do that, either. I thought she was one in a million.'

'Of course she was good, that's why we put her on your business,' Roe said crisply. 'But we've got other people.

And as I said, nothing is definite yet. She could decide to stay.'

'I see,' Harrell said. 'Could you help her decide, do you think?'

Roe's pulse skipped a beat. Could he? God knows he'd tried. Christ, he'd said everything he could think of to stop her running off on her crazy plan. And he was still angry enough to want to shake her, letting a silly office battle push her out of a good job, brushing off his deep feeling for her with hardly an answer. But how the hell could he help her decide?

'I'm on the board, but only just,' he said. 'There's a meeting soon, end of the year. I'm the new boy, but I'll be fascinated to hear what the top guys say about her, the ones who've dealt with her before. She was our prize lady, you know. There's not another woman in the company anywhere near a job like hers.'

'Tough to replace, then,' Harrell said.

'I suppose.'

Roe looked at his watch. Getting close to time now, and the security lines here were slow. They didn't have the equipment New York airports had; they did hand searches of baggage, patted you down, things like that. He'd hate to miss this plane. He signaled for the check.

'Those other people in the meeting,' Harrell said while they waited. 'Godwin? He's on the board, right?'

'You bet,' said Roe.

'And that young girl, the assistant? Would a girl like that want to go with her boss, follow her to another agency? What about the others, the writer and the art guy, how about them?'

Something in Harrell's voice signaled to Roe, trained as he was in catching signals, reading minds, making guesses about what people were really getting at.

'The young one is M.J. Kent. I don't think she'd want to follow Domina. I think she'd want to move up in the company on her own, see how she'd make out with a different boss,' he said.

'I see,' said Harrell as he stood up.

They walked to the lobby of the hotel. At the door to the

airport, Harrell turned to face him. 'I'd like to see Domina hang in there,' he said. 'Tell that to your board, to Godwin, if you think it might help any. And I'd just as soon that Kent girl went off my business. Tell them that, too.'

Roe was thunderstruck.

What was Harrell really saying? He tried to sort it out fast. Somehow Harrell had heard Domina wanted to leave Jackson. Somehow he'd decided he couldn't stand M.J. So M.J. *had* insulted him, just as Domina said. And if M.J. had done that, Domina had a right to want to fire her.

'Good game,' he said, reaching for Harrell's hand. 'Call you tomorrow. Don't worry, we'll straighten it all out.'

He tried to put conviction into his voice.

But he noticed that Harrell wasn't smiling.

He ran for security, for the gate. They shut the door just behind him. The stewardesses bustled him into his seat, fastened his seat belt for him, grabbed their own little seats. Then everybody waited on the ground for thirty minutes, stacked up in a row of planes waiting to take off. Never fails.

He wormed more comfortably into the broad seat, waited for his martini. He was feeling keyed up now, the warm fullness in his belly from the beer helping him think, letting him concentrate.

In his apartment, M.J. had said Domina was angry at her because of her overhearing Domina's plans.

In the Yale Club, which he firmly intended never to visit for the rest of his life, Domina had said she was angry at M.J. for insulting Harrell.

And that, he thought, led to her whole battle with Godwin and David. And they think it's just a quarrel between two women, predictable, embarrassing, something to wave off. I thought so myself. Until Harrell.

So I'm just as bad as they are. No wonder she's angry.

That thought needed mulling. Roe decided that another drink would be helpful. Another appeared in front of him as soon as he asked.

Hey, that was no woman's quarrel. That was my wife. I asked her to be my wife. Only, she's done that, didn't like it. What she wants is to run an agency. Today's woman.

311

They've only been in advertising forty years or so, now they have to run agencies. That Mary Wells started them all thinking. She married the client, that Braniff guy. Domina won't even marry her account man.

A rotten account man, over that breakfast. Didn't listen. Started paying attention only when Harrell brought it up. She *is* the only supervisor who's not a senior vice-president. And I know from the cost-accounting sheets, she makes less than the men supervisors on my business. A good twenty thousand dollars less.

Christ, where have I been?

Paying attention to her legs under my hands, to that right breast that's a little bigger than the other one, to those handfuls of shiny hair. Not listening.

But I'll tell her. Explain. I'm a great explainer, that's my business. I'll call the minute we get on the ground. I'll go where she is. Even if both her kids are sleeping home, all their friends, I don't care if Brady Godwin is sleeping there.

I've been a dumb jerk. Like over Belle Rosner. She showed me then. Maybe she'll show me this time, too. Could she manage an agency? What the hell, she's smart, young enough to have the energy, old enough to know how to use it. I'm a fool. But better than that prick of a husband she had. And better than anybody else she'll latch on to. I'll talk to her, tell her. The first phone when we get down.

Over the plaintive protests of the stewardesses, he stood firmly planted by the door the whole time they were taxiing in to the gate, while the seat-belt sign was on, the loud-speaker urging passengers to remain seated for their own safety. Fuck safety. He was going to be the first person off that plane.

Domina

The New York Times:

SLADE, MARAN. Suddenly on December 16,
funeral services Frank E. Campbell, 11:00 A.M.
Burial private. Please omit flowers.

When Domina's taxi rolled up to the corner of Madison and Eighty-first Street, crowds were on the sidewalk, even though the day was windy and cold. The strangling sensation at her throat returned, making her swallow hard. If only she could walk invisibly through those masses of people, get to an alcove alone for this terrible funeral.

Instead, she pressed through the crowd with her eyes down, straight through to the big double doors, past two men in black at the entrance. In the foyer she went straight to the guest book, scribbled her name, moved on into the chapel.

From the steps she could see Maria and Michael already seated at the front. Their dark heads were together, both aimed straight ahead, neither moving. They're just like me, Domina thought, they're here for Maran, for me, but hating the bustle, the fuss of it. She blessed them both, blessed Maria's instant response to the news about her beloved Aunt Maran, borrowing a car, picking up Michael at school, sweeping down to help her mother bear this funeral.

New York's most elegant funeral parlor was jammed, noisy in a subdued way. Though people tried to whisper, little bursts of sound would erupt each time a famous face appeared at the doors. As Domina moved to the front she noticed that no one seemed grief-stricken, even sad.

Dear God, she thought, her throat hurting, at least let this be something Maran could have stood, not overblown, not gummy with sentiment, tasteless. She had the best taste. I'm wearing her taste right now, this black wool crêpe she chose for me, best damned dress I can see in this room.

Oh, Maran. Domina kept remembering the note Maran

had sent with the flowers, to encourage Roe when he'd first come to the apartment. When will I see you again? Maran, when will I ever see you again?

Domina sat between the kids, touched their hands briefly. No one was near the three of them. Everyone wanted to be at the back of the room at a funeral. Then they could see people arriving, get satisfying looks at grieving relatives, survey the whole scene. She felt the odd pressure of a hundred pairs of eyes staring into the back of her head, but she didn't turn. Domina expected no relief from this funeral, no banishment of the terrible choking feeling that attacked her when she didn't expect it. She'd much rather have stayed quietly at home to mourn, or walked into any Catholic church, lighted a candle, sniffed the soothing incense.

Michael shifted beside her as Janie Hitch came down the steps, bringing a ripple of noise from the crowd. The rock star was wearing a white dress, white boots, white gloves. They all emphasized the ebony of her face, the black halo of hair. Well, Domina thought, that's Maran too, she'd love seeing Janie get all the attention.

Once she'd turned her head, Domina began to notice who was there. Fashion editors, wearing their ultra-chic clothes like uniforms, models' clothes without models' faces. The press, big men in dark suits, bright girls whose eyes were everywhere. Seventh Avenue had turned out. In every row elderly men in double-breasted suits, gawky old lady secretaries, the mainstay of those small businesses, dress firms, fur houses, shoe manufacturers. Maran's girls had flown in from everywhere; Domina recognized the one who ran Maran's Paris office, another who covered fabrics in Germany and Switzerland. Everyone looked perfectly dressed, chic in black, wine, chocolate. Maran, she thought, you'd like that, too.

Peter Bosch came through the doors in his safari jacket. Martha Bartos wearing Mexican black. Belle Rosner, plump in a wide black cape, her emerald gleaming on its broad front. Good, Domina thought, the fashion world has turned out for my Maran. Almost everyone who worked with her adored her, and they're proving it, they're all here.

The organ began sending out discreet chords.

Bill came in from a side door. He looked flushed, over-dressed, confused. Everybody stood up. Domina reached across Maria to take Bill's hand. It felt lifeless, strange, as if he were wearing rubber gloves. From the way he glanced around, Domina guessed that the planning wasn't his. Maran's girls must have moved in their usual speedy way to produce a funeral, as they had produced so many events in their working lives.

The curtains were opening on the platform in front of them.

Hold tight, it's a stage show. I must keep my face blank, I can't look horrified.

She looked up at the casket. With great relief she saw it was covered with daisies. Daisies in winter, exactly right. Good for Maran's girls.

Out of nowhere Jake Sternn appeared. As he walked to the little pulpit, Domina noticed he was wearing the most incredible black jacket she'd ever seen, deep velvet, Chesterfield collar, nipped in at the waist, almost a cutaway. Fashion, Domina thought – how much better that tiny man looks in his jeans and sneakers.

She lifted her chin to face Sternn, ready to listen, as the room quieted down.

Then, with that special feeling she always had when someone was staring at her, she glanced left, away from the doors she'd been watching.

Roe, standing way at the edge of the crowd, looking at her.

The sight of him sent a great stab of pain into her body.

Why Roe? He'd never even worked with Maran. He'd been so dead stubborn about her. But they'd been together at the Israeli show, the party. He'd liked her, everyone always liked Maran. But still, to her funeral? Had Roe come to be with her? To help her when he knew she'd need help? Darling Roe. She almost smiled at him, before she remembered.

Then she steeled herself, made her mouth still again. Damn Roe. Where had he been while she'd been grieving? Looking for business? Suffering a million problems? Sleeping alone in that huge bed? Damn him. She wasn't melting just because he'd come to her friend's funeral.

When she turned to the front, Domina saw that Maran's daughter had slipped in at the side. Must have flown in from somewhere. She's aging, looks used up, her face older than Maran's.

Sternn began speaking. Daisies and Jake Sternn, that was fine, Domina thought. He told about the day Maran had walked into his studio, like Diana, tall, glorious, magnificent. He spoke of traveling the world with her, crowds following her in the Rue de Rivoli, paparazzi stalking her in the nightclubs of Rome. Chanel dressing Maran with her own two hands. Domina relaxed. It was all right. Maran would have liked that speech.

Though she kept her head turned away from Roe, shrank behind Michael, she knew he was watching her, she could feel his eyes on the side of her face. She wondered how she looked. For days she'd forgotten her looks. Tear-stained, probably, sallow, pink in her eyes, lined. Who cared? He hadn't once tried to get to her. Takes a lot to get Roe Rossen to come back, she thought, your best friend has to die. That thought made her angrier at him. Did she have to lose everything at once? Roe. Her work. Maran. Life really clobbers you, she raged to herself.

The organ played smoothly as Maran's chief employee who ran the Paris office spoke of her feeling for her boss.

Finally it was over.

The curtains closed on the casket, so they could take it away unseen, as Bill wanted. Domina leaned over to touch Bill's arm. 'Call you later,' she whispered. 'I'll be home. Come over if you want, or I'll come down, be with you.'

He seemed speechless, overcome.

'She'd have loved this funeral,' Domina added, helplessly. She could almost hear Maran's voice saying, 'Fucking A.'

Domina kissed Maria, put a hand to the smooth, dark hair that fell over the girl's shoulder. Michael hugged her roughly, and she whispered good-bye to both of them. They'd done enough, she thought, let them drive back, go on with their work, their lives. She felt a pang. If something didn't come through for her soon, what would happen to the kids? Michael's school cost as much as Maria's college. Maria planned on a summer in Europe, had saved to help pay for it all year long. The strangling sensation came back, and she tried to cough it away.

In the crowd moving out, suddenly Roe was in front of her.

He looked huge, massive, wonderful. She wanted to put her arm out, to melt into him, curl up in his arms. She could almost feel his pull, drawing her toward him.

'Come on,' he said, briskly. He took her arm, moved with her toward the door. Michael, Maria, she thought, he's seen them. I wanted them to meet him, wanted to see them all together. But the kids had vanished.

Surprisingly there was a car with a driver, right out front. Roe pressed her in the back seat, slid in beside her. He pulled the door to as if he'd finally caught her, boxed her safely in. But he said nothing more, and he didn't seem to notice that she wasn't talking, either..

All the way to her building Domina looked steadily at the back of the front seat. She memorized every swirl in the upholstery pattern. There was an ashtray in the armrest. She desperately wanted a cigarette, but didn't trust her hands not to shake if she tried to get one from her bag. And she mustn't let her hands shake.

They stopped at her door. As the doorman moved to the curb to protest anyone parking there, Roe leaned across her, put a bill in the man's hand, said something. An ingratiating smile replaced the frown on the doorman's face.

Roe opened her door, pushed her gently out.

'Thank you,' Domina said through her constricted throat. 'Good-bye.'

'Never mind good-bye. Have to talk to you. Let's go.'

I can't talk, Domina thought. My throat won't let me. I can't show him I've been wretched without him, furious that he hasn't called, miserable about my plans falling apart. And about Maran. I've lost Maran.

'Domina. Move.'

He looks concerned. Sorry for me. I hate people feeling sorry for me. Especially him. Now he'll turn lofty and commanding, the way he was at breakfast. I'll choke, I'll sob, and he'll want to rescue me, and I'll let him, for all the wrong reasons. No.

'Roe,' she said, her voice sounding peculiar to her own ears. 'This isn't the time. That funeral. Not now.'

She had tried to sound cool, remote, but the words seemed whiny and self-pitying. Damn. She began feeling angry, to notice with amazement that anger helped to clear her throat, loosen the strangling bands.

Roe took her arm, pushed her roughly toward the elevator.

The push did it.

Domina had little experience with self-pity. But she knew all about rage. And until she felt the fury spilling over in her, she hadn't realized how much rage she'd held back these last weeks. No wonder I was choking, she thought, I'm furious with this bastard.

'Listen, my executive vice-president friend, just get your arm away. Where the hell were you when I wanted to talk? When I needed you?'

'I'm not going to wrestle with you in this lobby,' Roe said. 'Tell me upstairs.'

They were in the elevator, the doors were shutting.

Domina looked full at him, welcoming the feeling, knowing the first deep breaths she'd drawn in days. Adrenalin flooded through her, revving her up.

When she wouldn't get her keys out, Roe rang the bell.

Leota opened the peephole, then the door. She looked at Domina's face. Then she meekly took their coats and retreated into the kitchen.

Domina thought, if she comes back with drinks, ice, I'll fire her, make her take them straight back to the kitchen.

'Okay,' Roe said. 'Now listen to me, please.'

He seemed to be trying to control his own anger, she thought. He's remembering we've just come from a funeral, thinking how upset I am. I'll show him, making me glad to see him, making me want to touch him, the bastard.

'Domina. I'm really sorry about your friend. It must have been terrible for you, I know what you thought of her,' he began.

She'd been right. Her fury expanded.

'Please hear me out. I've been trying not to want you, not to think about you every five minutes. I can't stop wanting you. You shook me off so fast that morning, you didn't seem to be hearing what I was saying to you. I love you. I asked you to get married, for God's sake. And all you could think about was your fucking agency. It took me a while to settle down. I only just heard about Maran Slade, I got to you in minutes after I heard, believe me.'

'That was noble,' Domina said. 'You're sorry for me. Is that why you pushed me just now?'

'Come off it, Domina, let it go a little. We've got serious things to talk about. Listen. I was in Detroit yesterday, spent the day with Harrell. We had a long talk about you, he thinks you're the greatest thing since the Rolls-Royce. Wants to help you, he told me so. And about M.J., just what you said, Domina. He's going to help, don't you see what a difference that could make? When I tell Brady? They'll get rid of that kid so fast no one will even remember she was around They'll do just about anything you want, if he pushes for you. You've got an ally, a big Ford client. Everything's going to be different.'

It was the final push. White-hot fury. Harrell wants me to stay at Jackson. Roe comes back after Harrell tells him to. And he thinks *now* I'll relax, stay in that hellhole. *Now* everything's fine?

'Roe Rossen, you're a Jackson man, aren't you, all the way,' she burst out. 'It's still *your* way you want, isn't it? You back me up, but only when your Oreo-cookie client says to, and *then* you figure out I can stay, smooth it all over, forget it happened. Can't you get it through your account-man head? Those bastards wouldn't let me do my job. They wouldn't take my word. They treat me like a flighty, female idiot, and you go right along with them, till some bigshot says to stop. And for that, I'm supposed to love you back?'

He looked confused, she thought.

320

'You're taking it wrong,' he said. 'You're deliberately misunderstanding me.'

'Well, you made yourself pretty clear at that breakfast,' she pressed on. 'I remember it all perfectly, losers, flouncing out with accounts, all that stuff. You were exquisitely articulate, no misunderstanding.'

She could see he was stung.

'Oh, knock it off, Domina. How's it going, your agency? Clients rushing to sign up? Your billings mounting up? Can't you see sense? You're just on the edge of really big stuff at Jackson, isn't that what you've wanted since I met you? Since long before I met you?'

'You *are* a Potter Jackson man,' she said. 'They've never caught on about changes, people changing. You neither. Sure, once I wanted to be something big at Jackson. That was before they showed me what fifth-rate people they are, what nothings. Once, I wanted you. That was before your speech at the Yale Club. I've changed. You and Jackson can both get out of my way. I've changed.'

'I don't believe you,' he said. 'You hummed songs when you walked into that office in the morning, I heard you, more than once. Did you know you sounded so happy at eight in the morning? Do you know how rare that is, being happy to go to work in the morning? What's more, Domina Drexler, you smiled in your sleep when you were in my bed, looked young and relaxed and happy in bed. That was real. The hell you've changed. If you think that, you're just kidding yourself.'

Rage bubbled up in Domina. 'I see. I don't know my own mind. Probably need a good lay, isn't that what you guys always think? Then I'd smile in bed again, we'd go back to work together again, right?'

'Domina,' Roe began.

'Well, forget it,' she said, her voice strong. 'I don't need you to keep me going.'

'I didn't mean that,' he interrupted.

'And I don't need your magic lovemaking.' Her voice rose. 'I got this far all by myself. I'll manage the rest just fine alone.'

It felt good to shout, to let her anger go. The choked

321

feeling was gone. She took a little breath to think of something really devastating to say next. But then she saw the peculiar thing that was happening to Roe's face.

It was crumpling. His eyes were narrowing, his chin going down, his neck creasing. A little vein pushed in his temple.

'Manage then. Jesus, Domina, maybe what they say about you is true. Maybe you do have balls.'

The ugly words hit at her, started a pain in the pit of her stomach. It felt so sharp she had to bend over a little.

When she looked up again, he was in the hall, grabbing up his coat from the chair, reaching for the front door.

There was still time to take it back, she thought. Run to the hall, smile, explain. But she stood absolutely still while the elevator rumbled up to fetch him, closed its doors on him, took him away.

When she heard this, the pain swelled and twisted in her middle. Then, like a labor pang, it subsided, lingering where she could feel it ready to grow and hurt again. She kept very still, careful not to move and make it begin all over.

So fast. Everything blown up so fast. One minute she'd had Roe, a marvelous life, good job, hope for a better one. Now everything changed. Roe, gone, finished. He'd never have flung those words at her if he weren't finished. The worst thing he could have said. Balls.

And it's not true. No! I'm not that way.

After a while Domina got up and moved slowly into the kitchen, a cup of soup, tea, something hot. She tried not to breathe, not to shake up the pain waiting inside her.

She boiled water, found two bouillon cubes, crushed the little squares into grit.

The bouillon tasted like warm water with sand in it.

She poured it into the sink and went into the bedroom. The phone rang just as she reached the bed.

Hope shot through her. Roe? He'd regretted it?

'Mrs Drexler? Mr Bonnell's office,' said the voice at the other end.

The hope died.

Domina tried to rally herself for Mr Bonnell. He meant

hope, too. She couldn't hope for Harrell, and there wasn't anyone else. But this old man, she could talk him around. She always had, hadn't she?

'Yes, hello,' she said, making her voice firm.

'We've been trying to get you,' the secretary said accusingly. 'Mr Bonnell wanted you to know he's had to go away for a little.'

Domina's stomach lurched.

'Away? He can't make time to see me?'

'When he's back, he said, of course. He said to tell you he really felt the winter this year, wasn't as young and enterprising as he used to be. Puerto Rico, sit by the pool, you know. We'll be calling you.'

The winter. Mr Bonnell, who traveled to Minnesota and Washington and North Dakota to make money, felt the winter? Domina felt the pain increase again. Now she recognized what it was. Terror. It was inside her, growing.

'Thank you,' she managed to say, and hung up, while she thought, Jesus, what's going to happen to me? If even Bonnell is telling me no? He was my rock. There can't be anything without him. What can I possibly do now?

Domina was going cold, starting to shake, her teeth chattering. Michael will go to public school, get into knife fights, hard drugs, she thought. Maria will stand behind a counter in a store like Trimble's, she'll have to do what I did all over again. And what have I done? Nothing, I've got nothing, now.

She pulled her knees up on the bed, clasped her arms around them to help stop shaking.

All gone, she thought. I can't do it. Too much. I'll have to go back to Jackson till I get myself together. Have to.

She could do it. Women were expected to change their minds, be flighty. She could pretend she'd calmed down, regretted being so impulsive. Brady would forgive her regally, if she acted humble. M.J. was probably in some other group by now. If they met in the halls, Domina could just look away. And with Harrell's help, things might be easier.

While she forced her mind to think about going back, her

323

body rebelled. Chills and fever, she thought, this is what that's like, fever and chills.

Back to Jackson. To sit in a room with Roe, try to talk with Roe in a meeting.

I couldn't, she thought. I couldn't speak a coherent word, I'd dissolve into tears the moment I saw him.

She was crying now, tears melting into her hands, spilling onto the bed. Her feet felt like cold stones, like Michael's cast must have felt, pinning her to the bed.

Maran would have helped. But there was no more Maran.

The hugeness of her loss suddenly knotted her stomach with pain. For so long Maran had been there, listening patiently, dissecting every problem carefully, hearing every confession, offering funny, wonderful solutions for everything.

Now misery was attacking her, beating at her head, her stomach, making her gasp for air.

Brandy, she thought. Brandy will stop this, make me hurt less, maybe sleep.

She stumbled to the hall, the liquor cabinet. Without waiting for a glass she opened the first bottle she touched, tipped it to her mouth and drank. The liquor burned her tongue, made her shudder as she swallowed.

Back in the bedroom, her head ringing with alcohol and misery, she lay uneasily on the bed.

The dark felt eerie, full of menace, and she shut her eyes to keep it out.

Dozing, then dreaming, she suddenly heard a rapping, knocking noise, like an urgent summons. Domina opened her eyes, terrified, and was somehow a child again, in a threadbare nightgown, waking in the parlor in Elkhart. The front door was moving inward, slowly opening for someone in the blackness outside. When she tried to get up, to run and hide behind her chair, she realized that there was a cast on her leg. She struggled, wanting desperately to run away up the stairs, but she couldn't move the enormous cast. And then she saw she wasn't alone. Her mother was sleeping on the torn couch, a tumbler of dark red wine on the floor near her. Domina called out, 'Mamma, the door,

someone's coming in!' Slowly, her mother stirred, stretched up and then turned into Roe, waking and running his
hands through his hair, staring at her. Domina felt so
relieved, so safe, she turned to him. But her mother was
behind her, strong, frightening, clutching in her, dragging
her toward the door, away from Roe. And Domina began
to scream, 'Stop, stop,' but her mother paid no attention,
kept pulling her fiercely toward the door, the blackness, the
outside, where something hideous waited, and she
screamed and screamed.

The telephone roused her, sweating and dizzy, to a
gentler darkness and night quiet.

'Domina? Jake Sternn.'

She shuddered awake, still filled with the dream's terror.
The aftermath of the brandy dizzied her, and she pulled the
phone beneath the quilt where it was warm.

'I knew you'd be feeling rotten. Dreadful thing, Maran. I
can still hardly take it in, she's really gone. Seems crazy she
won't call, walk in the studio. Anyway. I have news for you.
Maybe make you feel better. Listen. The Revlon people?
At the funeral?'

Domina tried to focus her attention. He spoke so fast,
the words were full of skips and jumps.

'We went for a drink after,' Sternn was saying. 'Top guys.
Talked about Maran, how great she was, who could replace
her. There are new shots coming up soon.'

Naturally, Domina thought. Everything keeps going.
Except me. I'm losing my grip, helpless, floating around in
nightmares, becoming a child again, with a mother too
drunk to help her.

'Listen,' said Sternn. 'They're talking about a new line,
natural cosmetics. They want to break it away from their
regular agencies. Teen girls. They need everything, Domina, product ideas, names, packaging, advertising concepts.
Fresh, different ads. So I told them, you.'

Domina still felt the horror inside her, but now it was
diminishing. She knew it was still there, waiting, but it had
taken a little recess.

'I said Maran thought you were the best in the business.
That you were planning to go out on your own. Had a few

325

top clients. They knew you'd take Bonnell. And they want someone different from what they've got. So, what with sentiment and all, they're ready. You call them in the morning, you hear?'

The pain vanished.

Suddenly Domina felt her ears pop open. Everything seemed loud: the clock, the washing machine humming way in the kitchen, Sternn's breathing at the other end of the phone.

'Jake,' she said. 'Oh, Jake.'

'That's all? I expected you to start managing this right now, call tonight.'

Because I've got balls, she thought, they say I've got balls.

'Jake,' she said. 'I love you.'

'That's just what Maran used to say,' Sternn told her.

And hung up.

Maran, you always make things right, Domina thought.

She shoved the quilt away. Leota will make it like new tomorrow, she thought. And me, we'll make me like new. Revlon. No better name on anybody's client list. Teen girls. Who knows more about them than me? I'm Maria's mother. Experimental cosmetics. Earth colours. Fresh-air fragrances. Sexy ads so they'll feel old, sure of themselves. Wonderful.

Balls? You just bet I've got balls.

She stood by the bed thinking furiously.

Harrell. Wait till he hears this. And he could just be next. I'll go back to work, chip away at him till he tumbles into my hands. Then they'll all see what I can do.

All, she thought. And Roe Rossen.

326

Brady

Memo to: New York office,
The Potter Jackson Company

This year the annual Christmas party will take
place on December 22, from eleven o'clock until
one, when the office will be officially closed for
the holiday. There will be food, drinks, prizes,
and festivities, on the thirty-eighth floor. Children
are welcome. Come one, come all!

John Wingard Croft
Chairman of the Board

Brady Godwin sat with the other board members on a platform, trying to keep a drooping branch of the Christmas tree from tangling with his hair. No room to move his chair any farther away from the tree. So he sat, keeping his composure, and waited for the festivities. They were nearly ready, he could sense.

He smiled from the height of the platform down on the celebrating crowds. The Jackson party was delightful. And this one would be exactly like all the other parties since he'd come to the agency as a young man. Wonderful, he thought, that some things don't change in this world.

There was the famous Jackson punch. After all, Brady thought, executives can handle the stuff, with a few exceptions. He looked earnestly around the room for those exceptions, but so far, none. It's the troops we worry about. Little secretaries having one too many and acting like fools. Mailroom clerks, porters, all those men who check newspapers and do detail work, swilling down drinks from an open bar. Those are the ones to worry about.

The decorators had done their usual magnificent job in the big central room, he noticed with approval. No plastic stuff. Only good, natural pine branches, red satin ribbon, candy canes, that sort of thing. Like a good old-fashioned Christmas. Hard to find nowadays. Terrible plastic Santas everywhere, tinsel, neon.

He shifted his weight in the uncomfortable chair, slowly, imperceptibly. Agency executives are well trained in the survival of boredom, he thought. Like royalty. We sit through so many things we've heard before, presentations we've already reviewed, meetings with outspoken, aggressive people saying the same things over and over, advertising some young person thinks is absolutely new, simply because none of them read the old ads anymore, don't know their history. Every young copywriter reinvents the wheel, he thought. What was that campaign they showed me the other day? Cosmetics with milk in them? Well. The ladies were writing ads like that for Woodbury, Pond's, years ago. Everything goes in circles. I'll be away from it soon. Not too many Christmas parties left.

Brady looked over at the long buffet tables, where maids and stewards were readying the food. It would be served after the announcements and speeches, nothing long or burdensome, just the right words to set the tone for the agency. This party took up three floors now, piped by television sets to the other floors from this main place, food and drink set out in three different areas. Well, he'd certainly seen tremendous growth in his time at Jackson.

The children were getting impatient, too, he noted. Dressed in their best, most of them, no blue jeans today, he saw with approval. More children than there used to be, he thought. Well, more employees. Priscilla had brought the children when they were small. Good for them, he thought, to see where Daddy worked all day, where the money comes from. Inspiring for the boys. Fun for his daughter. Those had been pleasant years.

The loudspeakers were crackling now. Brady wondered why no one could ever seem to get this sort of equipment working properly. Never an agency screening in which a film was not shown upside down or backward, a tape screeching out at top volume, a blackout. Well, union men ran these things. Never cared the way regular employees cared. They couldn't be fired, had regular, prescribed raises and bonuses, retirement benefits. Pity.

Finally it was starting. Noble was on his feet, at the mike. The noise subsiding politely.

While David welcomed everyone, made a few little jokes and introduced Mr Croft, Brady sat. But when Croft stood, he assumed a more earnest expression. Sometimes Croft would leave hints about the agency's well-being, whether or not the profit-sharing would be its full fifteen percent, if people needed to worry about being fired, if accounts might be loose. Just hints, but Brady could pick them up.

As Croft, wizened, small, impeccably tailored and turned out, spoke in his dry tone, Brady listened carefully. He knew this had been a good year, bonuses would be ample, all should be well. And so it seemed. If there were hidden meanings in the speech, he couldn't sense them.

Brady applauded politely with the others. Now Pete Platt was on his feet. As president, he came after the chairman, second in command of the entire agency network. His role this morning would be nominal, as was his role in the company. A figurehead. Big, handsome, florid from outdoor sports, fond of boasting that he'd golfed his way around the globe. A banking man most of his life, he'd come to Jackson to straighten out a financial mess five or six years ago. His connections and money had made him a natural choice for the presidency. Platt's fresh viewpoint had been hailed as an asset. But Brady knew he'd failed to come up with much, once he'd muddled through the problem he'd been hired to solve. Nevertheless, he remained. Brady knew that companies do not make mistakes. People who rise above their level of competence are rarely removed. They either stay in jobs that keep them out of trouble, or in jobs that keep them out of sight. Manager of the Sydney office. Director of the Lima branch. Backwaters where American know-how helps them keep their branch offices solvent among less practiced types. But Platt had too much backing. He stayed, firmly under Croft's thumb. The board understood. But to the people in this room, Platt was the agency president.

If Platt wasn't really reading Dickens, he certainly sounded as though he was. Good cheer rang out with his voice. Appropriate, of course. Someone had to say those things officially at Christmas.

Finished, thank the Lord. Now left to come, only the raffle prizes and the squeals of joy. Then they could all pick up plates, fill them with delicious shrimp, roast beef, Virginia ham, turkey, biscuits, pastries, and salads, all waiting on the decorated tables. Everyone went home from the Jackson Christmas parties stuffed with good food.

Brady shifted position once more during the handing out

of prizes. Boxes of clients' products to a large number of people. Show tickets to a smaller group. Gift certificates to New York stores. Gift certificates to florist shops, restaurants in the neighborhood, camera and radio stores. With thousands of employees, hundreds of prizes. They all waited for the big prizes. Trips. Brady knew that with an airline account, travel cost the agency very little to give away, off-season seats at low rates. A weekend in Paris. Squeals of delight from the winner. A week's trip to Rome. Handshakes, applause, a rather unseemly yowl of pleasure from the young man who captured that one. A two-week trip to London. Everyone of a vice-presidential rank and over was excluded from these. Jackson aimed at fairness. Years ago, Brady remembered, it had always seemed that the big trips had gone to men who had just returned from business voyages to Bangkok or Hong Kong. Now things were evened up. It seemed right to him.

When the paper was drawn from the huge glass bowl for the top winner, it was someone Brady knew, for a change. Among so many, most of the winners had been men and girls he knew only by sight, from the other departments – media, checkers, account groups, all those. But the London trip was being handed out to that lovely little thing, M.J. Kent. There she was, coming out of the crowd to take the tickets in her little hand, the crowd parting for her. Such a beautiful girl, Brady thought, especially this morning, out of those dreadful jeans. M.J. had a jolly pink silky sort of dress on. Tiny strapped shoes, too. Odd, Brady thought, Priscilla always said that redheads ought not to wear pink. Perhaps M.J. didn't know that. Nice, he thought. A real party dress, the kind a child would want. She wasn't much more than that.

Watching M.J. accept her prize with a face suffused with joy, Brady felt uncomfortable. M.J. reminded him of Domina Drexler. He fervently hoped that Domina's absence, unexplained, of indeterminate duration, would be formalized at the year's end. Bad form, he thought, simply taking off and not coming in, at the rates she was paid. The woman was impossible, always had been. He'd be delighted to see the last of her. It would make his last years much

331

more pleasant. This time he'd handled her well, he believed. She had chosen not to inform him of her plans. He, in turn, had chosen not to inquire. A few extra salary checks meant little, compared to the risk of making Domina's behavior public. The board had always wanted him to cater to her whims. Now, if she stayed away without explanations long enough, they'd see things his way. Sulking. She was simply sulking at home, he was positive. Women always sulk when they don't get their way. Well, he was prepared. He'd had her separation papers drawn up, her severance pay calculated. A little longer, and he'd have David handle the woman. She would simply disappear. Over the years, a number of thorns in his side like Domina Drexler had simply disappeared. Helping them do it had got him his position. The board liked smooth transitions, quiet moves. Jackson disdained publicity. We're a family, he thought, and good families don't go public with their problems.

Loud applause and cries of good cheer greeted the end of the speeches. Everyone shuffled and headed toward the food. On the platform the men rose.

While Brady was stepping down, he noticed his own Princeton friend John Carroll at the back of the room. Some of John's people were with him – Brady recognized one or two of the interviewers, the researchers. Worried, he looked around to see if he'd missed any other important outsiders, clients. Sometimes a good many showed up at the Jackson party. But this year, he reflected, Christmas fell on a weekend, and few out-of-town clients would be around. He waved in Carroll's direction and kept on toward the buffet.

Lolly stood up thankfully, just behind Mr Carroll.

She was in a flush of impatience and eagerness, couldn't wait to move around the room. She desperately wanted to find Roe.

She wanted him to see how marvelous she looked now.

For three months Lolly had worked on her looks.

On the Monday after her disastrous blowup with Roe, she had sneaked the table silver, in its tarnishproof felt wrapper, out the door with her in the morning. At noon she had taken it to Fina's. Counted and weighed, it had brought her eight hundred and twenty-two dollars in cash. Bill wouldn't notice for months, she had thought, because they ate quick meals these days and used the stainless steel. She had expected to get more for the silver, but there was always such a hideous gap between what you spent to buy something and what people gave you when you sold it back.

She had gone to the bank and deposited four hundred dollars in a special one-year account at seven percent interest, in her own name. Freedom money, lawyer money, divorce money, she'd thought, a start.

The rest she'd taken straight to the New York Health and Racquet Club, becoming a member on the spot. The club offered enough different ways to lose weight and grow beautiful, she thought, to work even in her case. She would go at lunchtimes, instead of eating. That would slim her doubly fast.

Now Lolly was delighted with the way her plans were working. Her new, pared-down body, trim in black pants and sleek turtleneck top. Her hair different, too. She'd watched the models at the club come out of the steam room, work on their hair sitting naked at the dressing tables, take half an hour over their makeup. She'd learned. She'd talked to some of them, asked for suggestions, even begged for some of their beauty secrets. Gradually, over the months, she'd grown her hair a little longer, swirled it up in front for height, twisted it neatly into a roll in back. Made her look older, more poised. She'd added eye makeup, which she'd never bothered with, darker lipstick. And today, in the hope of bumping into Roe, she'd spent a full hour in the ladies' room at Carroll's, getting ready. Bill had never seemed to notice. But Roe, she was positive, would be astounded.

But wander as she would, from group to group in the big room, roving down the halls where people had spilled over with their plates of food and glasses, she couldn't find Roe anywhere.

Lolly went farther afield. She poked into corridors, looked behind half-closed office doors, moved away from

333

the merriment and cheer. My, she thought, Jackson is big. These offices go on and on. Two thousand employees? Or is it more? And I just want to bump into one person. Oh, Roe, where are you now, this minute? She felt her heart sink, her eyes cloud over with disappointment. A moment later, she could feel tears gathering. Oh, God, she thought, this mascara. I'll cry and it'll run and *then* I'll walk straight into him, with black smudges all over my face.

The ladies' room must be somewhere along here, Lolly thought, though she knew Jackson ladies' rooms and men's rooms weren't marked. Because years ago, management had thought it embarrassing to have signs on the bathrooms. People who worked at Jackson, they'd said, would learn their location, while outsiders had no need to know anyway.

Fortunately, a group of secretaries fluttered out of the big party room, laughing together and walking straight for one of the doors. Gratefully Lolly followed them and found a place for herself in front of one of the big mirrors. She'd get fixed up again perfectly, and then go out and *ask* people if they'd seen Mr Rossen anywhere.

As she was carefully wiping the black away from beneath her eyes, the door swung inward.

Carrying paper tote bags full of books and papers, dressed in worn blue jeans and a rough sweater, her hair actually falling across her forehead, Domina Drexler, coming straight toward her at the mirror.

Lolly's heart stopped. She even felt a little sick.

She couldn't believe it. She couldn't find the one person she wanted anywhere. And the one person she *never* wanted to see again in this world had to turn up right next to her. Domina Drexler. I'd like to punch her. Take this mascara stick and jab it right in her eye. Look at her, the old bitch, a pure mess. How could he want her? She's nothing, looks about a thousand years old.

Somehow Lolly went right on fixing her eyes, fussing with her lipstick while she thought furiously. Why wasn't Domina at the party? Why was she way down this corridor carrying all that stuff? Looked like she was taking a lot of things home, cleaning up her office. How come?

What she wanted to say was, 'Why do you look like the cleaning woman today, Mrs Drexler?'

What she finally said, as she put her lipstick down, was, 'Mrs Drexler, do you remember me? I'm Lolly Moss, you interviewed me for a job here.'

She watched Domina glance over, smile automatically. 'Yes, of course. How are you?'

The automatic smile made Lolly still angrier.

I'm standing here hating you, she thought, and you can't even bother to remember me. Pay attention to me, you bitch.

'Whatever have you been doing?' Lolly said. 'Why, you're a mess. I've never seen you look such a mess.'

At least *that* turned Domina's eyes back again to her.

'I suppose,' said Domina. After a moment, she went back to fixing her hair.

Fury, jealousy, hatred all boiled up inside Lolly. 'Roe Rossen specially asked me to come to this party,' she said viciously. 'He says it's so jolly, old-fashioned Christmas and all. Roe knew I'd enjoy being here, seeing where he works, meeting all his friends. But it's such a crush, I think.'

She had the satisfaction of seeing Domina wince, really react to her words. There, Lolly thought, glad of her smooth new figure, her perfect outfit, there, for once I look terrific and you look used up. You're not dressed for any party, for any lover. Now you know Roe has another girl, besides you.

'Can't keep him waiting,' she said. 'You know how Roe is.'

And she walked straight past Domina, out into the corridor. Good, she thought. It was worth coming here, to say that to her. She felt better than she had in days. Smoke, she thought, now I really want something besides that punch out there.

She edged up to a trio of young men standing just inside the doors to the big party. Two of them were sandy-haired and conventionally dressed. One was dark, bearded, blue-jeaned. He had the kind of curly hair that grew right around into his beard. Lolly thought he looked interesting.

'Hi,' she said. 'Anybody know where there's a little pot?'

All of them smiled. But the bearded guy looked at her closely, and detached himself from the others. He took her arm and turned her toward one of the empty offices.

There'd be dope in someone's desk, she was sure. When she calmed down, when she'd savored her nastiness to Domina, she'd get moving again, get herself some Scotch.

Lolly looked back once to locate Mr Carroll, protect her job while she enjoyed herself, have her fun far from where he was standing. There, she saw, he was over with some old men, important ones from Jackson. He seemed engrossed.

She turned back to the guy with the beard. Since she'd been snippy to Domina, let her feelings loose a little, something exciting was happening inside her, stirring her up, letting her feel free. Go with it, she thought. If you're going to have a whole new life, start it right, what the hell.

'Listen,' she said to the man. She felt daring, but determined. 'Listen. Are you Jewish?'

Within the mass of hair, his face looked startled for a moment, and his eyes snapped to her face. Once he'd really looked at her, he seemed to relax. To her relief, he nodded yes.

Lolly let Mr Carroll disappear from her sight as the guy closed the office door behind them.

Carroll and the chairman, John Croft, were approaching Brady. Brady got ready to congratulate Croft on his little speech, say a few words to his old college friend.

'Godwin, I have something to say to you,' said Croft.

Brady grew instantly wary. When Croft spoke, he paid attention.

'Over here,' said Croft.

He led Brady to the side of the room, toward the private offices that lined the window walls. Already people were taking food and drinks into those offices, Brady noticed with a frown. Every Christmas, somebody got in a mess in one of those offices. Somebody's husband kissed somebody else's secretary. Or worse.

When they neared an office, Croft stopped.

Good, thought Brady. Whatever it is, it's not confidential enough for him to want me alone.

'Listen, Godwin, I'm damned annoyed,' said Croft.

336

Good God, thought Brady, pain stabbing suddenly through his middle.

'Been talking to Carroll,' Croft went on. 'You know John Carroll, of course.'

'Of course,' Brady echoed. 'Princeton, you know.'

'Yes, well, never mind that. The thing is, he's got a lot to say about Domina Drexler.'

Oh, for God's sake, thought Brady. Has that woman talked to Carroll about a job? Impossible. She knows how closely we work with them. She'd never go to them, she'd realize I'd hear about it right away.

Croft watched Godwin's expression change from respectful interest to wary panic. Fool, he thought. Past his time. Can't manage the troops. How old is Brady? My age, I think, have to check it. But I'm as sharp as I ever was. Actually, so is he. Never was quick. Just defensive enough to hang on all these years. Well, let's see how he deals with this.

'Were you aware,' said Croft, 'that Mrs Drexler is in his special files? That she's evidently consulted one of their executives about new employment? And told them, obviously, that she'll go anywhere, take a salary cut even, to leave here quickly? Carroll actually saw her here today packing up, looking a sight, he said. He thinks it looks dreadful for us, a top executive like that. Press gets hold of it, we'll have questions, Godwin. I thought you had the woman under control.'

Brady felt ill. The fires inside him were burning, might flame up. He could clearly imagine a hole burning straight through his worsted vest, a small hole with black edges rapidly growing larger, like a burn in a piece of film on a screen.

He coughed into his hand. 'Odd, I lunched with John only last week. Never said a word about Domina. Not one word. And after all, I'm her immediate superior.'

'Yes, well, that's just it. You're the person who's supposed to know what's going on. Evidently she decided to go all-out for a new job quite recently. Something happen with her lately? Haven't you got her on Ford? Things not well there?'

337

Brady cursed Domina, while the pain swelled in his belly. Damned Italian bitch, trouble from the start. Confrontations, hysterics, never satisfied. Office wasn't enough. Money not enough. Greedy, demanding little bitch.

'Ford is going fine, John. I attended her presentation myself a couple of weeks ago. Everything went nicely. By the way, interesting client we have there. A Negro. But very bright, Ivy League, Harvard Business School. He seemed quite pleased.'

'Well, then, maybe she's making a grandstand play for something else,' said Croft. 'We know she wants a title, we've discussed it. Higher salary? But Carroll says she's definitely interested in leaving, ready to go at a moment's notice. Peculiar. You should stay on top of these things, Godwin. It's your bailiwick.'

'I'll certainly find out immediately what the problem is. Women, you know. Could be anything, some small slight, some silly idea, anything.'

The fire was in his head now, burning behind his temples. He could murder that woman. How dare she take her problems outside the agency? No loyalty, no gratitude. What was the matter with people today? Women, Negroes, Jews. Rossen's a Jew, and where's he this morning, by the way? He's her account man, he's supposed to know what's going on.

Croft was looking at him sharply, his small eyes staring into Godwin's face.

'It doesn't sound small,' he insisted. 'John Brinnin Carroll doesn't sound alarms for no reason. He's the best. You know how he hates errors. I've never known him to make one, come to think of it. You'd better get busy, Godwin, do some checking. These women's groups are all over now, making fusses. We don't want that sort of thing. If she's listed with Carroll on an urgent basis, she must be wrought up about something. Today, women who are wrought up bring those lawsuits, those human-rights affairs. Trouble. Stockholders, newspapers, we have a mess on our hands.'

What the devil was John Carroll doing, telling Mr Croft before he told me? My old friend, Cottage Club, too. He knows how we're organized. Knows I need smooth sailing here for just two more years. He ought to have warned *me* about this woman. And why didn't he? Could he think I'm not worth warning?

'Don't give it another thought, John,' Brady said. 'I realize the pressure, the serious nature of this, of course. Right on top of it. I'll handle it. Don't give it another thought.'

'I give everything thought,' said Croft in his nasal voice. 'Everything. Wish everyone did the same. All right, Godwin, get to it.'

Old bastard, thought Brady, wizened old bastard. Fear shook him, made his knees feel out of control. A spasm racked him, twisting in his bowels.

Thank God it passed. Two years, Brady repeated to himself, smooth sailing for two more years.

'Of course,' he said. 'And Merry Christmas, John.'

Croft had turned away, didn't reply.

The noise and bustle in the room overwhelmed Brady, made him feel nauseous. He walked unsteadily, as fast as he could, away from the party.

ies for just two more years. I ought to have waited
about that woman. And why they _____ Carol _____ with Tim
_____ he'd be annoyed.

'Don't give it a second thought,' John Gray said.
_____ sense the program. The fellows hurry of this of cup he
Sight to top of it I'll handle it' Don? It's it another
_____ though.

'I've even thought though it,' said Don in his anorak. '
Everything. Wish everyone did the same.' As Frost, Clerk
on his feet.'

Old rascal, thought Shade, warmed all he had. He'd
adore him, made him let his kill out of control. A guest
was more than enough to hurt.

Thank God it passed. Two years, Shade reasoned in
himself, should suffice for two more years.

'Welcome,' bespoke. And Merry Christmas, John.'
Clerk bid out red appropriate reply.

The snow and people in the room overwhelmed Frost;
made him feel nauseous. His eyelid contracted, as far as
he could a way from the party.

The Board

The Potter Jackson Company Profit-Sharing Club

Domina di Santis Drexler, # 112-22-6738
Computation date: December 31

The total value of your interest in The Potter Jackson
Company Profit-Sharing Club as of the above date was
$127,562.10. By reason of your separation from the
Company as of January of next year, and in accordance
with the election form you have filed with the Trustees,
your interest has been allocated as follows:

Total Trust Interest	$127,562.10
Vested Percentage	100%

$127,562.10

Less: Remittance to Company for debits, loans, bills outstanding, etc.	-o-
Cash distribution:	$127,562.10

This distribution comprises the following items, each of
which must be taken into account in the preparation of
your income-tax return(s) for the year.

Company deposits prior to January,
covering ten years of service, including
salary base, bonus checks twice yearly,
management-incentive-plan

membership, prorated-stock-plan
percentages $115,562.10

Company deposits for present year,
covering total annual compensation at
$80,000 at 15% declared profit-sharing
percentage including redistributed
forfeitures $12,000,000

Your voluntary contributions   -o-

This statement reflects the current status of the financial
market, and may represent either a gain or loss of
cumulative interest in total. It is subject to federal, state,
and local taxes.

                                        Club Committee

They gathered in the boardroom, the sanctum, the center of the Jackson universe.

The room was small, brown, perfect. Once it had been the heart of a vulnerable merchant bank in the City of London. It had been brought over piece by piece, carefully unpacked and fitted together by clever men with gentle hands. The carved wainscoting and paneled fireplace had been jigsawed in place. The windows were deeply recessed, the glass in them old, flawed, curved in small panes. Velvet cushions covered the window seats. A secretary, the most polished and perfect of all Jackson secretaries, sat white-haired and white-collared, her lined face expressionless, waiting to record the meeting.

Around the table, a museum piece of carving, they sat. Every man had a crystal glass and a small covered water pitcher. Each place held a leather blotter with a silver pen laid on it. In the precise center of the table, fresh flowers foamed out of a low Imari bowl. There was almost no sound in the room. Small Oriental rugs rested on top of thick carpeting, the soundproofing was excellent. Cool air flowed in from tiny vents carefully matched to the carving in the wainscoting near the decorated plaster ceiling.

John Wingard Croft sat in the armchair at the head of the table. A special folder was at his place, of rubbed burgundy velvet.

Peter Platt sat on his right hand.

Around the table sat the board members. Godwin. Temple. Williams. Rossen. Murchison, Murphy. Lester. Harrison. O'Hara. Johnson.

Roe thought: twelve good men and true. Jury. Deciding people's fates. Well, the decisions made in this room affected hundreds, maybe thousands of people, all around the world. So many offices, so many countries, he thought, waiting for them to begin. So many decisions. And I'm part of them. One-twelfth of the board. Don't get your hopes up, he thought then, we all know Croft makes the decisions. We second him. The guy runs this place like Napoleon. Take your time, you just got here.

Roe was restless in his beautiful, uncomfortable chair. He hadn't slept, had walked his terrace in the bitter December cold for half the night. Now he felt drained, empty, thick-headed.

He'd spent every ounce of energy in the last two days trying to get back to Domina, worrying about Domina, with no results.

Nobody answered at her apartment.

He'd gone back to the building, got past the stern doorman to the house telephone. Buzz after buzz, nobody picked up, nobody home. He racked his brain to recall Leota's last name, to call her and ask, but he couldn't remember, wasn't sure he'd ever heard it. He'd even handed the doorman a story of worry and fear, along with another large bill, after the one he'd given the man to let him leave the car at the door when he'd brought her home from the funeral. The doorman had let him go up in the elevator with the lobby man to ring Domina's doorbell. There was no mail outside her door, a good sign. But there had been no answer to his ring, either. When the lobby man had grown impatient, Roe had had to leave.

Inspired, he'd placed a call to Maria Drexler at Brown, in Providence. After the endless delays of calling a dormitory, the lost connections, the idiot young voices who answered phones, nothing. Miss Drexler had left for vacation, for Christmas. Nobody was there who knew where she had gone.

Roe tried to remember how to get in touch with Domina's son. He couldn't. Anyway, he thought, it would be the same thing, he was a school kid, too.

Only the board meeting had got him to the office. He was new enough on this board to want to be there, be part of it. Institutions like Jackson went serenely on doing business,

344

even when its members felt utterly frustrated, totally inept. Where the hell could she be? Could she have gone away without a word? She'd flown off to Israel that time, without a clue. Maybe she'd gone somewhere warm, taken the kids away for the holidays. But her mail had been picked up. And her newspapers. Tonight he'd get a good sleep and figure it out when he wasn't so tired. He'd just get through the board meeting. Then he'd find Domina.

Call to order. Minutes of last meeting. President's report. Secretary's report. Treasurer's report. They all paid special attention to that one. Money was the most important, the bottom-line statements of profit and loss, income and outgo, where all of them stood. Everything translated into money. New accounts meant more money. Departing accounts meant less. Inflation, economic conditions in a dozen markets, changes all over the world; in the end, all that mattered were the personal fortunes of the men in this room. Roe's interest was caught for a moment when they looked at the charts for the Buenos Aires office. The charts were adjusted to accommodate the fantastic rate of inflation in Argentina. Graphs that illustrated profits were backed up by other graphs that showed the real value of those profits. Roe remembered the Buenos Aires office from the one time he'd been sent there on an errand for Ford. Spacious, elegant, in the best section of the huge, modern city. Inflation, he thought. It was the only place I ever traveled where the menus in restaurants had no prices, the waiters calculated the cost of your dinner after you finished, according to the day's rates of exchange. The price tags in shops had changed from day to day, for the silver spurs and the cowboy boots, always rising. Nothing at a fixed price was in working order, Roe remembered, you couldn't make a phone call from a pay booth because nobody could figure out the proper coin to use. Crazy. Well, what good was a coin in a phone booth, if the person you wanted to talk to didn't pick up at the other end? Domina. Where? Where has she gone?

Suddenly, stunningly, the door opened and Domina walked into the room.

Everything stopped.

345

The treasurer paused almost in the middle of his sentence. He didn't trail off or wind down. He just froze, his mouth open.

The man turning the pages of the big flip charts froze, too. He almost seemed to stop breathing.

O'Hara had half-risen to ask a question, his hand half-raised to interrupt the speaker. He stood, his gesture half-complete, arm extended in air.

Roe saw all the heads on his side of the table, near the door, turn and freeze into stillness. The heads on the other side remained fixed. Nobody even seemed to blink.

There had been no knock. Only the sound of the hardware turning once, definitely. And there she was, looking down at them all around the conference table.

Unheard-of, for anyone to walk in on a Jackson board meeting. And without even knocking, Roe thought wildly. Jesus. If he hadn't known her, known she was in a state of some sort, he'd have thought the building was on fire, a bomb scare, lightning. Even Croft sat frozen in place, his little eyes staring straight at the source of this amazing intrusion.

Then Roe looked, really looked at Domina. He drank in her presence, searched her with his eyes, up, down, up again. He began to feel a strange relief. She didn't belong here. But it would be all right, because he was here, too. He could take care of her when she came to grief. He felt as if, after holding his breath for a long, long time, he had exhaled.

Domina looked tremendously excited. Her hands were trembling a little, and her eyes were wide open. She was dressed in her most Domina manner, he thought, her highest heels, most elaborate silver belt, sleekest jeans. Her cream silk shirt was unbuttoned almost all the way down its front. It showed nearly half her breast, and that breast was moving up and down, as she breathed quickly. Her chin was firmly up, her eyes burned into the room, her mouth was slightly open. Open for business, Roe thought crazily.

Croft broke the silence. Who else? thought Roe. None of these guys would dare.

'Well, Mrs Drexler,' he said, without intonation of any kind. 'You are surprising even those of us who know you. Why?'

Roe watched as Domina turned toward the head of the table. She was thinner, he realized, much thinner for such a brief piece of time since he'd seen her. A wave of misery and guilt washed over him. Domina had been growing thin while he'd been away from her. Roe wanted to get up, take her arm, hold her. He wanted to go and stand by her side.

'Because I have something to say to you, all of you, Mr Croft,' said Domina. Her voice sounded strong, low, clear.

'I see. They've told me you are impulsive. But this? Well. Here you are with something to say. Go on.'

Roe could see Domina gathering up all her forces.

'All of you, everyone on this board together, you're the company,' Domina said. 'I only know a few of you. But I've heard of all of you. Collectively, standing together as this board, you've been a wall, a wall I have no way of getting past.'

Roe glanced at Godwin. His face was a mask, bland, smooth, handsome. But a vein was throbbing in his temple. Roe could see it pulse in and out.

'For quite a while, I thought I could break through,' said Domina. 'I thought very hard work, a lot of success, strength, meeting every standard, all that sort of thing, would let me break through. But I've been learning I was wrong. I'll never get through. I'll never prove how good I am, how good I could be, for this company. You won't allow it.'

There was a noise across the table as Johnson started to get up. A big man, Viking-blond, his mouth set in anger now. Roe thought: Jesus, he's going to get her out of here, that's why he's on his feet.

Then, a sharp look from Croft snapped in Johnson's direction, and the man sat down again. Croft turned back to Domina.

'I can remember twenty times, thirty times,' Domina said. 'There'd be some job nobody could do, a speech to write for a client to give, a campaign to sell to somebody tough like my food people, a problem to figure out. And I'd do it. I sat up an entire night once writing a whole new speech for you, Mr Croft, because whoever Brady got before had made a mess of it. And nothing worked, none of it worked for you gentlemen. You never, never forgave me for being different. Special. A woman. A strange, unpredictable, untrustworthy creature.'

Croft leaned forward. 'Come on, Mrs Drexler,' he said. 'This is very dramatic. Your sisters in feminism would be most impressed. But you're being very one-sided. You've done quite well out of this company. You make a handsome living. You've moved along quickly here. You've had special privileges, too. Your office. Do you know how many men coveted that office space? A corner? And how much money was spent on decorating that office for you? To your specifications? No. You're seeing this company from a very limited viewpoint.'

Croft was staring at Domina steadily.

Roe could sense that the other men were restless, nervous, embarrassed. Christ, he thought, why don't I sweep her out of here before she makes a total mess?

'No, Mr Croft,' said Domina. 'Even the office. You're proving my point. A number of men wanted that office. You couldn't figure out how to give it to one of them without annoying the rest. So you took it out of competition. You gave it to me. You knew the men would subside, because I'm different, special. That's what I object to. I don't want to be special because I'm a woman. I want to be special because I'm good at my work.'

Croft looked at her. Slowly he dropped his gaze to her shoes. He looked at them for a long moment. Then slowly he ran his eyes up Domina's body until he met her eyes again. 'You have always received notice. That is valuable in a large organization. It's what men battle to achieve. You've been fortunate to be a woman. It's given you a number of special advantages that carried over into your work,' he said.

'Any advantages I've had have been balanced by disadvantages,' Domina said. 'My invisible boss? Do you think I don't know I'm the only supervisor with an extra boss? Or that I don't understand that you wrote his name on a chart so you could reassure clients that I'd have a backup? It's insulting.'

'Sensible chains of command always have backups,' said Croft.

Roe could see Domina getting pinker, breathing more deeply. He thought she was gathering up her forces for an assault, a big one.

'Mr Croft, a while ago I fired somebody in my group. For good cause. If I'd been a man, that firing would have taken place. I'd have been backed up. I wasn't backed up by anybody. There were discussions, was I being temperamental, flighty, that kind of slur. Backed up? I'm stopped. I can't get past a definite boundary in this company. Nothing I do, say, produce, earn, succeed at in this agency seems to make any difference. It makes me furious. It makes me outraged, frustrated, terribly angry. Even at that, I've been pretty strong. I don't have ulcers. No high blood pressure. I've never lost my grip on the work. But I've been angry for a long time. I want the title that should have come to me a year ago. I want a crack at this board. Not as a token lady, with a special title like consumer-affairs director, but as a genuine member. I want what I've earned, proved, what I'm capable of handling. And that's precisely what you will *not* give me. I can bring in new business, win creative awards, sell products past all predictions, you still won't give it to me.'

'In my time we waited our turn,' said Croft.

Roe could see that he was fast losing patience. Color had come up in his withered cheeks. His head was down like an angry mastiff's.

'Goddammit, I haven't got a turn,' said Domina furiously. 'I'll never have a turn here. There's no point waiting any longer.'

'Yes,' said Croft viciously. 'We know you are looking for new employment. Presumably, you have found it. Is that why you have the bad taste to come to this meeting? Where you don't belong?'

Domina seemed startled. 'New employment? You've heard wrong from somewhere. I'm not looking for a new job.'

She paused. Roe could see her chin come up, more firmly than he'd ever watched her make that gesture.

Domina looked at them all. She'd only once before been in the room, when one of the directors had tiptoed in, turned on a lamp, and pointed out Chippendale, Queen Anne, Hepplewhite, Imari. Now it was being used for its single purpose, a board meeting. So this was the way they looked, old, tired men, most of them, handsomely dressed, wonderfully groomed. By now their expressions amused her. They looked as if a rattlesnake had slithered in here, as if a snake were coiled, hissing at them. Well, I've managed to get their attention. Feels marvelous. Thought I'd be petrified, doing this. Thought I'd shake, stammer, get the words out wrong. Mr Croft put steel into my knees, my back. He's a horror. Smart, though. Like being in a courtroom, arguing with him. Did I make myself clear? Mother of Christ, if he couldn't understand, who could get it through to him? I said it all, and clearly, I think. But not the big thing. Let's see what happens when they hear that.

She tried to keep her eyes forward, not to see the one person she'd looked for as she'd come in. Roe. She felt his presence, could almost sniff his outdoor smell, hear his breathing speed up as she stood there. In the glimpse she'd had, walking in, he'd looked dreadful, older, thinner. Strain on his face, a slump in his carriage. She had resolutely kept her eyes toward the head of table, toward Mr Croft. A frightening presence, she thought. She'd participated in only one or two meetings exalted enough to hold his interest. With Mr Bonnell, when the budget had been increased. When they'd included her in the management-incentive financial program. The man almost gave off power, she thought, a concentration of strength and force. Don't give him one place to drive a wedge in, she told herself, he'll use it, he'll split you in two, you'll be devastated. Take care, talk slowly, keep your voice strong. You can call Maran when it's over. Oh, God, she remembered, not Maran, not ever again. If she thought about Maran now, she'd never be able to do the rest. Go, she thought. Ready, set, go.

'I'm not looking for any job,' she said clearly. 'I'm going to start my own agency.'

Even while Roe could feel her joy in saying it, he knew the men weren't reacting the way she would want. Relief seemed to flood over the table. Everyone relaxed a little, shifted in his chair. He knew they were all thinking: Thank God she's leaving. A little agency, no matter, no trouble. At least she's leaving the agency. After all, he'd expressed his own opinion clearly on that subject. Their opinions would be the same.

Domina must have felt their reaction, known what it meant. She took a step forward, closer to the conference table. In her high heels, she towered over Croft's chair, over all of them sitting around the table.

'Yesterday I went to Ford,' she said.

Roe watched all the men turn to stone. Instantly frozen again, instantly wary, they all stared at her. He caught a look at the elderly secretary sitting erect by the window, her pad clutched to her wide bosom. Her face was a picture of shock, outrage at this unseemly disturbance. Sisterhood, he thought, whatever happened to sisterhood? That woman is angrier at Domina than any man in this room.

'I went to see Harrell Barber, my client on the Blossom,' Domina was saying. 'You may know that he's black. An outsider, like me. So he understands outsiders. He knows a little about walls that can't be scaled. Harrell promised to talk to management at Ford for me. About quotas, government demands on agency affiliations in the next few years, spreading the work around, that kind of thing. Evidently he was persuasive. He called me at noon today, and he has something for me.'

Roe stopped looking anywhere but at Domina's face. She looked radiant, beautiful, triumphant. They'll kill her, he thought. How can I get her safely out of here, away from this poisonous room, these lumbering ciphers?

'Harrell couldn't give me what I really wanted,' Domina went on. 'The Blossom. It's too big. I couldn't handle it in my agency.'

Jesus, thought Roe. Jesus H. Christ.

'But he managed to get something loose for me. The car

351

coming after the Blossom. The one you took for granted, for next year. It hasn't a name, even a design yet. It's still on the drawing board. But I have a contract coming by registered mail, it's already left the Rouge. Signed. Two years' work on that car. They'll spend about two million. Small for you, big for me. Contract renewable subject to my performance. And that, with Bonnell of course, will be all I'll need to open.'

Triumph, Roe thought. How long has she waited to say this to these bastards? Her triumph. She's hit them all. Me, too – Ford's my responsibility. She's even hit me.

'That's why I interrupted you this afternoon,' Domina said. 'To tell you myself. To give you my resignation. To make you pay attention. And to fix things a little for the next woman who comes along. That's why.'

And she went out. As suddenly as she'd appeared.

They all stared at the place where she had been standing. Then pandemonium.

Everyone seemed to burst at once into talk.

Godwin turned to the secretary and spoke urgently, motioning her out of the room. She went, scampering.

Roe thought: she'll tell, this is much too good not to tell. She'll tell her best friend, and that friend will pass it along to someone, and it'll all be out. No secrets in this business. Even in the boardroom. Especially in the boardroom.

Harrison, manager of the Chicago office, large of face, crimson with rage, was loudest. 'Women. If they didn't fuck, there'd be a bounty on them.'

Croft, pinched around the nostrils, seething with outrage. 'This is your responsibility, your fault, Godwin. The girl is in your department.'

Murphy, for fifteen years the secretary, older, steadier. 'Always the same story. Give one of them a boost, and this sort of thing happens. Like unions. It's unions all over again. Look where we are with the unions.'

Pete Platt, simpler, more direct. 'She must have fucked for that client to get a piece of Ford, must have.'

Godwin, white, shaken, trying to pull himself together. 'Oh, no. It's a colored client. She wouldn't have done that.'

Murchison, looming, menacing. 'If any woman would lie down with a nigger, she would. She's tough as nails.

Roe felt dizzy, as if they were all hurling stones at him, hitting at him with heavy blows. What had Domina set off? These well-dressed, pleasant-looking men, talking this way? The board members of The Potter Jackson Company?

Croft again, breaking through the babble. 'It's the times we live in. Used to be a damn fine business for a man, decent people making a good living for their wives, families. Now anyone can get in – blacks, women, Jews, anyone.'

Roe shot to his feet.

He felt murderous now. Watergate, he kept thinking as his anger swelled, like on the Watergate tapes. We didn't believe our president could talk like this, but we learned. That's why this stuff seems familiar. I've heard it all before, even while I can't believe it. Blacks, women, Jews. Twelve good men and true. What am I doing here? With these shits. Why am I listening to this?

Lester, from the London office, quieter, brighter than most. 'Wait one moment, let's discuss this. Why is the woman so upset? Why did she approach a client? Unethical, actually. What set her off?'

Croft intervened. 'I don't want to hear any more. The incident is over. It's Godwin's job and he's botched it. Gentlemen, we've lost accounts before, big ones. Two million is nothing to this agency. Williams, talk to our law firm, see what they say. How can we put a spoke in her wheel. No danger with Ford. A lot of people have tried getting that away from us, and they can't. The client is too big for almost anyone else. That woman will never last.'

Lester persisted. 'With all respect, John, I think we should consider a countermove. We should really do something for the women here, the good ones, to show them, to point out to the press. Our image to the public, you know. I honestly think we should throw open the dining room. That's always been a sore point for the ladies. It would make a big splash in the papers. Photographs, luncheons, you know.'

Roe stared at Lester. A Neanderthal, he thought. He doesn't begin to see what Domina meant. None of them do. Even Croft. They're too old. Rigid in their thinking. They don't get it. Can't separate her work from her looks. Her sex. They cannot forgive her for being a woman.

Croft's head had turned sharply toward Lester. 'Absolutely wrong,' he said. 'There will be no giving in. No handouts. Forget it. From now on, we're tough. We promote none of them anywhere near to a supervisory job. We take no chances.'

Williams, from the Chicago office, plainer, blunter than most. 'John is right. It's all a lot of nonsense. What happened? A little cunt came along and grabbed for something. That's what cunts do, they grab for your balls.'

Roe's anger, like an explosive set alight with a fuse, sizzled and blew up. Light went off behind his eyes, crashing sounds in his head. He wished it were a real explosive, a weapon to blast at these men, turn them into charred, writhing bodies. What's taken me so long, he kept thinking, why haven't I seen what they are? Where have I been all this time? Too close to my work to see these shits? They're not fit to work for Domina, let alone the other way around. And just what the hell am I doing here with them?

Tell them, he thought. Blast them. Tell them they're finished, dinosaurs, too dumb for today's world. No. What for? Enough for today. They didn't understand what Domina was talking about. Why would they understand me? Women, Jews, their minds seal up. Words have no effect. Actions. Act. Get out. Now.

He moved, shoving aside the beautiful chair next to him. It was heavy, hard to move, and he needed a hand to shift its weight, let him escape from the table. Solid, this furniture, he thought. I'm leaving behind a lot of things, old things, that felt solid. But they aren't. They're old, full of dry rot, past their prime.

In three broad steps he was at the door.

Roe

Congratulations!

You are the grand winner in our Christmas
raffle. In this envelope are two tickets
to London, hotel reservations covering a
prepaid two-week stay, a check for one
thousand dollars to cover your expenses.
Bring check to Payroll with your identifi-
cation card to be made out directly to
your name. The company wishes you a Merry
Christmas and a happy journey as part of
the tradition of holiday giving at

The Potter Jackson Company

Roe went through the door of his office at double time.

'Forget everything,' he said to his secretary as he passed her. 'Get on the phone to Mrs Drexler's apartment. Call her. Call her every five minutes until you connect. It's urgent. I'll be inside.'

He was already inside as he said the words. He went straight to his desk and yanked open the middle drawer, where his personal things were. Briefcase. Where the devil did I put my briefcase?

His heart was pounding like at the end of a tennis game, his shirt felt as sweaty as after tennis. He pulled his jacket off, threw it toward a chair. It slid to the floor, a crumple of tweed. Fuck it. I'm signing off, out, going to Domina now. Got a hundred things to tell her, ask her. Got to get to her, nothing here matters anymore, just speed, just movement out.

The briefcase was in the corner where he'd tossed it that morning. He got up to fetch it, and began putting things from the drawer in it by the handful. One day, he thought, I'll learn to be neat, tidy. But not now. Got to get to Domina. That's the only thing that matters. All the years here? Funny, they don't matter now.

He found the gold pen he'd been missing for a year, stuck at the back of the drawer. He aimed outdated papers at the wastebasket, missing some. Didn't matter. He wasn't going to be around. Take the small stuff, he thought; the rest they can send after me. Why the hell don't they get her on the phone? Never mind. In five minutes I'll grab a cab and go there. Sit on her doorstep till she comes. Get Leota to let me in. Doorman. What time is it? My God, it's late. Quitting time. Past quitting time.

He heard the door click open, and looked up, annoyed. M.J. Kent.

Behind her, his secretary, fussing, protesting ineffectually. She could no more have barred M.J. than she could have blocked Mr Croft, he thought.

'It's okay,' he said. 'Just stay on that phone. I'll take care of this.'

When M.J. came through, Roe could see the determination on her lovely little face. She radiated will and determination, excitement and demand, standing there framed by his doorway. She closed the door behind her and stood looking at him, at what he was doing.

Roe put a hand up and loosened his tie till the knot hung inches below where it should, till he felt comfortable. Funny, he thought about tennis. The start of a game. Opponent walking onto the court with three, four rackets under his arm, springing across the court, young, strong, handsome, alarming. The opponent taking off the racket cover, bouncing a ball to test its spring, turning to rally with him, speeding a swift, bullet-hard ball in his direction.

'Quit doing that,' said M.J. 'I've got a little something to say to you, Roe. You quit doing all that.'

She moved to the window and began turning the long stick that controlled the vertical blinds, blocking out the lights from the other buildings, closing him in. She moved around his windows, one by one, blanking them all out. She shut out sound, as well. The office felt padded, quiet, like a single tennis court in a country place, net taut, ready for play.

Finished with the blinds, M.J. went to the door and turned the snap lock. Then she came back toward his desk.

Linesmen ready, thought Roe. Play.

Looking straight at Roe, M.J. put her beautiful small hands to her belt buckle and opened it. Her fingers reached for the zipper of her jeans. The denim scrunched down under her hands. She stepped out of the pile of fabric. The tiny bikini underpants she wore seemed to Roe to expose an endless expanse of perfect legs, shapely, fine, gleaming pale in the electric light.

With one stretch she put her hands to her T-shirt in a

357

crisscross, and stretched harder upward, slowly expanding like a flower blossoming on a stem. Then the shirt was on the carpet too, and she stood straight again. Under the flesh-colored smoothness of her bra her breasts swelled, spilled over the top where the lace was. She reached back to unhook it.

Roe thought: hit back, swat, do something, don't just stand there.

'Knock it off, M.J.,' he said.

'That's what I'm doing, honey.' The bra was off, then the scrap of bikini. She stood next to his mahogany desk.

She was glimmering like a pink pearl, he thought wildly.

She came around his desk. Suddenly she dropped to her knees, startling him. She was reaching across for her blue jeans, for the pocket. Something in her pockets. She yanked out an envelope.

Christmas. Oh, Lord, everybody had told him. This year M.J. had won the prize trip, the London tickets.

M.J. put the envelope on his desk and sat down on the closest chair. Wine leather. Against it, her body seemed to glow. Pink pearls in a wine-velvet case.

His body was responding to her nakedness now, the familiar heat rising up in him. His head began to pound, he heard the smallest sounds.

When she spoke, the noise seemed overwhelming. 'Forget her,' M.J. said. 'Forget that old lady now. She's past. She really blew it today in your boardroom, right? We'll never see her around here anymore. But I'm here. And I'm staying.'

Roe could smell the warm rosiness of her body, the sharp lemon scent of some fragrance she wore. Her skin seemed almost iridescent, gleaming. He felt that if he touched her body, the iridescence would stay on his hand, turn it pink and glowing.

'I came right up, because I knew you'd be thinking things over. Heard you stomped right out of the meeting. Thought you might be going away somewhere. So I brought a Christmas present for you. In this envelope.'

Envelope. He'd forgotten already. He looked at it, white against his green blotter.

358

'You come with me,' said M.J. 'There's tickets for two in there. David March Noble did something cute in the drawing to get them for me. He thinks I'm going flying with him. But I can fix that. I'll tell him I'm taking my poor old mama with me. Never been anywhere, poor thing, how she'll love tripping off with her baby girl. And meanwhile, you and I will have ourselves a time. Bet you know London places. You can show me. In between loving, you can show me.'

Roe thought: it's like listening to a guy with a bribe, a neat proposition you can't lose on, a little retainer if you'll just throw some business his way. M.J. thought that up fast. Reacts fast, this little girl. He stared at her breasts. Her dark red nipples seemed to be enlarging, like a photograph being cropped into its center, growing, and shimmering in the chair. Until there wasn't any chair, nothing but M.J.'s ripe breasts, her glorious hair falling around them.

'Well, say something, honey,' she said.

Roe tried to. His brain seemed to be dissolving, his tongue weighted down. He felt all eyes, zeroed in on those breasts, that orange hair. He was sweating now, he realized, neck, hands, damp, hot. The thing he wanted to say, only thing that seemed to make sense was: let's fuck.

He wrenched himself away from that idea, turned his body away from her, got himself together a little by curling his hand and driving his nails hard into his palm. The moistness of that palm disturbed him.

No. Danger, he thought, clap, poison, she's poison.

'M.J., you're making a fool of yourself,' he tried. 'Just what do you think you want?'

She smiled. 'You know real well what I want. You. I've spent all this time looking for somebody smart, who could get it up. Like you.'

Roe drove his nails farther into his palm. He took a good deep breath. 'Oh, I don't think I'm smart enough,' he said. 'Not nearly smart enough for you.'

While he said it, he could feel sanity returning, strength flooding through him. She was smiling, this little bitch. He began to feel cool, steady, almost cold after a moment. He wanted to stop her smiling. Slap, hand across her mouth?

No. She's too dangerous to touch. Probably likes getting hit. Don't put a hand to her. Do it with words.

'You're maybe the one guy around here who is,' she was saying. 'Let's just see, now.'

'Listen, M.J.,' Roe said, feeling together by the second, making himself see how ridiculous they would look if anyone came in. 'Changed my mind. You're not smart. You're a little nothing around here. Busy watching everybody, sniffing around people, you haven't got any idea what anyone thinks about *you*. Come on, M.J. You think the other girls in Domina's group don't understand you? Think you're fooling people with that smile and that cute drawl? Fooling Domina? She knows all about you. Harrell Barber knew the first time he set eyes on you. All the smart money, the really bright people here, have your number. You're pretty good at the beginning, but you don't last, baby. You can't fool us for long.'

M.J. only smiled and started to uncross her legs slowly.

Roe went on resolutely, trying not to look anywhere but at her face. 'You haven't learned anything from advertising, have you? People aren't dumb. You can fool them for a while, but not long. Like a new product, baby, you can start it with a lot of noise, but if it's rotten, everyone knows it fast. You're rotten, M.J. It's all over, you smell. We're not stupid here. We make a living reading people's minds. I can read yours.'

'That's what I said, Roe. You're smart. Now, about getting it up.'

'M.J.,' Roe said. 'I wouldn't fuck you if they made me president of this place.'

She was still smiling, but didn't move.

'Why the hell didn't you just do your job? David Noble. I might have known. I bet his secretary knows. And if she does, so does the whole typing pool. You think you're the first little dumbbell he's fucked?'

'Oh, come on, Roe Rossen, you don't know it all,' M.J. said. 'You don't even know I've been living with your Dan Trueman since I came to New York. Your own guy. Takes good care of me, too, thinks I'm the cutest thing on two feet. What do you think about that?'

Roe remembered now, a tennis game, his opponent was lobbing up an easy one. Smash it.

'I think he's worth fifty of you. He'll wake up soon, especially if you hand him that shit about your poor mother. He's got to have noticed you don't waste much time on your poor mother. Nice of you to tell me about him, by the way, he'd like knowing what you did. You think what goes on in bed takes care of everything. Baby, you've got things to learn. Works for a while for kids like Dan, old farts like David. But not for men, M.J. I'm fifty-one. You think there's anything under your shirt, your jeans, I don't know about? And I like to talk after I fuck, M.J. You haven't got any talk I'd want to hear.'

He'd gotten to her, he could see it. The pretty face was frowning now, the little mouth pinched into a line. Now, start serving, Roe thought, hit a few for Domina.

'This place isn't going to be much good for ambitious ladies, good lays or not, for quite a while, M.J. And if you got the news, *all* the news from the boardroom, you know that. No, they're not going to promote girls around here for quite a while. You're going to be stuck, no matter who you fuck. Assistant art director, is it? Pretty small potatoes. What the hell, you're hardly worth explaining it to.'

She burst out at him, furious, her eyes narrowing, her body hunched over. 'I was plenty worth it in your apartment the other night. I know what happened to you when I kissed you. I could feel what happened. You were all ready to go, that's something I know all about, you can count on it. I know when a man wants a piece of me, all right.'

He was smashing the tennis ball, darting around the court to reach every ball, returning them easily and gracefully, while she panted and labored. I'm controlling this now, he thought, standing easily at the center line and running her all the hell over the place. Hit this one, now, hard.

'Anybody can get a rise out of a guy, try hard enough, like you try. The trouble isn't getting it up, baby. The trouble is keeping it up. I start thinking about who you are, what you are, M.J., I couldn't keep it up. It would be like fucking a snake.

361

Smash. Game, set, match.

She turned her back and picked up her jeans, a little unsteadily, he thought.

He didn't watch her dress. He picked up the phone on his desk. 'No luck on that call to Mrs Drexler? Well, I'll be out in a second. I'm going over there. You keep on calling, just keep trying, and if you do get hold of her, tell her I'll be there in ten minutes, she's not to move. I don't care if there's an earthquake, anything, she's got to wait till I get there.'

From the corner of his eyes he could see M.J. yanking on her jeans, reaching for her T-shirt. All her motions looked jerky, cross. Childish, like a little girl angrily dressing after the doctor had pinched and poked her. One of her tiny sneakers was near his foot, half the size of his shoe. He almost kicked it over to where she stood, head down, looking around for it. Her face was red, crumpled like a child's, and everything about her posture suggested that she was ready for a temper tantrum.

He reached down for the small sneaker, took it by the toe, and reached over to whack her hard, just once, across her little bottom.

Brady

This bill is seriously overdue.
If there are any errors in these
charges, please let us know. If
our figures agree with your own,
we request immediate payment, and
remind you that your charge account
was granted on the basis of payment
within ten days of our billing date.
If we do not hear from you, we will
have to report your account to our
attorneys for legal action.

Godwin yanked angrily at the cord of the blinds on his office window. The sun came in, but not in the way he was used to. Now the building across the street had soared past his level. He had to tilt his head back to see the men on the highest floor, the yellow crane endlessly swinging loads of wire and wood to the top. Today the whole construction made him more furious than ever. With all the irritation he'd suffered, he would never see it completed. He would be gone before it rose even one more floor.

Whenever he thought about yesterday's board meeting, and the brief interview with Croft that had followed it, Godwin's mouth filled with a nauseating, sour taste, as if he'd gulped a glass of milk that had curdled. The taste seemed to choke him, sicken his stomach, even stop him from speaking properly.

He'd been ushered into Croft's private office, a small room, dark, after the magnificence of his outer reception rooms. In the little room, Croft sat at a plain wooden desk with a wall of shelves behind him. On the shelves were hundreds of owls, made of wood, glass, stone, feathers, metal. When Godwin sat opposite, he'd felt that Croft had a thousand small eyes, all staring him down.

He had not stayed long. It had taken Croft about four minutes to announce, in his menacing voice, that he would expect Godwin's resignation.

The sour taste had sprung up then, rising from his belly, filling his mouth, making his eyes water a little. Though he had forced himself to sit straight and look Croft in the face, even managed to say that he'd been considering early retirement, terrible thoughts had begun to whirl about in his head. Embarrassment. Disgrace. Fifty thousand dollars profit-sharing over the next two years vanished. No office. No position. No reason to get up in the morning. There was the real terror. Priscilla. She would be distraught having him home before they'd planned retirement. His friends would all guess he'd been forced out early. The worries swirled in his mind. A sour-milk taste pumped up into his mouth.

Godwin had spent the night at the Princeton Club, to delay giving the news to his wife until he'd settled down a little, decided how best to tell her.

Today he'd come to the office to tough out the complexities of leaving Jackson. Termination forms. Financial choices, disposing of company stock, arranging profit-sharing distribution. Packing decisions. A press announcement. Retiring is a job for a young man, he joked bitterly to himself. But he didn't feel like joking. He felt weak, weary, old.

The walk from the elevator around to his corner office had seemed endless. Did the executives in the offices he passed know? Even their secretaries outside those offices, did they know? Did the whole agency realize he'd been pushed out, called off the field in disgrace, after playing such a long, arduous game? They must know. Everyone must have heard, that woman, bursting into a board meeting, thumbing her nose at the chairman, stealing a piece of Jackson's best account. A nightmare, the kind he'd most dreaded. And he'd hired that damned woman, nurtured her, put her in position to ruin him. Should have fired her the first time she'd opened her mouth to complain. Ever since, she'd grown into a monster, feeding on the very opportunities he'd given her. How he loathed that woman. Loathed all the damned women who used their looks, tantrums, to destroy the men who helped them. No loyalty, no standards, no gratitude. The image in his head of Domina striding into the boardroom kept returning to his mind, bringing the sour-milk taste back disgustingly.

Godwin turned and looked at his bright office. The packing would be impossible. So many years of accumulating little things. Pictures. Awards. Desk accessories. Books. Gadgets, like his antique barometer. Well, his secretary could handle it, ship it all home. They could store everything in the attic. Good God, thought Godwin, I'm sixty-three. My father reached ninety-one. Twenty-eight years to fill. The whole room seemed to darken for a dreadful moment.

The telephone buzzed.

Damn, he exploded inside, his orders were worth nothing this morning. No calls. And there was the buzzer, urgent bursts of sound. Godwin grabbed at the receiver.

'I'm terribly sorry, Mr Godwin, but they said important, very urgent, so I thought –'

'Well, what?' Godwin snapped.

'Downstairs in the lobby,' the woman's voice said with a tremor. 'The chief lobby guard, Mr Godwin, he says it's terribly important.'

'My God,' he exploded. 'Does *everything* come to this office? Lobby guard? For heaven's sake, get hold of Noble, someone else. I will *not* be disturbed, can you understand that?'

'I'm sorry, Mr Godwin, truly, but the man, the chief, insisted you'd want to see him. Something about one of our creatives, trouble. He's on his way up here now, says he must see you.'

'On his way up here? Well, you just head him off, whatever it is. For God's sake, *handle* it, understand?'

He slammed down the telephone.

Let them find out, he thought, wait until I'm gone and let them see who does all the work around here, who manages the sticky problems, the impossible situations.

In a matter of minutes there was a burst of noise outside his door, and it was growing louder. Someone screaming.

Good Christ, Godwin thought, don't they know this is a business office? Sounds like a zoo out there. Of all mornings. He felt ready to tackle everyone, ready to lower his head and charge heavily into whoever was making that damned racket.

He walked to his door and yanked it open.

The scene in his reception room was extraordinary.

An enormous black man in a dark uniform with a badge was struggling with someone, someone who kept twisting and shouting. At first glance Godwin thought the man had hold of a small boy, a teenager in blue jeans. But as the slight figure twisted toward him, he could see it was M.J. Kent.

When her head turned his way under the man's arm, he could see her face, crimson with rage, her mouth open for screaming, her hair streaming back against the navy blue of the man's uniform.

'Stop that noise,' Godwin shouted.

He reached over to slam the outer office door, then turned to push the guard and his struggling prisoner into his private office.

Godwin's fingers ached to slap the silly girl quiet. Now he could hear the words M.J. was yelling, a string of foul words. Black bastard. Nigger prick. More, all aimed at the man who was holding her firmly with one hand.

The guard's other hand held one of Jackson's big flat black carrying cases, zipped half-open at the top and side. He clung to it just as firmly as he did the hysterical girl.

Godwin took hold of M.J.'s shoulders, pushed off the man's arm, shoved her roughly onto his couch.

Ignoring her noise, he looked sternly at the guard. 'What the *hell* goes on?'

The enormous man, his black face shining with sweat, his uniform torn in front, his expression absolutely impassive, began setting himself to rights, slapping down his jacket, settling his collar in place.

'Mr Godwin, sir, she's had the whole lobby in a mess carrying on this way, screaming her head off, gone crazy down there. Brought her up in the service elevator, howling and fighting. You see, it's the case, sir, we'd have taken her right to the nurse on fourteen, called an ambulance even, but she had this case. That's why we thought here, sir.'

What was the idiot talking about? Godwin thought. What on earth would make them want to bring a screaming woman to his office? The executive floor. Where clients visited. Good God, if Croft got wind of it, he'd have Godwin's head.

But then he remembered that everything was over for him at Jackson, that nothing really could harm him more.

They couldn't fire him twice. The notion relaxed him, amused him a little. After all, he was a problem-solver. Godwin's last problem he thought.

On the deep couch, M.J. was quieting down. She still shook, still wept tears that ran down her little face, spilled from her small nose. Sobs still came, the round breasts rose and fell fast with her breathing. Her shirt was sopping, clinging.

Horace Sutton stood quiet, watching Mr Godwin's face.

He felt quite calm. He knew he'd done right. Pity was he hadn't taken that little girl's neck in the crook of his arm, choked the sound out of her. But there were rules. He could grab someone, even a woman, get her where she'd be taken care of, police, doctor, nurse, bosses, whatever was called for. He couldn't take it on himself to stop the cursing and noise. But he could stop the mischief. This little piece of trash had something coming. And she'd picked the wrong man to call those names. Well, wait till this smooth white man got a look in that case. Horace knew he'd done right. Not since last month's grab of the guys who were moving out typewriters after hours had he been so dead sure he was right, stopping this bitch, getting her where she belonged.

'Well? What happened?' Godwin said impatiently.

'Happened to notice her coming in real early this morning, when I started my stretch. Hour, hour and a half later, Mr Godwin, she came back down, but in the service elevator, with this case. Struck me funny, her going up regular, sneaking back down in that dirty elevator, young lady like her. But I didn't think anything much, just made a little joke when she came past me, asked her did she have a building pass. You know, every big thing like that case has to have a building pass, it's the rules.'

'Yes, well?' said Godwin.

'Well, she gave me a look, then she picked up her hand and punched me out, started in screaming. Just lit right into me, you wouldn't believe the names – filthy nigger, cocksucker . . . Excuse me, sir, but you see. Well, then I thought something was fishy, so I took that big case, started to look in. She went just crazy. And when I saw inside, I just turned her right around, told one of the guys to call up here, brought her right along.'

Godwin thought: must have been some scene. The man was built like a defensive tackle. M.J. weighed about ninety pounds.

He leaned over and unzipped the case, turned it on its side.

When he began spreading out the papers, the words 'Top Secret' seemed to multiply by the dozens before his eyes. Top secret? What was this? Memos, call reports, statistics. Ford papers, every one of them something to do with Ford. Research documents. Engineering drawings. Image studies. But top-secret papers *never* left the office. There were shredders at the back elevators on every floor, so that papers like these never got out of the building, never even baled into ordinary trash. What the devil was M.J. Kent doing?

He kept rummaging. Beneath the papers were larger, heavier things. Layouts, photographs, specification sheets. Godwin could see instantly that they were layouts for the Blossom. Farther down, there were yellow copy sheets, full of erasures and X's. Idea copy.

What was this girl doing with any of this? An art assistant. She had no business even *seeing* top-secret papers in the agency.

He looked up at the guard. Horace Sutton, he noted, from the man's badge. Well, get Horace Sutton the hell out of here, handle this yourself, he thought. We'll never hear the end of it if he talks, better keep it in the family, handle it. Thank him. And don't call him Horace.

'Mr Sutton,' he said. 'You've done a good morning's work. I think you can safely leave this to me now. Please give my secretary your name when you go out. We'll want to be in touch, see you're suitably rewarded. Right on the ball down there, you fellows. Good work.'

He opened the door and held it for Horace Sutton, who saluted gravely and walked out without a backward look for his prisoner.

All through the talk, M.J. had been thinking furiously,

frantically trying to get herself together. While she kept up the sobbing, her mind ran this way and that, urgently searching for a way to talk, a way that could help her with Mr Godwin. She'd never felt so terrible, so shaken up in all her life.

Everything had gone wrong, right since Roe had spanked her with her own shoe, making the memory of her father snap back into her head. She'd stood in that big office feeling just like way back in Eufaula, crunched between her father's knees, helpless, tiny. Damn, damn. Roe Rossen might have put her on a silk pillow the rest of her days. Painting what she wanted, shopping for nice clothes, pretty things to wear for him. And quit worrying herself sick about money, payments overdue on her sapphire, nasty letters from credit people. A fix. Roe wasn't going to come through. David sure wouldn't give her money. Dan didn't have all that much. Domina gone, who knew what kind of boss she'd be getting now? Might take months to get a good raise. And anyway, raises were too slow. Time they took taxes out, medical, all that slop, there wasn't enough. She needed money, a lot of it, and fast.

A big drawing of the Blossom on Roe Rossen's wall had given her the idea.

The car was a secret. Secrets were worth something in advertising. Other car people sure might like knowing all about the Blossom. When it was coming out. What it looked like exactly. What extras it had. How the engine worked. And best of all, what the ads would be like. Could be worth money, M.J. decided.

She'd gone back to her cubicle, walked around her whole group's offices, choosing proofs, sketches, memos, pictures. From Domina's she'd taken yellow copy paper in a folder, old roughs for ideas that had been lying around since Domina had gone off. Everywhere, she'd found tons, secret reports and memos, information for the creative-group head, all valuable, she thought, to a competitor. She hadn't quit looking till she'd rounded up a whole rundown on the new car.

She'd packed all the stuff up in a big Jackson carrying case and then taken the case to her cubicle and jammed it

370

behind her desk, where it would be tough for anyone to open.

Last night she'd asked Dan casually who was Jackson's biggest car competitor. He'd told her Connally and Curtis. They had most of the lines for Chrysler, just like Jackson had most of Ford. And he'd confirmed her on the value of secrets. Rival agencies, he'd said, guarded their stuff as long as they could, to surprise each other at publication. Another agency would be wild to get top-secret Ford stuff, especially about the Blossom. That car had all Madison Avenue wondering.

M.J. had slept restlessly, and gone to work at the crack of dawn. She'd been ready, exactly at nine, to call the creative director of Connally and Curtis for an appointment. Naturally, he had five assistants in between him and telephone callers, but M.J. had managed to wrangle a date right away with one of those assistants. Whatever he was like, she'd thought, I'll hang on there till they take me to the top guy. When a Chrysler creative director sees what I've got for sale, well, I'll get my money. But how much? she'd worried. She sure could use about ten thousand. But suppose the stuff was worth lots more? Well, she'd see how badly the man wanted to look in that portfolio. And if he turned her in? Why would he? All those big men hated each other. Men, they didn't usually turn her in. Most often, they'd wanted to hang on tight to her.

Then, that prick had stopped her carrying out the case, and here she was in the worst place of all, Mr Godwin looming over like a fierce father.

Best stay close to the truth, she thought. Say I'm scared to pieces for my future. Domina fired me. Rossen wouldn't help me. Say I got so scared I went crazy, took that stuff to show someone the kind of big thing I was working on, meant to bring it straight back.

The nigger bastard was gone, and Mr Godwin was still quiet.

M.J. slipped to the floor and looked up into his face. She felt startled to see how red that face was getting.

'Mr Godwin,' she sobbed, 'you just have to help me out. I need help so bad.'

Godwin looked down at her. The feeling of power was coming back to him. It had been fading for so long, had been snuffed out completely in Croft's office yesterday. Now he could feel it running like blood through his veins, pumping strongly from his heart, circulating all through his body.

Women. Women in business, where they should never have been. Weeping, howling, breaking into men's affairs, disturbing everything, distracting everyone. Taking kindness, returning betrayal. Stealing, actually stealing. Domina Drexler had stolen an account. M.J. Kent had stolen top-secret papers. Domina was gone. M.J. was at his feet.

'You little slut,' he began. 'We helped you. We took you from whatever country trashpile you came from and we made you a Potter Jackson colleague. We paid you far more than you deserved, far more than you'd have gotten anywhere else. And we gave you raises, bonuses, put you on our finest accounts. We helped you plenty. And what did you do about it? You stole. Valuable papers right here in our own building. And you're asking for help?'

Power, righteousness, anger rushing to his head, Godwin felt better, stronger than he had in months.

'Get up off that floor,' he said in his sternest voice.

The girl looked really scared. Her skin was paper white. The tears had stopped, but her violet eyes were big in her tiny face.

'I could get the police. They put people in prison for stealing, you know. You could go to prison. Except we don't need publicity about silly, wicked little thieves. But you should be warned. It's a criminal thing you've done.'

He was rewarded by the fear in the girl's face. Now she looked absolutely terrified. Godwin began feeling the way he had in the old days, when he was a power at Jackson.

'You're fired, as of this minute. Finished. Out. You go out of this building today, pack your things immediately. And make sure they're *your* things, not ours. No severance pay. No extras. What's more, you'd better not look for a job in any New York agency, anywhere I can reach. No references, of course. And I'll tell anyone who inquires what you've done. Better find yourself another line of work, young lady. We have no room in advertising for thieves.'

He turned away and pressed the buzzer for his secretary. Godwin's last problem, he thought. He felt the power slow down, stop coursing through his body. The end. He would never feel powerful again.

M.J. sat petrified. My God, what will I do? Who can help me? Dan? He'll kill me when he hears. David will be scared shitless. It's not fair. I lost my head with that nigger guard, and who wouldn't, with worries like mine? That black asshole. But now? No money, no job. I wish I could go home, sit on the porch, and draw pretty pictures again. I can't. My father would kill me after all this time. Never even wrote a letter.

While she heard the secretary's step coming closer, saw the handle turning in the door, M.J. twisted her fingers together and thought. She searched desperately for something hopeful, *anything*. No light anywhere.

Wait. There was one thing. The London tickets. Safe home at Dan's with her things. Two tickets. One could be cashed in. A thousand dollars. Hey, there, you pricks at Potter Jackson. No severance pay? You gave me severance pay. And there's a whole big world out there across the ocean. There's agencies in London. And there's men in London, men have always helped me out. The bill collectors will *never* find me. Fuck you, Mr Brady Godwin.

M.J. went meekly out the door with the secretary.

Roe

The Ring-Again Feature.

Our new computer telephones
offer the convenience of
stored dialing. If the number
you want is busy, press the
Ring-Again button. Next time
you press, your number will be
dialed automatically with one touch.

After Roe's secretary had quit trying to get an answer at Domina's house, and gone home, Roe took over the calling.

Seven o'clock, no answer. Seven-thirty. Eight-ten. Eight-fifty.

He left the telephone, went out to the nearest neighborhood bar where he could get a drink, a steak sandwich, and keep trying her on the wall phone.

Up until eleven-thirty there was still no answer. Sometimes Roe clicked off impatiently after two rings. Other times he waited, letting the ring sound over and over.

Where the hell is she? he kept thinking. Why do I always have to be tracking her down? For once, can't she stay put?

At midnight, when there was still no answer, he walked home. His head held the endless buzzing sounds he'd heard all evening. His gut held more martinis than he'd intended.

Once home, Roe used the heel of one shoe to push off the other, scuffed the second shoe off on the sofa leg. He let his jacket slip to the floor, yanked his tie off, and put his head on the sofa pillow.

He'd meant to go on trying the phone, but sleep knocked him out. At five in the morning he woke, rumpled, aching, his head still pounding in rhythmic ring of the telephone.

Maybe now?

This time the phone had barely sounded when someone picked it up.

'Domina,' he said urgently without waiting for a voice at the other end.

'No. Leota. Who's this?'

He remembered Domina's unusual arrangement with her maid. Leota was there at five, left at one, served that breakfast Domina adored. Fine, he thought, she'll know where Domina is.

'It's Roe Rossen, Leota. I've been trying God knows how long to get Mrs Drexler. Where the devil is she?'

He heard her rich chuckle. 'Bed, like all smart people. What are you doing, calling this hour? I thought I was the only one crazy enough to be up five in the morning. And I get to sleep early evening.'

'In bed? She hasn't answered the phone since I don't know when. I've called since yesterday afternoon, for God's sake.'

He rubbed his eyes, bent to find his shoes while he pulled the phone with him.

'She was with that Mr Sternn yesterday, big doings, papers, lipsticks, perfume stuff all over the living room, some kind of work. Didn't want dinner home. Must have stayed out. Now the phone's outside her door, means she doesn't want breakfast till she wakes up. She hasn't been working regular, you know. Keeps different hours.'

'Right,' he said, hanging on to the idea that Domina was in her bed, where she belonged, and that he wanted to get to her, fast.

'We haven't seen you in a while, Mr Rossen,' said Leota's voice.

'You'll see me in ten minutes flat,' Roe said. One shoe was in plain sight. The other seemed to have taken off. 'Lock her in. Don't let her move till I'm there, you hear?'

'I'll make extra coffee,' Leota said. 'Sounds like you need it.'

He took a minute for the bathroom, avoiding the mirror after one look showed him a grim, unshaven face, a wild mass of hair. He smoothed the hair with wet hands, grabbed his coat up, and left.

Taxis were everywhere. He waved one down, pulled the ice-cold door handle shut, and told the driver to *drive*, goddammit.

At her apartment he went past the doorman on the run, past the lamps and tables that blurred in his sight, into the elevator and up. At least the doorman knew he'd been there before.

377

At her door he touched the bell. It chimed way inside somewhere, two notes echoing idiotically, like some strange bird call.

It's going to be all right, he told himself. She's here, sleeping. All I have to do is get to her, hold her, tell her I'm with her all the way. I'll make her listen this time.

The apartment looked strange, shadowy, the windows black rectangles, panes rattling in the wind. Behind Leota, the kitchen blazed with fluorescent light. While she smiled hello, he smelled fresh oranges on her hands, noticed a little orange dot on her apron front.

Suddenly Roe was starving, hungry for food, thirsty for the cold sting of orange juice in his mouth, ravenous for Domina. He got hot with wanting to pull her close, get right into her, wrap all around her and hang on.

'In here,' said Leota.

While he blinked at the bright light, she pushed a chair toward him, handed him a mug. Roe gulped the fragrant coffee, feeling it settle him down and stir him up, both at the same time.

'Thanks,' he said. 'I'm going in there and wake her up, one minute, all right?'

'Mr Rossen,' said Leota, 'things have been kind of down around here. You come to fix that? Get her back to that job used to make her so happy? Comfort her for Mrs Slade? Or more trouble? What?'

He put the mug down.

The whole last day played through his head in flash pictures, Domina staring at Croft, Domina keeping her eyes away from him, Domina striding out the big door with her back straight and her head high.

He stood, the longing to be with her burning up from his insides, tingling in his cock.

'No more trouble,' he said.

He moved fast down the long hall. One more picture flashed in his mind, of himself taking the breakfast tray and bringing it to Domina like an offering.

If I had any style, I'd do it, he thought. But I never had that kind of style. And I don't want anything in my hands when I open that door. I want Domina's face, her shoulders, her hair, her soft breasts, that's what I want to hold.

He turned the door handle and pushed. The room was turning gray, dawn coming. A few lights from the building across the way showed him her form in the big bed. Away to one side, taking no space at all, Domina was curled in sleep, her head nearly under the quilt.

His heart turned over.

I've waited for this so long, he thought. Every damn minute since that boardroom, since I left that office, since I left Louise. Maybe since I was old enough to want to hold a woman.

He put out his hand. 'Domina,' he said.

She sat up like a shot, straight and tall. Roe had never seen anyone, even in the army, wake so fast, so completely. Her eyes were wide, her hair fell neatly over her shoulders as if it had just been brushed, her whole body was tremblingly awake.

He was so surprised, he laughed. 'You're supposed to wake gently after I kiss you,' he said.

He put his head down, smelling the fresh air in her marvelous hair, feeling the satin smoothness of her bare arms. But when his mouth reached hers, her lips were tight.

'Wait. No,' Domina said, when she freed herself.

She held him away.

Domina looked at Roe, shadowy in the dark room, only his face lit from the pale glow at the window.

She saw the lines carved in his face, the stubble on his chin, the rumpled collar. She saw the unkempt hair, the little cowlick standing free behind the crooked part. She saw everything wrong with Roe's face as his smile broke through, and it seemed like the best face she would ever see, the most marvelous surprise she would ever wake to.

Get hold of yourself, she thought, don't just fall in his arms because you're battle-worn and beaten up, don't melt because you're lonely and desperate to hold him.

Cigarette, quick, she thought, and leaned past him for one from the bed table. Never had she wanted a cigarette so much, to fuss with, to put between her mouth and his.

He was taking the cigarette away, shaking her a little, and not gently.

'Listen to me. Come back and hear me out, don't mess with cigarettes now.'

She forced herself to rally.

'Why must I always listen to you?' she got out. 'Why don't you ever listen to me?'

His hand dropped. Domina began to feel more in control, steadier.

'Sweetheart,' Roe said. 'You're so thin. Your shoulder blades are sticking out, you're so thin. Oh, Domina, how I've missed you.'

She felt the control go.

Dear Lord, she thought. He's real, warm, sitting on my bed. His jacket is rough against my hand, he smells of gin and locker rooms and coffee. I've missed him so terribly. I thought I knew how much, but now he's here, I know in my bones.

Still not moving, she looked at him.

'Domina . . .' He lifted his chin, shifted his weight on the bed. 'I'm leaving Jackson too. I walked out of that room right after you. Stayed just long enough to hear the talk. They're total bastards, I'll tell you sometime. Now I just want to say, you were right, have been right all along. They proved it, every word they said.'

Oh, thought Domina, how I've waited to hear that from you.

Her hand flew to his face, her heart began to beat faster, to skip a little. Against her hand his cheek felt rough, stubbly.

'They didn't really hear you. I did, every word,' Roe was going on. 'Once I had a lot of good advice for you. Now I take it back. Don't do anything my way, Domina, don't do anything but be there for me. I've got to hold on to you. Especially now I'm beginning to see what you really are.' Dear Jesus, had she really got through to him? Had Roe finally understood her? And if he had, who cared about anyone else?

Roe, she thought, I love you so. I ache to grab onto you, hold you, take your head against me where my breast is soft, smooth your funny hair, kiss your tired eyes. I want to wrap my arms and legs all around you, use my knees to hold you close, hold you so hard you'll never leave me.

Dizzy with his reality, his actual nearness, she caught herself, pulled herself back from surrender, drove her nails into her palm until she could speak as she wanted to.

'Losers,' she said. 'You told me only losers. And that I had –'

Before the ugly word could come out, his mouth was on hers, blocking it, kissing her roughly. His tongue circled the inside of her mouth, pressed into her lips.

Domina dissolved. She felt herself melting, going limp on the bed. Weakly she pulled at his jacket, reached for his shirt buttons. Roe was holding her with one hand, using the other to tug at his clothes. When that failed, he took away his hand, ripped off the shirt, kicked his clothes away. He swept back the covers and was on her, pulling at her nightgown, burying himself in her. She arched to help him, felt him strain to fill her body. She sensed sweat, gin, his special outdoor smell as he pushed at her, lost herself totally in a sunburst as he went quiet. She wrapped her long legs around his body, doubled her arms behind his damp back to pull him as close as she could.

He's my home, she thought, my real home. It will never be dark and cold while he's there with me. Nothing like him has ever happened to me, couldn't happen with anyone else. He is what I will never leave.

Roe was on an elbow now, his finger tracing her hair line, his hand in her hair. The little tug seemed to pull her against him again. She felt little pinpricks of joy, tingling going all down her spine.

'While you're in my power, listen. I take all of it back. You could never be a loser. You've got courage and grace and wisdom, that's what you got. More. And I haven't said yet why all that's important to me.'

His voice sounded terribly close, as if it were coming from inside her head. Domina lay quietly, feeling his rough bulk against her side, warm, damp, pressing close. The room seemed so still she could hear the smallest sounds outside her door, the clock way in the living room, the subdued chink of the coffeepot against the cup way out in the kitchen, a pigeon flapping suddenly off the terrace fence.

'Let's go, Domina,' Roe said. 'Partners. Best damned agency the world ever saw. I'll match you. Equal time. We'll do it piece by piece, show everyone how. My money, my training, your talent and dazzle. Partners. Say yes, say it now. I want to hear you say yes to me.'

He was shaking her now, and she knew he wanted a response from her mind as eager as the one she'd given him with her body.

Domina turned her head, touched her tongue to his hand. It tasted salty, warm. She began feeling her strength gather up again, little electric shocks of excitement starting up again behind her eyes.

Partners? She and Roe fitted together in work the way their bodies had fitted together just now? Marvelous. How they could astound everybody, announcing *that* to everyone.

She kissed his hand, turned her face back to look up at him, beginning to shiver with anticipation again.

How they could match each other, she thought, how wonderfully they could act without explaining, speak each other's mind, look at each other in meetings and know what to do next, the way they'd been able to by the end of the Israel show, the start of the Ford work.

She lifted her head to put her cheek against his face, to rub against the scratch of his chin. The roughness convinced her he was real, solidly there in her bed.

Partners. Harrell already liked them both, he'd be pleased. Bonnell? He'd adore Roe, they were two of a kind, promoters, idea men. Revlon? Who could hold them better than Roe Rossen, just as smart, tough, resilient as their people?

Partners.

We may never go home, she thought, we won't ever have to go home. If we're working together as closely as that, we'll *be* home.

That thought was so fantastic that her mind seemed to expand and fill with sparks till there was no more room, and the little sparks cascaded down her neck, her back, swirled around in her bloodstream.

Close as Roe was, it wasn't close enough.

She tightened her arms around his back, pulled hard. The sparks made her hands tingle, her head fizz.

'Come,' she said.

The New York Times

Advertising
Philip H. Dougherty

Drexler Rossen is the latest addition
to the New York agency roster. Domina
Drexler is the well-known Potter Jackson
executive who moves out with a Ford
promise, a Revlon project and Boutique
Bonnell. Roe Rossen, also of Jackson's
executive team, leaves an Executive Vice-
Presidency and a Board spot to join in
the new enterprise. Miss Belle Rosner
will consult for fashion and cosmetic
accounts. Offices are open at 767 Third
Avenue, and both partners say new business
is being actively pursued.